Call Me

Duchess

By
Maggie Dove

E
P

Eternal Press
A division of Damnation Books, LLC.
P.O. Box 3931
Santa Rosa, CA 95402-9998
www.eternalpress.biz

Call Me Duchess
by Maggie Dove

Digital ISBN: 978-1-61572-286-0
Print ISBN: 978-1-61572-287-7

Cover art by: Amanda Kelsey
Edited by: Devon Towry
Copyedited by: Erin Cramer

Printed in the United States of America
Worldwide Electronic & Digital Rights
1st North American and UK Print Rights

To three exceptional women named Silvia,
who will always remain in my heart.

To my two wonderful friends and
invaluable critique partners, authors
Mariana Betancourt and Victoria Koch.
I couldn't have done it without you.
Thanks for the laughs, girls!

Prologue

England, 1870

Ah, the London Season—how glamorous, how debauch!

Staring at his image in the gilded mirror on top of the marbled staircase, the nobleman adjusted his black mask over his eyes and smiled with approval while surveying the fine-looking picture he presented. As usual, his appearance was faultless. There was not a hair out of place. It was time to make his grand entrance, but he couldn't help but linger a while longer as he looked over the banister at the massive ballroom below.

The magnificent Bentley House boasted the most exquisite of ballrooms, and tonight the festooned and tinseled room did not disappoint. What would the London Season be without the Dowager Duchess of Wallingford's annual masquerade ball, held every year at the commencement of the Season? He had looked forward to it for months.

His heart pounded with anticipation as he slowly descended the staircase, his keen eyes surveying the magical grandeur before him.

There she was now—the bejeweled and crusty dowager, dressed in black silk and lace, smiling at her doting son, the Duke of Wallingford. The duke's escort, Lady Lorena Bonner, giggled and blushed while speaking to Lord Christopher Jackman, who looked more enamored by her than ever.

Entering the room, the nobleman recognized Lord and Lady Hardwood and their delectable daughter, Samantha, from last year's Season. He accepted a flute of champagne from one of the numerous silver trays being passed around by uniformed waiters. He glanced at the dance floor and noticed the Countess of Salesbury waltzing with a young dandy while her aged husband watched silently. Was that not the exquisite Marchioness of Albester in lively conversation with the Earl of Deville? Where were their other halves? No doubt enjoying a lovers' rendezvous in the terrace while their spouses conversed for all to witness. The nobleman smirked, remembering how the four had scandalized the ton with their blatant behavior last summer. That was last year's gossip. He wondered what tidbit this year would bring.

The marchioness called him over, but he could not go and speak to her now. He pretended not to notice, for he had more pressing matters at hand. The nobleman was not interested in the guests he recognized. He was more fascinated by the guests he had yet to meet.

Looking to his side, he observed a large group of young ladies standing by the north wall. So many of them! Giggling and hoping they'd be noticed. This year's pretty pickings—such beautiful, dainty flowers just waiting to be plucked. Where would he start? Knocking back the champagne with one quick gulp, he headed toward them.

The London Season—how glamorous, how debauch, indeed! The time of year when the upper crust departed from their country manors and brought their young daughters to London to partake in the marriage mart, all anxiously hoping the young debutantes would meet eligible bachelors from good families such as theirs.

He wondered which one he would rape tonight.

Chapter One

It was unseasonably chilly for a spring evening when Archibald Wiggins, after a long day of gambling, finally arrived at the modest cottage he called home. Cursing the painful gout that denied him a moment's peace, he hung his frock coat in the entryway and dragged his aching, heavy body to join his three daughters in the study.

The cozy room welcomed him with the warmth of a flickering fire as Archibald stepped inside to find the three young women engaged in different activities. He quickly took a deep breath and fixed a smile. "Hello, darlings!"

Winifred put down her stitching at the sight of him. "Papa, where have you been?" she asked. "We ate supper without you."

Penelope ceased playing the piano and ran into his arms. "Papa, did you hear me play? Isn't it wonderful how I've improved?"

Marguerite, enthralled in her book, did not bother to acknowledge his presence.

"Yes, love, it sounded wonderful," Archibald lied. Unlike his dear, departed wife, Lydia, who had been quite the talented pianist, Penelope had not inherited the aptitude for the instrument. Penny's music grated so heavily on his ears, he had tried to gamble away the piano for years. Unfortunately, unlike Marguerite's horse, no one had been interested in wagering for it.

"Be careful, love. You are standing too close to my bad foot." Disentangling himself from Penelope, he addressed his other daughters. "What have you been doing all day, my loves?"

Winifred shrugged her shoulders. "What are we to do, Papa? It is too cold for outside activity. We are quite bored, I'm afraid."

"I'm sorry, ducklings. I've had a miserable day, too. I'm in bad need of a drink," Archibald declared, making his way to the last expensive bottle of imported port left in the cottage.

"Haven't you had enough, Papa?" Marguerite inquired, still not bothering to look up from her book.

"Bah—it's never enough!" Archibald replied, waving his hand in a gesture of dismissal. Bringing the bottle with him to the sofa, he uncorked it and poured himself a glass. "I'm going to savor every last drop. There's hardly any left."

He loosened the small bow tie of his slim cravat and opened his vest, allowing his large, protruding belly to expand. "I have something interesting to tell you, girls."

Marguerite finally turned her attention away from her book. Her dark blue eyes narrowed suspiciously. "The last time you had something interesting to say, Papa, your creditors had come for Mother's valuables, and my steed was being dragged away from the stables."

Smirking, Winifred returned to her stitching. "Marguerite is right, Papa," she murmured. "I am beginning to dread the word 'interesting.' You never say anything worthy of note. It is always interesting for you but never for us."

"The arrow has pierced my heart, Winnie." Archibald touched his chest, pretending to be hurt. "You wound me!"

"She's right. You've managed to gamble everything away," said Winnie.

"Not everything, my love, I still have you and your sisters," Archibald retorted, chuckling at the incredulous, shocked look Winnie gave him as she looked up from her stitching.

"He would put a wager on us if he could," Marguerite remarked before returning to her book. "Short of the cottage, there is nothing left to barter."

Damn the little chit! Even unaware of the extent of his gambling debts, Marguerite had just spoken the awful truth. Archibald had no one to blame but himself. Last month, he managed to gamble away the cottage. This afternoon, he gambled the last of Lydia's jewels. His creditors were at his heels, and he had a month to hand over the cottage. Bloody hell—the chit was a bloody mind reader. Try as he might, he could never put anything past his middle daughter. She read him like the book she held in her hands.

Actually, he hoped one of his daughters could snatch herself a rich husband and deliver him from the financial mess he brought upon them. Maybe if his dear Lydia were here, he would not be in such a penurious state.

Now that there was nothing left to barter, he had no choice but to move in with his sisters, Hyacinth and Lavinia. They would welcome him, he was certain, but moving in with those two controlling spinsters would not be easy for him. How long could he keep his sanity? Was he destined forever to be the only male in a household of doting, exasperating women? Hopefully not. If things worked out, there would be a rich son-in-law in the near future to save him from this terrible fate.

Penelope looked disapprovingly at her sisters. "Never mind them, Papa. I want to hear your news. What is it?" she asked excitedly. "Tell me."

Archibald touched her cheek. "Let me rest first, duckling. Be a dear and allow me to finish my port," he said, hoping the sweet, dark wine would help him gather his thoughts. He needed to find a way to tell his girls what he had done, but no amount of liquor would make him eloquent enough to pacify them once they heard the truth. The words "you are now destitute" would sound the same no matter how well expressed or how careful the delivery.

"Papa, I'll play a piece from Mozart while you rest."

He cringed as Penelope ran to the piano and her cumbersome fingers began to massacre yet another brilliant composition. *Wolfgang Amadeus must be turning in his grave,* thought Archibald, rolling his eyes as he tried his best to concentrate beyond the dreadful noise.

His copper Penny, as he often referred to his youngest child, had inherited Lydia's rich, glowing auburn hair, green eyes and fair skin. She was pretty enough, sweet enough and kindhearted, but yet...so very daft. Would there be a man in England able to ignore her constant chatter, her feeble mind and, worse, the odious piano playing? He seriously doubted it, wagering his Penny would not bring him luck.

Imbibing the last drop of his fine port, Archibald's eyes traveled to his other daughters, wondering which of the two could bring him out of his predicament.

Ah, Winifred. Intelligent, serious, full of integrity. Dependable Winnie, diligent to the bone. If only he could depend on her now. He leaned back and sized up his eldest daughter, trying to be as optimistic and generous as possible under the circumstances. Tall and rail thin, her mousy brown hair pulled back in a high knot and worn with a cluster of ringlets at the sides, Winifred's austere features resembled those of his spinster sister, Lavinia's.

Archibald shook his head miserably, exhaling a breath. Why did he bother to deceive himself? There was no hope where Winifred was concerned. Poor and dowdy was no recipe for finding a man. *Her shortcomings will keep a prospective husband at bay,* he thought sadly as she adjusted her wire-rimmed glasses and concentrated on her stitching.

His eyes moved from Winifred to Marguerite. *Yes, that one!* If he were betting solely for appearance's sake, he would place his wager on his middle daughter. There would be no hesitation on his part. Although she exasperated him to no end, she would win hands down.

Marguerite's high, exotic cheekbones, large sapphire eyes, smooth, ivory skin, and hair black as coal had turned many a head. From the day she was born, Archibald and his middle daughter had been butting heads. Archibald had to admit that, at eighteen, she was exquisite. Not quite as tall as Winifred, but, nevertheless, tall and proud. She carried herself confidently, aware of the appreciative glances cast her way. Unfortunately, the chit was stubborn to the core. Now, when he needed her to focus on making a realistic match, she had it in her mind to marry none other than Phillip Lancaster, the Duke of Wallingford.

As was her usual custom, Marguerite had not confided in Archibald about this silly attraction of hers. He would have been in the dark had he not overheard her sisters giggling and discussing it behind her back. Ordinarily, he would have dismissed her infatuation, but Marguerite's imperious aspirations worried him. She was foolish to think the duke would consider her. The man was way beyond her reach; he did not even know she existed. Marguerite might as well have set her sights on the next king of England.

Closing his eyes, Archibald Wiggins sadly shook his head. In the game of cards that was his life, he had been dealt a full house with three queens, but no winner. It was time he folded and called it a night. With this thought in mind, he put down the empty glass of port.

"Gooselings, I need your attention," he announced so suddenly he caused Penelope to cease her assault on the piano keys and Winifred to look up from her stitching. "Are you ready for my big surprise? It involves London."

The dark, heavy lashes that shadowed Marguerite's cheeks flew up with interest. Giving her father a quizzical look, she closed her book and put it aside.

Archibald smiled. "Your Aunt Elizabeth has graciously asked that you join her in London for the Season. You are coming out at last. Imagine the balls, the dinner parties, the nights at the opera. You'll do it all."

His announcement ignited the little study. Afraid he would lose his courage, Archibald tried to ignore the gasps of excitement, followed by the incredulous, happy looks on his daughters' faces.

"Oh, Papa—the London Season!" Penny jumped from the

piano bench. "It's everything I've ever dreamed!" Delighted, she began to waltz around the room.

"Settle down, my sweet ducklings, there is a catch. You'll not be returning home. You have four months to find husbands, or you'll be working as governesses by Season's end. You see, I've lost the cottage. We have a month to pack up and leave."

Paying no heed to their collective gasp, Archibald continued. "Don't look so shocked, ducklings. London is full of eligible bachelors who are desperate for wives," he fibbed, quickly unfolding a piece of paper from his trouser pocket. "I've categorized these lucky fellows by age, title, and, of course, wealth. I think you will find this list quite helpful."

"But, Papa...the cottage," Marguerite objected, "our home."

Archibald waved away her objection. "Nonsense, child, one roof's as good as another. You should be happy. I've just handed you the opportunity to pursue that duke of yours. Marguerite Lancaster, Duchess of Wallingford. Now, doesn't that sound splendid? You'd never have a chance at him, hiding in this old cottage."

Contemplating his daughters' confusion, Archibald felt a slight pang of remorse, but he quickly shrugged it off. He may have gambled their dowries away years ago, but he had managed to give them something much more valuable. He was a resourceful fellow, and his blood ran through their veins. If they couldn't find husbands, they would manage somehow. Why wouldn't they find husbands? The Duke of Wallingford was way beyond their dreams, but there were other, less notable prospects. Surely one of his three daughters would come through for him.

Shame on him! He was starting to believe his own lies. Pity he wasn't this good at cards.

* * * *

Edmund Kent had been gone too long. As the coach made its way up the steep, rutted road, his spirits began to soar. Through the rows of trees, he could see the ivy-shrouded Windword Hall, surrounded by its reeded moat. Soon he would be home—home at last, amid acres of tended lawns, topiary gardens, evergreen sculptures, mazes and laborer's cottages. Indeed, he had been gone too long!

While his thriving shipping business took him to exotic and interesting places, the Gothic beauty of Windword never failed to take Edmund's breath away. This time his return home would be different. The stately manor would not be the same without Julianna, his only sibling, who was now in London, partaking of the London Season. Selfishly, he wondered why he had given permission for his sister to spend the summer with Lord and Lady Hardwood.

Once again, his persistent neighbors had offered to present Julianna to society, as they had presented their daughter, Samantha, the previous year. Last year when the Hardwoods had invited her, Edmund had refused, thinking Julianna a bit young for the Season. But now his sister was of age. Although he would have liked nothing better, it would have been selfish to keep Julianna cooped up at Windword Hall forever.

Accusing him of being overly protective with Julianna, Ruth, his beloved governess, had written to Edmund in India, chastising him for trying to delay the inevitable. The governess, who had lived at Windword since Edmund was a child, offered to accompany Julianna during her stay in London as her chaperone, insisting that it would not do for his sister to miss such an opportunity yet again.

Edmund had no choice but to relent, and he had regretted it ever since.

The London Season, or "the marriage mart," as he liked to call it, was a necessary evil he would have liked to postpone as long as possible. Thirteen years Julianna's senior, Edmund was more like a father than a brother to her. Since their parents' death, twelve years ago, Edmund had been Julianna's sole guardian. Damn it, he *was* overprotective when it came to his little sister, but he would not apologize for it. She was his only family.

Although Edmund hated the idea of Julianna in London, he did have to admit he was somewhat grateful to the Hardwoods. His sister's coming out was a task he would not have enjoyed witnessing. Julianna's thoughts were those of any wellborn, aristocratic girl of marriageable age—very different from his. The notion of Julianna parading herself before strange men, hoping to catch a husband, gave him pause. He found the practice demeaning. What need did Julianna have of a husband at eighteen?

Indeed, Lord and Lady Hardwood saved him from a dreaded undertaking. Where other young lords looked forward to the revelry and gaiety of the London Season, Edmund shirked London's gilded society, favoring the uncomplicated, simple life at his family's country estate. He had always looked forward to returning home.

This time, Windword was different. The hounds that always greeted him at his return were nowhere to be seen. When Godfrey, the butler, opened the heavy wooden doors, his usual detached expression seemed more nervous than dour. The moment Edmund stepped inside, a sepulchral silence seemed to envelop the marbled halls of the grand manor.

Servants moved quickly by him, averting their gazes. There was a chill in the air, and some of the furniture in the rooms had been covered with sheets, as though no one had expected him home. Then he saw her coming down the stairs: Ruth! Was this ghostlike woman Ruth? Had she aged so much in so short a time? What the bloody hell was she doing here?

The usual welcoming embrace was now one of deep anguish. Her arms tightened around him, as though she feared she would collapse if she let go. "Oh, Lord Edmund, I'm so sorry—I'm beside myself with worry!"

"What's happened, Ruth? Where's Julianna? Why aren't you with her? Did the Hardwoods object to your presence?"

"No, of course not. The Hardwoods were wonderful to me. They think that Lady Julianna is with you. They sent her luggage today. It is in her room. I arrived last night. When I read your telegram this morning advising us of your arrival from India, I almost—dear God!" Ruth flung out her hands in despair. "It's Lady Julianna. I don't know where she is—we thought she was with you!"

Edmund's chest felt as if it would burst as fear knotted inside him. "With me? Why would you think that?"

"Because that is what we were led to believe."

Dread tore at his gut. "Damn it, Ruth, where the hell is Julianna?"

"I don't know!" Ruth cried out in anguish, cradling her head in her trembling hands, deep sobs racking her shoulders.

Trying not to panic, Edmund took the grieving woman in his arms, handing her a handkerchief to wipe her tears. "Ruth, calm down, and tell me what happened. You said her luggage arrived from London today. Let's go to her room. Maybe there's some clue."

Taking the stairs two at a time, Edmund reached the landing before Ruth. When he entered Julianna's room, he noticed the faint smell of his sister's perfume still clung to the air. He inhaled deeply, needing the reminder of her youthful presence. The usually bright and cheerful bedroom seemed cold and uninviting, as though it had been uninhabited for months. The plush, heavy curtains, kept opened on a typical day, were drawn shut, hindering visibility.

Walking to the window, Edmund yanked open the curtains then sat on the bed beside a slumped and weepy Ruth. "All right, Ruth," he demanded, terror thickening his throat. "Start from the beginning. What happened?"

Trying to compose herself, Ruth wiped her tears and blew her nose with Edmund's handkerchief. After a few seconds, she finally found her voice. "Five nights ago, Lady Julianna wanted to attend the first ball of the Season, a masquerade ball. I was not feeling well and could not accompany her."

Ruth took a deep breath before continuing, "Lord and Lady Hardwood were adamant that Lady Julianna not miss the ball. I didn't see the harm. They assured me she would be closely chaperoned at all times. Unfortunately, that was not to be."

Numbed with rage, Edmund swallowed hard. How could they have lost his sister at a masquerade ball? "Go on," he insisted, his voice deceptively calm.

As though reading his thoughts, Ruth quickly added, "Lady Julianna told the Hardwoods she was leaving the ball with you, that you had surprised her. Later that evening, the Hardwoods received a note from Lady Julianna."

"What did the note say?"

"It said that she would not be returning to the Hardwood townhouse. She had decided to travel abroad with you, and that you would both be leaving in the morning. We didn't question it, knowing how you felt about the Season. We all thought you had changed your mind about her being in London."

"When did you realize she was missing?"

"This morning...when the two telegrams arrived."

"Two telegrams?"

"Yes, yours, advising us of your arrival from India. I realized you had never come to London, and you were not traveling with Lady Julianna. Could she have been kidnapped for ransom? The sister of the Earl of Windword—I should have never let her out of my sight!" Ruth shook her head in despair and resumed her crying. "This is my fault. I shouldn't have allowed her to go to the ball."

"Ruth, concentrate. Where's the other telegram?"

"In the study. We did not open it. It was addressed to you." Ruth gasped. "Could it be a ransom note?" she asked, her eyes widening with fear.

Edmund jerked to his feet, quickly exiting Julianna's room with Ruth following close behind. Descending the marbled staircase, he ran through the hallway, into the study, then rushed to his desk. He tore open the telegram. His blood started to boil as he read until a searing hot fury almost blinded him—a fury greater than any he had ever known.

"The bastard!" he raged, unable to control his anger. He read the telegram a second time, and then a third. The more he read it, the more astounded and furious he became. The telegram was no ransom note. It was a marriage announcement from his friend, Diego de Cordoba, the Marques of Altamares.

The bastard took Julianna to Spain and married her in the process.

Chapter Two

The train whirred through rolling hills and green pastures. Every now and then, grazing sheep and quaint stone cottages dotted the rural landscape. Wrapped in her thoughts, Marguerite stared out the train window at the passing English countryside, wishing her father had not insisted on accompanying them on the train trip to London.

Traveling coach, the three sisters sat cramped together while Archibald's rotund body took up most of the tiny compartment. He sat across from them, looking quite comfortable with his coat opened and his knees spread wide, eating chocolates out of an opened box he held in his hand. For the last hour he had done nothing but eat, and talk incessantly about their future plans, embarrassing Marguerite with his total lack of discretion or privacy.

Marguerite wondered what the man seated next to Archibald and directly across from her must be thinking. When entering the compartment, the tall, handsome stranger, whose knees she had become quite familiar with, had greeted them with a polite nod, but, after opening a newspaper, had not uttered a word since. She didn't blame him; she wished she could hide behind a newspaper as well.

"It didn't have to be like this, Papa. We are so tight in here; I can't work on my stitching. Aunt Elizabeth paid for us to travel in comfort," Winifred chided. "You should not have traded the first-class tickets and pocketed the difference."

"Don't complain, my little duckling. Here, have one of these," Archibald said, extending the nearly empty box of chocolates. Winifred shook her head, but Penny reached out and took two of the chocolates.

When Archibald offered some to Marguerite, she declined, once again readjusting herself as she tried to find a more comfortable position. Sharing the seating with her two sisters made her feel cramped and hot. *It won't be long now,* thought Marguerite, excitement rushing through her veins.

She had never agreed with her father on any issue, but this was different. Archibald was right; opportunity had come knocking at her door. This was all she had dreamed about for years. Soon she would be in London, waltzing in the arms of the most sought-after bachelor in all of England. Lord Phillip Lancaster, the Duke of Wallingford, the only man she could ever love. *Marguerite Lancaster, Duchess of Wallingford.* It certainly was a splendid name. Work as a governess—never! She would become Phillip Lancaster's duchess or die trying.

"Aunt Elizabeth would never have us travel under these conditions," Winifred persisted, shaking her head in disgust. "I can't even breathe."

Marguerite smiled when she heard Aunt Elizabeth's name. What would she have done without her late mother's sister? As usual, Aunt Elizabeth and Uncle John had come through for her. After her mother's death, her godparents had been Marguerite's only source of happiness. Not only had Marguerite spent every summer at their country estate as a child, but now they were making it possible for her and her sisters to partake of a London Season. She would never be able to thank them enough.

Generous to a fault, and wanting their only daughter, Samantha, to share a sense of family, Aunt Elizabeth and Uncle John had often asked Marguerite and her sisters to spend summers at Hardwood Manor. Why Penny and Winnie had preferred to spend their summers with their Brighton relatives instead, Marguerite would never understand. She did not care much for Brighton or her father's relatives, who were loud, boorish and unschooled in the social graces. Instead, Marguerite absolutely adored her cousin, Samantha, with whom she shared much in common. Willful to no end, both loved horses, and neither could refuse a dare.

"Papa, when Aunt Elizabeth finds out what you..."

"Please, Winnie, let it go. We have more important things to discuss," Archibald announced, reaching out to pinch Winifred's cheek. "Penny, call out the names on the list. I want to go over them one more time."

Mortified, Marguerite turned her head from the window. "Papa, we are not alone," she insisted, referring to the stranger who sat next to Archibald, reading his newspaper. "Can't it wait?"

"Hush, my darling," Archibald said, with a wave of his fat hand as he popped the last chocolate into his mouth.

"Please, Papa. This is not the time," Marguerite persisted, wondering why she should care what the stranger thought of them. His traveling accommodations certainly indicated that he was not of high social standing. Although his appearance was well groomed, his hands were not elegant and pale as a gentleman's would be. Instead they were big, square and calloused as though used to hard labor. The man would not be intimate with the gentry on Archibald's list. Still, she found it highly embarrassing for her father to speak of something so private in front of a perfect stranger.

Looking appalled, Winifred raised her eyebrows at Marguerite. Her eyes shifted nervously from the stranger, to her father, to the list in Penny's hand and back to the stranger again. "Marguerite is right, Papa. We'll have plenty of opportunities to go over the list in London. This is a private matter."

Undeterred, Penny lifted her chin in defiance. "Papa, I intend to meet every last one of these lords." To Marguerite's and Winifred's mortification, she waved the wretched list in her hand before reading out the names, "Lord Albert Lansing, Duke of Raleigh, two and sixty, very wealthy…Papa, this man is old!"

"Precisely, my dear. He will die soon, and he has no heirs. If I could, I'd marry him myself," Archibald said, chortling. "There's a few more on the list with one foot on the grave. If you ask me, I'd fancy those first, put my money on the old ones."

Winifred's brow furrowed. "No more, Papa. You're embarrassing us."

Using a handkerchief to wipe the chocolate off his walrus mustache, Archibald challenged, "Stop interrupting. I'd wager you'd be more embarrassed toiling as governesses. Penny, continue."

"Yes, Papa. Sir Richard Adams, nine and twenty, wealthy. Lord Arthur Armstrong, Earl of Chesterfield, three and thirty, wealthy," Penny recited proudly. "Lord William Bentley, Marquess of Sutherland, eight and twenty, very wealthy. Lord Stanley Rutherford, Viscount Rutherford, one and forty, last resort, not so wealthy. Lord Edmund Kent, Earl of Windword, one and thirty, extremely wealthy."

Penny's eyes widened with sudden interest. "Marguerite, isn't he Julianna's brother?"

"Yes," Marguerite begrudged through stiff lips, trying to ignore the stranger who had put down his paper and was watching them, highly entertained. The stranger glanced at Archibald and her sisters from time to time, but his gaze always returned to Marguerite. She found him vaguely disturbing as his dark-lashed, warm brown eyes observed her, pleasure softening his granitelike features. Feeling flushed, she dropped her eyes before his steady gaze.

"Gooseling, since when do you know the Earl of Windword?"

"I don't know him, Papa," Marguerite muttered. "I-I know his sister," she managed to say, before raising her eyes to find the stranger watching her still. The insolent stranger's rugged masculine appeal was too unsettling for her. She tried not to notice his thick brown hair and square jaw; his massive shoulders, which filled the frock coat he wore; his hard, manly thighs in closely fitted gray trousers; and those firm, sensual lips.

"Lady Julianna Kent is Samantha's best friend. They often played together at Windword Hall," Winifred contributed. "Marguerite has mentioned her many times."

Archibald gave Marguerite a sidelong glance of utter disbelief. "You've been to Windword Hall?"

"Of course she has," Winnie replied. "You forget Marguerite has spent every summer with Uncle John and Aunt Elizabeth. Julianna Kent lives in the neighboring estate."

"Well, what do you know? My little gooseling kicking her heels and hobnobbing with the titled few at Windword Hall," Archibald remarked proudly. "Forget summers. If I'd only known such a distinguished notable lived so close to Elizabeth, I would have sent you there permanently. Lord Windword would be a splendid catch. Why hasn't he sought you out, Marguerite?"

Highly flustered, Marguerite tore her eyes away from the stranger, wishing the earth would open up and take her with it.

"Papa, I don't want to disappoint you, but I'm afraid you'll have to take the Earl of Windword off your list," Winifred said hastily, noticing Marguerite's distress. "We will not see him in London. The earl shuns London society and much prefers his country estate."

Archibald frowned. "How do you know all this?"

"His sister told Marguerite. Winifred and I don't know the Kents, but we know much about them through Marguerite," Penny elucidated. "Can we get back to the list, Papa?"

"Marguerite, have you met the man?" Archibald demanded.

"No," Marguerite replied honestly, much to her father's disappointment.

"Why?" he snapped.

"His shipping business keeps him quite busy," Penny interjected before Marguerite could respond. "The earl spends his time traveling the world. Poor Lady Julianna, all alone in that huge castle with only the help for company. Now can we go back to the list, Papa? I think this one sounds promising," she announced, pointing to a name on the list.

"All alone in that huge castle with only the help for company...I should be so lucky! So, my little copper Penny, which one of these wealthy notables has caught your eye?"

Penny read proudly, "Lord Jonathan Bradley, Viscount Bradley, four and twenty, quite wealthy. Papa, the list does not advise on their physical characteristics. You do not tell us what they look like. As it is, most of the gentlemen on this list are too old for me."

"Nonsense, my child—a wealthy notable is never too old."

"But Papa, I have not seen this viscount. He may be fat and unappealing."

Archibald chuckled. "My sweet duckling, you are too young and innocent to realize the appeal of a fat purse. Time passes way too soon, my dear. Most pretty young lords grow paunchy and wrinkled. Look at me, I was handsome once."

Penny began to object, but Archibald interrupted her. "Yes, Penny. Handsome men grow old, but wealthy men grow wealthier." Trying to prove his point, he took her hand. "Learn to love with your hand outstretched, like this. Not with your heart or with your eyes, but with your needs, and what he can provide. Just make certain he finds you appealing. He'll give you anything."

Marguerite and Winifred exchanged mortified looks. "Please stop, Papa. No more of the list," Marguerite insisted, keeping her eyes on Winnie, too embarrassed by her father's crude remarks to dare look at the stranger.

Archibald struggled with his girth to get to his feet. "Did I hear the conductor say Crawley? This is my stop, girls."

"You are leaving us, Papa?" Penny protested, wide-eyed. "I thought you were coming to London with us? What are we to do without you?" she asked him, tears beginning to form in her eyes. "I'm going to miss you so!"

"Crawley is near London. I'm only a short train ride away. Let me be the first to know if and when you snatch yourselves a husband. Good luck, ducklings!" Tipping his stovepipe hat, Archibald made a triumphant exit onto the platform.

Waiting for him at the depot were Aunts Lavinia and Hyacinth. Wearing black bustle dresses with matching black bonnets and parasols, Marguerite's aunts seemed delighted to see their brother as they opened their arms to embrace him.

Smiling, Archibald pointed to Marguerite's window, and the elderly aunts began to wave good-bye. It was difficult to watch. As the train began to move, Marguerite waved back, hoping the poor souls would hold on to the little black purses that hung from their wrists and not soon regret their decision to lodge her father.

Marguerite turned her head from the window to find that Winifred had changed seats and had accommodated herself beside the stranger.

"Thank God, no more list," Winnie commented as she took out her stitching.

"Yes," Marguerite agreed, smiling. "No more list."

Penelope frowned. "Oh, Marguerite! You are not interested in Papa's list because you fancy the Duke of Wallingford. Papa has worked hard on this list, and I appreciate all the effort he has put forth. You better look at these names, duckling, and set your sights on someone more attainable," she blurted out angrily. "Papa told me that the man is a confirmed bachelor."

Winifred stopped stitching and glared at Penelope. "Leave her alone."

"I will not," Penny insisted. "Lord Phillip Lancaster does not know Marguerite walks this earth. I'll wager she'll never marry that duke. Why, Papa did not even bother to put his name on the list. The man can have any woman he wants."

Marguerite stiffened, momentarily taken aback by Penny's biting words. Her embarrassment quickly turned to annoyance. "You are wrong, Penny. He'll marry me," she managed to say, more for the stranger's benefit than for Penny's. "I will be the next Duchess of Wallingford, if it is the last thing I ever do."

The stranger seemed to take pleasure in her response. His mouth quirked with humor, and his laughing eyes studied her with curious enjoyment. She would not let him intimidate her. Marguerite arched her brows and met his gaze boldly, before he returned to his newspaper.

Papa's abandonment did not deter Penny. Cringing from time to time, Marguerite and Winifred decided to ignore their youngest sister as she continued to read from the list, peppering it with silly comments until she enunciated the very last name.

Grateful that she would soon be in London, Marguerite leaned her forehead against the glass of the window and closed her eyes. She could not remember a more trying day—a perfect stranger made privy to her and her family's most intimate details. Damn Papa, Penny and the dreadful list. Damn the insolent stranger and the amusement written all over his face. In this small compartment, his presence was compelling—so compelling she wished she could jump off the train. The more she recalled everything the stranger had heard and witnessed, the more she wanted to jump, run, and hide from her mortification.

In London it would be different. The stranger was plebian, common, a nobody. So what if he had an air of authority and the appearance of one who demanded respect? She certainly didn't respect him. Without uttering a single word, he had mocked her, ridiculed her. Why should she let him bother her? He was of no importance. In London, she would never set eyes on him again.

She straightened her spine and lifted her chin with optimistic resolve. *Marguerite Lancaster, Duchess of Wallingford.* It wouldn't be long now.

* * * *

Marguerite felt a sense of disappointment when the carriage came to a full stop outside the Hardwood town house. The open carriage ride from Victoria Station to Grosvenor Square had been nothing less than exhilarating. Never in her life had she witnessed such excitement. The hustle and bustle of the crowded city with its architectural beauty had left her speechless. The busy London streets were teeming with horse-drawn vehicles going in all directions. Vendors hawked their wares, street sweepers tried to keep the streets clean, beggars and vagabonds coexisted with elegantly dressed men, women and children.

To her delight, the carriage passed right in front of Buckingham Palace. The coachman had reverently removed his cap and had stopped the carriage, taking great pleasure in informing them that it was Queen Victoria's official residence. When Penny stuck out her tongue at the Queen's Guard, Marguerite and Winnie had both stiffened, momentarily taken aback by Penelope's appalling behavior. After the initial shock, the two sisters were unable to control their laughter as the coachman almost fell off his seat while Penny nonchalantly insisted the guards were "way too serious for their own good," and suggested that "the Queen reprimand them at once."

When the footman opened the carriage doors and set down the steps, Marguerite wished their ride had not come to an end. Descending the carriage, she looked up in awe at the red brick, terracotta townhome before her. The towering manor house with its tall windows, pointed arches, and curved black iron balconies exuded unlimited wealth and space. How different from their own modest cottage. Theirs no more, she ruefully remembered, having been so cavalierly gambled off by Papa.

"Welcome, my dears!" Uncle John exclaimed as he assisted Marguerite, Penny and Winifred out of the carriage. "My apologies for not meeting you at the station as planned, but we were detained by an unexpected visitor. He is in the drawing room with our Samantha."

Holding her arms out to them, a smiling Aunt Elizabeth hugged each sister as they stepped from the carriage to the pavement. "My dears—I've longed for this day! If only your mother could be here," she said wistfully, and then shook her head. "I refuse to think of sad things today. We have wonderful news. I'll let Samantha tell you. It's her news to tell. Take the luggage inside," she instructed the footman who held a small suitcase with their meager belongings. "Inform the staff the ladies have arrived."

The footman bowed his head in acknowledgement and quickly disappeared through a side entrance.

"Uncle John, Aunt Elizabeth, we are so grateful, so very happy to be here," Marguerite spoke for her sisters. "Honestly, we don't know how to thank you."

Smiling, Aunt Elizabeth kissed her cheek. "Nonsense, Marguerite. It's our pleasure, darling. Penny, Winnie—I always blamed Brighton for keeping you away from us. Let me have a look at the three of you. My, what a pretty trio—I must hug you again, my dears. Penny, you are the image of Lydia. Winnie, you remind me of my mother, your late grandmother, Olivia."

Winifred smiled. "Papa always told me I remind him of Aunt Lavinia."

The tensing of Aunt Elizabeth's jaw betrayed her deep frustrations. "Such gibberish—why would he say such a thing? You look nothing like Lavinia. You are lovely, the spitting image of my dear mother," she blurted out, before turning to Marguerite. "My dear, Marguerite, you are breathtaking. You look more like my daughter than Samantha, who resembles her father. I only wish Lydia were here to see just how lovely her daughters turned out."

Chuckling, Uncle John opened the wrought iron gate and allowed the women to pass through, following close behind.

Coloring fiercely, Aunt Elizabeth gasped at the realization of her words. "I only meant Marguerite has inherited my black hair and blue eyes. I certainly was not suggesting..."

"Of course not, dear. Although you know you are quite lovely, you certainly weren't calling yourself that. Marguerite, we missed you last summer," Uncle John said. "Wished you had joined us in London, but your father insisted you stay and take care of him during his inopportune illness. How is dear old Archibald?"

Confused, Marguerite turned to her uncle as they ascended the steps and approached the front door of the town house. "I don't understand, Uncle John, what do you mean you missed me last summer?"

Before Uncle John could reply, the door opened, and Mortimer, the butler, allowed them into the hall.

"Hello, Mortimer," Marguerite greeted the butler with a wink and a smile. "I dare ask—have you missed me?" For years, Marguerite and Samantha mercilessly teased the stuffy butler, knowing it bothered him greatly. "I present my sisters, Miss Winifred Wiggins and Miss Penelope Wiggins. Penny, please be gentle. Mortimer is Uncle John's and Aunt Elizabeth's own grenadier guard. You can try to make him laugh, but to no avail. He is most proper."

"Miss Marguerite, Lady Samantha is expecting you and your sisters in the drawing room," the butler informed, most stiffly, proving her point. Before he could say another word, Samantha came running from behind, pushing him to one side in order to embrace Marguerite.

"Excuse me, Mortimer, please move aside...Marguerite! I couldn't wait any longer. I've missed you," she exclaimed, before turning to hug her other cousins. "Penny, Winnie—finally—Brighton's loss is our gain! Come with me. I can't wait for you to meet Steven."

Uncle John and Aunt Elizabeth exchanged smiles.

"Samantha, we will join you later. I need to speak with Cook about tonight's dinner, and your father must attend to an urgent matter," Aunt Elizabeth informed them, smiling. "Hurry, Samantha—Lord Steven is waiting."

"I can hardly wait for them to meet him. Follow me, cousins," Samantha instructed as she led them to the drawing room.

They were walking so fast, Marguerite hardly had a chance to admire the beautiful tapestries and paintings that hung in the hallway. "Who is Lord Steven?" she asked, noticing Samantha seemed lovelier than usual. There was a certain glow about her cousin that had not been there before. Samantha's dark brown hair seemed shinier, her hazel eyes brighter. Even her walk had a jaunty cheerfulness.

Samantha dimpled, biting back her lips as though she were

dying to say something. Pausing, she took Marguerite's hands. "Lord Steven Bradstone—my fiancé," she burst out proudly.

"Sam, really?" Marguerite asked, delighted. "How marvelous! You never mentioned him in your letters."

"That's because I was embarrassed to mention him. I waited all last summer for him to declare his love for me. I had finally given up, and today...today he appeared out of nowhere and asked for my hand. I thought my heart would burst."

Winifred smiled. "Samantha, how marvelous—how wonderful!"

"Thank you, Winnie. I'm grateful I have my cousins with me to share my joy. I don't think I could be any happier." Samantha continued, a bit breathless, "Steven was serving in Australia. It took him all year to sell his commission and make the proper plans for us to be married."

Penny remained silent. Frantically searching through her purse, she tried to keep pace with the others as they swiftly walked through the long hallway.

"A cavalry officer?" Winifred asked. "How splendid. He must be quite handsome."

"Indeed," Samantha agreed. The cousins burst out in giggles, except for Penny, who was not paying attention and was now actively searching through the folds of her skirts.

Samantha had not lied. When she opened the drawing room door, there stood Lord Steven Bradstone in all his tall, blond glory, his piercing blue eyes regarding his fiancée warmly.

The ladies entered the room, but before Samantha had the chance to introduce Steven to her cousins, Penny, with a determined look upon her face, rushed past Lord Steven and dumped her purse on the escritoire.

"Found it—what would I have done if I'd lost it?" Penny exclaimed, waving the dreaded list. She took a pen and dipped it into an inkwell. "Lord Steven Bradstone, second son of the Marquess of Greyleigh, six and twenty," she read out loud. "One less," she said, to her sisters' mortification, as she scratched Lord Steven off the list.

Chapter Three

After a celebratory meal, Uncle John asked everyone to join him in the study for a champagne toast. Once he had toasted the newly engaged couple, Uncle John and Aunt Elizabeth quickly retired to their chambers. Feigning fatigue, Marguerite accompanied Penny and Winnie to their bedroom, giving Samantha the opportunity to spend time alone with her fiancé.

"Winnie, this room is perfect—just perfect!" Penny exclaimed as they entered the lovely pink chamber.

Winnie huffed. "Really, Penelope, now that we're alone, I can finally get this off my chest. I shouldn't even be speaking to you after your abominable behavior earlier! For the life of me, I don't understand how you can—"

"What behavior?" Penny interrupted her, looking confused. "What have I done now? Tell me, what did I do?"

"You really don't have an inkling, do you?" Winnie asked exasperated.

Penny lifted her chin, meeting Winnie's icy gaze straight on. "Not a one."

Winifred turned to Marguerite and rolled her eyes. "What are we to do with her?" Without waiting for an answer, she turned back to Penny. "Let it be the last time, Penelope."

"Last time for what? Just tell me what I did."

"Let me see." Winifred inhaled deeply. "Let me start with what you said to Lord Bradstone earlier, that's what. We've never been more embarrassed in our lives," she replied, raising her voice. "You have to think before you speak. We've told you this before. Your discretion leaves much to be desired, Penelope Wiggins."

Insulted, Penny threw back her head and placed her hands on her hips. "Oh, hush. Lord Steven thinks I'm delightful. I heard him tell Samantha."

"What did you expect him to say? The man's in love. He certainly isn't going to speak ill of his fiancée's cousin," Marguerite said, chuckling. "If I were him, the wedding would be off. What must he think of us? Give me the list, Penny. This idiocy stops now, before you embarrass us any further."

Taking a frilly pillow and hugging it to her, Penny ignored Marguerite's command as she plopped onto the four poster bed. "Oh stop. Can't I enjoy my good fortune without having to be censured by both of you for every single thing? Look around, I've never seen such luxury. My bed is big enough for two. I'm going to sleep like a queen."

Penelope is right, Marguerite thought. They had never experienced such luxury. Her sisters' huge bedroom was identical to the one Marguerite would be sharing with Samantha. Both rooms were painted pink with white trimming and had elaborately designed mahogany furniture consisting of two four poster beds separated by a nightstand, two chiffoniers, a washstand, and a writing desk. If that weren't enough, the rooms were connected by a large dressing area with large mirrored dressers, wardrobes and two brocade dressing screens.

Winifred opened the large suitcase comtaining their personal effects and began to unpack. "Samantha told me when Mother died Aunt Elizabeth refurnished both her homes, hoping we would come live with her. That is why Samantha's bedroom is exactly like this one. She wanted us to feel like her daughters."

Penny's eyebrows shot up in surprise. "Well, what happened? Why didn't we come live here?" She sat upright at the edge of the bed.

"Papa refused her," replied Winnie as she handed Marguerite and Penelope their clothes. "After Mother's death, he couldn't part with us, too."

Putting the items aside, Penny grinned. "Sweet Papa, why does he love us so much? We could have been sitting in the lap of luxury all of these years. Why couldn't he have parted with us?"

"He puts himself first, that is why," Winifred said, frowning. "That wasn't the only time. Marguerite, do you know you and I were invited to London last summer? Aunt Elizabeth wanted us to come out with Samantha."

Penny objected, "What about me? Why wasn't I invited?"

"You know the answer to that. You are barely old enough to come out this Season. Go on, Winnie," Marguerite insisted. "Uncle John mentioned something on the way in this afternoon. I didn't have a chance to ask him later."

"Samantha told me her Uncle Archie refused their invitation. He allowed Penny and I to go to Brighton and kept you with him to take care of him. Papa lied to us. He told us that the Hardwoods had withdrawn their yearly invitation to Hardwood Manor because they were taking Samantha to London for the Season. He should have let us go to London and kept Penny with him to take care of him."

Penny stomped her foot. "Why me?" she protested vehemently.

"Penelope, Marguerite already told you. Last summer, you were not of age. You would have been the perfect candidate to help him with his illness. Instead, he sacrificed Marguerite and me."

"I don't know why you are complaining," Penny said as she began to put away the few items of clothing in a drawer. "You went to Brighton. Remember? If anyone should grumble, it should be Marguerite."

Marguerite smiled. "Well, I'm not grumbling. Let's forget about last summer and Papa. Instead, let's think of what awaits us this summer."

Winifred agreed. "I can't wait for our first ball."

"We've already missed a few balls," Penelope said, pouting. "I have no ball gown. I feel like Cinderella at the mercy of her mean stepsisters before the fairy godmother came to save her. I'll never find a man without the proper attire."

Marguerite and Winifred exchanged knowing looks.

"Penny, our ball gowns are ready. They just need to be fitted to our sizes," Marguerite reassured. "Last month, when Papa accepted Aunt Elizabeth's invitation, she bought the fabrics and went to a modiste on our behalf. Tomorrow, we go to Bond Street, to Madame Collier's shop, to make the adjustments. The gowns should be ready in no time. Samantha also needs to be fitted for her wedding dress and trousseau."

Penny gasped with delight.

Carrying her few belongings, Marguerite stood by the door and smiled. "Aunt Elizabeth is our very own fairy godmother. She is going to make certain we all marry princes."

Closing the door, she walked past the connecting dressing room. She entered the bedroom she would share with Samantha.

* * * *

After putting out the light, Samantha twisted and turned in bed. She punched her pillow as she tried to adjust it just right. Punching it one more time, she placed the pillow beneath her head. "Oh, Marguerite, what's the use? I'm too excited to sleep," she exclaimed suddenly.

Amazed at how soft the silken sheets and fluffy down pillows were, Marguerite luxuriated in the comfort of her four poster bed. "Have I told you how grateful we are?" she asked dreamily.

"A million and one times," Samantha replied. "I'm the one who is grateful, Marguerite. You are here with me. The only thing marring my happiness is that Julianna isn't with us."

"Was Julianna supposed to be here, too?"

"Yes, she was supposed to come out this Season but her brother put a stop to it."

"Why?" Marguerite asked, confused.

"I don't know. Edmund refused to allow her to come with us to London last summer. Finally, this year he relented, only to whisk her away during the first masquerade ball. He then insisted she travel the world. I'm so angry with him, Marguerite," Samantha confessed, taking out her frustration on her poor pillow, pummeling it as though it were Lord Edmund Kent, himself.

"Why would the Earl of Windword do such a thing?"

"Why indeed? That man is so overprotective. I don't know how Julianna puts up with him. He won't allow her to come out to society. She's our age, Marguerite. She's more than ready. How does he expect her to find a husband?"

Recalling how selfish her father had been last Season, Marguerite fumed inwardly. "Never mind, Sam. You shouldn't be angry on such a special night. Steven is wonderful, by the way."

"Oh, Marguerite, he is...He really is. I can't wait for you to meet someone just like him."

"I already met the man for me, or have you forgotten?"

"His Grace, Lord Phillip Lancaster. How can I forget?" Samantha replied, giggling. "The three of us developed such an attraction for him. Now that Julianna's in love with a Spaniard and I'm in love with Steven, you can have him all to yourself."

Marguerite sat up on her bed. "A Spaniard? How did she manage to fall in love with a Spaniard?"

"Right under Edmund's nose, too." Samantha laughed. "Diego de Cordoba is Lord Edmund's good friend. He often visits Windword Hall. He's a widower, and he has a little daughter named Sofia. Julianna is absolutely mad about her. Edmund has no idea."

Fatigue beginning to overtake her, Marguerite lay back on her pillow. "It serves him right for being so domineering," she commented, realizing it had been a long day.

Samantha yawned. "Who?"

"That strict and overbearing Earl of Windword—that is who.

Does he love her?"

"Of course, he does. Edmund loves his sister very much."

"No, silly, Diego. Does Diego return Julianna's feelings?" Marguerite asked, yawning.

"I don't know, but since when has that stopped Julianna? When she wants something, she fights for it."

"Sounds like me."

"Do you remember the first time you saw him?"

"Who?"

"Lord Phillip Lancaster, silly. Your duke."

Marguerite sighed, remembering the first time she laid eyes on the Duke of Wallingford, the most perfect man she had ever seen. "How can I forget? Six years ago, this summer. I can't wait to see him again. You don't think he might remember me?"

"I seriously doubt it. He had never seen you before, or since. You, me and Julianna: the Three Musketeers. How we laughed that night." Samantha giggled devilishly. "I never told my parents. They would have locked me up and never let me out, if I had." She suddenly gasped. "Never mind my parents—Edmund Kent! Poor Julianna, I don't want to think what would have happened if he had not been on one of his trips."

"Ouch!" Marguerite shuddered in jest. "Thank the heavens the grouch never found out. Most importantly, how fortunate the Duke of Wallingford never mentioned it to the Shendlys or to your parents afterwards. I find it hard to believe. He must have known I was from a neighboring estate."

"I think the duke would not have wanted to call attention to the incident." Samantha continued with a yawn, "What I find hard to believe is that you actually interrupted the handsome Lord Phillip during a romantic interlude. On a dare, you did the unthinkable and fell in love with the Duke of Wallingford in the process. Julianna and I never thought you would go through with it."

Marguerite chuckled, recalling how she heard their neighbors at Shendly Manor would be hosting a ball in honor of the Duke of Wallingford, who was visiting on his way to London. Samantha dared Marguerite and Julianna to spy on the Shendlys' ball and their most renowned guest. Julianna refused, but Marguerite could never pass up a dare.

Once Aunt Elizabeth and Uncle John had left for the ball, the Three Musketeers had walked to the neighboring estate. While Julianna and Samantha waited by the gate, Marguerite had entered the estate unnoticed.

Climbing up a tree to watch the guests, Marguerite had come across the Duke of Wallingford and his paramour in a lover's tryst. Shocked, but fascinated, her innocent eyes had witnessed passion between a man and a woman. She remembered how the woman had moaned and called him "Phillip" and how Lord Phillip had kept calling out the name "Louise." So enthralled was Marguerite, she had not noticed the tree branch was about to break until it was too late.

Her skirts raised, her thighs wrapped around the duke's tall form, Louise's bodice was opened wide, her large breasts exposed, when Marguerite fell from the tree and landed at Lord Phillip's feet. The duke, entwined within his lover's embrace, cursed at the sudden intrusion. His angry gray eyes were like silver lightning as he stared down at Marguerite.

All Marguerite could do was stare back at him. Riveted by his handsome face, thick black hair, and his tall, manly form, she had never seen anyone more magnificent.

Poor Louise had screamed and tried to cover herself as he came off her. Still cursing, the duke had demanded Marguerite's name, but she had darted out of there so quickly, he had not been able to race after her. Marguerite cringed. What would have happened if she had broken a bone? What if she had not been able to flee? The thought mortified her.

She had never forgotten the duke's handsome face. She hoped he would not remember hers. That was six years ago. It was dark. She was a child. She had changed much.

Since that day, Marguerite had followed the Duke of Wallingford's love life from the various newspapers Samantha and Julianna had been kind enough to mail to her. From those same society pages, she had recognized Lord Phillip's lover as the infamous and very much married Louise Shasner-Blake, Countess of Salesbury.

Lord Phillip Lancaster was not too happy to see Marguerite then, but she would make him happy now. He would be the one to fall at her feet.

With that blissful thought, Marguerite drifted into sleep.

* * * *

Later that night, at an inn across town, Edmund Kent lay wide awake in the room he had rented under an assumed name. His thoughts kept him up, making him toss and turn in bed as he had every night since reading the telegram from Diego de Cordoba informing him of Julianna's whereabouts. Punching his pillow for the umpteenth time, Edmund cursed under his breath. "Bloody hell!"

Julianna's predicament was the reason that Edmund now found himself in the middle of the London Season, pretending to be someone else, and having to endure all he had shunned in the past. The Season, with its frivolous merrymaking and endless festivities, reminded him of the senseless accident that had taken his parents' lives twelve years ago. Crossing the street after attending the opera, the Earl and Countess of Windword had been run over by a carriage full of young, drunken revelers. At nineteen, Edmund had witnessed the tragic accident from the sidewalk. The image of his parents lying in a pool of blood on the cold cobblestone street would remain with him until his dying day.

Since his parents' untimely death, Edmund had lost his enthusiasm for London. He had seldom returned, opting to send his aides when it came to business matters. Ironically, his travels and his absence from previous Seasons now allowed him to go incognito amongst the aristocracy. They knew his name, Edmund Kent, and his title, the Earl of Windword, but no one recognized his face.

He had changed much in the last twelve years, but there was one thing that would never change, and that was his love for his sister, Julianna. Four weeks ago, livid with her for marrying a difficult and complicated Spanish widower with a prone-to-tantrums, spoiled little daughter and in-laws sure to make her miserable, Edmund had wanted to wring Julianna's neck. He had been even more furious with his supposed "best friend," the Marques of Altamares for taking advantage of Julianna, who was but a child herself.

At the time, his only thought was of Julianna's future as an English marquesa. Sweet, innocent Julianna, who had been sheltered from English society, would find herself thrown headlong into the intricacies and chicaneries of the Spanish court. The Spanish Inquisition would be mild compared to the trials his little sister would suffer married to Diego de Cordoba.

According to Diego, his life in Spain was more than a bit thorny with family intricacies, bickering over inheritance, and plenty of fiery squabbles more absurd than any clear-thinking, red-blooded Englishman could possibly comprehend.

Earlier that year, when they had crossed paths in Italy, Diego had confided that his family was insisting he marry his late wife's sister, Inés. To complicate matters even more, Inés had taken residence at his home with the excuse of caring for his eight-year-old daughter, Sofia. Julianna's home life would be wretched, having to share her house with newfound relatives who would resent and not appreciate her. Worse, having had the misfortune of knowing them quite well because of his friendship with Diego, Edmund had been convinced that the passionate Spanish clan would make mincemeat of his dear sister.

Set on rectifying the situation by annulling the marriage and bringing her back to Windword Hall, Edmund had rushed to Madrid, only to find his sister's marriage to be the least of his problems.

Julianna's motivation for eloping had nothing to do with love. Instead, it involved something so vile, so dark, so awful that, when thinking of it, Edmund's fury consumed every part of him. Diego had assured him the marriage was in name only, and its sole purpose was in keeping Julianna out of harm's way. Their union would be annulled once it was safe for Julianna to return to Windword Hall.

Apart from Diego's daughter, Sofia, who knew Julianna well from their travels to Windword, Julianna's true identity had been kept from the rest of Diego's family and friends. For the time being, she could hide in Spain as the Marquesa of Altamares, where no one in England would be the wiser. Having learned the ugly truth, Edmund had no choice but to return to England without Julianna and trust his sister to Diego's care.

No longer furious with her, or with Diego, Edmund's rage was directed elsewhere—at a vile, depraved animal whose identity Julianna had refused to divulge, but that Edmund was determined to uncover. Watching his sister reduced to a trembling, frightened victim—so terrified she would not return home or give up the bastard's name for fear of her life—had broken Edmund's heart. It also made him even more determined for revenge.

No matter how interminable or unpleasant the Season, he would find the filthy bastard who had tried to rape his sister and threatened her with death—and he would make him pay dearly.

* * * *

The next morning, Marguerite heard a knock at the door, but before she could respond, Flora, Samantha's personal maid, entered the room carrying a pail of water.

"You've overslept, child," Flora announced, trying not to lose her equilibrium as she struggled with the heavy bucket. "You surely are a sight for sore eyes."

Marguerite threw back the covers then stood from the bed, rushing over to her. "Nanny, how good to see you!" she exclaimed, genuinely happy to see the plump, elderly woman who had been Samantha's nanny for years. "You mustn't carry that. It's too heavy."

Relieving Flora of the bucket of water, Marguerite walked to the porcelain washstand and filled it to the rim. "You can hurt yourself doing such strenuous work," she persisted, placing the half-empty pail on the floor.

"Do I seem out of breath?" Flora asked as she opened the drapes and began to make Samantha's bed.

"No, Nanny, you don't, but..."

"It's not strenuous, miss. Moving about is good for my circulation. I don't want to be idle," she commented, stretching the sheets and plumping the pillows. "I won't be replaced with some young filly and be sent out to pasture. Especially now that Lady Samantha is getting married."

There was no use in arguing with Flora. She was stubborn and would never change. Aunt Elizabeth had tried to "send her out to pasture" for years, but the elderly nanny had insisted on staying on as Samantha's maid, no matter how arduous the work. Samantha tried hard to alleviate the workload by picking up after herself or secretly having some other maid do Flora's chores behind her back. The more Sam tried to lighten the load, the more her dear nanny persisted in proving herself. Finally, the Hardwoods had decided to let Flora have her way. She would let them know when it was time to retire.

"Let me have a look at you." Flora stood back, her eyes narrowing speculatively as she surveyed Marguerite. "I always knew you would grow up to be a beauty, but you have surpassed my expectations," she said. "You've got curves in all the right places, child. You'll be a married woman before the Season is over, or my name isn't Flora Hemmingdale!"

"I hope so, Nanny." Marguerite blushed, covering herself with her robe. "If I don't get a proposal of marriage, I'll have no choice but to become a governess by Season's end."

"Nonsense!" Flora laughed. "Don't try to fool me with feigned modesty, child. You know they won't be able to resist you. Look at the time," the nanny said suddenly. "Lady Samantha will be angry with me for keeping you. There are fresh towels in the dressing room, behind the screen. When you're finished dressing, you may join the others downstairs in the breakfast room for a bit of nourishment. You are going to need it. My lady has planned quite the day for you. She is waiting downstairs."

"I missed you last summer, Nanny," Marguerite said, smiling. "You never change."

"I suppose that is a good thing. I missed you, too. The summer was not the same without you. Now hurry, you don't want to be late. London awaits you, dear. Now where's that hug you owe me?"

Smiling, Marguerite hugged the old woman. "Flora, are Penny and Winnie downstairs?"

"No, I've woken them twice, but they are still in their beds. Too much excitement, I suppose, traveling and all."

"They must hurry. We have an appointment with the seamstress this morning."

Flora agreed. "Indeed, they must. After Madame Collier's, you will visit the Bond Street shops for accessories, and then, if there is time, you are going to do some sightseeing."

"Sam is taking us to Hyde Park and then to Westminster Abbey. I can't wait to see the Serpentine! Nanny, wake them again. Winifred is usually quick, but Penelope takes her time getting dressed."

Picking up and gently swinging the half-empty pail of water back and forth, Flora walked to the door. "Don't worry, miss. If they insist on staying in bed, I know what to do." She smiled devilishly. "There's enough water here to wake the dead."

Marguerite giggled. "Nanny, you wouldn't!"

A half hour later, a famished Marguerite, tired of waiting for her sisters to finish dressing, knocked on their bedroom door and told them that she was going downstairs without them. Once she descended the staircase, she was surprised to find Uncle John, Aunt Elizabeth and Samantha, all with somber expressions on their faces, whispering amongst themselves in the hallway.

"Marguerite, come dear. We need to speak with you," Uncle John beckoned when he saw her walking toward them. "I'm afraid we've just received troubling news."

"Is it Papa—is he ill?" Marguerite asked, alarmed.

With a nervous smile, Aunt Elizabeth took Marguerite's hands in hers. "No, dear. It's not Archibald. It does not involve you. You need not worry."

Uncle John looked at his wife and firmly shook his head in disagreement. "You are mistaken, dear. It does involve the girls. Marguerite, the troubling news concerns an employee of mine, Alpert Cummings, a loyal and faithful man who has just passed away."

"I'm sorry for your loss, Uncle John," Marguerite replied, confused. "My memory fails me. Was I acquainted with Mr. Cummings?"

"No, dear, but I would like to introduce you to his replacement, Ashton James, who is waiting in the study. Ashton has worked under my employment for some time, and I trust him implicitly. He will take over Alpert's duties. I have every confidence in him."

"Uncle, I would be happy to meet Mr. James, but I fail to see how this involves me."

"Your aunt promised Archie you would be well chaperoned during your stay in London. You see, dear, we will be quite busy with the preparations for Samantha's wedding, but we mustn't forgo our duties as guardians. Things have changed since we made that promise. We can no longer keep it."

Marguerite's stomach knotted, and she stiffened with dread. *Dear God, this cannot be happening!* She could not go back to her father. Not now, when all her dreams were about to come true. She would never have another opportunity to meet the Duke of Wallingford.

"Have you changed your minds? Do you want us to leave?" she asked, trying to swallow the lump in her throat.

"Of course not. On the day you leave us, you will have a wedding ring on your finger, my dear. Until that day, you are ours to keep," Elizabeth quickly reassured her. "We have hired a chaperone, that is all."

Elated, Marguerite exhaled a long sigh of relief.

As they all headed toward the study, Marguerite noticed her cousin was unusually quiet. "Sam, were you close to him?" she asked.

"Close to whom?"

"Your father's employee, Alpert Cummings...the one who just died."

"I never met him. I don't approve of the chaperone, that is all," Samantha snapped, most uncharacteristically. "I'm sorry, Marguerite. I guess I'm acting like a spoiled and nervous bride."

Marguerite had heard brides could be a little trying, but why would a chaperone cause Samantha such distress? There was more going on here, but she knew better than to press her cousin. Samantha would let her know soon enough if there was something wrong. For now, Marguerite was more than happy to be staying in London. A chaperone sounded perfectly fine to her—as long as the woman did not get in the way of her meeting Lord Phillip Lancaster.

Smiling politely, Marguerite followed the Hardwoods into the study.

There was something vaguely familiar about the man who stood at the window with his back to them. No—it couldn't be! Could it? Her eyes froze on his tall, broad-shouldered physique.

"Ashton, this is my niece, Miss Wiggins. Her sisters will be joining us shortly," Uncle John said, before turning to Marguerite. "As a favor to us, along with Albert's many duties, Mr. James has agreed to be your chaperone during your stay in London."

When the stranger turned around, a soft gasp escaped Marguerite as she recognized him immediately. His features were hard and chiseled, just as she remembered. He was to be her chaperone—him?

Ashton James's eyes grew openly amused once he recognized her. With a wry smile, he strolled forward and extended his hand. "Ah, yes, your chaperone," he said, as though he could read her thoughts.

The warmth of his hand and the burr of his manly baritone sent a tingle up Marguerite's spine. She stood stock-still, instantly mesmerized, as she looked up into his deep, dark brown eyes. He was so devilishly handsome, he nearly took her breath away.

"Hello, Meggie," he drawled, releasing her hand.

Marguerite could not find her voice. She did not know if she was more shocked by his casual familiarity or by the teasing, almost mocking glint in his eyes. All too vividly, the embarrassing train ride came back to haunt her.

Samantha's eyes shifted from Marguerite to Ashton James. "You know my cousin's name? I was not aware you were acquainted with one another."

His lips twitched. "Oh, yes. I'm quite familiar with Miss Wiggins and her sisters. Right, Meggie?"

Under his watchful gaze, Marguerite felt herself blush. "I don't know him." She managed to shrug offhandedly.

His grin was lazy—irresistibly devastating. She became aware of the attractive laugh lines that crinkled at his eyes, the sensual lips that twitched with mirth, the clean, masculine scent of his cologne. He was much too attractive—too attractive for her own good.

Feeling flushed, Marguerite desperately wanted to leave. Her eyes scanned the room for a way out. "I'll go see what is keeping my sisters."

Aunt Elizabeth's brows furrowed. "Before you go, Marguerite... which is it? Mr. James, I do not understand. Do you or do you not know one another?"

"Mr. James thinks he knows me, but he doesn't know me at all. A train ride does not a person make," Marguerite noted haughtily.

It was evident by the confused looks on the Hardwoods' faces that she was not making any sense, but she could not help herself. She did not want to be affected by him, but it was hard to remain coherent when this stranger was so close. Except he was no longer a stranger. His name was Ashton James, and he suddenly become her chaperone.

Satisfied she put him in his place, Marguerite turned her back to him, eager to get away.

"So long, Meggie," she heard him call out.

Meggie, indeed—the audacity of the man! He was but a mere employee of Uncle John's. How dare he address her in such a familiar way? "Don't call me Meggie. I don't like it," she said over her shoulder as she walked out the door.

"Would you prefer I call you Duchess?" he asked, a trace of laughter in his deep-timbered voice.

Chapter Four

Marguerite sat before the mirror, her mass of silken black hair pulled back in a soft chignon, as Winifred stood behind her, adjusting her tiara. Was that really her, Marguerite Wiggins, Archibald's daughter? Was she truly in London, getting ready for her first ball? Could it be a dream? It certainly felt like one. She hardly recognized her image in the mirror. Aunt Elizabeth's sapphire-and-diamond tiara made Marguerite appear almost regal. The cobalt blue chiffon bustled gown, which matched her eyes, was the most exquisite she had ever possessed. If she barely recognized herself, she could not believe her eyes when it came to Winifred, who stared into the mirror with an awed expression on her face.

Wearing an amethyst silk gown and a pearl crown accented by tiny lilac roses, her sister had been transformed from a gooseling, as Papa would say, into a beautiful swan. Her glasses tucked away, Winnie stared at herself before the mirror with rounded brown eyes. Loose tendrils of silky brown hair softened her face. A smile trembled over her lips.

"Oh, Marguerite, is it really me?" Winnie asked. "I feel as though I'm going to wake up at any minute."

"Yes, Winnie, it's you. You look so beautiful—you take my breath away. Aunt Elizabeth was right. You look just like the portrait of Grandmother Olivia in the hallway," Marguerite said, smiling. "I was just thinking the exact same thing. If this is a dream, please don't wake me."

An hour earlier, the dressing room had been a chaotic throng of everything female. Ball gowns with large trains hung perfectly pressed as the young women, in various stages of dishabille, prepared themselves for the most exciting of evenings.

While they giggled and recounted the week's events, Flora, who was highly skilled with the hairbrush, had worked her magic on each and every one of them. Their giggles soon turned to compliments and mutual admiration once the exquisite gowns had been draped over the various corsets, crinolines and bustles.

"My, look at the four of you—I've never seen so much beauty

gathered in one place before...like a lovely bouquet of flowers! Don't you agree, Flora?" Aunt Elizabeth exclaimed as she entered the dressing room.

Flora, who just finished fixing Samantha's hair, heartily concurred. "Miss Penelope, pink is most assuredly your color, and Miss Winifred, violet does you fine. Miss Marguerite, that blue gown sure brings out the blue in your eyes. Lady Samantha, tonight you will be Lord Steven's lady in green. Everyone else will be green with envy when you dance in his arms."

Marguerite noticed Samantha smiled halfheartedly and did not respond. Her cousin had seemed preoccupied, very different from the Samantha who had greeted them at the door the day they arrived in London. It worried Marguerite to see her dear cousin so troubled, especially now, when she should be walking on air. What could be weighing so heavily on Samantha's mind?

Smiling proudly, Aunt Elizabeth said, "Speaking of my future son-in-law, he is waiting with his parents in the drawing room. The marquess and marchioness are anxious to take you to the ball."

"Oh dear, I mustn't keep them." Samantha stood from the mirror, quickly gathering her purse and shawl. "I can't wait for the three of you to meet Steven's brother, Roland. He'll be at the ball. Mother, I wish you were coming, too. What a shame. How's Papa?"

"He'll be fine. He's a little under the weather, nothing serious," Aunt Elizabeth replied. "We were looking forward to attending the ball, but I'll wait up tonight, and you can tell me all about it." She turned to her nieces. "Are you almost ready, my dears? Mr. James is also waiting in the drawing room. Oh, Penny, I would like you to wear my ruby earrings and necklace. They will match perfectly with your gown."

"Mr. James is here?" Penelope gasped. "I'm far from ready! He won't leave without me...will he, Aunt Elizabeth?" Copper ringlets meticulously curled on her forehead and at the nape of her neck, Penny, dressed in pink taffeta, nervously bit her lip and shook her hands. "Aunt Elizabeth, could you help me? The excitement is turning my fingers into jelly. My bodice has so many buttons, I can't get to them all. Can you also put the earrings and necklace on me? I'm afraid I'll drop them. They're so beautiful—Aunt Elizabeth, thank you!"

"Of course, my dear," Aunt Elizabeth replied, walking over to Penny. "Try to collect yourself. Mr. James will wait for you. Remember his one rule: you are to arrive with him, and you are to leave with him."

"We cannot disappear from the ballroom without him...not even for a breath of fresh air," Marguerite added, rolling her eyes.

She had enough of Mr. Ashton James. The past three weeks, although exhilarating, had been somewhat torturous for Marguerite. She had been presented at court, had flirted with many interested and eligible bachelors, had picnicked in Hyde Park, had been to the opera and theatre, had promenaded up and down Rotten Row on horseback, all with her sisters and a multitude of single women who were also drawn to the same places in order to catch a husband. She had done all that and still no Duke of Wallingford. Lord Phillip Lancaster was nowhere to be found... nowhere at all. Instead, the one thing she could count on was having Mr. Ashton James constantly looking over her shoulder.

The man was insulting and exasperating. At one point she had come close to slapping his face. He'd had the nerve to suggest that they stop "peacocking their wares" in order to find husbands, insisting that they keep their dignity and not look so desperate. To make matters worse, Penny and Winnie, instead of feeling slighted, were absolutely thrilled with him. They could not contain themselves, gushing with compliments about how wonderful he was, and how absolutely handsome he was, and how incredibly heavenly it was to have him as their chaperone.

Her sisters seemed to look to him for advice, obeying his every command. The man commanded plenty. Penny was right—they were Cinderellas. No matter where they were or how they felt about it, at twelve o'clock, midnight, Ashton James would usher them out and deliver them home.

Tonight would be different. Tonight they would attend Lady Wimberly's ball. The Duke of Wallingford would surely be there, and Marguerite vowed to herself not to leave without being formally introduced to him. She did not care what Ashton James had to say about it. Tonight would be the beginning of a beautiful romance and the end of Mr. James's tyrannical dictatorship.

* * * *

Marguerite looked up from the dance floor and noticed the time on the huge grandfather clock at the top of the stairs. It was close to midnight. Soon Ashton James would come looking for her, and he would insist on leaving the ball. Out of breath from dancing yet another waltz with yet another clammy young lord, she excused herself and decided to hide from her ogre of a chaperone in the powder room. Although she would have liked nothing more than to return to the Hardwood townhome, she was not ready to call it an evening—not yet.

Lady Wimberly's ball was magnificent, everything Marguerite had dreamt of and more, but she was no longer enjoying herself. The ball had been in progress for some time, and unlike her sisters, who waltzed past her with dreamy expressions upon their faces, Marguerite's mood had worsened by the minute. If she had to feign one more smile or hear one more foolish accolade, she would scream.

The lavish surroundings did little to improve her disposition. It was warm—too warm. The stifling scent of thousands of blossoms fused with heavy perfume and sweat was making her ill. She needed to get away for a minute or two, and the powder room was the perfect place to sort out her thoughts. After all these years, her duke was here, so close, yet so unattainable.

Hours earlier, when Uncle John's carriage had waited in place behind the line of coaches depositing guests outside the Wimberly mansion, she had been overwhelmed with excitement. Recognizing him instantly, she could hardly contain herself as she'd watched the Duke of Wallingford step out of his crested carriage. He was as she remembered, absolutely magnificent. How splendid he looked with his top hat and cloak as he ascended the red carpeted steps. She could not take her eyes off him as she watched him enter the opened double doors into the well-lit mansion.

Fighting the urge to jump out of the carriage and run after the duke, she had waited with her sisters and Ashton James for what seemed an eternity for their turn to dismount. Ashton James had descended first, and after helping her sisters out of the carriage, their chaperone had offered his white-gloved hand to assist her. Eager to go inside, she had taken his hand and had tried her best to ignore the glint of humor in his dark brown eyes as she stepped down onto the pavement.

"Don't trip over yourself trying to get to him, Meggie. He's probably had his share of adoring females. Try not to look so eager."

Marguerite had quickly pulled her hand free of his, but he had offered his arm to escort her up the steps. "It is Miss Wiggins to you—must I remind you again, Mr. James?" she had asked, begrudgingly placing her hand on his arm.

"What can I say, Miss Wiggins? I lost my head."

The knowing grin on his handsome face confirmed Marguerite's suspicion that the man was not the least bit contrite. "I was not aware that you were an expert on the Duke of Wallingford," she had whispered angrily as they had ascended the steps to the mansion. "How do you know about his women? Have you read about them in the society pages?"

"Society pages, Miss Wiggins? Certainly not. The silly look on your face gave away his identity, that is all," Ashton replied, chuckling, as they entered the festive mansion, and after handing his cloak and hat to the attendant, he led her and her sisters toward the crowded staircase to the ballroom below. "I'm no expert on your beloved duke, but I'm a good judge of character. The man appears to be well into his forties. He could have married by now."

"Why do you suppose he hasn't married?" Marguerite had wondered out loud, and had regretted her words the moment she had spoken them. The last thing she'd wanted was to encourage Ashton James's opinion on such a personal matter. Now that she had given him an opening, she knew he was going to offer it to her nonetheless.

"Maybe your duke is bored. Look around. There are plenty of women here who would kill to be called 'Duchess.' Make him want to choose you, Meggie. Play hard to get. You've been doing it for weeks with all the others. I've seen you with plenty of men, and not once have I witnessed such a wistful expression on your face. Your father would be furious if he knew the number of potential suitors you have discouraged since your arrival in London."

Was she that obvious? The man was infuriating and annoying, but, regrettably, quite accurate when it came to her. At first, Marguerite had been hard-pressed to admit that he was, indeed, a very good judge of character. It was as though the exasperating Mr. James had an uncanny ability to read her mind, and it irritated her to no end.

This time, while he had a point, her chaperone was not entirely correct.

Contrary to his beliefs, she had not been playing hard to get. She desired none of the gentlemen who had shown the slightest interest in her, and simply considered these men obstacles in her plan to marry the Duke of Wallingford. By some miracle, she had been given this one London Season to make all her dreams come true. She would not waste it by encouraging anyone other than Lord Phillip. She could not afford to do so.

"Enjoy your ball, ladies. We leave at midnight and not a minute after," Ashton had stated the moment they had finally entered the ballroom. "Go find your duke, Meggie. The clock is ticking," he had said, pointing to the grandfather clock at the top of the stairs.

Marguerite had not failed to catch the sarcasm in his voice. Her chaperone's impertinence had reached an even higher level than usual, but she had been too irritated with the man and too enthralled with the magical milieu of the ballroom to give Ashton James another thought. Taken aback by the grandiosity of it all, she, like the wide-eyed Penny and Winnie, could only admire the large flower arrangements that seemed to be everywhere and the beautiful crystal chandeliers that hung from the painted ceiling and illuminated the room. Not to mention the landed gentry who mingled and watched as others waltzed on the dance floor to the orchestra's music.

For the rest of the evening, she had tried her best to stay clear of Ashton James, concentrating mostly on getting close enough to the Duke of Wallingford for an introduction. Unfortunately for Marguerite, the crowd of guests between them, the doting females circulating around him, and the eager bachelors who continued to claim dance after dance with her, had made it impossible. For four long, exhausting hours, Marguerite had pretended to enjoy herself, all the while becoming more and more frustrated as the night went by.

Entering the spacious powder room, Marguerite smiled at the two young ladies who stood at the corner of the room before an oval floor-length mirror. So absorbed were they in their conversation, the women did not acknowledge her presence. In fact, Marguerite believed that they had not even noticed her when she took the empty chair before the mirrored vanity table.

She was not familiar with the petite, dark-haired girl who fanned herself and primped before the mirror, but she recognized the tall, buxom blonde as Lady Lorena Bonner and felt a sudden pang of jealousy. She had read about Lady Lorena often enough in the society pages and had seen her image in the papers.

Always smiling, always on Lord Phillip's arm!

Without ever meeting her, Marguerite had loathed the woman for years. The fact that Lady Lorena Bonner was even lovelier in person, and the rumor that one day Lorena would become the Duchess of Wallingford, did not help matters any. Dressed in an elegant aquamarine gown, Lady Lorena's large blue-green eyes glimmered brighter than the expensive diamond jewelry she wore. Her stylish chignon lay at the base of her long, graceful neck. Marguerite's fingers itched to pull hard on that golden chignon and scratch out those very eyes. It was all she could do to sit and listen.

Lady Lorena stared at her image in the mirror while she powdered her nose. "Emily, I've been a fool. He's never going to marry me. He has been dangling that marriage proposal before my eyes for years. If it is Louise he wants, he's welcome to her. I mean it this time. I told him so earlier."

Emily's eyebrows shot up in surprise. "I can't believe my ears," she exclaimed. "You've been pining for years!"

"True, but he's been pining after that married countess like a sick puppy dog longer than I for him."

Emily turned to her friend in amazement. "Lorena, you actually broke things off?"

"There was nothing to break off. I've waited years, and what have I to show for it? Nothing—not so much as a betrothal. I've been just one of many ornaments on his arm. If there's a woman out there who can make him forget his beloved countess, I wish her the best."

"Why tonight? Are you angry that he's been flirting with Louise all evening? "

"No, I'm used to Phillip's flirting with the countess. Someone else has gotten my attention, that is all," Lady Lorena admitted with an air of calm and self-confidence as she pinched her cheeks. "He is gorgeous—those dark eyes, the square jaw, those generous lips! I want to find out all about him. I get goose bumps just thinking about the man."

Emily shook her head in awe. "I never thought a man existed who could make you forget the Duke of Wallingford. Who is this miracle worker?" she insisted, her eyes wide with excitement. "Is it Lord Jackman? Don't think I have not noticed how you look at him when he is not watching."

Lady Lorena flicked an imaginary speck of dirt from her gown. "I'm not certain I'm ready to reveal his name, Emily Middleton. After all, you haven't told me about the mystery man who offered to take you home."

Emily Middleton blushed as she smoothed her hair and flattened her palms against her dress. "I told him it was out of the question unless a few of my friends came along. It wouldn't be fitting to be alone with him. He agreed."

"So who is he? I've never seen you look more excited."

"Oh, Lorena, I've never been happier! I've longed for this day, but I'm not going to tell you his name. You wouldn't believe me."

Giving Emily a cool, appraising look, Lady Lorena shrugged. "Well, I'm not as secretive as you. You've always been silly that way. I hope it's not James Ashton or Ashton James—I don't remember which," she replied, giggling. "I begged Lady Samantha Hardwood for an introduction, but when she finally got to it, I was too mesmerized by his physical attributes to pay any attention to his name. Emily, I think he's the handsomest man I've ever met."

"Oh dear, no—not him! I was introduced to him earlier, and I don't think I like him," Emily said, her brows furrowing. "Don't you find him a bit daunting? He towers over the other men by a full four inches. He is so...so..."

"Magnificent?" Lorena chuckled devilishly. "Let's go, Emily. I can't wait to feel his arms around me. I've been dying to maneuver a dance from him all evening."

"I agree he is quite pleasing to the eye. I tingled all over when Mr. James was presented to me, but he was not the least bit interested in anything I had to say. I don't know for certain, but there were times during our conversation when I felt the man was silently mocking me."

Lady Lorena gave a burst of laughter. "Good—I'm delighted you find him intimidating and he finds you boring. I want him for myself."

"Don't get too confident, Lorena, dear," Emily replied, tucking her fan into the small beaded purse matching her pink gown. "He has not danced all evening. Every time I see him, he is trailing behind those two country bumpkins. I swear the Wiggins girls couldn't look more out of place. I wonder what he sees in them."

Lady Lorena's lips puckered with annoyance. "Emily, don't be cattish. Lady Samantha introduced me to her cousins earlier, and I find them delightful. They may be a little green, but their manners are impeccable."

"Maybe Miss Winifred's manners, but that red-haired Miss Penny is more than a little rough between the edges," Emily insisted. "I wonder what she finds so interesting in the piece of paper she carries with her at all times. Have you met the third sister, Lady Marguerite?"

"No, we have not crossed paths. It's a tight squeeze out there. Speaking of tight squeezes," Lorena said chuckling, "I'm ready to find that handsome devil, Mr. Ashton, and make certain I get my dance."

Emily Middleton's tone hardened. "Honestly, Lorena, if I hear one more sugary accolade about that country bumpkin, I'm going to scream. The men have been fawning over Marguerite Wiggins for weeks. Did you see the way Lord Roland Bradstone was eyeing her tonight?"

"Emily, if I haven't met the woman, how on Earth am I supposed to notice the way Lord Roland looks at her?"

"I haven't met her either, but gossip has it that Lord Roland is quite taken with her and is going to call on Miss Wiggins this week," Emily went on heatedly. "Now that his brother is engaged to Lady Samantha, Lord Roland's parents are eager for him to take a wife. After all, as firstborn, he is the one who should be begetting heirs. I fear that Miss Wiggins is going to snatch him for herself."

Lady Lorena's eyes widened with concern. "Oh no—Emily, please tell me your mystery man is not Lord Roland Bradstone! He's notorious for his womanizing. I don't like the way he looks at me. He undresses me with his eyes."

Before Emily Middleton could respond, a breathless Penny burst into the powder room. "Marguerite, where have you been? It's half past twelve! Mr. James has been searching for you everywhere. He is really angry with you."

At the mention of her name, both Lady Lorena and Miss Emily stared at her, then at each other in stunned silence.

"Marguerite?" Emily Middleton finally found her voice. "Marguerite Wiggins?"

Marguerite was so furious she could hardly speak. Shooting the mortified ladies a look of cold hauteur, she took a deep breath and rose fluidly from the chair. *It would not do to make a scene,* she silently repeated over and over in her mind while trying to control her emotions. Straightening herself with dignity, she walked over to the door to stand beside her sister.

"Penny, dear, how long has he been searching for me?" she asked smiling.

Penny frowned. "Don't act the innocent, Marguerite. You know he's been waiting a half hour. He told us not a minute past midnight. Congratulations, you have managed to disobey him yet again."

All color drained from Lady Lorena's face. "I'm so sorry, Miss Wiggins. Please accept our apologies. We didn't mean to offend you."

"Miss Wiggins, we did not realize it was you sitting there,"

Emily contended. "Please accept our—"

Purposely snubbing Miss Middleton by not allowing her to voice an apology, Marguerite addressed Lady Lorena with feigned gaiety, "A pleasure to make your acquaintance, Lady Bonner. We have finally crossed paths. You need to pinch those cheeks a bit more. You look awfully pale. Now if you'll excuse this country bumpkin, your handsome devil is waiting for me."

* * * *

"Penelope, I can see him with Winnie at the top of the stairs. Go and tell him that I am not leaving without an introduction to Lord Phillip. The crowd has thinned. It will be easier now."

"I'll do no such thing. He's angry enough," Penny spat out. "Marguerite, what did I interrupt in the powder room? You look as though you are about to burst."

"Never mind that—you are wasting precious time. Do as I say, Penelope Wiggins," Marguerite demanded angrily. "Go, or I'll burn that silly list of yours."

"You and your stupid duke!" Penny stomped her foot. "I wouldn't blame Mr. James if he came down and grabbed you by the hair. I don't know what those women said to you, Marguerite, but whatever it was, you had it coming." Huffing, she walked across the dance floor and began to climb up the grand staircase.

Consumed with indignation, Marguerite's fists bunched at her sides as she recalled the odious, but informative, tête-à-tête she had just been made privy to in the powder room. With the Countess of Salesbury proving to be too great a rival for Lady Lorena, Marguerite had one less formidable competitor in the contest to win the duke's heart. She should be ecstatic, but instead her feelings puzzled and disturbed her.

Why did she detest Lady Lorena more than ever when the woman was no longer her nemesis? Emily Middleton had mocked Marguerite and her sisters by calling them "country bumpkins." It was understandable to feel insulted, but to Marguerite's befuddlement, this was not the reason for her fury. Instead of wanting to claw Emily Middleton's eyes out, Marguerite's anger was directed solely at Lady Lorena Bonner, who had been nothing short of kind when referring to her family.

Kind, but daft!

Lady Lorena had eyes, but she certainly lacked brains, thought Marguerite as she watched Lord Phillip lead the Countess of

Salesbury into a waltz. Granted, Lord Phillip's affair with the married countess was no ordinary flirtation. It had lasted years and had still not run its course, but surely, with a little bit more patience on Lady Lorena's part, plenty of charm and an overabundance of guile, the countess was an obstacle that could have been overcome. She would never understand why Lady Lorena would give up her quest to become a duchess to set her sights on Ashton James—of all men!

What exactly had her chaperone done to make Lady Lorena readily accept defeat after years of pining after the duke? Could her rude, overbearing chaperone have personal plans of his own? The possibility that he could have planned a lover's tryst with Lady Lorena or others like her turned Marguerite's stomach. The thought repulsed her, but it made perfect sense. It was the only explanation she could come up with as to why Mr. James insisted on leaving early every time they attended a function. The scoundrel was using his outings with Marguerite and her sisters to seduce ladies of the upper crust, ladies he would otherwise never dream of meeting.

Marguerite fumed. The man had no business cavorting with Lady Lorena Bonner or Miss Emily Middleton. Although he looked the dashing gentleman in his black evening wear, the man was not of noble birth and not of great means. Mr. James was solely an employee of Uncle John's. She would have to speak with that grand, dandy Casanova and set him straight. He was being paid to act as her chaperone and not to arouse the passions of the giddy females who surrounded him.

She did not have to wait long for Ashton James to react to Penny's words. Quickly ascending the steps, his chiseled features set in irritation, he strode to her side. Truth be told, she could hardly blame Lady Lorena for noticing him. Even in a crowd, Mr. James's presence was compelling.

"You knew we were supposed to leave at midnight. Did you conveniently forget?" Ashton asked brusquely, his expression one of contained anger. "Let's go. You've kept me waiting long enough."

Marguerite lifted her chin in defiance. "I'm not going anywhere without an introduction to Lord Phillip. Your rendezvous can wait, Mr. James."

"What rendezvous?" he asked, a muscle clenched along his jaw.

"Don't act the innocent with me. We both know why you want to leave early. I figured it out when I came out of the powder room."

"Damn it, Marguerite. You exasperate me. What the devil were you doing in the powder room all that time? Were you hiding from me?"

"What I do in the powder room is none of your concern," she replied heatedly. "About Lady Lorena..."

His eyes flashed in a familiar display of impatience. "Who?"

"You heard me. You are here to chaperone. Don't do it again."

"Do what?" he snapped.

"You know exactly what I mean. I don't care what you do on your own time, but don't use our outings to set up assignations with unsuspecting women who have no inkling of your position or background. It is not fair to them, or to my uncle, who is paying good money for you to watch over us."

Ashton James stiffened at her words, his brown eyes darkening like angry thunderclouds. "Are you finished?" he demanded.

"No," Marguerite replied as she pointed to the couples on the dance floor. "Samantha and Steven are waltzing, and so is the duke. I'm certain Lord Steven is familiar with the Duke of Wallingford. The moment the waltz is over, I'm going to ask Samantha for him to introduce us. Go back and wait upstairs with Penny and Winnie. I'll join you as soon as I get my introduction. You are dismissed."

Ashton's mouth dipped into an even deeper frown. "Bloody hell, woman. You try the patience of a saint."

Marguerite was about to retort when, to her complete surprise and indignation, Ashton caught her by the elbow and firmly escorted her to the dance floor. Incensed, she turned to go, but before she could do so, she felt herself being spun around to face him. With his powerful hands, Ashton yanked her against him, and before she knew it, he was twirling her to the rhythm of the music.

"Let go of me at once!" Marguerite fumed. "How dare you force a dance on me?"

He looked briefly over his shoulder. "I've a mind to take you over my knee. Now shut up and waltz."

The scowl on his face told Marguerite that he was completely serious. Wanting to stomp on his foot, she averted her gaze and, for what seemed an eternity, tried to calm herself by concentrating on the beautiful orchestral music and the movement of her steps.

"Where did he learn to dance so gracefully?" she muttered, then realized she had voiced her thoughts out loud. Her cheeks burned as she raised her eyes to find Ashton staring down at her, his expression a chiseled mask of stone.

Marguerite was not certain if it was the exhilarating waltz, the tantalizing scent of his clean, masculine cologne, the nearness of his tall, hard body against hers, or the intimacy of being held within his strong, muscular embrace—but she was feeling more than a bit dizzy as his dark eyes bored into hers.

Instead of resenting Ashton James like she had all her other dance partners for keeping her from the duke, she found herself enjoying the waltz. Lady Lorena was right. The man was, indeed, devastatingly handsome. The very air seemed electrified as everything around her disappeared and she saw only him.

She felt an odd twinge of disappointment moments later, once the music stopped and the waltz came to an end. Her disappointment soon turned to horror when Ashton, without giving her a chance to catch her breath or regain her equilibrium, suddenly let go of her. Turning blindly, she stumbled—to her mortification—right into the Duke of Wallingford and his countess, Lady Louise Shasner-Blake.

"Who have we here?" asked a smiling Lord Phillip as he caught Marguerite in his arms. His gaze riveted on her face, then moved over her body slowly. Her embarrassment was replaced with a tingling in the pit of her stomach as she recognized the admiration in the duke's gray eyes. "Who is this beauty that luck has brought me at so late an hour?"

Her pulse pounded. Could she be hallucinating? She dreamt of being crushed within his embrace. Here she was in his arms, and his eyes were making passionate love to her. Phillip Lancaster, the Duke of Wallingford, actually found her attractive!

"You look familiar, my dear. Have we met?" Lord Phillip inquired, his gaze raking boldly over her as he released her.

Tongue-tied, Marguerite merely stared at Lord Phillip. This could not be happening! Had the duke recognized her? If he hadn't caught her, she would have fallen at his feet, like years before, when she'd fallen from the tree and interrupted him and his countess—the same countess who now stood beside him, her eyes shooting daggers at her.

"Your Grace, I would like you to meet Miss Marguerite Wiggins." Marguerite heard Ashton's deep voice behind her. "She is leaving with me...now."

Something in her chaperone's voice cautioned Marguerite to obey. Without speaking, she gave Ashton a forced smile and a tense nod of consent. Both the Countess of Salesbury and Lord

Phillip looked surprised as she abruptly turned and walked away without so much as a curtsy. She couldn't help herself; she was too flustered to say a word.

Marguerite heard Ashton excuse himself. With a few quick strides, he caught up with her. "You wanted an introduction. I gave you one."

"Throwing me at him—only to drag me away before I had a chance to say anything. How could you? Lord Phillip must think I'm as rude as you."

Marguerite walked with stiff dignity, nodding at a few people as Ashton pulled her along the dance floor and up the stairs to where her sisters were waiting.

"I'll not warn you again, Marguerite. Never talk down to me. The next time I won't be so accommodating," Ashton said coldly, his contemptuous tone sparking her anger even further.

Marguerite ignored him as they approached an open-mouthed Penny and Winnie, who quickly rushed over to her, full of excitement, as they had witnessed everything from the banister.

Ashton James would not spoil her evening. Tonight, she had accomplished her goal. The Duke of Wallingford knew her name. He smiled at her, had found her attractive. She waited years for this moment. Nothing her chaperone could do or say would ruin her good mood.

Chapter Five

Uppity little thing, Miss Emily Middleton, and feisty, too, just as he preferred them! Earlier, when he had pushed her into his coach and had driven off, the bewilderment on her face had been almost endearing. Miss Middleton's confusion soon turned to horror when he tied a handkerchief around her mouth, making certain no sound could come from her. She kicked and screamed once she grasped he had tricked her. To his good fortune, she realized too late her friends were not waiting for her in the coach, and he wasn't taking her home as he offered at the ball.

The poor, delusional Miss Middleton had been circling him for some time, waiting eagerly for him to notice her. Like all the others before her, she'd had her heart set on a courtship that would undoubtedly lead to their marriage. Indeed, he had noticed her, but he had other plans for the pampered and spoiled Miss Emily. His lust demanded an outlet...and she was it.

No longer able to ignore the fever that raged within him, he had sought her out. As was usually the case, it had not taken him long to lure her away from her friends. This time he had been more cautious. The last time the fever consumed him had been most unfortunate. His captive escaped from the coach. To make matters worse, his driver offered no assistance. The self-righteous old fool walked away, leaving him alone to hunt for the girl. He searched for her everywhere, but it was as though she evaporated into thin air. Damn bitch! If he had caught her, he would have killed her. Where could she have gone?

He could have had his pick of women that night. Why had he chosen her? Who would have thought she'd have such strength? She had not given him the chance to tear off her clothes. Instead, she fought him, biting and scratching until he was a bloody mess. The slaps he dealt her had not stopped her from kicking him in his most vulnerable place. When he doubled over in pain, she ran away.

After the episode, the coachman had been given a stipend and banished to the countryside, his life and family threatened with death, if he ever breathed a word to anyone. Shortly thereafter, he had hired a new driver, one he could trust. The man's wife, Gertrude, along with her parents, had been employed under his domain for years. Fresh from their honeymoon, Edgar Mason and his pretty little wife were hungry and ambitious, in need of funds to start an orphanage. In exchange for Mason's silence and assistance, he would provide all the funds Mason needed.

He smiled, remembering earlier. Never before had he invited his coachman to watch or to participate. But he needed to implicate the man further. It wasn't enough that the coachman drove the coach while the girl was getting fondled—the man needed to get his hands dirty. Allowing him to join in the pleasure would ensure Edgar's silence. He was certain of it. Besides, he was not a greedy man. Women were a penny a dozen.

After driving to a secluded place, he had called the driver into the coach, and to his surprise, encouraging the salacious coachman to watch as the virgin was being molested had heightened his own pleasure.

Emily, sweet Emily! He had thoroughly enjoyed her look of terror as his hand slid inside her bodice and he began to fondle her young breast, exposing it for the driver to see. Oh, the pleasure she had given him when he tore open her bodice and put his mouth to her nipple! He had also enjoyed sliding his hand up her thigh and finding the core of her femininity. Terrified, she had wriggled against him in protest, but the more she squirmed, the more his finger had penetrated her.

It was after four in the morning when he had finally carried her out of the coach. They had ridden for hours, and he had degraded her in all sorts of delicious ways. But he had waited until now to take her completely.

He was confident no one had seen them enter the town house he kept for just this very thing. Bordellos on Fleet Street were out of the question. He did not enjoy willing and dirty prostitutes. His tastes were more refined. He did not want to visit where others had been before. He liked them young, virginal, and begging for mercy.

Not like the bitch who escaped. He wouldn't think of that now. The incident only served to infuriate him. He hated loose ends. He would find the bitch and deal with her later. At the moment, he had more pleasurable things in mind. Tonight belonged to Miss Middleton.

His mouth watered. Taking his time, he stood at the edge of the bed, simply feasting his eyes. Lovely she was as she cowered naked against the headboard on the far corner of his bed. He couldn't wait to have her. Such pretty breasts, small but firm, her rosy nipples like perky little rosebuds just waiting for him to suckle and bite.

"Stop trembling, Emily. Come, open your legs for me. Let me have a look. Such a pretty little thing you are, Emily dear."

Emily wept as he grabbed her legs and pulled her toward him.

"No one will hear you, my dear. Stop your crying. You might as well enjoy it. I've had my eye on you for a while. You, my dear, have had your eye on me."

With a deep chuckle, he opened his robe, allowing her to view his naked body. Her gasp of fright hardened him all the more. "Don't fret, my dear. You'll accommodate me just fine."

He laughed as she screamed and tried to escape. Reaching out and taking her by the hair, he caught her before she made it to the door. He pulled her to him and spoke into her mouth, "You don't want to make me angry. I can make this most unpleasant for you."

Chapter Six

Following a late lunch on the afternoon after the Wimberly ball, the women of the Hardwood townhome retreated to the drawing room. When Penny headed for the piano, Marguerite made a beeline for the wing-backed leather armchair closest to the window and furthest from Penny's playing, besting Winifred, who resigned herself to the chaise lounge by the fireplace. Aunt Elizabeth reclaimed her usual seat on the tapestry sofa next to Samantha, where they both resumed work on their respective petit points.

"That's lovely, Penny, dear," Aunt Elizabeth called out, rather loudly, hoping to be heard above Penny's pounding on the keys. "Do come and sit by me," she said kindly, patting the seat. "The piano can wait—my curiosity can't. I want to hear everything that went on in that ballroom last night. I tried my best to wait up for you, but you arrived so much later than usual."

Frowning, Penny reluctantly rose from the piano bench and walked across the room, plopping down beside Aunt Elizabeth on the sofa. "That's because Marguerite kept us all waiting. She wouldn't leave until she got her introduction to the duke. Served her right falling into the poor duke's arms. I'm not surprised she had to run off in mortification."

Wide-eyed, Aunt Elizabeth set aside her needlework. "I don't understand anything you're saying, Penny," she said, shaking her head. Turning to Marguerite, Aunt Elizabeth asked, "Do make sense of this. What does Penny mean, my dear? Did you finally get to meet Lord Phillip? Please tell me, and don't leave anything out."

Marguerite looked up from her book and pondered her aunt's request. Why did Penny have to mention the embarrassing episode? She had intended to tell Aunt Elizabeth all about her introduction to Lord Phillip, but she had planned on leaving out the part where she had almost plowed him over. As usual, her younger sister was making a muddle of things.

Before Marguerite could elaborate, Penny's accusing voice stabbed the air. "Yes, she met him, and she also insulted him by—"

"Marguerite," Samantha interrupted, thankfully changing the

subject. "Steven is under the impression you stole his brother's heart last night. Roland may not be your duke, but he would make a great catch nonetheless. Don't you think he looks an awful lot like Steven? Everyone says so."

Marguerite smiled politely. "Yes, he does," she managed to say. "Lord Roland is a fine-looking man. I think Emily Middleton is quite taken with him."

"Emily Middleton is not the only one, Marguerite. Roland is extremely sought-after. According to Steven, his brother could have married long ago, but has been waiting for the right woman. Wouldn't it be wonderful if he chose you? Sisters-in-law—oh, Marguerite, it would be wonderful indeed!"

Wonderful for whom? Certainly not for her. Marguerite kept silent. She did not want to hurt Samantha's feelings, but she had decided well into the evening Lord Roland Bradstone, although handsome and well-to-do, was not to her liking. Definitely not! Lady Lorena's assessment of the man in the Wimberly powder room had been correct. His lecherous smirk and the salacious gleam in his light blue eyes had given Marguerite the jitters, and, like Lady Lorena, she had felt naked every time Lord Roland had looked at her. Physically, the brothers had much in common, but, fortunately for Samantha, the caddish Roland was nothing like his gallant and loving brother, Steven. No—there was no possible way she and Samantha would ever be sisters-in-law.

Aunt Elizabeth's face seemed to radiate pleasure at the prospect of a possible match. "Marguerite, Lord Roland Bradstone—how splendid!"

A deep crinkle furrowed Penny's forehead as she shot Marguerite a cold look. "Lord Roland Bradstone, Lord Benjamin Kincaid, Lord William Bentley, Lord Stanley Rutherford, Lord Jonathan Bradley, Lord Joseph Bonner...the list goes on. It's not fair. Marguerite has single-handedly appropriated herself to all the eligible bachelors on my list—and she doesn't even want them! Isn't that right, Winnie?"

At the mention of her name, Winifred, who was languidly stretched out on the chaise lounge, became instantly alert. "Honestly, Penny, I've had enough of your whining to last me a lifetime. Just for once, can't you be happy for Marguerite?"

Aunt Elizabeth's eyes shifted nervously from one sister to the other. "Penelope, what about that nice Mr. Pennington?" she asked, trying to avoid further bickering. "Samantha told me he claimed many a dance with you last night."

Pouting, Penny gave an impatient shrug. "Well, yes, but he does not count. I only danced with him because my dance card was practically empty."

"Whatever do you mean?" Aunt Elizabeth looked at Penny with amused wonder. "Of course he counts."

"Mr. Scott Pennington is not on Papa's list. He holds no title. I would rather work as a governess than be married to him."

"Has Mr. Pennington proposed, my dear?" Aunt Elizabeth inquired, looking surprised. "It does seem awfully sudden since you were introduced only last week."

"Well, no, he hasn't proposed. If he did, I certainly wouldn't accept. I refuse to be called Mrs. Penny Pennington for the rest of my days."

"No need to worry about that now, my dear," Aunt Elizabeth said to mollify her.

"I met someone last night, and I don't care that he is not on Papa's list," Winifred suddenly announced. "He's simply wonderful."

Penny's mouth dropped. "Who is he? Was he introduced to Marguerite?"

A secretive smile softened Winifred's lips. "Yes, Penny, he met Marguerite. At the risk of sounding vain, I'm most pleased to announce that Mr. Damian Cummings only had eyes for me."

"Winnie, Mr. Cummings may not be on your father's list, but he is quite the wealthy merchant," Samantha said, smiling. "He owns several shops on Bond Street and throughout London. It is of no surprise that he attended the ball last night. Lady Wimberly only invites the most eligible bachelors. Penny, Mr. Pennington might not hold a title, but he is an affluent banker who has many shares in the American railroad."

Temporarily speechless, Winnie and Penny looked as though their eyes were about to pop from their sockets. Reading their thoughts, Samantha responded with a mischievous grin. "You see, cousins, I have a list of my own. When Mother announced that you were coming to London, I quizzed Steven on all future prospects."

Penny slumped back into her seat. "Well, I don't care if he is wealthy—I do not like Mr. Pennington. We resemble one another—like brother and sister. His face is always pink with eagerness. A man should not have freckles."

"How absurd! Where is it written that a man should not have freckles? Is this another one of Papa's mandates?" Winnie demanded, heatedly. "Marguerite, are you listening to this?"

Marguerite suppressed a giggle. "Winnie, if she prefers her fate as a governess rather than marriage to Mr. Pennington, who am I to criticize?"

"Marguerite would rather starve than to marry anyone but the Duke of Wallingford. You, Winifred Higgins, are an ungrateful daughter," Penny retorted. "I don't understand what Mr. Cummings saw in you last night. It certainly could not have been the biting tongue that mocks our Papa."

Shaking her head, Aunt Elizabeth attempted to end the squabbling once and for all. "Now, now, my darlings, it won't do to argue. Penny, dear, you are entitled to your opinion. No one is going to force you to marry Mr. Pennington against your will."

At that precise moment, the drawing room door opened, and Mortimer, the butler, entered holding a silver tray filled with calling cards. "Mr. Scott Pennington to call upon Miss Penelope Wiggins, Mr. Damian Cummings and his sister, Miss Desdemona Cummings, to call upon Miss Winifred Wiggins."

"Is there anyone else?" Aunt Elizabeth asked.

"Oh yes, my lady...there are many more." Taking a deep breath, the butler continued, "The Marquess of Sutherland, the Earl of Ainsely and his sister, Lady Lorena Bonner, the Viscount Drake, the Viscount Rutherford, Lord Jonathan Wesley, Lord William Chesterfield, Lord Anthony Featherstone, Sir Frederick Brown, Sir John Daly, and the Viscount Bradstone, all to call upon Miss Marguerite Wiggins."

Marguerite's heart sank when Mortimer did not announce Lord Phillip's name.

"So many?" Aunt Elizabeth sprung from the sofa. "Mortimer, don't keep our guests waiting in the vestibule. Bring them to the drawing room, and ask Cook to prepare some refreshments." She turned to her nieces. "My darlings, you are taking London by storm."

Penny corrected her aunt. "You mean Marguerite is taking London by storm. Winnie and I have only one caller each. Mr. Cummings's sister does not count."

Winifred rose from the chaise, quickly removing her glasses and hiding them in her skirt pocket. "How do I look Marguerite? Do you think Mr. Cummings and his sister will approve of me?" she asked, pinching her cheeks to bring out her color.

Marguerite smiled. "You are perfect, Winnie. I'm not worried about Mr. Cummings's opinion of you. It's the poor, unwanted Mr.

Pennington I'm nervous about."

Winifred suddenly looked horrified. "Penelope, I'm warning you. Please treat Mr. Pennington with respect, and do not say anything that will later reflect on the rest of us. After all, he is a guest, and he is rich beyond your wildest dreams. Mr. Pennington should grab you by the shoulders and shake some sense into you."

A furious Penelope was about to retort when Marguerite walked over to stand before the stiff, white-gloved butler. Believing she had caught the duke's interest last night, she had been foolishly hoping that Lord Phillip would call on her today.

"Mortimer, may I see the cards on the tray? Are you certain there is no one else?"

Marguerite instantly regretted the question the moment she voiced the words. How silly and presumptuous of her to think the Duke of Wallingford's calling card would be hidden amongst the other cards and Mortimer could have possibly overlooked it.

"Never mind that silly duke, Marguerite," Samantha said, guessing her thoughts. "You are now the most coveted woman in London, and the envy of every other woman of marriageable age partaking of the Season. Enjoy it! Penny's right; you *are* taking London by storm."

"She certainly is, my dear. She certainly is!" Uncle John's deep voice resounded in the room. "Don't you agree, Mr. James?"

Marguerite hardly recognized the cool, reserved Ashton, who stood in the threshold alongside Uncle John. Mr. James did not even bother to respond to her uncle's question. His brown eyes, usually warm and approving of her, were now cold and distant as he measured her with the same passionless expression etched on his face since their dance the night before. The amused, crooked grin that had irritated her to no end just last night had been replaced by a total lack of interest. It was as though she were invisible. Never mind his grin; a scowl from him would have been preferable to the indifference he showed her now.

Marguerite attempted a conciliatory smile, but her smile quickly faded when she noticed it had no effect on him. His impassive countenance made her raise her chin and return his stare with defiance, as she had been doing since they had walked out of the ball. The slight furrow of his thick eyebrows above a keen, hawklike gaze made her squirm, and she had to look away, too flustered to keep up the pretense.

Why should she care what Mr. Ashton James thought of her? Her chaperone's opinion should be of no importance, but, to her surprise, Marguerite found she did care. In fact, it had bothered her most of the night. She knew he was angry with her—and rightly so. She acted like a spoiled, unpleasant child, determined to get her way. Deliberately ignoring his wishes, she had kept him waiting at the ball and had treated him horribly—insulting him and dismissing him, insisting he not use his position as chaperone for romantic opportunities.

What bothered Marguerite most was, after all that, Ashton had still been willing to help her. Although her introduction to the Duke of Wallingford was certainly not what she envisioned in her dreams, Ashton James made it possible for her and the duke to be introduced nonetheless. Instead of expressing gratitude, Marguerite had shown her chaperone only disdain.

The awkward silence during the coach ride home had been almost unbearable for Marguerite. The knowledge she was the cause of Ashton's foul mood kept her much too preoccupied to enjoy her good fortune in meeting Lord Phillip. Once they arrived at the Hardwood townhome, her chaperone walked them to the door and quickly said his good nights to Penny and Winnie. Ignoring Marguerite, he turned on his heel and left, making it clear he couldn't wait to be rid of her.

She waited all morning to apologize to Mr. James, but she never had the opportunity to catch him alone. To her dismay, her apology would have to wait a while longer given that the drawing room was filling up with guests.

* * * *

Several days later, Marguerite had still not apologized to Ashton. She tried to approach him on a number of occasions, but had been interrupted by the constant flow of visitors filing through the doors of the Hardwood townhome. The invitations and activities that followed each visit had made it even more difficult to speak to her chaperone alone. After a few more awkward and botched attempts, Marguerite finally decided to leave well enough alone.

Ashton no longer sought her out to give her advice, but he seemed less angry and did not ignore her as much. The passing of time helped soften him a bit. Why bring up her behavior and make him furious all over again? She needed to focus her efforts on luring the Duke of Wallingford to the Hardwood townhome, and not worry so much about her chaperone's low opinion of her.

Since the Wimberly ball, Desdemona Cummings and Lady Lorena became regular fixtures at the town house. So had Mr. Damian Cummings and Mr. Pennington. Of course, the outrageously flirtatious Lord Roland Bradstone had not missed a single afternoon to turn Marguerite's stomach with his sugary, inappropriate comments. Indeed, their home had been inundated with eligible bachelors, but sadly for Marguerite, Lord Phillip had still not graced her with a visit.

Today had been no different from any other afternoon at the Hardwood residence. After the midday meal, the women had retired to the drawing room, while Ashton and Uncle John had withdrawn to the study. Soon after, Mortimer walked into the drawing room and announced the names of the visitors who waited in the foyer.

An hour later, most of the guests made their departures as the customary "at home" calling period of a half hour had come and gone. Unfortunately for Marguerite, the five guests who remained in the Hardwood drawing room seemed not at all concerned of wearing out their welcome by extending their stay. Least of which was Lord Roland Bradstone, who joined Marguerite on the tapestry sofa.

The young and attractive Miss Desdemona Cummings, who had hardly spoken two words to Winifred since entering the drawing room, had quickly followed suit. Fashionably dressed, the haughty brunette's shameless flirtation had become more transparent with each passing day. She had not wasted a single second before crossing the room and wedging a place for herself beside Lord Roland on the sofa.

"Lord Roland," Desdemona gushed, "please tell me all about your stay in Bath this year."

"There's not much to tell, Miss Cummings. I'm afraid it was much of the same. I'm more anxious to hear what Miss Wiggins thought of last night's ball."

"Oh," Desdemona said, seeming a little taken aback by Lord Roland's obvious snub. She turned her attention to the delicacies arranged on the silver tray that rested on the rosewood table before them and opted for a dainty finger sandwich. Carefully taking it from the tray, she placed it in her mouth and chewed seductively, fluttering her eyelashes and trying once more to entice Lord Roland in conversation. "My lord, I do hope you are enjoying the Season."

"Hmm...oh yes." Lord Roland bit his lip, devouring Marguerite with his eyes while she poured him his second cup of tea. "Most assuredly, my dear. I always enjoy myself in the presence of a beautiful woman. You certainly are a beautiful woman...a very beautiful woman."

"Really, my lord, you mustn't say such things. Your words may go to my head," Desdemona said, giggling like an idiotic schoolgirl.

Inwardly amused by Desdemona's misplaced flirtations, Marguerite grinned. Her amusement was short-lived when Lord Roland rudely turned his back on Desdemona and concentrated his attention solely on her.

Squirming in her seat, she tried to inch away from him toward the end of the sofa. Undeterred, Lord Roland moved all the closer. "Where are you going, little one? Don't you want to be near me, my dear? I want to be near you," he whispered for her ears only. "Very near, indeed."

Marguerite wanted to slap his face, but she quickly reminded herself that the horrid man was Steven's brother. Under no circumstances could she cause a scene. Trying to control her temper, she did her best to ignore Lord Roland's insinuations by concentrating her attention elsewhere.

Her gaze fixed on Lady Lorena, who conversed by the mantel with Ashton and Samantha. Her poor cousin could very well be having a conversation with herself. By the starry-eyed expression on Lady Lorena's face, Marguerite could tell she was completely ignoring poor Samantha and drooling over Ashton's every word. Had the woman no decency? Marguerite did not know which of the two guests was the more shameless, Lady Lorena or Desdemona Cummings?

Revolted, Marguerite turned away from the trio and focused her attention on a sulking Penny, who sat on the windowsill looking completely bored as the freckled, redheaded Mr. Scott Pennington tried his best to impress her by mentioning the numerous investments he had recently made in America. Not more than two inches taller than Penny, the burly man was not particularly handsome, but he seemed good-humored and quite taken with her. Not that Penelope cared one way or the other. Rudely yawning while inspecting her fingernails, she turned her back on him and stared out the window, disregarding him altogether.

During their visits, Penny had been determined to flirt with most of Marguerite's callers, hoping to procure for herself a "lord on Papa's list." Despite all of Penny's efforts, the men had not shown interest. The more Penny vied for their attention, the more the equally determined Mr. Pennington vied for Penny's, making certain to monopolize all of her little sister's time with endless, tedious conversation only a banker could find interesting.

On the other side of the drawing room, Marguerite observed a completely different picture. Sitting quite cozy on a pale-blue Queen Anne love seat, Winifred seemed enthralled with the tall and pleasant-looking Mr. Damian Cummings. Mr. Cummings seemed even more captivated with Winifred. Marguerite hoped Mr. Cummings's courting of Winifred would lead to a proposal of marriage. She also hoped Mr. Cummings was nothing like his twin sister, Desdemona, who now inched closer to Lord Roland on the sofa.

"Don't be coy, my little tulip," Lord Roland whispered ever so softly for Marguerite's benefit alone, his eyes like devouring piranhas fixed on her bosom.

If only the sofa were a rowboat! Maybe then it would tip over and she could swim away. Had she imagined the slight flicker of his tongue lasciviously wetting his upper lip? Marguerite's skin crawled at the thought, and she shuddered, turning her head away in disgust. Had anyone else noticed?

As if drawn by some magnetic force, Marguerite's eyes immediately locked with those of Ashton James from across the room. The slight nod of his head and the knowing look on his face told her nothing had escaped his notice. The knowledge soothed her, and, for a second, she felt a camaraderie with him. Could one short afternoon with Lord Roland make her appreciate her infuriating and formidable chaperone?

She smiled at Ashton, and although he did not smile back, she noted his eyes and the harshness in his features momentarily softened. *Good!* For some inexplicable reason, she needed to feel his goodwill, his protection. He looked so strong and capable; she had to stop herself from running into the safety of his arms.

"Miss Wiggins, I wonder if we could step out to the patio for some fresh air?" Lord Roland suddenly whispered in Marguerite's ear. "I want to be alone with you."

Jolted from her musings, Marguerite stiffened. "It would be rude of me to leave my guests, my lord," she said, not caring if she sounded a little sharp.

"Your guests have gone, my dear. At present, I am your only caller," he replied, his eyes blatantly staring at her bosom. "I'm most definitely in need of fresh air."

"Would you like to borrow my fan?" she asked.

Lord Roland's face reddened. Just as he was about to speak, Ashton, Lady Lorena and Samantha walked up to them.

"I'm about to give Lady Lorena a tour of the house," Samantha announced. "Miss Cummings, would you care to join us, too? I'm sure Mr. James would be happy to escort us."

A wave of apprehension swept through Marguerite. What was Samantha doing? Was she out of her mind, leaving her alone with this wolflike libertine? Oh, why did Samantha have to take Lady Lorena for a tour of the house now? Why did Ashton have to accompany them? Marguerite knew she was not thinking rationally, but Lord Roland's inappropriate behavior was not all in her mind. She should not feel the need of a chaperone in her own home. If he acted this boldly in a room full of people, God only knew what Lord Roland would do to her if they were unaccompanied.

If only she could confide in Samantha! Anyone could see Steven thought the world of his brother. Marguerite would not cause a rift between Samantha and Steven, not now when they seemed so very happy together. She was probably overreacting. What exactly had the man done? Nothing, really. Nothing at all, except to look at her insolently, as though she was his morsel to devour.

"I'll pass, Lady Samantha, thank you just the same. I'm still a little fatigued from last night's ball," Desdemona replied.

Marguerite breathed a sigh of relief, never imagining a time when she would have welcomed Desdemona's company more than at present. If Desdemona was staying behind, maybe Ashton would do the same.

Ashton smiled politely. "Lady Samantha, it would be my pleasure to escort you and Lady Lorena, but first I must have a word with Miss Wiggins."

Marguerite felt safe the moment she touched the warmth of his outreached hand. His fingers were strong, firm and protective as he helped her from the sofa and ushered her to a corner of the room where they would not be overheard.

"How long are you going to let that fool ogle you?" Ashton demanded between clenched teeth. "How long am I supposed to watch and do nothing?"

The depth of his fury took her by surprise. "As long as it is necessary," Marguerite replied tartly, reacting angrily to the challenge in his voice. "We cannot cause a scene—the man is Steven's brother."

"To hell with that. I'm going to throttle the living daylights out of him. If he doesn't stop staring at your—" Ashton bit out, his gaze momentarily captivated by her bosom before traveling back to her face. "Never mind, I'll take care of it."

A slow, warm flush infused her skin as their eyes met, and she looked down, trying to hide her embarrassment. "Please, don't do anything. I won't be the one to jeopardize Samantha's happiness with Steven. I beg you."

Ashton gave an impatient shrug. "Then you're on your own, Marguerite." He stepped back and with a slight nod motioned for her to rejoin the others on the sofa.

"You can't leave me alone with him! You're being paid to chaperone," she blurted out in a desperate attempt to keep him at her side, but her words had the opposite effect on him. The muscles in his jaw tensed before he grabbed her by the wrist. Marguerite wanted to explain, to tell him that her words were spoken out of fear and not because she was talking down to him or giving him a command. The look on his face told her, in no uncertain terms, he would not give her the opportunity.

"As you constantly remind me, it's what I'm being paid to do," Ashton said, pulling her alongside him. "By all means...go ahead and handle the louse yourself." He deposited her back on the sofa and walked over to Lady Lorena and Samantha. His dark eyes held hers captive for a few seconds, before he turned to leave.

Don't go. Please don't go! She opened her mouth to protest, but only a gasp escaped her lips as she watched them exit the room.

"Where were we, my dear? Ah, yes, we were about to go out to the balcony before we were interrupted," Lord Roland insisted.

Marguerite looked away. It wasn't Lord Roland's words that made her uneasy. His praise was innocent enough, not any different than the compliments she had received from the other gentlemen callers, but it was the way he continued to stare so shamelessly at her bodice that made her skin crawl. How could Ashton have left her now, when he knew how anxious she was?

"Miss Wiggins, will you be going to Ascot? I would not miss it for the world. How about you, my lord?" asked Desdemona before biting into another sandwich.

"Ascot is a must, Miss Cummings, quite the social function," he replied. "Now that our families are about to unite, I do hope Miss Wiggins and her sisters accompany me to Berkshire for this year's event. There are many places I'm longing to show Miss Wiggins. On the other hand, Miss Wiggins refuses to show me her balcony."

Starting to panic, Marguerite stared at the drawing room doors, hoping to see Ashton walk through them. Why hadn't she worn another dress? She had an armoire full of dresses and blouses. Why hadn't she picked a bodice that was not as tight—one that would have hidden her curves and not call attention to her bosom? Why did she have to have such generous breasts? Why couldn't her breasts be small like Winnie's?

"Penny, won't you play the piano for us? I'm certain our guests will be delighted to hear your music." Marguerite could hardly believe those words had come out of her own mouth, and neither could Winifred, who looked at Marguerite as though she had suddenly grown another head.

Without hesitation, Penny rushed to the piano and, true to form, began pounding out pieces that even the world-famous composers who wrote them would not recognize. Several excruciating minutes later, she stood proudly, curtsied and returned to the windowsill to join a most enthusiastic and complimentary Mr. Pennington, whose freckled face was redder than ever as he stood applauding and bowing to her.

By the looks of the horrified faces in the room, Mr. Pennington was clearly Penny's only fan.

Lord Roland appeared offended, as though Penny had personally insulted him. "My dear, your sister is quite the piano player. After that rendition, I really must insist we retire to the balcony at once."

"After that, I think we're all in need of air." Desdemona gave a labored sigh. "Mr. Pennington's reaction to your sister's playing made me recall a phrase from *The Merchant of Venice*. Are you familiar with it, Miss Wiggins?" she asked Marguerite.

"I'm not certain to which phrase you refer, Miss Cummings. *The Merchant of Venice* is rather lengthy."

Desdemona persisted, "It goes something like this: 'Love is deaf and lovers cannot hear.'"

"I'm certain you are referring to 'Love is blind and lovers cannot see,'" Marguerite replied, realizing too late that she had made Penny a laughingstock in order to deter Lord Roland's advances.

One corner of Desdemona's mouth pulled into a tight smile as she commented dryly, "Not when it comes to your sister, Miss Wiggins. She must feel like a fish out of water in our lovely city. This must be quite the adventure for her, but also a little trying, no doubt."

"What are you alluding to, Miss Cummings? Are you calling us country bumpkins?" Marguerite asked absently, her eyes fixed on Ashton, who had finally returned and was walking across the threshold with Samantha and Lady Lorena. "It is not the first time someone has referred to us as such."

"Why, no, I would never dream of it, Miss Wiggins! I'm only saying that London is a lovely city. Don't you agree, my lord?"

Lord Roland was too busy eyeing Marguerite to respond, and Desdemona had finally had enough. "My lord," she insisted, putting down her teacup and gathering her belongings, "I asked a question."

"Yes, she's lovely."

"My lord, I did not ask if she was lovely, I asked if—oh, never mind. Damian," she called out to her brother, "look at the time. We have overstayed our welcome. We need to leave."

Taking out his gold pocket watch, Damian Cummings stood from the love seat he had been sharing with Winnie. "Indeed, Mona, I didn't realize the time. I do hope we haven't been too rude. Please, Miss Wiggins," he said turning to Winifred, "before I take my leave, won't you allow me the honor of escorting you tomorrow afternoon? My sister will agree to be our chaperone. Won't you, Mona?"

"If that is what you want," Desdemona replied stiffly.

"Will you come to the park with me?" Mr. Cummings asked Winnie again.

Winifred smiled. "Why, yes, Mr. Cummings. I would like to go very much."

Mr. Pennington cleared his throat. "Miss Penelope, won't you grant me the same honor? I'm sure Mr. Cummings would not mind if we join them."

"I would be delighted," Mr. Cummings replied, most eagerly.

"I am not going anywhere until Miss Wiggins agrees to let me escort her to the park tomorrow afternoon as well," Lord Roland added.

Before Marguerite and Penny could decline the invitations, Samantha exclaimed, "Of course Penny accepts! What a wonderful idea, Marguerite. You and Roland can ride with Steven and me."

"Of course, Lady Lorena and Mr. James will be most welcome to ride with us," Damian Cummings offered politely.

The idea of having to fight off Lord Roland in the park both frightened and repulsed Marguerite. She felt the man's hot breath on her neck as he whispered softly, "Hyde Park will be filled with people, but do not worry, my dear. We'll find a way to be alone."

Horrified at the prospect, Marguerite jerked to her feet, and to everyone's amazement, she ran over to Ashton and blurted out before she could stop herself, "Mr. James will be riding with me."

A bemused smile tipped the corner of Ashton's mouth. "Why, Miss Wiggins, such enthusiasm. How can I refuse? Thank you, Mr. Cummings, but Miss Wiggins and Lord Bradstone will ride with me." His voice was firm and final as he shot Lord Roland a cold look. "I'm sure Lord Bradstone will have no objection."

"None at all," Lord Roland grudgingly mumbled under his breath.

Marguerite watched with smug delight as an angry Lord Roland turned on his heel and left. She looked up at Ashton. "Thank you," she whispered, drinking in the comfort of his nearness and feeling completely secure.

"Don't thank me, Miss Wiggins," Ashton whispered back. "It is my duty to protect you. We wouldn't want your uncle's good money going to waste, now would we?"

The man was mocking her, but Marguerite did not care. He could mock her all he wanted as long as he kept her safe.

Chapter Seven

The next afternoon, Marguerite, dressed in a frilly pink bustle gown, sat rigidly holding her matching parasol next to Lord Roland, whose sexual innuendos were becoming more and more blatant as the open carriage strolled through Hyde Park.

Beside them sat Samantha and Steven, too enthralled in each other's company and the plans they were making for their upcoming engagement party to notice Lord Roland's behavior or the discomfort Marguerite was feeling because of it. Directly across from her sat Ashton James. His square jaw visibly tensed, his tight expression growing more menacing each time the lecherous Lord Roland whispered in her ear and hinted of a private walk in the park.

Next to Ashton, resembling a golden goddess in all her summer splendor, sat Lady Lorena Bonner. Marguerite had to admit the woman had never looked more beautiful. Clad in a yellow silk poplin dress that matched her blonde chignon, Lady Lorena was fluttering her eyelashes as she expertly maneuvered her lacy yellow fan and smiled up at Ashton as though he were the only man left on earth. She was using all her feminine wiles trying to get Ashton's attention as the carriage sauntered along the Drive, but to no avail.

Poor Lady Lorena, thought Marguerite, smiling inwardly. If it was Ashton's interest she vied for, the foolish woman should not have joined them today. Ashton's glower, directed at Lord Roland, confirmed that Lady Lorena Bonner was far from his mind. This pleased Marguerite greatly, but she told herself it only pleased her because she needed him to keep her safe.

It was no wonder Lorena found him appealing, though. Rugged and handsome, her chaperone had never looked more splendid. The narrowly tailored afternoon attire fit his manly form just fine...too fine, making Marguerite acutely conscious of his tall, muscular physique. Lorena could not take her eyes off him, but Marguerite could hardly blame Lady Bonner when she, herself, was suffering from the same malady. It was hard not to notice how his hands were long-fingered and strong, how his rich brown hair was ruffled by the breeze, how his dark, beautiful eyes were sharp and assessing, how his chin was cleft most attractively, how his lips...Damn him! Why did he have to be so devastatingly handsome?

It had been many weeks since their initial encounter on the train to London, when she had been first captivated by his looks. One would think by now his appearance would not rattle her so. Instead, to her disconcertment, she found him better-looking with each passing day.

Closing her eyes briefly, Marguerite reminded herself that Ashton was not the Duke of Wallingford, and, no matter how handsome, captivating or virile she found him to be, she should not be harboring an inappropriate physical attraction for her chaperone—especially when she was heart-set on marrying another man.

"My dear, it will not be long now," Lord Roland whispered, placing his hand on her shoulder in a possessive gesture, bringing her attention back to the inevitable walk in the park. Worriedly, she wondered what she could do to stall Steven's brother without causing embarrassment and making it known to the happily betrothed couple sitting beside her. She turned her attention to Ashton.

Preoccupied with her thoughts, Marguerite had not realized that Lord Roland had not removed his hand from her shoulder or that she was openly staring at Ashton. She felt her flesh color when Ashton quirked his eyebrow questioningly, catching her in the act. Quickly turning away from him, she tipped her face to the sun, taking pleasure from its warmth and from the fact that this stubborn, arrogant, overwhelmingly attractive man was looking out for her welfare.

Jerking her shoulder from Lord Roland's grasp, she watched with interest as the aristocracy paraded on foot, horseback, and carriage to stroll, chat, flirt, notice and be noticed. Indeed, the usual crowd had turned out for their daily afternoon promenade in the park where gossip and fashion reigned supreme. If it weren't for the company she had been forced to endure, she would have enjoyed the outing immensely. Hyde Park, with its profusion of trees, was certainly lovely. It created a feeling of home for Marguerite, almost making her forget that she was in the middle of London and that Lord Roland had every intention of spending time alone with her.

Marguerite loathed the actual moment when the carriage

finally reached its destination near the Serpentine Lake, where Mr. Pennington and Penny, Mr. Cummings and Winnie and their reluctant chaperone, Desdemona, had spread blankets on the grass underneath a shady oak tree and were waiting with refreshments for them to arrive.

As Lord Roland helped her out of the carriage, Marguerite relaxed a bit knowing Ashton was very much aware of her situation. She would not be left alone with the lecherous lout. Ashton would make certain of it.

Penny waved at them as they approached the group. "Marguerite, come and see. Mr. Pennington brought champagne! I thought we'd be having tea, but he brought champagne. Isn't the Serpentine magnificent? I just want to jump in. What took you so long? We've had a glorious time. Isn't that right, Winnie?"

"Yes, Penny," Winifred agreed, smiling shyly at Mr. Cummings as she patted the empty space beside her for Samantha and Steven to sit. "I'm afraid we've drunk the entire bottle."

"Don't worry, Miss Winifred, there's more," replied a smiling Mr. Pennington as he refilled Penny's and Winnie's flutes. "Come join us, Miss Wiggins. Your sisters have been highly entertaining. I don't remember ever having a more splendid time."

"Entertaining is not the word," Desdemona mumbled under her breath. "Refill mine too while you're at it," she said, raising her flute to Mr. Pennington. "I can't remember a more tiresome time. Lord Roland, on the way here, I noticed a garden party. I don't suppose you would like to accompany me for a quiet stroll? Maybe we can spot a few of our mutual friends."

"Mona, has the champagne gone to your head?" Damian Cummings objected, looking abashed at his sister's behavior. "Lord Roland is here with Miss Wiggins, and they have only just arrived."

Lord Roland and Marguerite took their seats on an empty blanket and were promptly joined by Ashton and Lady Lorena.

"Indeed, I am here with Miss Wiggins," Lord Roland agreed, ignoring Desdemona's invitation. "I am going to deflower her in our lovely park," he mumbled, almost inaudibly, under his breath.

Ashton's face darkened. "What did you just say?" he demanded, his mouth slanted in an incredulous frown.

The anger in Ashton's tone made everyone turn to look at Lord Roland, who seemed momentarily out of sorts, like a naughty schoolboy suddenly caught in the act of a misdeed.

"I want to show Miss Wiggins the lovely flowers," Lord Roland answered quickly. "They are spectacular at this time of year."

"In that case, we can all join you," Ashton replied, his tone still heated.

Lord Roland did not answer. Instead, he took the flute of champagne Mr. Cummings handed to him and brought it to his lips.

Leaning toward Ashton, Marguerite whispered only for him to hear, "Please don't leave me, Ashton."

"I won't," he assured her, clenching and unclenching his fist. "Flowers be damned, the cad wants to show you how they pollinate."

* * * *

An hour later, Marguerite found herself being escorted by Lord Roland on the dreaded walk. At first the stroll had been pleasant enough, as they stopped every few yards to converse and exchange pleasantries with their many acquaintances who were strolling the crowded park before returning to their homes to change for dinner. Soon Marguerite found herself on a less-traveled path in a dark and heavily wooded area of the park. Panic set in when she turned around to find that Ashton and Lady Lorena were not behind them.

"Where are you taking me?" she demanded of Lord Roland.

"Never mind, my dear. We are finally alone. No one will find us here. I've looked forward to this. You are such a treat."

"Mr. James and I heard what you said earlier." Marguerite straightened herself with dignity. "I am not a treat, my lord. I'm Samantha's cousin, and I have never given you any indication that I'm willing to—"

"Willing to do what?" Lord Roland interrupted her, seeming very pleased with himself. "What is it, exactly, you think I want you to do? Shall I dare hope?"

Marguerite gave him a hostile glare. "We are not alone, my lord. Mr. James and Lady Lorena are trailing close behind us. Let us go back."

"Go back? Do you know how long it's taken me to get you here?" Lord Roland laughed and pulled her toward him. "Of course we are alone. I made certain of it, little one. I lost them in the crowds, and then I took this path...No one comes through here. He is probably going insane looking for you. Now, be a good girl and give in to me."

Marguerite backed away from him. "I will do no such

thing—release me!"

Lord Roland ignored her command. "Imagine that pesky Miss Cummings insisting I intrude on a private garden party. You and I shall have our own garden party, once I get you near the Serpentine, my dear."

"We were near the lake before you insisted on this stroll," Marguerite said, panic rioting within her. "Let go of me at once."

With a slimy smile, Lord Roland licked his lips. He looked down at his crotch and then back at Marguerite. "It's not the lake I'm referring to, my dear." He pulled her even closer and tried to kiss her, but Marguerite evaded his kiss by turning her face from side to side. She tried to knee him in his most sensitive area, but it was to no avail, for he was holding her much too close.

"Bloody hell—get your hands off her!"

Quickly releasing Marguerite, Lord Roland spun around to find Ashton and Lady Lorena standing behind him. "Mr. James? What are you doing here? How dare you use that tone with me?"

Curses fell from Ashton's mouth as he rushed over to Marguerite. His face, a glowering mask of rage, yielded to concern when he took her in his arms. He looked questioningly into her eyes. "Did he hurt you, Marguerite?" he inquired in an odd, yet gentle tone, touching her trembling lips with his finger and gently smoothing a loose tendril of hair from her cheek.

"I'm fine," Marguerite reassured him, gazing up at him, thinking she had never seen anyone more perfect or wonderful. "Oh, Ashton, if you hadn't come..."

"Mr. James, not many know of this path," Lord Roland insisted. "How did you find us so quickly, and why are you here? Miss Wiggins and I were having a wonderful stroll, and you had to ruin it."

"Lorena, take Miss Wiggins back to the group," Ashton commanded. "Lord Roland and I have business to discuss."

"What business, Mr. James?" Lord Roland looked genuinely surprised. "The women—we cannot leave them alone. What kind of a gentleman would I be if—"

"Shut up!" Ashton slammed one fist against the other before forcing Lord Roland behind some shrubbery. "We've already established what kind of man you are."

* * * *

Lady Lorena smiled at Marguerite as they made their way back to the Serpentine to find the rest of their party. "Don't look so worried, Miss Wiggins. Lord Roland deserves whatever he has coming to him. He's been throwing himself at you in the most unmanly way for days," she said, breaking the silence between them. "I'm happy he'll crawl out of here today with his tail between his legs."

Marguerite was more shaken than she cared to admit. "I'm not worried. I'm furious with myself. I should have told Samantha about him days ago. Mr. James should not have to fight Lord Roland in Hyde Park in broad daylight. It is scandalous."

"What is a London Season without a bit of scandal? Don't worry, Miss Wiggins. The miscreant picked a path less taken. No one will be the wiser."

"What if Lord Roland makes trouble for Ashton? He is, after all, the heir to the Marquess of Greyleigh. His family is quite prominent, and Mr. James has no such influence."

Lady Lorena shrugged off Marguerite's concerns. "Don't be ridiculous. The last thing Lord Roland wants is for his family to find out. Anyway, your chaperone looks as though he can handle him just fine."

Marguerite sighed. "I suppose you are right, but I will never question the value of a chaperone again. I'm not sure how far Lord Roland would have gone if you and Ashton had not found us. If you ask me, I think the man is a bit crazed."

"Crazed? That is not what I call it," Lorena said angrily. "The man is a lecherous coward, and he has no respect for women. Nevertheless, I'm sure there are plenty of women who would love to tend his wounds and bruised ego."

"I don't understand it. Why would they want to, crazed or not? The man is a salacious libertine," Marguerite declared.

Lady Lorena smirked. "The licentious lord is not to be trusted, but there are many like Emily. The poor girl has been attracted to him for years."

"Do you think Lord Roland is her mystery man?" Marguerite asked, suddenly recalling the conversation between the two women the night of the Wimberly ball.

"Miss Wiggins, about that night...I'm sorry you overheard us in the powder room. Emily loves to ramble on. She doesn't mean half of what comes out of her mouth," Lorena insisted, coloring fiercely. "Speaking of Emily, there's her brother, Frank. Actually, I'm a bit worried about Emily. The poor girl has been under the weather since the night of the ball. I tried calling on her, but she's not taking any visitors. I think I'll stop to speak with Mr. Middleton and find out how she is doing, if you don't mind."

"You'll excuse me if I don't accompany you," replied Marguerite. "I'm a bit rattled."

"Of course. Wait here. It won't take long," Lorena assured.

Sitting on a stone bench, Marguerite watched as Lady Lorena approached Frank Middleton. She wondered how Lady Lorena had found the time to call on Emily Middleton when she had been spending every waking hour in the Hardwood drawing room rivaling Marguerite for Ashton's company when Marguerite had needed him most.

"How about a stroll, my dear?"

Marguerite stiffened, gasping at the odious words. Fear and anger knotted inside her as she sensed Lord Roland's presence behind her and felt his hot breath upon the back of her neck.

"Miss Wiggins...what a lovely creature I've found in these woods." His voice sounded deeper than usual. Perhaps his throat was swollen from crying out at the pummeling Ashton had given him. She covered her ears, not wanting to turn and look at him. "Such a beautiful woman should never be left alone without a man to protect her," he continued.

Shock yielded quickly to fury. *No more.* She had enough. She was through being polite to Lord Roland for Samantha's sake. The man was relentless. Not even a thrashing from Ashton could deter him. She hated herself for having put up with his advances for so many days. This time she would give Lord Roland a piece of her mind.

Keeping her back to him, her stomach clenched tightly as she heard herself say, "Listen to me, you libertine—not one more word. You are not to be trusted, taking advantage of a defenseless woman. Leave me alone, and never bother me again. You disgust me."

"As you wish, Miss Wiggins, I won't come near you again."

"Good! What kind of animal plans to have his way with a woman whether she wants him or not? You filthy scoundrel!"

"How dare you speak to me with such disrespect?" he said in a low, menacing voice.

Marguerite turned to face him, to further insult him, but the moment she saw him, her knees turned to jelly. She gasped, but this time her gasp was not from fear or anger. This time is was from sheer horror.

A furious Duke of Wallingford stood before Marguerite, his beautiful gray eyes staring daggers at her before he stormed off, leaving her in open-mouthed distress.

Recovering from the shock, Marguerite tried to follow him, but his long strides were too quick for her. "Your Grace!" she yelled after him, but it was no use. He could not hear her. He was too far away. Frantically, she continued to run after him, but he did not realize she was about to reach him as he jumped into his carriage. Seconds later, tears of frustration blinded her eyes.

"Don't go, my darling Phillip," she managed to say, but it was too late. His ducal carriage disappeared within the multitude of other carriages, horses and pedestrians that were participating in the daily procession.

This was much too awful. It couldn't be happening. Marguerite felt an acute sense of loss. She had wanted the Duke of Wallingford for what seemed a lifetime, and in a few seconds, she had ruined any chance she could have had with him. Disappearing with his carriage were all her hopes and every dream she ever had of becoming a duchess. She felt weak, as though she was going to faint, and she would have if Ashton had not grabbed her from behind and held her against his strong, hard body for support.

"Let him go, Meggie."

With tears in her eyes, Marguerite gave a choked, desperate laugh. "You saw?"

"Yes."

"You heard?"

"Everything."

"So did everyone else in London. Look around, Ashton. I am a laughingstock! They have all witnessed my shame. They will be gossiping about me for years...running after the Duke of Wallingford like a madwoman only to be ignored by him. The duke despises me, and my reputation is completely ruined. Oh, Ashton, what have I done?"

"You've done nothing, love. Now let me take you home."

Chapter Eight

The Salesbury ball had started hours ago. As usual, he had made his grand entrance, only to be surrounded shortly there-after by a flock of foolish women vying for his attention. Tonight someone in this extravagantly adorned ballroom would be chosen as his next victim. It had been a while since he had been unable to control his appetite and had forced Emily Middleton to surrender to him. Since that night, he tried to curb his dark desires, but they recently returned, stronger and more potent than ever. The demon inside him was restless once more. Tonight there would be no stopping him.

Smiling graciously, he pretended to listen to the ladies' silly prattle, but he was too excited for effortless conversation. They bored him with their machinations and devious ways...all want-ing to possess him. If they only knew his thoughts were of a more sinister nature. Tonight he would be the possessor!

Excusing himself, he walked to the terrace for a breath of fresh air and a cigar. While enjoying his cigar, he looked down to the street and noticed his coach parked by the curb with his driver, Edgar Mason, waiting patiently for him.

Staring down at Mason, he sneered inwardly, wondering who of the two was more eager for tonight's occurrence, Edgar or himself. The scrawny little man had enjoyed himself tremen-dously, watching and participating in Emily Middleton's rape. Tonight would be even more enjoyable for both of them.

As usual, there were plenty of beauties most willing to spend time with him. It was always like that, and it bored him to no end. Not until he had them naked and bound with the look of horror on their innocent faces did it make it all worthwhile. His member hardened as he recalled how little Emily Middleton had begged him for mercy.

It was time to choose the lucky one. Walking back inside, he smiled as he perused the ballroom once again and noticed all the pretty little flowers just waiting to be plucked.

His eyes rested momentarily on Louise Shasner-Blake, the beautiful Countess of Salesbury. What a lovely specimen she made on the old count's arm, conversing and greeting all of her guests. Indeed, she knew how to throw a party, but he would not bother with her tonight. She was too busy to even notice him. Not that it mattered. The others noticed. Tonight there would be no stopping him.

His gaze scanned the room. Ah, just as he thought! There they were—the Wiggins sisters, minus one. The lovely Marguerite was missing from the ball. It had been several days since the afternoon in the park. No doubt the twit was hiding out at the Hardwood townhome, crying her eyes out. He licked his lips, knowing it wouldn't be long before he would take her against her will and make her pay for the indignities she had made him suffer. He would wait for the right moment, when she would not have her chaperone around to save her.

His hardness strained against his trousers as he thought of the pending sport of bringing the little fool to her knees—literally. Indeed, Marguerite Wiggins would be his soon enough, but tonight belonged to another. He looked around and finally decided on the one.

Ah, yes! There she was, smiling and looking quite attractive, just begging for his attention. Hadn't she thrown herself at him for what seemed a lifetime? The hussy had been more than blatant with him, following him and openly suggesting they spend time together. He was finally going to give her what she wanted. He licked his lips with relish.

She would be easy enough prey. Her lovesick brother was much too occupied with the girl on his arm to notice his sister gone. Before the morn he would take her against her will and make her pay for Miss Marguerite Wiggins's disparagement of him.

Excitement mounting with every step, he made his way toward his unsuspecting victim...Desdemona Cummings.

Chapter Nine

"How long are you going to keep this up, child?"

Marguerite heard Flora's voice and woke to find the old nanny standing over the bed with a look of concerned disapproval. "Nanny, what time is it? Never mind…I don't care," she mumbled before turning on her side and closing her eyes again.

"You should be ashamed, wasting away in this dark room," Flora insisted as she walked over to the window to draw the curtains. "The sun is shining. You cannot ask for a more perfect day."

Marguerite begged over her shoulder, "Go away, Nanny. It can rain all day, for all I care. Please don't wake me again."

"Still feeling sorry for yourself, are you? You've been locked up in here for the past week, sobbing and wailing over that duke of yours. Your tears could fill the Thames, child. How long are you going to cry over him?"

"As long as I need to," Marguerite replied, yawning. "Did Samantha leave?"

"Hours ago, with Lord Steven, as did the others. She's deliriously happy. I'm glad you chose to keep your mouth shut. It would ruin everything if she found out about that awful Lord Roland and the part he played."

"Hours ago?" Wiping the sleep from her eyes, Marguerite turned and rose slightly from her pillow to look at the mantel clock from across the room. "One o'clock in the afternoon." She whispered the words with a resigned shrug before slouching back against the headboard.

Flora began to make Samantha's bed, stretching the sheets over the mattress and fluffing the pillows. "You haven't changed your mind about telling her, have you?" she asked. "It would make things easier for you. You could clear everything up and—"

Marguerite interrupted, "The man is a filthy animal, but don't worry, Nanny. I haven't changed my mind, especially now, with Sam's engagement party coming up. Mr. James and Lady Lorena are the only ones who know. I simply told you the truth because you kept hounding me."

"I didn't believe for a second that you would offend the Duke of Wallingford for no reason." Flora smiled. "Not with the way you've carried on about him all these years. You would have to be insane."

"Maybe I am insane. I single-handedly ruined my future. I'll never become the Duchess of Wallingford, and all other chances for a prosperous match have dwindled down to none. Nanny, the image of those who witnessed my behavior in the park as I insulted him, and then raced after him, constantly plagues me. I can't stop thinking about it."

"Ah, my child, you don't deserve this. It's all Lord Roland's fault. Once your cousin is safely married to Lord Steven, you can make things right with the duke. Once he has forgiven you, the others will follow. Now, please get up? Your bath is waiting in the adjoining room. It is nice and steamy at the moment. I can't guarantee that for long."

"I'm not getting up, Nanny. My life is over. I just want to sleep."

Flora's mouth tightened. "Your life is far from over. I'll be back with a tray."

For one week, Flora, bless her heart, had drawn Marguerite's bath and had brought her meals, but Marguerite could not recall the last time she had eaten. Food was the last thing on her mind. How could she have confused the Duke of Wallingford for Lord Roland? Why hadn't she turned around to look at him before spurting out insults? Lord Phillip Lancaster was the darling of the *ton*. Anyone imprudent enough to disrespect him in public would be spurned for life. They would never forgive her.

Longing to go back to sleep, Marguerite, once again, turned on her side, placing the pillow over her head to quiet the same old self-recriminations that played in her mind since the awful day in the park. "Don't bother. I can't stomach a thing."

"Force yourself," Flora said before closing the bedroom door.

Flora was right. She should be ashamed for sleeping the morning away, but she was not ashamed. Only in dreams could she forget her miserable existence. Before the "unfortunate incident in the park," Marguerite had adjusted quite nicely to her life as a society debutante in London. Normally, by this time in the afternoon, she would have had her early horseback ride in Rotten Row, would have attended a breakfast party, gone shopping or visited an art gallery.

On a typical day, she would have already changed outfits twice—from her nightgown to her riding clothes to her morning dress—and would now be donning an afternoon gown to receive her many gentlemen callers. Ordinarily, she would have been up and about hours ago, enjoying the constant activities that filled her day. This was no normal, ordinary day, and there were no activities in store for her. Today was Gold Cup at the Royal Ascot races, and, at her insistence, her family had gone to Berkshire to partake of the Ladies' Day festivities without her.

Hot tears rolled down her cheeks when she thought of the elaborate white hat, pretty white gown and matching parasol Aunt Elizabeth carefully picked out for her to wear on this most special of days. The elegant outfit hung in the cabinet, along with all the other beautiful gowns she would never wear again.

Marguerite took a handkerchief, dabbed at her eyes, and blew her nose. Try as she might, she could not stop crying. The past week had been the worst of her life. Since the "unfortunate incident in the park," which was now the term used by her family to describe the terrible misunderstanding between her and Lord Phillip, Marguerite had craved only solitude and isolation, and, though devastated that she would miss the Royal Ascot, she was also somewhat grateful. The townhome would be empty for hours; her actions and emotions would not be scrutinized by well-meaning relatives. Should she venture outside her quarters, she could roam about the house and not have to avoid Ashton James.

Ashton James! The thought of him made her cheeks burn in remembrance. She could never face him again. It was much too mortifying to be near him, especially as she had not seen him since her emotional breakdown during the carriage ride home that awful afternoon.

Promising to send the driver back for the others, Ashton had walked her back to Mr. Cummings's carriage and delivered her from the gawking gossips in Hyde Park to the safety of the Hardwood townhome. Cringing, Marguerite pressed the pillow over her face, recalling her inappropriate and unladylike behavior during the ride home, how she had desperately clung to him and how, without saying a word, he had held her in his arms while she wept and lamented her misfortune the entire way.

She had not bothered to thank him upon arriving at the townhome. Once he had helped her out of the carriage, she had gathered her skirts and taken the town house steps two by two, almost trampling the butler in the foyer as she rushed inside, leaving Ashton to explain to Uncle John and Aunt Elizabeth, who stood open-mouthed at the marbled staircase while she, sobbing hysterically, and without an ounce of dignity, raced past them, up the stairs, to lock herself in her room.

As though the "unfortunate incident in the park" and the carriage ride home with her chaperone had not been embarrassing enough, the aftermath had been all the more humiliating.

Since that day, her suitors had stopped calling on her. When she had arrived in London, she had been so completely sure of her ability to snatch the Duke of Wallingford as a husband that she had discarded all other suitors, casting them off just as they now ignored and discarded her. No more invitations to afternoon garden parties, riding or strolling in the park with friends. No more theatre or opera. No more dinner parties, reception or soirees...no more balls. Marguerite Wiggins, daughter of Archibald Wiggins, niece of the perfectly proper Lord and Lady Hardwood, had been officially shunned by the upper echelon of English society, and she had no one to blame but herself.

Could she have been more foolish?

Marguerite gave her pillow a good punching and then placed it behind her back as she accommodated herself to a sitting position. Grabbing her novel from the bedside table, she opened the book and tried to read, but her thoughts would not allow her to focus on the written word.

After several futile attempts at reading, Marguerite shut the book and returned it to the table, cursing Lord Roland under her breath. Flora was right. If he had not practically attacked her in the park, she would have had her wits about her, and everything would have turned out differently. She would never have insulted the duke and would never have ruined her life in the process.

Suddenly a heavy knock at the door interrupted her dismal thoughts. "Nanny, go away." She pulled the sheets over her head and heard another knock. "Flora, I'm not hungry. Please take the tray back to the kitchen."

"I'm not Flora."

The hoarse, manly voice from behind the door startled her.

"Mr. James?" Marguerite demanded from underneath the sheets. "You shouldn't be here. My uncle would highly disapprove."

"Your uncle is not here to disapprove. He's gone to Ascot, or have you forgotten? I came back for you, Marguerite. I'm taking you to the races. Now let me in."

"I will do no such thing!" Marguerite rushed to the door, quickly turning the key and locking it. "I am not the one with loss of memory, sir. It is *you* who has forgotten gentlemen are not allowed upstairs."

"Since when have you considered me a gentleman?" he asked with a deep chuckle. "I'm just a lowly chaperone."

"Go away, Ashton. Or I'll...I'll..."

"You'll what, Marguerite? We are going to Ascot, even if I have to drag you all the way. Get dressed or I'll break down the door and dress you myself."

* * * *

The ninety-minute coach ride to Ascot with Ashton seemed interminable. Furious with him, Marguerite refused to be lured into conversation. Instead, she kept her thoughts to herself, concentrating on the beautiful Berkshire countryside while trying to ignore his presence.

Pretending complete indifference to Ashton's existence was no easy task. Marguerite never wanted to speak to him again, but it had been almost impossible to tear her eyes away from him. Sitting close beside her in his elegant gray morning coat and top hat, the man had never looked more virile. A quiver surged through her as she recalled how soothing his hard body felt against hers when she cried in his arms the last time they were alone in a carriage.

Marguerite felt herself blush. She did not want to remember that horrible afternoon in the park and the embarrassing carriage ride home. It should not matter that Ashton had been kind to her or that his muscular chest had felt most comforting against her cheek. Regardless of his thoughtfulness that day, Ashton James was a brute—an extremely handsome brute, but no less a brute. He should have left her in her room and not dragged her to Ascot against her will. She only agreed to come with him because she knew he was serious about breaking down the door and dressing her himself.

Still, sitting this close, his nearness was overwhelming; his clean, masculine cologne tempted her senses. She could not help but wonder how it would feel if he were to gather her in his arms and kiss her. They were alone...No one would be the wiser. Her pulse quickened, and her cheeks warmed at the speculation. Blushing, she continued to stare out the coach window, not daring to look at him, fearing, somehow, he would be able to guess the sensuous, wicked thoughts that passed through her mind.

"We're almost there," Ashton suddenly announced. His deep voice interrupted her reverie, channeling her thoughts from being kissed by him...to being snubbed by the nobles attending the

Royal Ascot. She felt butterflies in her stomach just thinking of what was in store for her at the races.

The story of her "unfortunate incident in the park" had spread through London like a raging firestorm. Marguerite had suspected as much, but Penny had confirmed it after returning from the Salesbury ball two nights ago. Almost waking the entire household, a furious Penny had burst into Marguerite's bedroom, shouting how she would never forgive Marguerite for ruining the Wiggins's name, letting her know exactly what was being said about her. Apparently, Marguerite was now the butt of everyone's jokes. It had taken Aunt Elizabeth, Samantha and Winifred to calm Penny down and return her to her own room.

If only they could turn back to London. She must have been crazy to allow her chaperone to bully her so. She was not ready to face society. It was close to four o'clock in the afternoon. The race had probably already taken place. She would not be welcome in any of the celebrations that followed.

"How long are you going to give me the silent treatment, Marguerite?"

"As long as it takes for you to instruct the driver to turn the coach around," Marguerite admitted, frankly.

"Why would I want to do that?"

Exasperated, Marguerite expelled a heavy breath. "Because I have no business in Ascot. I have been shunned, remember? I've lost any chance I ever had with the Duke of Wallingford. I have no prospects or suitors. I face a lightless future as a governess," she spat out, not bothering to look at him. "You shouldn't have forced me to come."

"I disagree."

"You think the duke will forgive me?" Marguerite turned from the window.

He let out a throaty chuckle. "Sorry, Duchess. You pretty much ruined that. I was thinking, who in England would be mad enough to hire a scandalous governess to rear innocent children?"

Shocked by his cruel comment, Marguerite raised her hand to slap his face. He was much quicker than she. Grabbing her hand in midair, he placed it against his hard cheekbone. "Go ahead, slap me," he dared her. His mouth curved as though on the edge of laughter. "I only repeated what was going through your head. I can't help it if you've suddenly become a defeatist."

"You are laughing at me, sir, and I don't find it amusing," she said, yanking her hand away from his clutch.

"Neither do I, Marguerite. I find it pathetic. The Royal Ascot is only the halfway point of the Season. You still have time to catch a husband. You're not going to find one withering away in your room. Let me help."

"I fail to see how you can be of any help, sir. The invitations have ceased. There are no more gentlemen callers. I don't need a chaperone."

"I agree. You don't need a chaperone. You need a suitor. There is nothing more tempting for a man than to see a beautiful woman on another man's arm. It makes him want her all the more."

Marguerite took a quick, sharp breath as realization set in. Staring up at him in amazement, she shook her head. "You must be joking! You can't be suggesting that..."

The knowing smile on his handsome face confirmed to her exactly what he had in mind. He intended to court her. Collecting herself, she managed to shrug and say offhandedly, "I did not know you harbored such feelings toward me, Mr. James. I don't need you as my chaperone, and I certainly don't want *you* as a suitor. It is most improper of you to even suggest it."

Her words amused him. He chuckled most attractively, and, again, Marguerite wondered what it would feel like to be kissed by him. She quickly shook her head, trying to erase the thought from her mind.

"Such distaste for me, Miss Wiggins? Don't flatter yourself. I harbor no romantic feelings for you. I assure you, I only want to help you find a husband," he added dryly.

Marguerite felt the blood rise to her cheeks. Her thoughts had nothing to do with distaste—quite the contrary. She found him much too appealing for her own good. She also found him to be the most arrogant man she had ever met.

Help her find a husband—of all the brazen suggestions! The man must be mad!

Maybe she was the one who was mad? What could she have been thinking earlier, imagining his kiss with such fervor? She had saved her lips for a duke. She would not allow a chaperone, employed by her uncle, to be her first kiss, no matter how handsome or how virile she found him. No matter how sensual his full lips, or how appealing, this man would never be her suitor.

Turning away from him to look out the window, Marguerite folded her hands in a guise of tranquility. "It seems you are the one who flatters himself, Mr. James, if you think that I will agree to this," she calmly managed to say. "Why do you insist on helping me?"

"I don't know. You certainly try my patience. I suppose, if I had a sister, I would want someone to help her if she were in need." His voice was oddly gentle. "Now, sweet Duchess, pretend you're crazy about me. We're finally here."

Marguerite did not reply. She was much too enthralled by the happenings outside the coach window to speak. Everything Aunt Elizabeth had told her about Royal Ascot was true. Society's garden party was what she had called Gold Cup Day—the embodiment of opulence and fashion, a most sophisticated affair. The women outnumbered the men at least four to one with their colorful outfits and matching hats as they paraded through the lawns, taking refreshments and exhibiting their elegant wares. The horses... the horses were magnificent! So excited was Marguerite to join in the festivities that, for a split second, she forgot she would not be welcome. The split second of happiness vanished all too soon. She looked at Ashton and bit her lip, her stomach churning with anxiety and frustration as she remembered her predicament.

"Come with me, Meggie. It will be all right."

Before she could object, his strong arms grabbed her waist and helped her from the coach. Once she was on the ground, his eyes swept over her face approvingly, then roamed over her figure as she smoothed the frilly white dress and adjusted her matching hat.

"You look lovely, by the way." He gave her an irresistibly devastating grin before tucking her hand possessively in the crook of his arm. "I couldn't have done a better job if I had broken down the door and dressed you myself."

Chapter Ten

Gold Cup Day and the remainder of Ascot Week turned out to be surprisingly enjoyable for Marguerite. Her passion for all things equestrian allowed her to dismiss the open stares and wagging tongues of the *ton* as she concentrated only on the races and the magnificent thoroughbreds that vied for the cups. At Lady Lorena's insistence, Ashton and Marguerite returned to Berkshire for two more days of grandstanding, high fashion, and plenty of snickers. To her surprise, Marguerite had not regretted it one bit. In fact, she could hardly recall a more exciting time.

The days that followed the Royal Ascot proved to be equally gratifying. Once Ascot was over, her "pretend suitor" suggested they go riding every morning in Hyde Park. So a ritual began between them—a ritual Marguerite looked forward to the moment she opened her eyes each day.

Today was no different as she hurried down the Hardwood staircase in her riding habit to meet Ashton. When Marguerite spotted him in the foyer, she rushed toward him. Unable to deny the spark of excitement within her, it was all she could do to walk a little slower and not look so eager to see him.

"Good morning, Mr. James," Marguerite greeted him. Smiling impishly, she handed him her favorite book of poems. "You haven't forgotten, have you?"

"No, I haven't forgotten, Miss Wiggins," Ashton replied, eyeing her with amusement. "Should you win today, I will get on one knee and read poetry to you under the tree of your choice. Should you lose, Miss Wiggins, I'll be expecting to collect my winnings."

Marguerite giggled. "I'm afraid, Mr. James, that you will never hear me sing while Penny plays the piano. We have already established that I am better than you when it comes to racing. Prepare to inhale my dust, sir!"

Ashton winced good-naturedly. Standing beside the butler, clad in full riding gear, he looked big and tall. "Listen to the little chit, so sure of herself, so completely bombastic and determined. I ask you, is this any way for a lady to speak, Mortimer?" Ashton teased, winking at her.

"I suppose not, sir," the butler replied stiffly as he opened the doors for them.

Laughing and filled with confidence, Marguerite walked through the doors with Ashton behind her. "The next time Mortimer sees us, we'll have enjoyed a morning of poetry in the park," she proclaimed, tossing her head proudly while sliding on her gloves as she carried the horse crop under her arm. "I must admit, I'm looking forward to our little chase. I could hardly sleep last night just thinking about it."

Ashton grinned. "A morning of poetry in the park—such joy. I can hardly wait. It is a wonder I slept at all."

"Don't be cynical, Mr. James." Marguerite giggled, taking his hand as he helped her into his coach. "There are worse things."

"Worse than poetry in the park?" he asked. "What could be worse?"

"My singing," she replied. "I have never carried a tune and would rather die than sing for you."

Once in Hyde Park, Marguerite stepped out of the coach and inhaled the fresh morning air. Looking at her surroundings, she was overtaken by the mystic splendor of the park. It was still somewhat dark because the sun had not yet risen. There was haze in the air, and the surface of the Serpentine was covered by a blanket of mist resting on top of the water. A red-orange light filtered through the lush wooded area as they walked toward Rotten Row and met up with Simon, Uncle John's groom, who waited with the horses.

As was their usual custom, Ashton and Marguerite mounted their horses and rode at a leisurely pace for a short distance, but unlike the other days, when Ashton seemed relaxed and indifferent about the race, today he looked driven, raring to go. As soon as the race began, he took off like lightning, surprising Marguerite. For a brief moment, she actually felt she could lose the contest.

Competing to the best of her ability, she rode frantically. She was determined to win, and she did not give much thought to her appearance as she raced. She hardly noticed when her black silk topper hat flew away and her hair came undone from its tidy coiffure. Nor did she care when her long skirt began to gather up her thighs or when a button popped free from her bodice, exposing too much cleavage. She would worry about those things later. Now she had to catch up with Ashton and be the victor. This was all that mattered to her.

Enjoying the feel of her hair as it bounced free and wild in the wind, Marguerite raced past Ashton, yelling, "Poetry it is, Mr. James!"

The exhilarating air blew in her face, and she laughed with delight, knowing the wagging tongues would have a field day if they could see her now. Of course, the tongues would not see her. There was no one awake at this ungodly hour. As usual, their outing was perfect, absolutely perfect! The park belonged only to them. This morning was proving to be even more invigorating than all other mornings.

I won! Marguerite thought happily when she crossed the makeshift finish line where Randolph, another of Uncle John's grooms, stood waiting. With whip in hand, she jumped off her horse and, for a few seconds, basked in her victory as she waited for Ashton to cross the finish line.

After crossing the line, Ashton dismounted his horse. "You should be ashamed." He grimaced in good humor when they handed their horses back to the groom. "What sort of lady rides astride in Rotten Row?" he teased.

Pulling off her gloves, Marguerite shrugged. "The kind whose chaperone allows her to, and whose only suitor does not want to read poetry to her," she replied as she raised her arms behind her to twist her thick, unruly locks back into a chignon. "You are lacking as a suitor, Mr. James. I prefer you as my chaperone."

When he didn't come back with a clever remark, Marguerite looked up at him and, following his gaze, noticed she was almost spilling out of her clothes. Mortified, she turned around to adjust herself. "Shall I pick the tree or shall you?" she asked over her shoulder, shrugging to hide her embarrassment while her fingers unpinned a brooch hidden inside her bodice. She took it out and pricked her finger while trying to fasten it where the button had been.

"It's your win, Meggie. You pick the tree." Ashton's hoarse whisper finally broke his silence as she turned to face him. "You're bleeding," he said, taking her hand to examine her finger. "What happened?"

His warm touch sent shivers up her spine, but when he sucked gently on her finger to stop the bleeding, Marguerite inhaled sharply at the intimacy of the contact. The titillating sensation of his tongue on her skin was intoxicating, awakening feelings within her she had never experienced before.

Taking a handkerchief from his pocket, he pressed it to her finger. "Did I hurt you?"

"No. It's nothing," Marguerite stammered, feeling flustered and embarrassed. Obviously her little gasp had led him to believe that she was in pain when pain was far from what she was feeling. Once again, she had to remind herself that desiring her chaperone was foolish and impractical. Her intellect told her so, but the overpowering attraction she felt for him at that moment had nothing to do with reason. "It's only a little prick."

The moment she said the words, Marguerite wanted to take them back. In horror, she remembered her father's drunken buddies using the word to describe a certain part of a man's anatomy as they played poker at the cottage and did not know that she was within earshot. She felt her flesh color. "I meant I *pricked* my finger," she blurted as he released her hand. "I did not mean..."

"I know what you meant, Meggie." Ashton's mouth twitched with humor. "I've never seen you wear that pin before," he said, staring at her brooch, chivalrously changing the subject.

Her hand went to the brooch. "It is a miniature of my mother's image. I always wear it hidden next to my heart. Oh, thank you, Simon," she thanked the groom, who had retrieved her silk topper hat and had come running to hand it to her. Turning to Ashton, she pointed to the trees way in the distance. "We can sit over there."

* * * *

Settling underneath the large oak tree, Marguerite quickly adjusted her riding skirt over her knees.

"Shall I compare thee to a summer's day? Thou art more lovely and more temperate. Rough winds do shake the darling buds of May, and summer's lease hath all too short a date," she quoted, watching with smug enjoyment as Ashton stood staring down at her, his brows drawn together in an agonized expression.

His pained expression made her burst into giggles. "I was only teasing you, Mr. James. You don't have to read poetry to me," she said, choosing to put him out of his misery.

"You are generous, Marguerite. I would have made you sing."

She laughed. "Your eardrums would have ruptured at the sound."

An easy smile played at the corners of his mouth. "I've never weaseled my way out of paying a debt. Hand me the wretched book, and let's get this over with."

Delighted, Marguerite sat back against the tree trunk and closed her eyes. Ashton dropped down beside her and, in his deep voice, proceeded to lull her with her favorite sonnets, making her want to stay in the moment forever.

When he stopped reading, Marguerite opened her eyes to find him watching her.

"You are a romantic, Marguerite—too romantic for your own good. What made you fall so hard for that self-righteous peacock you are so intent on marrying?"

His words took her by surprise. "It pains me to talk about him," Marguerite objected. "What is the use? Phillip will never want me now." Shaking her head, she sighed wistfully. "If I had only refused Lord Roland's invitation and not gone to the park that afternoon, everything would have been different. He would have come calling sooner or later."

Giving her a sidelong glance, Ashton chuckled. "My, but we are sure of ourselves this morning," he ribbed. "Is that your hat, Miss Wiggins? It must be pretty big to fit that head of yours."

"Stop it!" She giggled, grabbing the black silk hat and playfully thumping him with it.

"You didn't answer my question."

Marguerite leaned lightly into him, tilting her face toward him. "What question?"

"What do you see in Wallingford?"

She shrugged. "What every other girl of marriageable age sees in him," she said, matter-of-factly.

Shutting the book of poems, Ashton put it aside. "Maybe you aren't so romantic after all, Miss Wiggins."

"What do you mean?"

"You don't know Wallingford, yet you are infatuated with him. You have just admitted you feel this way because he happens to be a duke."

"I admitted no such thing. I want to marry Phillip because I love him."

"Love him?" Ashton gave her a look of utter disbelief. "Did I not introduce you to His Grace the night of the Wimberly Ball? When did you magically fall in love with him? While I was dragging you out of the ballroom?"

Flattening her palms against her riding skirt, Marguerite stood to go, but Ashton stopped her by placing a restraining hand on her arm. His dark eyes glued her to the spot.

"Sit down, Marguerite. I'm only trying to figure you out. You are a woman. I should not judge you. I suppose it is your nature to want a wealthy man with a title to keep you in luxuries for the rest of your days."

"You know me little, Mr. James." Marguerite forced her lips to part in a curved, stiff smile. "Lord Roland is a man of title and his family is fabulously wealthy, but I would never consider marrying him," she managed to reply through thin lips.

His eyes grew openly amused. "True, but why marry Bradstone when you have set your sights on someone so much higher? It matters little to you that the duke is governed by his mother and only does what she demands. Don't look at me that way, Marguerite. I'm not saying anything you haven't heard before."

"I've heard no such thing! I've loved Phillip ever since I first saw him years ago, when I used to spend summers with Samantha at Hardwood Manor. One night, while spying, I fell out of the tree right into the duke's arms and interrupted his tryst with the Countess of Salesbury—oh, never mind!" She stopped talking when she saw the look of skepticism on his face.

Putting his arms behind his head, Ashton leisurely stretched his long legs before him and lounged against the tree, seeming to enjoy her struggle to recapture her composure. "If Wallingford were a butler, would you feel the same about him?"

Marguerite scoffed. "A butler? The Duke of Wallingford? Don't be silly, Mr. James. Of course I wouldn't feel the same way if he were a butler. I won't apologize for it. My mother had plenty of opportunities to marry well. Instead she chose a man who gambled away everything she brought to the marriage. She realized too late Papa loves no one but himself. Poor Aunt Elizabeth had to watch her only sister perish and die of a broken heart."

Marguerite managed to wipe the smug look off his face. "Do you want to know why I hide the miniature brooch? I've always been afraid Papa will pawn it or gamble it away, as he has done with everything I have ever treasured—including *my* horse!"

Ashton's expression stilled and grew serious. "Meggie, you have reason to be suspicious of men, but you can't judge every man by your father." He leaned toward her and gently pushed a wayward strand of dark hair from her eyes. "Not all men are gamblers, Meggie. Not all nobles are noble."

His mouth curved with tenderness. "I feel I've made you angry, and that is the last thing I wanted to do this morning, but it irks me to see you so heartbroken over the Duke of Wallingford when he does not deserve you. That pompous fool should have forgiven you by now. Serves him right you fell on him," he said, giving her a smile that sent her pulse racing. "You didn't say what Wallingford did when you interrupted his tryst with the countess. He must have been bloody angry."

Marguerite took Ashton's large hand as he helped her up. Rising to her feet, she brushed off pieces of dried leaves and dirt from her riding habit. She kept quiet, refusing to speak to him while she considered giving him the silent treatment, but it was useless. Try as she willed, she could not remain angry with him.

"I did not stay long enough to find out. I ran so fast I thought my heart would burst. It was exciting, I must say," she replied.

"You little minx. Nothing scares you, does it?"

"Lord Roland Bradstone scares me. He scares me very much."

* * * *

He heard his name and fumed inside. Hiding in the shrubbery, he hoped they had not seen him. Such an attractive couple they made: Marguerite Wiggins and that protective chaperone of hers.

Look at her now! So she wanted to marry a duke, did she? How presumptuous of her to think she ever could. She should be ashamed, laughing and gushing over her chaperone. How interesting the conversation between them. To think he had gone for a walk in the park to clear his head and come upon them, racing and merrymaking, and afterwards walking to almost the exact location where she rejected him a few weeks ago. The trollop!

How appetizing she looked earlier with her black, shiny tresses loose to her waist, her breasts spilling out of her bodice and her curvy, scrumptious backside bouncing up and down on the saddle while she had the nerve to ride astride.

So the hussy had been in love with the Duke of Wallingford since she was a child? Look at her, so brazen, flirting and laughing in that tight riding attire. She flirted so blatantly with that chaperone of hers it was a wonder the man didn't just rip her clothes off and take her in the woods. He wondered if the chaperone could see it. He would have to be made of stone not to notice that the girl was completely taken by him.

Ravish her, idiot! No one would know...only he, and he would do nothing. He would just watch. She deserves it! So proud, so arrogant, so delicious...He had dreamed of taking her for weeks now, but the opportunity had not presented itself.

Desdemona Cummings had not satisfied his need as he had hoped. Her endless pursuit of him had caused him to notice her, but the experience had been lacking. She had been attractive enough, and her screams had brought him to gratification while he pricked her virginal cavity, but the girl had lost consciousness before Edgar Mason could take her, and that had ruined the ritual he now so enjoyed. The ugly little man, with his pox-faced olive complexion, scared the girls more than he could ever hope to do. He had gotten used to Mason taking over once the girls thought he was through raping them.

Visions of the haughty Marguerite, so determined to marry a duke, lying spread-eagled before him and suffering the indignities Edgar loved to mete out restored his good humor.

Soon, darling, soon!

Chapter Eleven

Thinking of Ashton and the delightful ride they just shared, Marguerite smiled. She ascended the marble staircase, completely absorbed by how handsome he had looked earlier in his tan riding breeches and black Hessian boots. So absorbed was she in her thoughts of Ashton, she hardly noticed Flora and two young chambermaids carrying water buckets in the hallway.

"You sure look pleased with yourself, Miss Marguerite. Come back from your morning ride, have you? I'm glad to see that handsome devil has returned you to the living," Flora declared before turning to the maids. "What are you two giggling at?"

The younger and fairer of the two maids was brave enough to reply. "He sure is fine-looking, Miss Flora! Kitty and I almost keeled over when we saw him this morning before he took off with Miss Wiggins. Right, Kitty? Didn't we almost keel over?"

Knowing better than to respond, Kitty stood nervously holding the bucket, her eyes shifting from one person to the other.

The tensing of Flora's jaw revealed her irritation. "Silly chits, you are not paid to admire Mr. James or any other man who enters this household. There is work to be done. Go and see to Miss Winifred and Miss Penelope. Hurry—time's a-wasting!"

Shooing the chambermaids off, Flora turned to Marguerite. "Lady Hardwood insisted on hiring the lazy pair. It tires me more to train them than to fill the tubs myself."

"Nanny, it's wonderful you finally agreed to hiring them! Now you'll have time to play cards with me."

"I have no time for cards, and neither have you, child. I'm busy overseeing those ninnies, and Mr. James is keeping you busy as well," Flora said. "Your bath is ready. The water is hot, as you like it."

Marguerite smiled gratefully. "Nanny, you're a dear. I'm in desperate need of one."

"I suggest you step right in and not linger talking to your irritable cousin. She's in a tizzy," the nanny warned before walking away.

Smiling, Marguerite entered the bedroom to find Samantha

busy writing at her escritoire. "Hello, Sam, my favorite cousin," she said cheerily, tossing her riding whip and topper hat on the bed. "How are the preparations coming?"

"I'm your only cousin, and the preparations are endless," Samantha informed her, before putting down her pen to look up at Marguerite. "Oh, Marguerite, I'm beside myself. The engagement party is at week's end and I still do not know where to sit the guests. There is still much to do."

"How can I help?

"That's sweet of you, but there is really nothing you can do to help. Poor Mother is handling most of it. How was your ride with Mr. James?"

"Exhilarating. Ashton and I raced on Rotten Row, and, as usual, I won."

Samantha's eyes widened. "Have you lost your mind? Marguerite, if anyone catches you—"

"No one is going to catch us. Don't worry," Marguerite quickly said, noticing Samantha's disapproval. "We go at the crack of dawn. The park is empty, not a soul around to further ruin my reputation."

"Marguerite, tell me you didn't ride astride."

"Why not? It is more secure and much more invigorating," Marguerite replied, chuckling. "Don't look so shocked. I told you, no one saw us. Sam, if I rode sidesaddle, he would have the advantage!"

"Mr. James let you win. He most certainly let you win," Samantha insisted, returning to her writing.

Marguerite sat on the bed and unbuttoned her long-fitted button-down bodice. "He most certainly did not let me win," she objected, removing one riding boot at a time. "Have you forgotten I'm an experienced horsewoman?"

"Indeed you are, but he is quite the horseman."

Walking behind the changing screen, Marguerite removed the rest of her riding attire and stepped into the warm bath Flora and "the ninnies" had prepared for her. "Quite the horseman?" she called out as an afterthought. "He can hardly mount a horse."

"I've seen him ride many times. He rides as swift as the wind, Marguerite. You forget, I've known him for years."

"Yet you never once mentioned him to me."

"Should I have? You sound much too curious about the man. Is it possible, after resenting him for weeks, you, my dear cousin, could be taking pleasure in his company?"

Marguerite laughed. "Don't you dare tell him! I'll never admit to it."

"Yes, but you'll admit it to me. The two of you have been inseparable since the Ascot. If I didn't know better, I would say that you were quite taken with him."

"That is the plan. We are pretending. Although he cares not a whit for me, Ashton has it in his mind that he is going to find me a husband," Marguerite said, matter-of-factly. She took the scented soap from the soap stand and languidly began to lather her arms and legs. "I wasn't willing at first, but I've changed my mind. I'm grateful to him for forcing me to leave this room. If I'm destined to become a governess, I might as well enjoy my last few weeks of freedom."

"He is forcing you to pretend to court him?" Samantha asked, her voice raising an octave. "What inane plan is this?"

"Inane, indeed—it hasn't worked at all." Marguerite giggled. "None of my suitors are back, but Ashton has kept me so active I haven't had the chance to breathe, much less think of my prospects or lack thereof."

"It's just like him to have his way, Marguerite. I've always found him incredibly handsome, but terribly intimidating as well."

"Samantha, don't be ridiculous! He's your father's employee. Why on earth would he intimidate *you*?"

"Oh, I don't know, maybe because he's so firm, so stubborn and strict."

Smiling, Marguerite admitted, "I've grown to admire that about him."

"Are you certain you are *pretending* to be infatuated?" Samantha asked. "I can tell by the way you look at him you find him hard to resist."

Marguerite grew serious. "I told you, I am only pretending. Anyway, no matter how irresistible I may find him...I could never be infatuated with him."

"Why? Because you don't want to marry beneath you? You are not Aunt Lydia, Marguerite, and Mr. James is not Uncle Archie. The fact that Mr. James is in my father's employ should not make a difference if you should take a liking to him."

"Sam, it seems to me that it is you who has lost your mind, not I. Of course it makes a difference—a very big difference. Since when have you become so open-minded?"

"All I'm saying is I can understand your attraction to him, Marguerite. Whether or not he holds a title should not matter to you."

"That is easy for you to say. You are marrying the son of the Marquess of Greyleigh."

Rising from the tub, Marguerite grabbed the clean towel that hung from the screen. After drying herself, she slipped on her underclothing and donned the lilac skirt and lacy white chemise she had chosen earlier. Coming forth from behind the screen, she went to her chiffonier to look for her gold earrings and the lovely cameo she inherited from her mother, another piece she had successfully hidden from her father's pilfering fingers.

"Are you coming downstairs?" Samantha asked, rising from her desk. "We can endure a few hours in the drawing room with Mr. Cummings and Mr. Pennington, now that Desdemona has stopped coming to visit."

Why bother going downstairs? Marguerite thought, somewhat disappointed, as she pinned the cameo at the base of the high-necked blouse. Ashton would not be joining them for lunch. He had business to attend and would return in the evening to take her to the opera. She wished she could stay in her room and read until then.

Marguerite and Samantha walked to the door, ready to go downstairs, but before they opened it, Penny and Winnie burst in through the connecting dressing room door on the other side of the bedroom.

"I cannot believe our papa, Marguerite! I've sent him several missives, and he has not responded to one," Winifred complained. "How can a man ignore his own daughter? What will Mr. Cummings think?"

"That our papa must be a very busy man." Penny defended their father as usual.

"Doing what, I ask? Learning needlepoint? How busy can he be with Aunt Lavinia and Aunt Hyacinth? It is imperative Papa come to London at once. Mr. Cummings wishes to speak with him."

Marguerite smiled as she watched her sisters argue, feeling extremely grateful that her *faux pas* in the park had not ruined Penelope's and Winifred's chances as it had hers. Thanks to the enamored young Mr. Pennington and Mr. Cummings, Penny and Winnie had remained very much a part of the London scene and had not missed a single social gathering. Sudden realization overtook her.

"Imperative...Mr. Cummings wants to—Winnie!" Marguerite exclaimed. "Do you think, maybe...?"

Winifred smiled happily. "Yes, he proposed last week, but we wanted to keep it quiet until Mr. Cummings could formally ask Papa for my hand. I fear if I wait for Papa, I'll die an old maid."

"This is wonderful news!" a delighted Marguerite cried out, throwing her arms around her sister. "Penny, Sam...isn't this wonderful news?"

Shaking her head, Penny folded her hands over her chest. "Don't be so certain Papa will give his blessing. Our father does not approve of plebian wealth."

"Since when?" Marguerite took Winifred's hand in hers. "Winnie, no matter how mortifying, you will have to warn poor Mr. Cummings about Papa."

"I have—and he still wants to marry me," Winifred said, giggling. "It doesn't matter to him our papa is a...well, that plebian wealth will keep him gambling in style."

"How can you speak that way about him?" Penny cried out, her chest heaving as she pointed an angry finger at Marguerite. "You are the worst of the two, Marguerite Wiggins."

"Yes, yes, yes—we all know." Marguerite repeated the words that Penny had thrown in her face more times than she cared to remember. "I have ruined the family name. I should be ashamed."

Penny shook her head in agreement. "Indeed, and I will hold you personally responsible should I not find a husband this Season. It wasn't enough that you ruined us by insulting the Duke of Wallingford. You are now gallivanting about town and paying heed to Mr. James, an employee of our uncle's. Where's the wealth in that?"

Her face crimson, Winifred threw up her hands in disgust. "Don't you dare reproach Marguerite when you are no better than our own father. You've gadded about town with poor Mr. Pennington, who adores you, but you are only using him. You're the one who should be ashamed, Penelope Wiggins—you are Papa's daughter true and true."

"Why, thank you, Winifred. I take that as a compliment," Penny retorted, forcing a smile and shrugging offhandedly.

"It wasn't meant as a compliment, Penny dear," Samantha blurted out. "Don't blame Marguerite if you cannot find a husband. No one else is at fault if you are not content with the only man in London who has given you a second look."

Penny frowned with cold fury. "Pretty uppity now that you are both getting married," she spat back.

"Indeed, we are," Winnie gushed, fluttering her eyelashes.

"Like my mother, I will not wed a lord. I am proud to say I am marrying the man I love and it has nothing to do with his wealth."

"Only if Papa is of the same mind. He may not be a fancy lord, but he lords over you. Come to think of it, Papa should not have to rush to London at your beck and call. Mr. Cummings is the one who should go to Crawley. It is the proper way of it." Tilting her chin, Penny turned and stormed out of the room.

"I actually agree." Winifred giggled. "Mr. Cummings left for Crawley first thing this morning. Hopefully, he'll return this evening with favorable news."

Samantha rushed over to hug Winifred. "I'm so happy, cousin. We shall celebrate your good fortune as well as mine. My engagement party will be in honor of both of us."

"Damian and I would not dream of sharing your special day."

"Nonsense, it is even more special now. Let us go and find Mother. She is going to be thrilled!"

Winnie hesitated. "Don't you think we should wait until it is official? What if Papa objects?"

Rolling her eyes, Marguerite let out a long, audible breath. "Oh, please," she blurted out before she could stop herself.

The notion that Archibald Wiggins would object to a very successful, wealthy merchant for a son-in-law caused the three of them to burst out laughing. Chattering excitedly amongst themselves, despite Penny putting a damper on it, the three women left the room to share the wonderful news with the rest of the household.

* * * *

Marguerite and Aunt Elizabeth stared out of the coach window when it stopped in front of the Theatre Royal at Drury Lane. Aunt Elizabeth looked uneasy as they watched the bejeweled ladies and distinguished gentlemen, all dressed in their finery, crossing the street and making their way toward the entrance.

"Marguerite, maybe it was not such a good idea to bring you to the opera. You have been sad of late, with the incident and all. Lady Willis, who attended the performance last week, informed me it is quite the tragic story."

"Most operas are," Marguerite commented, amazed at the crowd of notables walking into the theatre, wondering if Lord Phillip or Lord Roland were amongst them.

"Mr. James, I trust you will deliver my niece without incident to Lady Lorena and her father," Aunt Elizabeth asked Ashton after he assisted her and Marguerite out of the coach.

Ashton's eyes caught and held Marguerite's, sending her a private message. "I'll take care of her," he reassured, his voice calm, his gaze dark and powerful. Marguerite was impressed with the confidence he inspired in her. Tragic story or not, as long as Ashton was by her side, she knew she would enjoy the evening.

Smiling, Aunt Elizabeth waved to a few friends who had waved to her from afar. "You are a godsend, Mr. James," she said, turning to Marguerite. "As I was saying, Lady Willis confided she shed more than a tear. When that poor Dutch captain loses Senta after she jumps in the water and drowns... Well, poor Lady Willis almost choked trying to contain herself."

"He drowns, too, when the ship sinks," Uncle John remarked, sarcastically, as he placed his wife's shawl over her shoulders. "Elizabeth, I hope you know you've completely ruined it for Marguerite. She might as well go home."

Aunt Elizabeth sighed heavily while the four of them slowly progressed toward the entrance. "I wish we could sit together, but Lord Hardwood and I must join Lord Steven and his family. Mr. Pennington and Mr. Cummings will be sitting in our box tonight with Penny and Winnie. I hear that poor Miss Cummings has taken ill. She'll have to miss the opera. Such a shame. Marguerite, before we separate...remember to be strong, dear. Like busy bees, the *ton* may sting...but they don't bite."

Amusement lurked in Ashton's eyes as he studied Marguerite for a moment. "Neither do bees. If they did, I'm afraid she'd bite back," he said, his lips curving most attractively.

Giggling, Marguerite tapped him with her fan. "I would do no such thing!"

Uncle John looked perplexed. "What the devil are we talking about? Elizabeth, you are not making any sense, all this talk about bees."

"John, dear—never mind. I'm too nervous to think straight. This is the first time Marguerite is out in society since the... episode."

"Elizabeth, he said he would take good care of her. Have you forgotten she managed to survive Ascot, my dear? After that, a night at the opera will be a breeze. Don't worry so much."

Uncle John turned to Ashton when they reached the foyer. "My wife is right, Mr. James. You are a godsend for helping us protect our niece."

Silently agreeing with her uncle, Marguerite couldn't resist another glance at the perfect stranger who had been hired as her chaperone and had suddenly become her pretend suitor. Employee of Uncle John's or not, Ashton was an eyeful in his opera cloak, white gloves and hat. By the covetous looks being thrown in their direction, Marguerite felt that many a proper lady would have given anything to trade places with her and be escorted by him to the opera.

"Don't worry, Aunt Elizabeth, I'm old news by now," Marguerite reassured her, sounding more convinced than she really felt. "They won't even notice I'm here."

Aunt Elizabeth raised an appraising eyebrow as she stared at Marguerite. "The rose gown is quite flattering, my dear. Good or bad, I'm afraid the tongues will always wag when it comes to you. You are much too beautiful to go unnoticed."

"True," Uncle John agreed, giving Marguerite a kiss on the forehead. "Try to enjoy the performance, dear niece. Elizabeth, are you certain you didn't leave something out?" he asked, good-naturedly. "Is there anything else you would like to reveal about the opera to Marguerite?"

Aunt Elizabeth ignored him. "Oh, look, there's Lord Bonner and Lady Lorena. John, darling, we mustn't linger. The Marquess and Marchioness Greyleigh are waiting."

After exchanging salutations with Lady Lorena and her father, the group dispersed, moving on to their respective boxes to watch the performance.

Marguerite had to confess the setting and costumes were impressive, and the actors' voices were equally so, but she also had to admit that she would never be a fan of the opera. No matter how much she tried to enjoy it, it did not move her spirit. On the contrary, it grated on her nerves. By the time the intermission came along, Marguerite could not wait for Senta to jump into the ocean and drown as she was tempted to end her own misery by jumping off the balcony and falling onto the audience below.

During the intermission, attendants carrying refreshments entered the Bonner box. Although starving, Marguerite and Lady Lorena graciously declined the wonderful tidbits. Aunt Elizabeth had warned her earlier that it was not looked well upon for a lady to eat or drink at an opera or play. *If only there weren't so many silly rules!* She seldom drank, but a little champagne would have made the woeful tale of Senta and her doomed captain much more palatable.

Several minutes later, Lord Eustinius Alpert Bonner IV announced that he was going to the foyer and graciously invited Ashton to join him for a drink and a smoke. Out of politeness, Lady Lorena invited Marguerite to join her in visiting the other boxes, as it was the custom for women to trade pleasantries with their friends.

Marguerite and Ashton declined respectfully, both opting to remain in the Bonner box for the rest of the intermission.

Ashton stood and waited for Lord Bonner and Lady Lorena to exit before retaking his seat beside Marguerite. "It is obvious you do not like *The Flying Dutchman*," he stated with a deep chuckle.

"I don't," Marguerite replied, observing the crowd with great interest through the mother-of-pearl opera glasses Aunt Elizabeth had let her borrow. "I don't like opera at all. Right now, I wish the insufferable Dutchman would just fly away."

"You better not admit that in these circles."

"True," Marguerite agreed. "Speaking of insufferable, you don't think Lord Roland is here tonight, do you? We've managed to evade him for days. There are so many people, I can't recognize a soul."

Ashton's brow furrowed. "Put the glasses down, Marguerite. Don't give the bastard another thought."

"I can't help but think of him. Everyone believes he is avoiding me, along with the rest of the *ton*. I fear Lord Roland will make an appearance the moment his face is healed. It is only a matter of time before he comes for me again. Oh, Ashton, he scares me terribly."

A muscle flickered angrily at Ashton's jaw. "I hate to ruin your evening, Duchess, but the bastard's face *has* healed. Lorena saw him with Desdemona at the Salesburys' ball the week before last. Don't look so frightened. Bradstone will not bother you again. I made certain of it."

Marguerite pressed her lips together in anger. "The hateful man does not have the sense to avoid me. Flora and Lady Lorena are the only ones who know exactly what he tried to do to me while strolling in the park."

"You kept quiet because of Samantha, even though it cost you everything you've schemed for since arriving at London."

"Since way before that," Marguerite admitted. "I told you this morning—I've been scheming for years."

"Indeed," Ashton said with a trace of laughter in his voice. "Lancaster has no inkling of your obsession. The fool must be blind as well as pompous. At the risk of having you grow an even bigger head, Duchess, I, too, must agree with your aunt. You are much too beautiful to go unnoticed."

Marguerite felt herself blush, embarrassed by how happy his compliment had just made her. "Please don't make fun of me, Mr. James. Don't mock me."

"Why would you think that?" Ashton demanded.

She raised her eyes to find him watching her closely. His dark gaze held her captive. When he spoke again, his voice was tender. "I'm not mocking you, Marguerite. You are beautiful and surprisingly generous. The latter is why I find myself wanting to help you. So does Lorena. If she stayed with you in the park, maybe you would have reacted differently to Wallingford."

Fighting the urge to be crushed within his embrace, Marguerite moistened her dry lips and looked to her lap. "Nonsense," she managed to respond. "I don't hold Lady Lorena responsible for my predicament. Unlike the rest of my new acquaintances, she risked being spurned for opening her arms to me."

Ashton captured her chin and turned her face toward him. "Have you forgotten who fathered the lovely lady and what he represents? Lord Eustinius is a most revered member of the House of Lords. I doubt anyone would dare snub her, even though she deems it fit to associate with the likes of us," he teased. "Seriously, Lorena is a good friend. Thanks to her generosity, we have attended the Ascot and the Royal Theatre in style."

A pang of jealously sprang through Marguerite. Ashton was right. Lorena had proven to be her only true friend in London, but no matter how grateful she felt toward the woman, she did not enjoy listening to Ashton mention her with such high regard. She should be ashamed, but she simply couldn't help her feelings. Try as she might, Samantha was right—she was finding Ashton harder and harder to resist.

Resist what? Marguerite chided herself. So he found her beautiful and generous. Those were his exact words to her, but those were also the exact words he had used to describe Lorena. No... she corrected herself. The word he used to describe Lady Lorena was *lovely,* not *beautiful.* Beautiful was a much better word, she thought, inordinately pleased.

"About Bradstone." Ashton placed his gloved hand on her shoulder in a protective gesture, and the tingling effect of the contact spread through her like wildfire. "The man knows the next time he so much as breathes near you his face won't heal so quickly," he reassured her, taking her hand and clutching it tightly. "Are you feeling all right?"

Try as she willed, Marguerite could not find her voice. She was no longer thinking about Lord Roland. She was conscious only of Ashton's nearness, her senses throbbing with the feel and scent of him.

Gulping a nervous breath while trying to calm the thrilling current racing through her, she finally replied, "Let's forget about Lord Roland. I'd rather talk about the way my horse outdid yours this morning."

"Oh?" he replied, firm lips twitching.

"Yes, you can try to prove yourself tomorrow, Mr. James, but I fear it will be to no avail. I'm too accomplished a horsewoman to allow you a win."

Before Ashton could respond, Lady Lorena returned with her father, and, to Marguerite's chagrin, the opera commenced once more. Trying not to yawn or shift in her seat, Marguerite pretended great interest as she looked through her opera glasses and endured another hour and a half of German opera, rising fluidly and most enthusiastically from her chair to clap with great appreciation when it was finally over.

Afterwards, Ashton and Marguerite conversed with Lord Eustinius and Lady Lorena while they waited outside the theatre for their carriage to arrive. As she was trying to spot Uncle John and Aunt Elizabeth in the crowd, Marguerite saw the Duke of Wallingford stepping into his crested coach with a beautiful blonde woman. The sight of him completely unsettled her composure.

"Her name is Claire Dumont. She is French, and she is not going to last a week."

Marguerite looked at Lady Lorena in surprise. "How do you know this?"

"I know Phillip." Lady Lorena smiled wisely. "He loves the very married Lady Louise Shasner-Blake. I'm glad I was able to tear myself away from him and not waste any more years at his side."

"Why is Miss Dumont going to last a week when you lasted years? She is just as lovely," Marguerite burst out without thinking, and then gasped. "You must excuse me, Lady Lorena. I did not mean to say that. You are much lovelier than she."

Lady Lorena's eyes grew openly amused. "Poppycock!" She waved her hand in a gesture of dismissal. "You meant every word. You speak your mind, Miss Wiggins. I so admire that. To answer your question, Lancaster strung me along because of my father's influence and good will. Poor Claire. She'll never become his duchess."

"Neither will I," Marguerite said as she watched his coach drive off. "He'll never propose to me now," she mumbled wistfully under her breath before realizing what she had just admitted to Lorena.

"Cheer up, Miss Wiggins. We've all been in love with him at some time or another. It may comfort you to know there won't be a Duchess of Wallingford unless her name is Lady Louise Shasner-Blake. He will never propose to anyone else."

A half hour later, Ashton and Marguerite followed Uncle John and Aunt Elizabeth up the Hardwood townhome steps. When Mortimer opened the front door, Ashton grabbed Marguerite gently by the arm and held her back at the threshold while Uncle John and Aunt Elizabeth went inside.

"Tomorrow at dawn, Duchess."

"At dawn it is!" Marguerite said, smiling up into his chiseled face. "You make it sound more like a duel than a race, Mr. James."

His chuckle was deep, warm and rich as he nodded farewell before turning to go.

"Good evening, Mortimer. What a glorious evening," she addressed the butler, before walking inside. Indeed, it was a glorious evening. Ashton had called her beautiful.

* * * *

The next afternoon, Edmund Kent waited inside Mitchell's Jewelers and Watch Repair in Bond Street, hoping Mr. Jonas Mitchell would give him a clue that would lead him to find Julianna's assailant. Edmund's patience was running thin. Unearthing the filthy worm had proven to be more difficult than he expected. It had not deterred him in the least. He was more determined than ever to find the bastard who threatened his sister with her life...even if he had to return to Spain and force her to give up the name.

Since his arrival in London more than two months ago, Edmund visited the Bond Street shop every week only to be told Jonas Mitchell was recovering from a heart episode and could not be reached. Thankfully, today Edmund found the old jeweler sitting quite happily behind the counter, totally recovered, and more than willing to help.

After several minutes, the old man returned. "I understand this is of the utmost confidence, my lord...a most sensitive issue. You may be certain I will not betray your trust. Should a customer enter the premises, we shall finish this conversation in the back office. For now, it is safe to speak here. I've had the chance to inspect the piece, and what I have found is startling."

"Tell me."

Jonas Mitchell nodded his head. "I wish I could have assisted you sooner. My sister and I are greatly indebted to you, my lord. Ruth considers Windword Hall her home. I remember when she was hired as your governess. So excited was she! That was quite a while back. It is only through your generous funds I was able to open this shop seven years ago. I'm glad I can finally show my gratitude face-to-face."

Edmund replied, "This is why I came to you, Mitchell. I trust no other. No one must know I'm here or that I have the piece. Do you recognize it?"

"Yes, my lord. Any knowledgeable jeweler would recognize it immediately. It is quite extraordinary."

"Whose is it?" Edmund demanded. "Do you know?"

"I can't say, my lord. It is intricate handiwork. The man who owns this cuff link must be quite powerful."

Carefully holding the cuff link between his forefinger and thumb, Mr. Mitchell encouraged Edmund to examine it underneath his jeweler's loupe. "The quality of the sapphire and diamonds is impressive, indeed, but it is the tiny inscription at the edge of the cuff link that tells the tale. Do you see it, my lord?" he asked, excitedly.

"Yes," Edmund answered, putting down the eyepiece. "It is a crown. What of it?"

"This sapphire is from the Royal Collection, my lord, only to be sanctioned and given as gifts to the most trusted and closest of friends. As Russia's imperial eggs were given to royal family members back in the day, these sapphires are England's version of the Fabergé eggs."

Carefully, the jeweler handed the cuff link back to Edmund. "The piece you hold in your hand, my lord, was a gift from our Queen or from one who ruled before her. The owner is probably a member of the royals or someone very close to them."

Bloody hell! No wonder Julianna had refused to give up the bastard's name. The man was much too powerful. It would be her word against his. No one would believe an individual of such eminence would stoop so low as to try to rape a lady. The only clue in Edmund's possession was this sapphire-and-diamond cuff link Julianna had accidentally grabbed on to while fighting the bastard off the night of the masquerade ball. Diego had rushed out and handed it to him just before he left Casa de Cordoba in Aranjuez.

"There must be some sort of registry for these gifts. An official record of who receives what," Edmund said. "The name of the person I'm seeking must be on that list—if not his name, the name of one of his ancestors."

"I would presume, my lord, but I'm not acquainted with the inner workings of Buckingham Palace or what takes place within its gates. If I could, I would rush right over to extract the registry from the elderly monarch myself."

Realizing he was now a step closer to finding Julianna's attacker, Edmund held the cuff link in his palm, squeezing it until it bit into his hand. "Mitchell, the information you've given me today is thanks enough. One way or another, I will get my hands on that registry."

"Before you go, my lord, won't you let me feast my eyes on it again?"

Edmund opened his hand and indulged the old jeweler, allowing him a last look at the cuff link.

"Have you seen anything more beautiful than the color of that sapphire?" Jonas asked, shaking his head in awe.

"Yes, I have," Edmund replied matter-of-factly before dropping the cuff link into a pouch and returning it to his vest pocket.

Jonas Mitchell grinned. "Ah, my lord. Could I venture to ask if she is one of a kind...like the sapphire she rivals?"

Edmund ignored the man's comment. He didn't need Ruth's brother to tell him what he already knew. He had not realized it until recently, did not know when or how she had accomplished it, but that spoiled, overconfident, proud slip of a girl with eyes that could turn and stare daggers at him without a moment's hesitation had managed to get under his skin. Sometimes she treated him as though he were nothing more than a scratch on the bottom of her heel, and yet...when she looked up at him with that enchanting smile of hers and those magnificent, trusting sapphire eyes, she could totally disarm him.

He'd had his share of women, but never before had he encountered anyone as exasperating as this chit. *One of a kind, indeed!* She was driving him insane, and, of late, he found himself fighting a battle of personal restraint, divided between wanting to wring her little neck and kissing the hell out of that sultry mouth of hers.

After thanking the jeweler, Edmund stepped out onto the sidewalk and into his coach. Once seated, he took the pouch from his vest pocket and dropped the cuff link onto the palm of his hand to stare at it again.

A jab of guilt stabbed at his chest. *Damn it!* The bloody stone should remind him solely of Julianna's plight and not of the beautiful girl with the sapphire eyes. His thoughts filtered back to the day he'd first seen her on the train to London. How puffed-up and determined she had seemed to him then, but how magnificent. He had never seen anything more beautiful than the resolute young woman who had every intention on marrying a duke. Damn it all to hell—Marguerite Wiggins was a distraction he did not need or want.

"Where to, Mr. James?" asked the coachman.

"The Hardwood townhome," Edmund replied. "I must speak with Lord Hardwood at once."

Chapter Twelve

Aunt Elizabeth had certainly outdone herself, thought Marguerite as she took in her aunt's meticulous selection of setting, exquisite cuisine and seating arrangements. The epitome of elegance and style, the Hardwood dining room sparkled in yellow and white tones from the lace tablecloths, the floral centerpieces and the assortments of candles to the hanging chandelier adorned with summer blossoms.

Indeed, Samantha's engagement party was proving to be a huge success, quite the extravagant affair filled with laughter and animated conversation between agreeable and like-minded intimate family and friends—like-minded and agreeable everywhere except at the oblong head table where Marguerite had the misfortune of being seated.

The ornate table of gold plates and polished glass, stunning gold centerpiece of yellow, orange and white summer roses and the gold-accented porcelain candelabras could not diminish the unpleasantness of the discordant people surrounding her. Not even the shining silver bowls overflowing with delicious fruit and cakes and the elaborate three-course meal her aunt had lavishly planned could whet Marguerite's appetite as the food was served *à la Française* by uniformed waiters. She could only lift her fork to nibble a morsel here and there. Ordinarily she would have had to restrain herself from wanting to devour the delicious *filet de boeuf à la jardiniére*, or the *canards à la rouennaise*, but tonight her stomach had been tied up in knots since the moment in the parlor when Lord Roland had come to escort her to the dining room. With mounting dread, Marguerite had realized Samantha and Aunt Elizabeth had bestowed her the honor of placing her at the head table with the engaged couple, their parents, and the most sought-after bachelor in the room, the only person Marguerite did not want near her, the hateful scoundrel who had cost her everything—Lord Roland Bradford.

Not that Lord Roland seemed to take any pleasure in her company. It was evident from the scornful glances he occasionally directed her way he now loathed her as much as she did him. For that much, Marguerite was extremely grateful. Ashton's pummeling of Lord Roland in the park must have done the trick. No more having to endure suggestive looks or inappropriate insinuations from the detestable cad. In fact, the man had not bothered to utter a single word to Marguerite since he had guided her into the room and taken the seat beside her.

Marguerite's covetous gaze traveled to the lively guests sitting at the numerous round tables about the room. Although Marguerite was flattered to have been placed with the guests of honor, she strongly wished Samantha and Aunt Elizabeth had refrained from doing so. At the moment, she felt very much like the naughty child who had been punished and forced to stand at the corner of the room while the other children played and ran free.

Mostly, she felt disappointment that Ashton was not at her side. For weeks, he had been her escort and companion. She had grown accustomed to having him by her side and would have much preferred to sit at his table, sharing the meal with Penny and Winnie, Mr. Cummings and Mr. Pennington, and the flirtatious middle-aged brunette who had been earlier introduced to Marguerite as Lady Rosalind Blythe, along with her timid daughter, Bernice.

Gazing at the voluptuous Lady Blythe, Marguerite wondered how much longer the woman's dress could hold up her ample breasts, which threatened to spill out of her low-cut gown for all to see.

Marguerite had to contain herself from going over and pulling the woman's hair out. The wanton tramp was out of control, fluttering her eyelashes and blatantly throwing herself at Ashton as though there was no one else in the room.

"That woman needs to cover her chest," she blurted out.

Uncle John addressed her from the opposite end of the table, "What about chess, dear?" he asked with furrowed brow, catching her by surprise.

Marguerite was so absorbed in the laughter, merriment, and flirting emanating from Ashton's table, she had not realized she had spoken the words out loud. She was grateful that, at that precise moment, the boisterous conversation in the room had made it difficult for the guests at the head table to hear her comment.

"I did not mention chess, Uncle John. I only said the party is a great success."

"What?" Uncle John asked, raising his voice. "What did you say, dear?"

"The party is a huge success!" Marguerite repeated, raising her voice and angry with herself for allowing the Blythe woman to get under her skin.

Uncle John smiled proudly. "Indeed it is, my dear. Indeed it is! Your aunt has surpassed herself. Why, even our serious Mr. James seems to be enjoying himself."

Staring at Ashton and wishing she were the one next to him, Marguerite drank the last of her wine and waited patiently for a uniformed servant to pour some more into her glass. She knew that she was breaking every rule of etiquette Aunt Elizabeth had painstakingly taught her. Instead of pretending to drink the wine by touching the glass to her lips, she had already gulped two glasses down while trying to ignore the shameless hussy flirting with Ashton.

Feeling sick to her stomach, Marguerite was about to turn her head so as not to witness any more of the woman's antics when Ashton, looking handsomer than ever, captured her eyes with his. Marguerite felt a warm glow flow through her when he raised his wineglass to her as both a sign of reassurance and a warning notice to Lord Roland. Relief overtook her. With a slow, secret smile, she nodded slightly, acknowledging him from afar. With that small gesture, Ashton had let Marguerite know his interest was not on the enticing seductress beside him. He was watching out for her and only her.

Still, it irked Marguerite that she was forced to observe the wanton trollop use her heaving mounds to gain his attention. She decided it was best to keep her eyes away from Ashton's table so she could celebrate the happy occasion and enjoy the evening as much as possible. Sitting with the Greyleighs proved no easy task.

A sour Lord Roland leaned toward her and muttered under his breath only for her to hear, "Mr. James can keep his threats to himself. I no longer have any interest in pursuing you, Miss Wiggins."

"That's a relief, my lord," Marguerite replied coolly. "With a room full of women to choose from, I'm delighted you will not waste your time on me."

"Listen to her, Lord Roland."

Marguerite heard Flora's voice before she turned to find the almost unrecognizable servant, defrocked of her usual light blue nanny garb and wearing a black dress with white, fancy apron and frilly white cap, standing at her side holding a crystal decanter. "Don't worry, Miss Marguerite, I've got my eye on the rotten vermin," she whispered before pouring the wine unto Marguerite's empty glass.

"Hush, Nanny, he'll hear you—they'll all hear you," Marguerite whispered over her shoulder. "What are you doing here?"

Glaring at Lord Roland's back, Flora responded, "I'm making certain the good-for-nothing rogue behaves himself. I hope they do hear. It would serve him right."

"I'll have some more of that hearty wine." Lord Roland raised his glass only to be ignored by Flora, who passed right by him and gave him a dirty look before refilling everyone else's glass and retiring to stand at the back wall with the other servants.

"Mother, the room is filled with servants. Why is Nanny here? Can she not sit and watch?" Samantha asked as she gazed over her shoulder at Flora. "She told me she would wait for me to tell her about the party once it was over."

"You believed her?" Uncle John asked, chuckling. "The woman has a mind of her own. We all know that."

Aunt Elizabeth looked heavenward and sighed. "You know Flora wouldn't miss this for the world, Samantha. I didn't have the heart to deprive her of being part of your engagement party. You know better than to ask if she'll sit and watch."

Preferring not to discuss the help in front of the Marquess and Marchioness Greyleigh, Aunt Elizabeth quickly changed the subject. "Lord Greyleigh, my husband tells me you are an avid hunter."

"Indeed, I am," Lord Greyleigh replied most enthusiastically. "I am not one to boast, Lady Hardwood, but I have been blessed with my share of skills, if I do say so myself. I'm quite adept at taking to the hunt. Just ask my sons. Isn't that right, Roland... Steven?"

"Ah, yes," Lord Roland mumbled absently, too busy ogling Lady Blythe to give his father an encouraging response.

Lord Steven cleared his throat. "Hunting requires much skill. I can testify that our dear father is quite adept at the sport."

"I'm very proficient at it," the marquess readily agreed. "Very proficient, indeed."

Not one to boast! Marguerite was soon discovering the slight and distinguished-looking marquess most enjoyed speaking about himself, unlike his hefty wife, who had no interest in conversation, but concentrated only on the food she wolfed down.

"Never mind hunting—Alfred, that shameful doxy is ruining my meal. The woman is making a public spectacle of herself," Marchioness Greyleigh suddenly managed to say between bites.

"Dear, naive Freddy should never have sent Rosalind to London without him. If only he had not taken ill at the last moment. Look at her. She belongs in a brothel! Her bosoms are falling out of her gown, right under Mr. James's nose. It is all the poor man can do not to inhale them along with his food."

The marquess smiled patiently at his wife. "Constance, try not to make a scene. Rosalind is your brother's problem. It is true she should have stayed in the country to tend to Freddy, but one can't blame the woman for wanting to share in our happiness."

Overlooking her husband's words, the marchioness continued, "The hussy should be ashamed. We all know she cares for Freddy as much as I care for that flamboyant red gown she is wearing! I don't know why he chose to marry her at this late stage. I feel sorry for the daughter. Freddy loves the shy little mouse as though she were his own. Poor thing must be mortified at her mother's behavior."

Marquess Greyleigh smiled benignly, as though he were dealing with a petulant child. Exhibiting great patience, he put down his fork and wiped his mouth with his napkin. "Bernice is a grown woman of nineteen. She must be used to her mother's behavior by now, dear."

"Don't you *dear* me. You are all alike, ignoring your wives to lust after women half your age," exclaimed the marchioness, her mercurial black eyes narrowing suspiciously as she watched her husband, who was now ogling Lady Blythe as intently as their son Roland.

"How can I ignore you?" the marquess remarked absentmindedly. "You make that quite difficult, my dear."

"I must say the color red does become her. Uncle Freddy must have his hands full with her," Lord Roland said, licking his lips. "I would love to trade places with the old bugger just for a night. I think I'll plan a trip to the country sometime soon."

"Roland, don't," Lord Steven gave his brother a dark, disapproving look before turning to Samantha and her parents. "I apologize for my brother. He's had too much to drink."

Lord Roland smirked at Flora as she refilled his water glass. "Too much drink? I've hardly had anything at all," he protested. "The insolent servant has refused to serve me and has been glaring at me all evening."

With one quick swig, Marguerite drank the last of her wine. Smiling, she came to Flora's defense. "Nonsense, Lord Roland. Why would Nanny refuse to serve you?"

"Why, indeed? Roland, behave. The woman is here to serve and nothing more," the marchioness reprimanded her son before taking yet another piece of fruitcake from one of the large silver bowls on the table.

Lord Roland shrugged dismissively and helped himself to his mother's glass of wine.

"Greyleigh—you must stop staring at Rosalind as well," the marchioness insisted, her brow creased as she concentrated on finishing her *filet*. "I will not be humiliated in this manner. It is bad enough my poor brother is being cuckolded right before our eyes."

"Don't be crass, Constance," Marquess Greyleigh retorted. Bending forward to look past his wife's heavy, sagging bosom, he winked at Marguerite with the same suggestive grin that Lord Roland usually gave her. "Why look elsewhere, when there is someone much more beautiful at this table?"

"Greyleigh!" The marchioness shot her husband a murderous glance.

"I meant you, my dear...only you. Now stop berating your poor sister-in-law."

"Poor, indeed! She will inherit Blythe Castle, and tonight she is wearing most of the family jewels."

"The rubies match her dress, dear. What is the poor woman to do?"

Uncle John and Aunt Elizabeth exchanged nervous glances.

"Dear, do you not think it is time for the toast?" Uncle John asked, most desperately, trying to waylay a family feud.

Aunt Elizabeth replied, "Not yet, dear. We have not served dessert. I say, don't Lady Lorena Bonner and Lord Christopher Jackman make an attractive couple? It seems they have been quite enamored for some time and kept their courtship a secret. I can't say I blame her."

"Why is that?" Uncle John asked.

"After the wasted years alongside the Duke of Wallingford, Lorena refused to be seen with the baron unless he offered her a proposal of marriage. She kept their courtship a secret."

Marguerite focused her attention on Lady Lorena and the handsome baron, who sat surrounded by the rest of the Bonner family at the corner of the room.

"A proposal? That's a bit harsh!" Lord Roland gasped. "Jackman will never fall for that ploy," he insisted, chortling. "A man knows when he's being led to the slaughter."

Aunt Elizabeth and Samantha exchanged knowing looks. "Mother, let me be the one to break the news," Samantha beseeched, turning to Marguerite, "Oh, Marguerite, you're not going to believe this. It is so romantic! The baron proposed to Lorena last night. We added a place for him this morning."

Surprised by the sudden news, Marguerite's gaze quickly traveled to Ashton.

"How wonderful—how simply wonderful," Marguerite exclaimed, genuinely happy for Lorena, and equally delighted that Lady Bonner was engaged to be married and not engaged in an amorous affair with Ashton. The man held no title, owned no land, was not of the aristocracy, but try as she might, Marguerite could not tolerate the notion of him with anyone else. During the past weeks, she had chided herself countless times for feeling this way, but had come to accept her thoughts were not rational or justifiable when it came to Ashton James.

Ashamed of her feelings, Marguerite, once more, reminded herself that her chaperone's love life was his own to have, especially since she never considered or desired him as a prospect. Nevertheless, as he was now rapt in conversation with the ardent Lady Blythe, Marguerite was elated to know at least one lady in the room would no longer be available to him.

"Indeed, what wonderful news," Aunt Elizabeth gushed. "She is such a good friend to you, Marguerite. Lord Eustinius is hosting a ball to celebrate the engagement, and you, my dear niece, are first on Lorena's list of invites."

With a sneer, Lord Roland remarked, "Jackman must be mad waiting years yearning for some silly woman. No chit is worth that much trouble. Isn't that right, Miss Wiggins?"

Marguerite ignored him. She was now convinced Lord Steven must have been left at the Greyleigh doorstep at birth. *Poor Samantha, how on earth will she endure her future family?* Samantha seemed to be immune to her surroundings. Her eyes were fixed on Steven. The dreamy expression on her face showed his horrid family was the last thing on her mind.

Watching the loving couple, Marguerite wondered what it would feel like to have Ashton look at her the way Steven was now gazing at Samantha. Not as her chaperone, but as a man in love. Dear God, why was she even considering such a thing? The next time Flora came around with the wine decanter, she would place her hand over her glass and decline. The alcohol made her think silly thoughts. It was time to stop drinking.

* * * *

Across the room, Edmund Kent tried to ignore Lady Blythe's fingers as they sensuously stroked his arm. For the past hour, he strived to overlook her unwanted advances, making idle conversation with the other guests while the married woman groped and caressed him in a room full of people—and in front of her own daughter. The poor girl, Bernice, turned every shade of pink as she watched her mother making a public display of herself.

"Your eyes have not traveled far from Lord Roland and Miss Wiggins, Mr. James. Why is that? Does the girl interest you? Say it isn't so, my dear man," Lady Blythe whispered in his ear. "She is much too young for you."

The lady's gaze went implicatively to her bosom. "Fruit is much more succulent when it is ripe," she said, grinning wickedly. "I'm sure I don't have to tell you that. A delicious morsel such as yourself must be well schooled when it comes to the opposite sex."

Edmund smiled politely at the overtly suggestive brunette. If he hadn't been so preoccupied with Marguerite and Bradstone, he would have actually given her what she wanted. It had been a while since he had satisfied his baser needs, and this one could satisfy him just fine. No stranger to women, Edmund knew an invitation when he got one. The signs were all there: the licking of her bottom lip, the wanting look in her eyes. He doubted she would object if he were to suddenly drag her upstairs, rip off her clothes, and take her up against a wall.

Unfortunately, at the moment, Lady Blythe was only a nuisance to him—a tempting diversion, but one he could not afford to indulge in.

"Well, Mr. James? Do you or do you not have a secret attraction for Miss Wiggins?"

"How observant of you, Lady Blythe," Edmund replied, his words loaded with sarcasm. "My interest in Miss Wiggins is that of chaperone and nothing more. I'm being paid to watch over Marguerite."

Lady Blythe's lips curved into a naughty smile as she eyed him up and down covetously. "You are also being paid to chaperone her two sisters, but you haven't given them a second look. It doesn't take much perception, Mr. James. Anyone with eyes can see Marguerite Wiggins is the one who interests you."

"Her sisters are sitting at my table. I can assure you they are well supervised at the moment," Edmund commented dryly, his eyes returning to Marguerite.

"Why does Miss Wiggins need a chaperone tonight? Surely you are not suggesting my dear nephew Roland would try to do anything improper to her while at his brother's engagement party? He is Freddy's godson. I trust him implicitly. I even gave permission for Roland to show Bernice the sights after dinner."

Edmund was taken aback by Lady Blythe's remark. "A ride after dark? Tonight? Do you think that is wise?"

"Why not? They are almost cousins," replied Lady Blythe, her eyebrow raising a fraction. "You look as though you disapprove, Mr. James. If Lord Hardwood can hand over his nieces to *you*, a man who is not even family, I can certainly entrust Roland to accompany Bernice for an innocent coach ride. What harm would it do for my daughter to see London in style? The poor girl has been cooped up too long in the country."

Unlike Lady Blythe, Bernice was conducting herself quite properly at the dinner table. Given Bradstone's roguish behavior had forced Edmund to come to blows with the cad, his conscience told him to try to warn the mother.

"It is certainly your prerogative, Lady Blythe, but I would not recommend the ride without a chaperone," he said firmly.

Lady Blythe disregarded his suggestion with a shrug of her shoulder and a sly grin. "You are an extremely attractive man, Mr. James. I thought chaperones were supposed to be old spinsters who accompanied young maidens and lived vicariously through their wards. Although you are much too serious for your own good, I do find you highly entertaining. I dare say I wish I had employed you first, and not to protect my daughter but to look after me."

Upon hearing Lady Blythe's remark, Penelope Wiggins turned her attention from Mr. Pennington and snootily addressed the woman. "You don't need a chaperone, Lady Blythe. Somehow I don't think you are too concerned with gossip. You seem quite adept at taking care of yourself."

"Penny!" Winifred admonished. Her eyes darted nervously from Lady Blythe to Penelope and back again. "Please do not pay attention to my sister, Lady Blythe. Most of the time Penelope does not mean what she says."

Penny retorted furiously, "Oh, I certainly do mean it. What business does *she* have with a chaperone?"

Rosalind Blythe let out a low, throaty laugh. "My dear Miss

Wiggins. I know that chaperones are for innocent girls who avoid scandal and do not want to get compromised before marriage. Why should I have to deprive myself of such a treat? I cared about gossip once. I avoided scandal *before marriage*. Tell me, how did your sister, Marguerite, get so lucky? She is not that different from me, you know."

"Lady Blythe, do not compare yourself to my sister," Penny said stiffly. "You couldn't be more different from her."

Edmund chuckled at the notion. Had he heard correctly? Penny was right. Marguerite Wiggins was far different from the woman beside him. For starters, his charge would never throw herself at a stranger she'd just met. He didn't know which statement was the more absurd, that Lady Blythe and Marguerite had anything in common or that her dear, precious nephew, Roland, could be trusted "implicitly."

"I suppose Miss Wiggins does have a point." Lady Blythe gave out a long sigh and pressed herself closer to him. "I certainly have no business with a chaperone. Would you, Mr. James, be interested in another position, not as a chaperone but as my bodyguard?" She smiled and gave him a little wink. "I'm sure we could find it mutually beneficial."

Bernice, who had hardly spoken a word since the beginning of dinner, suddenly objected, "Mother, please don't go on so. Mr. James is not interested in another position."

Edmund felt sorry for the daughter. Looking as though she would rather be anywhere but at the Hardwood engagement party having to endure her mother's scandalous behavior, the girl seemed mortified, her cheeks beet red, but she somehow managed a tremulous smile and continued, "My stepfather would never agree to it. Papa Freddy is such a dear. He would insist on guarding you himself."

"Don't you think Bernice is quite lovely, Mr. James?" Rosalind suddenly asked him, causing poor Bernice all the more embarrassment. "Now, Bernice, don't look at me like that. You haven't answered me, Mr. James. Isn't she a pretty little thing?"

"Yes, she is," Edmund answered truthfully. Although Bernice was not as striking as her mother, the daughter, with her light brown curls and big brown eyes, was, nonetheless, quite pretty.

"It is about time she finds a husband. Freddy should have made the effort of partaking of the London Season for Bernice's sake. Now I fear it may be too late. She is nineteen and counting."

Blocking Lady Blythe's chatter from his thoughts, Edmund's

gaze turned in Marguerite's direction. Almost as if she had read his mind, Marguerite's eyes suddenly locked with his, beguiling him with her liquid blue stare. Instantly, he felt the heat rise in his body, and the primal stirrings of his maleness began to undermine his resolve to keep his wits about him. *Damn!* Where had sanity and reason suddenly gone to? One look from her and he'd almost come undone. Almost? Who was he fooling? Lately he had not been able to think of anything but her. Many times he had imagined her beneath him, and he would bury his hardness deep inside her soft and willing warmth.

Edmund hated to admit it, but the Blythe woman was indeed perceptive—at least when it came to him. The feelings that Marguerite stirred in him were inappropriate for a chaperone. He was supposed to protect her, but he was beginning to feel Marguerite should be cautious of him. An unmarried man with primal needs and a beautiful woman of marriageable age needed to be watched closely. If conditions had been different, they would never have been left alone without supervision.

Smiling at him from across the room, Marguerite looked even more luscious and tempting than usual. Her silk, cream-colored gown was not provocative as was the red dress worn by Lady Blythe; Marguerite's dress was demurely elegant and tasteful, much as the girl herself, but his instinct told him that hidden beneath all her finery was a seductive young body waiting to be explored—silky skin and curves that would drive any sane man to distraction. He knew this like he knew the back of his hand, like he knew his name to be Edmund Kent and not Mr. Ashton James.

He had often wondered what his ward would do if she knew the truth about him. What if he had met her under different circumstances? Would Marguerite have dismissed the Earl of Windword as easily as she had Ashton James, the lowly chaperone? Ashton was no match for the Duke of Wallingford...but Edmund? Could he have had a chance with her? *Bloody hell,* he cursed himself. What did it matter anyway? Marguerite had made no secret to him that she loved the Duke of Wallingford, and Edmund would never stand for being used as a consolation prize, no matter how enticing he found her.

He had more pressing issues to resolve than to fantasize about a chit who cared nothing for him. His sole purpose for being in London was to find the bloody bastard who had tried to rape his sister.

Tormented by conflicting emotions, Edmund recalled that first morning, when he had arrived at the Hardwood doorstep to let his neighbors know what had actually happened to Julianna and swear them to secrecy of her whereabouts. Back then, Edmund had never contemplated he would end up being in charge of the Wiggins girls. Locked in the study with a distraught Lord and Lady Hardwood and their daughter, Samantha, Edmund had scoffed when Elizabeth Hardwood had suggested he chaperone her nieces, but he'd quickly relented after realizing it would make an excellent cover. Not only could he search out the rapist without arousing suspicions, but Lord and Lady Hardwood could rest easy. Their charges would be safe from the depraved bastard who was preying upon innocent and unsuspecting girls.

That was months ago. Edmund now wondered at the wisdom of his decision. How could he have guessed at the time that the Wigginses were the girls who had shared a train with him the day before, or that Marguerite Wiggins would cost him such sleepless nights?

His thoughts of Marguerite were suddenly waylaid when he heard Penny trying to caution Rosalind against Bradstone.

"Lady Blythe," said Penny, "if you wish your daughter to stay in London for the rest of the Season, I suggest you not let her alone with Lord Roland tonight. The man has a reputation with the ladies."

"Really? How do you know this, my dear?" Lady Blythe asked, appearing amused. She turned to her daughter. "Bernice, darling, Miss Wiggins is going to speak her mind once more. Let us listen to what she has to say."

Penny didn't fail to catch the sarcasm in Lady Blythe's voice. Her lips puckered with annoyance. "You may choose to make jest, Lady Blythe. I feel he has broken many a poor girl's heart. I noticed how Mr. Cummings's sister was all smiles when she conversed with Lord Roland at the Salesbury ball. I saw them together in the balcony. Now Mr. Cummings tells us Desdemona has left London for the country."

Damian Cummings looked uneasy. He cleared his throat before speaking. "Indeed, but her departure does not concern Lord Bradstone. Our mother is not well and has returned to Surrey with Desdemona. I can assure you, if that were not the case, Desdemona would be here tonight. She had so wanted to attend."

"Are you certain, Mr. Cummings?" Penny persisted. "Lord Roland must have broken Emily Middleton's heart, too. The last time I saw her, she was dancing with him at the Wimberly ball.

Her brother, Mr. Frank Middleton, told us that she has also re-tired to the country."

Winifred objected, "Penny, don't be ridiculous. Please stop."

"Don't be a hypocrite, Winifred Wiggins. The man is a cad. You said so yourself when he was pursuing Marguerite. Thank good-ness she was not the least bit interested in him, or Marguerite would now be in Crawley with our aunts Lavinia and Hyacinth and our dear papa. Lord Bradstone tried his best to compromise our sister for weeks."

"Well, I don't know about that, Miss Wiggins, but now that you mention it..." Mr. Pennington looked pensive as he scratched his chin. "There was another young lady, quite lovely, I might add. She was delightful, and we were having a most pleasant conversa-tion during the masquerade ball..."

Penny's jaw clenched and her eyes narrowed. "Delightful, Mr. Pennington?"

"Not quite as delightful as you, Miss Penelope. I dare say, Miss Penelope. I don't suppose we could have a word in the courtyard when dinner is over?"

"Of course, Mr. Pennington. We shall retire the moment the toast is given. Now go on with your story. Wasn't the masquerade ball the first ball of the Season?"

"Indeed, Miss Wiggins, it certainly was. As I was saying...the lady and I were chatting when Lord Bradstone interrupted us. I specifically heard Lord Roland invite her to the theatre the next evening, and she agreed to attend. Later I was told Lady Kent left with her brother to travel abroad. Odd, don't you think? Why would she leave so soon when the Season had just begun? I hope she did not leave with a broken heart. "

Edmund tried to maintain his composure the moment he heard his sister's name and asked as casually as he could manage, "Mr. Pennington, are you certain that it was Lady Julianna Kent you saw with Lord Roland at the masquerade ball?"

Mr. Pennington smiled. "Indeed, Mr. James. I could never for-get such an enchanting face."

Penny's brows drew together. "Enchanting, Mr. Pennington? According to Marguerite, Lady Kent is somewhat of a tomboy who enjoys climbing trees and riding horses in the middle of the night. Our sister bored us with silly stories of the summers at Hardwood Manor with Samantha and her neighbor, Julianna Kent. The 'Three Musketeers' is what they called themselves. How silly is that?"

Winifred disagreed. "Penny, I don't know how you can say their stories were boring or silly. We both enjoyed them, and you know it." Smiling, she turned to Mr. Cummings. "I would have loved to have met Lady Kent this summer. Unfortunately, her overprotective brother snatched her away before she had time to enjoy the Season. Samantha misses her greatly and wishes she were here. Marguerite is also disappointed Lady Kent left without getting the chance to spend time with her."

"Well, I, for one, am glad she's gone," Penny admitted bluntly. "I wouldn't want to share her with Mr. Pennington. He is my only suitor."

Lady Blythe threw her head back and let out a peal of laughter. "Didn't your mother teach you not to declare your feelings in public? Did you hear what she just said, Mr. James?"

Edmund did not answer her. He was too preoccupied wondering if Penny, without knowing, had uncovered the awful truth. He sat frozen, his eyes fixed on Lord Roland. Was Bradstone the one who had tried to rape his sister? He was about to interrogate Mr. Pennington further when he was interrupted by their host.

Lord Hardwood stood at the head table, enthusiastically clinking a silver spoon against a wineglass. "Ladies and gentlemen, join me in a toast! I drink to Lord Steven's continued good health and well-being." He turned to his future son-in-law. "My dear man, may my daughter, Samantha, bring you the same happiness her mother has brought me."

Absently, Edmund joined the others as they lifted their wineglasses to toast the engaged couple. Following Hardwood's toast, everyone stood and made their way to the head table to congratulate the pair. Afterwards, the men returned to their tables while the ladies began to exit the dining room to leave the men to their brandy and cigars.

Lady Blythe squeezed his hand before taking her leave. "It has been a pleasure, Mr. James. I do hope we can talk later."

Edmund hardly heard or felt her. Alarm and fury rippled along his spine. At least three women had precipitously and unexpectedly left London after attending a ball and spending time with just one person—and the bastard was now following Marguerite out of the dining room!

Chapter Thirteen

Unfortunately for Marguerite, no sooner had she left the dining room than Lord Roland approached her from behind. "I would like a word, Miss Wiggins," he said, grabbing her elbow. "We need to have a private talk."

"Don't touch me," Marguerite objected. Jerking her arm free of his grasp, she began to walk down the hall toward the parlor. "I have nothing to say to you," she said over her shoulder.

Halted by an iron grip on her wrist, she discovered Lord Roland would not be deterred. "Let's go in here. I doubt there will be any interruptions. Come with me," he insisted after he opened the door to the study and realized it was empty. "I daresay, Miss Wiggins, you've had your fill of drink this evening."

"Take your *filthy* hands off her, Bradstone. I'll not warn you again."

Closing her eyes with relief, Marguerite recognized the strong, menacing voice. She turned to find Ashton, his brows drawn together in an angry frown, standing behind them as she was being forced into the study.

Lord Roland stiffened, instantly releasing her. "I only wanted to apologize to the young lady, Mr. James. It is not necessary for you to watch over us. It was not my intention to—"

"Get the hell out of here, Bradstone," Ashton said curtly. "Miss Wiggins is not interested in anything you have to say. She has not forgotten what you tried to do in the park. Neither have I."

Lord Roland's expression was wary. "I just wanted to thank Miss Wiggins for her discretion concerning that afternoon. I will not bother her again." He turned to Marguerite. "Miss Wiggins, please accept my apology. I hope the next time we see each other you will not treat me as if I were carrying a contagious disease."

The loathing in his eyes revealed to Marguerite that Lord Roland was anything but contrite. He was going through the motions, no doubt, so that she would continue to be discreet. It would not do for his family to know his abominable conduct that day ruined her life.

Ashton shot Lord Roland a cold look. "She is not keeping quiet for your sake. Take your apology and get out."

Marguerite was about to give Lord Roland a piece of her mind, but before she could do so, Ashton grabbed Lord Roland by the coat collar and shoved him out into the hallway.

Once Lord Roland was out of the study, Ashton slammed the door behind him and turned to Marguerite. "Promise me, you won't allow yourself to be alone with this man ever again."

Marguerite blinked, feeling light-headed. "This is not a hard promise to keep," she said, smiling. "I despise him...I really do. The man is the cause of all my troubles. I'm terrified of him. Why would I want to be alone with him?"

"Promise me, damn it," he snapped.

"I promise," Marguerite assured him, taken aback by his fury. "I'm glad to see you were able to free yourself from Lady Blythe. I was beginning to wonder if I would ever see you again. Did that woman do something to upset you? Is that why you look so angry?"

"Never mind her. Just make certain you keep Bradstone away." His voice rang with command. "I'm dead serious, Marguerite."

"I can see. Don't worry about Lord Roland. Apart from a few off-color remarks regarding his 'dear aunt Rosalind' the man behaved impeccably. He did no harm tonight."

A look of astonishment flashed in Ashton's eyes. "Have you forgotten what the man is capable of? You couldn't have forgotten." His eyes narrowed suspiciously. He took her by the shoulders and looked intently into her face. "That bloody bastard is right. You're drunk. How much did you have to drink?"

"I'm just a little dizzy." Marguerite balked, disentangling herself from his grasp. "I admit I had a little too much wine during dinner, but no one would blame me if they knew what I've been through this past hour. Except for Steven, the Bradstones are not the kind of people you want as dinner companions. I feel as though I've been to war—a war of words. So don't judge me. Dinner was a nightmare."

"That may very well be, but you can't walk out like this. You need to sober up first."

Marguerite smiled impishly and crooked her finger. "Let's waltz instead," she beckoned him.

Ashton frowned. "Duchess, you can hardly stand, much less waltz."

"Honestly, Ashton, you are no fun." Humming *The Blue Danube*, she began to waltz on her own, before nearly colliding with his powerful body. Suddenly she felt queasy, as though she were going to be sick.

Ashton caught her in his arms and led her to Uncle John's favorite leather chair, where she fell into it with a moan. Holding her head in the palm of her hand, she watched as Ashton walked over to Uncle John's desk and poured a glass of water from a decanter. Seconds later, he returned to where she was sitting and held the glass out to her. "Drink this."

"Oh, Ashton, I don't think I can. My head is spinning. I need a moment."

"Drink it. Take tiny sips."

Marguerite took the glass he was offering and began to sip the water. How could she refuse him? He looked so handsome tonight, standing in his black evening attire, looking down at her with obvious irritation.

"Stay put. I'll be right back," he ordered.

"Where are you going?"

Without replying, he walked out of the room and returned a few minutes later with a plate of plain pound cake. "Eat this."

She knew better than to argue with him. Taking the plate from him, she attempted to eat the pound cake. After a few bites, she looked up at him. "I don't want any more. It's dry. I feel as though I'm going to choke."

Ashton shook his head. "Eat it all," he ordered. "Drink it down with water. You'll soon feel better."

Marguerite did as she was told. He was right. As soon as the cake hit her stomach, the queasiness began to disappear.

Thankful, Marguerite smiled up at him. She could not help but notice how deliciously masculine he was. She liked everything about him, the powerful set of his shoulders, his tall, beautifully proportioned body, the stubborn set of his chin. It was no wonder the Blythe woman found him so appealing and could hardly keep her hands off him.

Feeling her cheeks begin to warm, she gave an anxious little cough and tried to concentrate on finishing her cake.

"What exactly happened during dinner?" he asked. "What was it that drove you to drink?"

Having to watch that harlot throw herself all over you—that's what drove me to drink!

Grateful Ashton could not read her thoughts, Marguerite replied, "Please don't make me relive it. I'm glad I'm here with you and not with those horrid Bradstones. Please, Ashton, don't leave me again. I'm sure the men have joined the women by now. After my stomach settles, we can return to the parlor...together. I want to see the magic tricks Aunt Elizabeth has arranged for us. She has thought of all kinds of entertainment in order to keep Penny from playing the piano."

"*The piano?* I have no time to play the piano. Where's Uncle John?" Penny burst into the study, taking both of them by surprise. "I've been looking for him everywhere. Have you seen him, Mr. James?"

"Your uncle was in the hallway a few minutes ago," Ashton replied, taking the empty plate and glass from Marguerite and placing them on a small round table nearby.

"Where was he going? Do you know?" Penny asked, anxiously. Ashton shrugged. "Haven't a clue."

Penny, more wound up than usual, threw her hands up in the air. "Honestly, if that old man does not resurface, he won't see a penny of Mr. Pennington's worth."

Marguerite jerked to her feet. "Penelope—don't you ever refer to Uncle John that way. Honestly, what is wrong with you?" she demanded.

Huffing, Penny rolled her eyes. "Uncle John is not the old man I am referring to, Marguerite. It is Papa. He is not in Crawley. Aunt Lavinia and Aunt Hyacinth have no inkling of his whereabouts. I need to find Uncle John. He'll know what to do."

Marguerite did not understand why Penny was making such a fuss. The news of Papa's disappearance was more than a few days old. Earlier in the week, Mr. Cummings had informed the family that his trip to Crawley had been a waste of his time. Unable to locate Papa, Mr. Cummings had failed to formally ask for Winnie's hand. Her sister had been very disappointed, as had Aunt Elizabeth, who had looked forward to announcing Winifred's engagement this evening.

"Where can Papa be? The aunts have not seen him for more than a month. I must find our uncle immediately." Penny paced and wrung her hands.

Marguerite tried her best to reassure Penny. "Don't worry about Papa. He's fine. He knows how to take care of himself, Penny. He'll show up soon enough."

"He better. I promise, Marguerite, that old man will not keep me from the love of my life!"

Marguerite and Ashton exchanged curious looks. "The love of your life?" Marguerite asked, confused.

Penny's face lit up suddenly. "Mr. Scott Pennington has just proposed to me...and on one knee. I don't need Papa. My uncle can give us his blessing."

"Oh my—Penny! So you agreed to marry him?"

"What do you think, Marguerite?" Penny said with a sly grin. Before Marguerite could respond, she reached between her breasts and took out the treasured piece of paper Archibald had handed her during the train ride to London. Smugly, she tore it up into little pieces, threw them up in the air, and walked out of the study.

Turning to her chaperone, Marguerite thought she detected laughter in his eyes. "What just happened here? Did she just tell us she is engaged to Mr. Pennington...the Mr. Scott Pennington who is not on Papa's list? Indeed, I must be drunk."

"Then we're both drunk." Ashton's firm mouth twitched, a glint of humor finally surfacing. "I never thought she'd get rid of that list."

Marguerite giggled. "Neither did the rest of the household—never in a million years! She ran out so fast, I didn't get the chance to congratulate her."

"We just saw Penny in the hallway. She told us the news!"

Marguerite heard Samantha's voice and turned to find her cousin and Steven standing at the threshold. "Why is she in such a hurry? Steven and I could hardly pass on the good wishes."

Smiling, Marguerite nodded in agreement. "Indeed, I was just telling Ashton the same thing. She wants to find Uncle John so he can give his approval since Papa has disappeared."

"We are looking for Father, too. Mother thought he would be here, hiding away from the guests. I wanted to show him my engagement ring. Oh, Marguerite, have you ever seen anything more beautiful?"

Marguerite rushed over to Samantha. Taking her cousin's outstretched hand, she was genuinely awestruck by the beautiful diamond Steven had just so generously bestowed. "Sam, it's magnificent. Mr. James, come and see. Isn't it beautiful?"

Ashton walked over to them and smiled politely as Marguerite held Samantha's hand in front of his face. He was about to respond when Steven declared proudly, "Not nearly as beautiful as the woman who wears it. The ring doesn't do my Samantha justice."

"Well, I don't know about that. You know what they say: love is blind," Samantha said a little self-consciously, placing her hand on Steven's arm.

Steven insisted, "Nonsense, my dear. My eyes don't deceive me. You are the most—"

Blushing, Samantha interrupted him, "Steven, dear, let's go find Father. Marguerite and Mr. James do not want to hear about how beautiful you think I am." She gave him a little wink. "You can tell me that later...when we are alone." Without another word, the happy couple left the study and shut the door behind them.

Marguerite turned to Ashton. "They do make a great pair, don't they?"

"What's wrong?" Ashton asked her. "You look like you're going to be sick again. Do you want to sit down?"

"I'm fine. It's not that."

"What is it then?"

Sighing, Marguerite gave a resigned shrug. "I love her so much. Ashton, I don't want to envy Samantha...but I suppose I do. I envy her, and I envy my sisters. Everyone's engaged but me. Even Lady Lorena announced her engagement tonight."

Marguerite's spirits sank even lower when she noticed the look of disappointment on Ashton's face.

"For God's sake, Marguerite, I would think you'd be happy for them. Instead, you wallow in self-pity."

"I am happy, truly I am, for all of them, but my life is ruined— my fate is sealed. Thanks to Lord Roland, I'm going to spend the rest of my life as a lonely servant teaching children who are not my own."

Her words seemed to amuse him. Chuckling, he shook his head. "I seriously doubt it. There's always the theatre," he teased her. "You're quite dramatic, my dear."

Marguerite could not help but smile. Despite his obstinate and arrogant ways, she could always count on him to make her feel better. It didn't hurt that Ashton was the most attractive man she had ever laid eyes on, or that more and more his mere presence was making her feel things she had never felt.

She was about to return to the sofa when Ashton stopped her. "We better go too," he said, placing a restraining hand on her arm. "We've been gone too long."

Guiding her toward the door, he put his hand on the doorknob, but Marguerite was not ready to leave. She went around him and closed her hand over his to prevent him from turning the knob.

He raised his eyebrow questioningly as she leaned back against the door.

Looking up at him, Marguerite sighed. "I don't want to go yet.

I'd much rather stay here with you." Her hand traveled from his hand to his chest. "Since when have you cared whether we are alone or not? Are you afraid that I will ravish you, Mr. James?" she asked, playfully fluttering her eyelashes.

Marguerite was only teasing him, but Ashton remained silent. She tried to assess his unreadable features. The silence lengthened between them, making her uncomfortable. Hastily, she drew her hand away. She had never been this bold with him before. Obviously, he did not appreciate her attempt at joking, but she was tired of denying her attraction for him. What did it matter anyway? She had no prospects, no duke and no reputation. Why couldn't an abandoned spinster enjoy herself before retiring to a life of loneliness? Brazenly, she put her hand back on his chest, feeling a surge of excitement when his muscles tensed under her fingertips and she felt the steady pounding of his heart.

Leaning into him, she tilted her face toward him. His gaze was dark and compelling as he stared down at her. He grabbed her hand. "Don't do that, Marguerite. I'm not made of stone. I'm liable to forget I'm your chaperone," he admitted, his expression tight with strain.

"Would that be so bad?" she asked.

Her eyes fixed on his lips, and suddenly her whole being filled with the wanting of him. "Can you forget...if only for tonight...if only for a moment...just one stolen moment...Ashton...please."

Standing on tiptoe, Marguerite shamelessly touched her lips to his.

"Damn you, Meggie. I'm tired of fighting it," Ashton cursed, his voice raw and husky, before taking her in his arms, crushing her against his muscled chest.

Her knees weakened when his mouth descended upon hers. Slowly, his expert lips feather-touched hers several times, teasing her, lusciously tormenting her, becoming more demanding as they began to taste and explore the smoothness of her mouth.

Marguerite gasped when his tongue parted her lips, but she soon succumbed to his expert domination, and her tongue began to mate with his, shyly at first, but growing bolder as she followed his lead.

She had never felt anything more pleasurable. The warmth of his delicious lips caused a tingling in the pit of her stomach, and as the kiss progressed, the tingling traveled further down, causing sensations that were foreign to her and sending her senses into a wild swirl. Ashton growled low in his throat as she kissed him back, lingering, savoring every moment.

"Miss Wiggins, you are delectable," he drawled against her mouth.

He pulled back to look at her, but Marguerite tightened her arms around his neck and drew him down for another kiss. She could not think straight. All she knew was she wanted to stay in the moment. If only he could hold her forever. Powerless to resist, she had a burning desire, an aching need, for more kisses.

"Don't stop, Ashton," she murmured breathlessly against his lips. "Please don't stop."

He chuckled, his strong arms enfolding her against the length of him. "I have no intention of stopping, Marguerite."

She felt his breath close to her lips as he was about to kiss her again, when Marguerite whispered back, "It doesn't matter anymore—I'll never marry the duke."

Ashton stiffened. "The duke?" An icy contempt flashed in his eyes as he ground the words out between his teeth. "Were you thinking of Lancaster just now?"

She looked up disoriented, but Ashton didn't wait for an answer. He thrust her away as though she were poison. Her heart pounding wildly, Marguerite stared wordlessly as he turned on his heel and left.

Oh, Ashton—what had she done? She felt screams of frustration at the back of her throat. How could she have been so stupid? Why had she mentioned the duke when Lord Phillip Lancaster was the furthest thing from her mind? She called after Ashton, but he had already vanished.

Marguerite left the study, determined to find him. She needed to explain she had saved herself for Lord Phillip, but was now glad—*oh, so glad*—her first kiss had been with Ashton.

Desperately, she searched the first floor of the townhome. Realizing he left the party, she rushed toward the foyer, but it was too late. When Mortimer opened the front door for her, she saw Ashton inside a coach that was driving away.

* * * *

The night was infernally hot inside the leather confines of the coach, or maybe it was Edmund's temper that had him so steamed. Feeling like a caged lion, he cursed under his breath and damned Lord Roland Bradstone. For the last hour, he'd been spared none of the bumps and grinds of London's cobbled streets, trailing after the depraved bastard and Rosalind Blythe's daughter, Bernice.

It did not surprise Edmund that, before the party's end, and not bothering to watch the magic tricks Lady Hardwood graciously provided as entertainment, Bradstone made his escape and whisked Lady Blythe's daughter away with the same celerity of an African cheetah. What could one expect from a man who had the manners of an alley cat?

No doubt the filthy bastard had tricks of his own in store for poor Bernice.

Who other than a fool could believe Bradstone's intentions were purely altruistic, and his sole purpose was to show Bernice the sights of London? What sights, indeed, could Bernice see at this hour of the night? This was no tour of London, and Bradstone was certainly no tour guide.

Leaning forward, he slid open the partition window and ordered the coachman, "Make sure you don't lose them."

"Don't worry, Mr. James. I'm following a distance behind, and they have no notion."

"Good." Edmund closed the partition and leaned back against the leather seat.

Bloody hell! What kind of a mother would allow her only daughter to ride unchaperoned through the streets of London at this ungodly hour? Rosalind Blythe must be insane. He knew well enough the safety of Lady Blythe's daughter was not the reason for his foul mood. There was only one woman who could make him this angry.

Edmund slammed his fist on the leather seat. Damn her. Damn Marguerite—but damn him for being so careless.

Earlier, when he had followed Lord Roland and Marguerite into the study, kissing Marguerite had been the last thing on his mind. Hell, he tried for weeks to keep his hands off her. Undeniably, the exasperating Miss Wiggins proved to be the most tempting woman he ever laid eyes on. Needing his wits about him for his sister's sake, Edmund had been determined not to fall under Marguerite's spell. But this evening, she had made it impossible for him. She looked up at him with those beautiful sapphire eyes while she pouted those luscious lips, and he lost all control.

Damn it—the little temptress kissed him first. What the hell was he supposed to do? He never claimed to be a saint. Hardwood should have known better than to put him in this predicament. He, Edmund, should have known better than to play with fire.

The moment he held Marguerite in his arms, and she tempted

him with those sweet, beckoning lips, all rational thought left him. There was no denying her kiss unsettled him. Truth be told, Edmund couldn't recall when a kiss affected him this strongly—and the teasing little chit had been thinking of the duke while he'd been kissing her.

Damn it! He had only himself to blame. From day one, Marguerite had made no secret of her intention to marry Lancaster. Her motivation for kissing Edmund had stemmed out of self-indulgence—a means of consoling herself now that the duke was out of reach and uninterested.

The more he thought about Marguerite, the more he felt like throttling the little chit. From now on he'd keep that alluring would-be duchess at arm's length. Tomorrow morning, he would tell Hardwood in no uncertain terms he would have to find someone else to watch over his niece. Edmund's days of chaperoning were over.

Edmund noticed the coach had entered Hyde Park and was now traveling through a wooded path of giant oak trees. Where the devil was Bradstone taking Bernice?

No doubt, the bastard had told the poor girl he wanted to show her the Serpentine. Unfortunately for Bernice, in this darkness the only Serpentine she would see would belong to the snake himself! Edmund raged, recalling how Bradstone had referred to the Serpentine and used that same vulgar line when trying to ravish Marguerite in the park.

Suddenly the coach came to a halt. The coachman knocked on the partition, and Edmund opened it.

"Mr. James, it seems they have stopped underneath those trees at a distance. The driver has left the coach and is walking further into the woods. I suppose he wants to give his master some privacy."

Edmund replied, "Stay put. I'll be back soon."

He stepped out of the vehicle and started to walk toward Bradstone's coach. Suddenly he heard screams. As Edmund ran toward the coach, he distinctly heard the bastard's voice.

"You like it, don't you, little whore? Keep those milky thighs of yours open, and let me have my pleasure."

"No, no...oh...please...don't...stop!" Bernice begged, the sound of her voice resembling a whimpering, hurt puppy. "My lord, don't...please...don't...stop!" she screamed with a shuddering sob.

A sensation of intense sickness swept over Edmund. His heart pounding, he tore open the coach door only to find Bradstone's bare buttocks thrusting forward as his surging body covered a half-naked Bernice, her petticoats up to her waist, her bodice unfastened, leaving her small breasts completely exposed.

"Get off her, you filthy son of a bitch!" Edmund thundered.

A furious Bradstone looked over his shoulder. "Damn you to hell, Ashton James! What the devil are you doing here? I demand an explanation."

"I'm going to kill you, you bloody animal!" Edmund bellowed, thinking of Julianna. Is this what the bastard had planned for her the night she ran off for Spain?

Enraged, he was about to tear Bradstone off the poor girl when Bernice, not bothering to straighten her petticoats or button her bodice, suddenly smiled at him. "Have you come to chaperone us, Mr. James, or have you come to watch? Do come in, Mr. James—but only if you don't follow through with your threat to kill Roland...at least not until he satisfies me."

Too shocked to respond, Edmund could only stare as Bernice traced her fingertip around her dusky pink nipple and pulled at it until it pebbled in her hand.

Licking her lips, she lasciviously beckoned him, "Please join us. I don't mind."

"My mistake." A disgusted Edmund hardly got the words out before he promptly slammed shut the coach door. Striding back to his coach, he heard Bernice's girlish giggles until, shortly after, they turned to wanton squeals and moans.

Chapter Fourteen

Reeking of sex, he couldn't disrobe fast enough. Shedding his clothes, he quickly dismissed the valet and slammed the door behind him. He passed by a mirror and paused to admire his fine naked body, concentrating on his now flaccid, but large member. Few men could boast of such a generous size, he thought proudly, as he took it in his hands. He loved the way those horrified virgins shied away from it when they first saw it fully engorged. And later, the pain it inflicted while he took his pleasure inside their tight, satiny walls.

Tonight there had been no rape. It made him angry just thinking about it. The slut loved every minute of it. She had been so willing, so completely enthusiastic, it took him by surprise. Unlike the others he had forced, this one was no Emily Middleton, who cowered and cried at his bedpost. Nor was she anything like the delectable Desdemona, whose look of fright inspired him to be even crueler when he took her, or the wilting Sarah or...

Damn it—those times he enjoyed the aftermath, lingering in the memory of their pleas for mercy. Tonight was different. He was eager to put this one out of his mind! He needed a bath to wash the whore's sex off him.

Tearing himself away from the mirror, he walked over to the warm bath the valet prepared for him and slipped right in. It felt good, but not even the soothing bathwater could lighten his bad humor.

Earlier in the afternoon, when he asked her to join him for an evening ride, she looked so stunning, so alluring, that she'd quickly aroused him. He had been anxious to have her, but he had no idea when the Blythe whore raced out of the Hardwood townhome and jumped into his coach she enjoyed being watched as she took her pleasure.

He had thought her a lady like the others, but, to his complete surprise, the strumpet begged for more! Not at all frightened, she managed to irk the hell out of him.

Later, when Mason, the coachman, had entered the vehicle, the doxy had not screamed or pleaded with him not to touch her.

To Mason's delight, and his further astonishment, she had not shied away from him either. Instead, she had welcomed the slimy coachman with the same enthusiasm she had shown him earlier. The slut!

Not only had she opened her legs wide for Edgar Mason, she cried out in ecstasy when the coachman entered her. The memory of tonight sickened and disgusted him to no end. Her enthusiasm spoiled it for him. After a while, he' had to dismiss the coachman, as he took no pleasure watching Mason and the insatiable whore fornicate not once but twice.

Tonight, to his great misfortune, he had chosen wrongly. Who could have guessed, despite her noble birth, the lady would act no different than an East End prostitute?

The next time would be different. He would make certain of it. He smiled suddenly. Thinking of Miss Marguerite Wiggins always brightened his mood. Lately, he could not get the elusive, arrogant bitch off his mind. He wanted her badly, but that guard dog chaperone of hers never left her side. The man made it impossible for him to have her within his clutches. He had not forgotten the haughty Miss Wiggins. Far from it! The thought of Marguerite Wiggins begging for mercy while he tore her clothes off hardened his member.

As he stepped out of the tub, he no longer felt dirty...He felt invigorated.

He would have his way with her before the Season was over.

Chapter Fifteen

The next morning, Marguerite woke to find Samantha sitting at the corner of her bed, staring at her with an amused expression on her face. "Go away, Sam," she begged groggily, before turning on her side and placing her pillow over her head. "I don't want to wake up."

"I don't doubt it for a minute, lazybones," Samantha replied, giggling. "Sorry to disappoint you, but now that you're awake, I want to hear all about your dream."

Wiping the sleep from her eyes, Marguerite sat up against the backboard. "What dream?" she asked, yawning. "What are you doing on my bed?"

Samantha smiled wickedly. "Having a grand old time listening to you talk in your sleep. Unfortunately, you woke up and spoiled it for me. You were dreaming about your chaperone. No wonder you didn't want to wake up."

"I was dreaming of Mr. James?"

"Don't play innocent with me, Marguerite Wiggins. You know perfectly well that you were dreaming of him."

Heat rushed to Marguerite's face as she recalled the delicious, fiery kiss she had shared with Ashton the night before. "What did I say? What did you hear?"

"Not much, but you were moaning something about *'Ashton... oh, Ashton!'*"

Mortified and holding back a smile, Marguerite hugged her knees to her. "Hush—I did no such thing."

"You can deny it all you want, but I heard you." Samantha laughed. "I don't have the time to argue. Mother's waiting for me, but you're going to tell me all about that dream when I get back."

Marguerite looked at the mantel clock. "Where are you going so early in the morning?"

"To Madame Collier's. I'll finally get to see my wedding dress. I can't wait! Would you like to come along?"

"Thank you, but Ashton..."

"Oh yes." Samantha smiled knowingly. "Heaven forbid you miss your morning ride with Mr. James. We'll talk later." Giving

Marguerite a little wink, Samantha gathered her purse and walked out of the room.

Marguerite was about to get out of bed when she heard soft knocking. Winifred, still in her nightgown, walked into the room through the connecting door and sat at the edge of the bed.

"Marguerite, I'm glad Samantha is gone. I need to speak with you alone."

"All right. But first...what do you think about Penny's news? We didn't get a chance to talk last night. Isn't it wonderful? Where is she?"

"Sleeping like a log."

"You look serious, Winnie. What's the matter?"

Winnie took Marguerite's hand in hers. "I want you to know you will never have to be employed as a governess. I have discussed it with Mr. Cummings. We will be happy to provide for you for the rest of your days. Aunt Elizabeth insists Papa was only scaring us into finding husbands. She never intended for any one of us to work as governesses. She insists you stay with her, but I want you to live with me."

Marguerite was speechless. She'd been worried about facing an uncertain future, and now Winnie had generously offered her a place by her side. Her heart filled with love for her sister. "Winnie, I'm really grateful. I do not want to intrude. Are you certain Mr. Cummings has agreed to this?"

"Indeed, he has, or I wouldn't be marrying him. So it is settled?"

"Winnie, thank you—I couldn't have asked for a better sister." Marguerite hugged her. "I would love to live with you and Mr. Cummings, but only after your first year together. I'll stay with Aunt Elizabeth until then. Funny, last night I thought I was desolate, and this morning I find I am not." Glancing at the mantel clock, she gasped. "Look at the time! I would love to stay and talk all morning, but Mr. James is expecting me."

Winnie's brow rose inquisitively. "Marguerite, you seem awfully chipper. I would guess it has nothing to do with your future with me and Mr. Cummings."

Marguerite smiled. She felt her cheeks begin to warm. Winnie was right. Her good humor had nothing to do with her sister and Mr. Cummings. Indeed, while eternally grateful to Winnie, Marguerite did not want to think of her future as a lonely spinster. She was enjoying the present too much to think of where she would be living in two months or two years. Right now, all she wanted was to kiss Ashton again.

"Oh, Winnie, I'll burst if I don't tell you. Last night, I kissed Mr. James, and he kissed me back. Winifred, it was the most marvelous kiss. I can't stop thinking about it. I never dreamed a kiss could feel so...so...oh, Winnie!"

"Marguerite Wiggins, you didn't. You aren't even engaged. Nice girls don't—"

"I did." Marguerite smiled impishly. "I don't care."

Winnie gasped, staring at her open-mouthed. "What's gotten into you?"

"Ashton James, that's what. I can't stop thinking about him, and if I don't hurry, I'm going to make him wait. He hates it when I do that. He's already annoyed with me."

"Annoyed? What did you do?"

"Nothing I won't fix this morning," Marguerite said confidently. She had to make things right between them. Ashton was not just annoyed. He left angry with her.

A knock on the door interrupted their conversation. "It is me, Flora."

"Come in, Nanny."

Flora entered the room. "I have a message from Mr. James, Miss Marguerite."

"Where is he? Downstairs?"

"No, he came very early. Locked himself in the study with your uncle and left shortly afterwards. Before he left, he told me to tell you he won't be able to go riding this morning."

"Did he leave a note?"

"No, miss."

Marguerite's heart sank.

* * * *

Marguerite thought she would burst with excitement as she, along with Uncle John and Aunt Elizabeth, climbed the steps to the luxurious Bonner townhome. After standing in line for what seemed an eternity, they were finally advancing toward the entrance.

Soon she would see Ashton. He was probably already inside, hopefully waiting anxiously for her arrival.

As they passed the threshold, the white-gloved butler who stood at the door directed them into the foyer. Feeling as though she would die of anticipation, Marguerite handed her cloak to an attendant and watched as a delighted Lord Eustinius, alongside

Lady Lorena and Lord Jackman, welcomed his many guests.

"Oh, Aunt Elizabeth, I'm so happy for Lorena," Marguerite said. "I'll never forget how wonderful she's been to me. I hope Lord Jackman makes her very happy."

"Indeed, and doesn't she look lovely tonight? Lord Jackman is one handsome lord," Aunt Elizabeth whispered as they made their way toward their hosts.

"What are you saying, my darling? What about Lord Jackman?" Uncle John asked.

Aunt Elizabeth replied, "Never mind, dear. Move along now. There are others waiting behind us. We mustn't keep the line stagnated. They are as anxious as Marguerite to get to the ballroom. We are next to greet the Bonners."

"Finally," Marguerite blurted under her breath. "I don't know why it is taking so long."

Aunt Elizabeth chuckled lightly. "Marguerite, dear, I don't think I've seen you more excited. Not even when getting ready to attend your first ball. Remember how happy you were the night of the Wimberly ball, and how miserable you made poor Mr. James? At least according to Penny's account the next morning."

Marguerite was spared having to respond when the line moved ahead and she came face-to-face with their hosts.

Looking gorgeous in a golden chiffon ball gown, Lorena smiled graciously when Marguerite finally approached her. "I don't think I've ever seen you looking more beautiful, Marguerite. I'm so happy you came."

Marguerite smiled back, taking Lorena's outstretched hand. "Lorena, it is I who's never seen *you* looking more beautiful. Thank you for having me. Honestly, you are my one true friend in London."

"You have a good friend in your chaperone. Where is Mr. James, Marguerite? Isn't he with you?"

"He's not here?" Marguerite asked, trying to sound as casual as possible while attempting to hide her disappointment. "I know he'll come," she added, hoping desperately that would be the case. "Mr. James thinks the world of you, Lorena, and so do I. He wouldn't miss your ball."

After greeting Lord Eustinius and Lord Jackman, Marguerite walked alongside her uncle and aunt toward the grand staircase. She tried to calm her nerves. What were a few more minutes of waiting when she had waited all week for the opportunity to speak to Ashton? She hadn't seen him since their kiss and, to her mounting frustration, had not been able to explain or apologize for her dreadful blunder. Certain tonight she would get the chance, she looked over the balcony to the ballroom below and noticed the room already filled to capacity.

It would be difficult to speak to Ashton amongst such a noisy crowd. She would have to lure him to the terrace the moment he arrived.

Marguerite smiled wickedly, just thinking of how perfect it would feel to be alone with Ashton again. After apologizing to him for her insensitive and inane comment, she would be in his arms and they would dance until the wee hours of the morning. Later, Ashton would kiss her again...and again.

A delightful shiver ran through her as Marguerite began to descend the marbled staircase.

* * * *

The drive home from Lady Lorena's ball seemed eternal as the concerned, but silent, couple, Aunt Elizabeth and Uncle John, left Marguerite to her thoughts. Once in the townhome, Marguerite bade good night to her guardians and quickly entered her bedroom, shutting the door behind her. The night had been a total waste of time, as Ashton had not attended the ball. Greatly disappointed, she began to undress.

Shortly after, Flora knocked on the door and came inside to help her with the task.

"How was the ball, Miss Marguerite?" Flora asked while hanging the ball gown Marguerite had just discarded back in the wardrobe.

"I'm sorry, Nanny. I don't want to talk...I just want to go to sleep. I hope my dreams are better than the nightmare that was Lady Lorena's ball."

"Of course, miss. You are tired. Get in bed. I'll slip away when I finish putting away your belongings."

After ridding herself of her bustle and crinoline, Marguerite donned her nightgown and crawled into bed. "Good night, Nanny. Thank you." Just when she was about to close her eyes, Aunt Elizabeth opened the door and peeked her head through the opening.

"Marguerite, may I come in, dear?" Without waiting for an answer, her aunt came inside and walked over to sit on Samantha's bed. "I'm so sorry. I know tonight must have been difficult for you, Marguerite. You should have danced the night away like your cousin and sisters. Instead..."

To her dismay, Marguerite had no choice but to sit up against her pillow and reply, "Aunt Elizabeth, you can say it. Instead, I only shared a dance with Mr. Cummings and Lord Jackman. No doubt, Winnie and Lorena forced them into it."

"Don't say that, dear. No man has to be forced to dance with you." Staring at her with concerned, sympathetic eyes, Aunt Elizabeth took Marguerite's hands in hers. "Oh, dear, you look so despondent. I wish there was something I could do."

Marguerite tried to smile for her aunt's benefit, but she couldn't.

"That horrid duke. I'll never forgive that stuffy Lord Phillip for causing you such distress," Winnie hissed, entering the room through the connecting door with Penelope trailing behind her.

"It isn't the duke's fault. Have you forgotten she insulted him?" Penny corrected. "I certainly don't blame the man."

Her brows drawn together in an angry frown, Aunt Elizabeth disagreed. "It is his fault. He shouldn't have surprised her in the park that afternoon. He scared her, dear. The man should get himself a thicker skin. Honestly, I don't know why Lorena invited him tonight, much less spent so much time wrapped in conversation with him. If I were her, I wouldn't have given him the time of day. Did you notice, my dears?"

"Notice what?" Marguerite asked, wishing everyone had not congregated in her room. Why couldn't they just leave her alone? She did not want to relive the evening's events. She did not want their pity. All she wanted was to go to sleep.

Penny exclaimed, "Indeed! They were talking up a storm. Didn't you see them, Marguerite? With the way you feel about him, I would think your eyes would have been glued to him all evening."

"Penny!" Winnie scolded her. "Marguerite no longer cares for Lord Phillip, but I did see him talking to Lady Lorena. He was staring at you while they talked, Marguerite. Didn't you notice?"

"No," Marguerite replied. She hadn't noticed. She had not been interested in anyone or anything other than finding Ashton. Her face hurt from all the squinting and peering around the ballroom for any sight of him. How foolish of her to spend so much time looking for him when he never intended to make an entrance.

Winnie smiled. "It wasn't such a wonderful ball after all. I found it a bit boring," she said, sounding nonchalant. "This is why we are home early."

"Were we at the same ball?" Penny protested, "You practically dragged me out! I was having such a good time telling everyone about my engagement."

Winnie fumed. "You didn't! You cannot make a formal announcement without Papa's approval, and you know it."

"I know nothing of the sort. Uncle John approves, and that is good enough for Mr. Pennington and me. No one can stop us from professing our love. No one. Not Papa, not even you."

Trying to stop the bickering, Marguerite turned to Winnie. "I know you came home early because of me. You shouldn't have. I didn't want you to miss out on the festivities. I feel guilty for dragging my poor uncle and aunt away from the ball. It wasn't necessary that they accompany me. The driver could have taken me home and returned for them. They wouldn't have it. Now, to add insult to injury, you and Penny felt you had to follow me home, too."

"See, I told you so, Winnie," Penny burst out. "It isn't our fault she's miserable. Poor Mr. Pennington had more than a dance or two left."

Aunt Elizabeth snapped, "Stop it, Penny. There will be other balls. Can you not see you're adding to your sister's misery?"

"I'm sorry, Aunt Elizabeth," Penny quickly apologized, but Aunt Elizabeth ignored her.

"Marguerite, you look tired. Let's leave her to her sleep. Flora, are you almost through?"

"Yes, my lady," Flora replied. She turned to Marguerite as soon as Aunt Elizabeth and her sisters left the room. "If they only knew it's all Lord Roland's fault. Stuffy or not, that poor duke had nothing to do with it."

After adjusting her pillows, Marguerite laid back, covering herself with the bedsheets. "I know, Flora, but I don't want to discuss Lord Roland or Lord Phillip. I'm just glad the evening is over."

Flora shook her head while walking toward the door. "It must have been trying for you tonight, Miss Marguerite. It's one thing to be balked at with Mr. James by your side and another to be out in public without him. That handsome devil hasn't done much chaperoning of late. He should never have allowed you to attend the ball without him. Haven't seen him in days, but wait till I get my hands on him. Good night, now."

"I want to get my hands on him, too." Marguerite grabbed her pillow and gave it a good punch. "I haven't the foggiest where he is, Nanny, but I'm going to find out," she vowed, turning over on her side when Flora left the room.

* * * *

Early the next morning, Marguerite knocked on the study door.

"Come in," Uncle John's voice called out right before she entered the room to find him sitting behind his desk.

"Please, Uncle John, don't get up. I'm sorry to bother you, but I need a word."

"Of course, Marguerite." Uncle John smiled. With the tip of his head, he motioned her to the burgundy leather chair directly in front his desk. "Sit down, my dear. You are never a bother. I was just—"

"Uncle John, you must help me," Marguerite interrupted him as she walked toward the chair. "I need your assistance."

"What is it, my dear?" he inquired. "You seem desperate."

Once she was seated, she looked at him from across his big mahogany desk and said earnestly, "I am desperate. I must find him."

Uncle John folded his hands together in a comfortable gesture. "Who?"

"Ashton...I mean, Mr. James. Uncle John, it's been days since he resigned as my chaperone. Last week, I tried to press you for more details, but you had nothing more to say on the matter. I only kept quiet because I thought I would see him at the ball. Oh, Uncle, you cannot imagine the disappointment I felt when I did not see him last night."

"Marguerite, my dear, I know last night was hard on you, but—"

"Hard?" she interrupted him again. "It was excruciating, but not for the reasons you think. I don't care that I sat like a wallflower discussing the weather with the other spinsters-to-be while the popular ladies waltzed until their feet were numb. I could care less if I danced or not."

"My dear niece—"

"Wait, Uncle John, you must let me finish. Last night, my only thought was of Ashton and how much I miss him. I'm miserable without him."

Her uncle's eyes grew large. "Oh? I had no idea that you depended on him to such extent."

"Find him for me, Uncle John. We had a misunderstanding,

and I must apologize to him. Why do you suppose he didn't come to Lorena's ball?"

Uncle John pointed behind her. "Ask him yourself."

Marguerite turned around to find Ashton standing by the French doors that led to the outside gardens.

"Ashton!" She gasped in delight, her heart thundering at the sight of him.

Uncle John chuckled. "That's what I have been trying to tell you since you came into the room. Mr. James and I were discussing important business. He will be out of the country for two weeks. He was about to make his exit when you interrupted us."

"Out of the country? Ashton, must you go?"

"Of course he must go, my dear. There is urgent business he needs to take care of for me. Shouldn't you be calling him Mr. James?"

Marguerite turned to her uncle. "Can't you send someone else?" she blurted, scarcely aware of her own voice.

Looking surprised, Uncle John arched an eyebrow. "Marguerite, dear, I know you have come to rely on your chaperone, but the man has other duties."

She turned to Ashton. "We need to talk. Can we speak in the courtyard?"

A muscle ticked at his jaw as Ashton addressed Uncle John. "Lord Hardwood, if we are finished here. My ship is waiting."

"Ashton, did you hear me?" Marguerite asked, frustrated that Ashton had chosen to ignore her.

"Of course, Mr. James," Uncle John said, ignoring her as well. "We have covered all the issues. We'll talk when you return from your trip. Have a safe and fruitful one. I only hope you get the answer you are seeking."

Ashton nodded in agreement.

"What answer?" Marguerite asked, but before she could get a response, Ashton opened the French doors and exited the study. Too stunned to move or even speak, Marguerite could only stare after him as he descended the terrace steps to the courtyard below.

Confused, Uncle John tried to appease her. "Dear, we'll find you another chaperone."

Indignant, Marguerite jerked to her feet and rushed to the French doors. "I don't want another chaperone. I don't want anyone but him. Excuse me, Uncle John—he's going to listen to me whether he likes it or not!"

Rushing out of the study, she ran down the terrace steps and onto the gardens. She could see Ashton as he was about to turn the corner to the side of the townhome. Soon he would be at the front of the building and climbing into his waiting coach. She had to stop him. "Ashton!" she yelled after him. "Ashton, stop—Ashton! Don't go," she begged him.

Ashton turned around. "Damn it, Meggie. What the devil do you want from me?" he snapped, his voice hoarse with exasperation when she finally caught up with him.

"I want you to forgive me," she said breathlessly. She reached out and clutched at his hand. "Please say you forgive me."

"I forgive you, damn it."

"Well, it doesn't sound much like forgiveness to me," Marguerite retorted furiously, his tone sparking her anger. She turned to leave when Ashton reached out and swung her around to face him. Grabbing her arm, he pulled her alongside him and marched her across the lawns.

"Where are you taking me?" she asked, breathlessly trying to keep up with him until he deposited her behind a large oak tree and stood before her. "What are you doing?"

"Making certain we are alone and not being watched. We both know I can't resist you. I'm done trying."

Marguerite thought she would melt when he suddenly wrapped his arms around her waist and drew her to him. Caressing her cheek with his knuckles, he asked her, "Did you mean everything you said up there, Duchess? Or was it all poppycock?"

"Yes, I meant it. I'm miserable without you, Ashton."

He remained silent. His large fingers lifted her face to meet his gaze as his dark eyes narrowed speculatively, searching her face, reaching into her thoughts.

"I don't care a whit for the Duke of Wallingford. How can I when I can't stop thinking about you, Ashton?"

He smiled tenderly, tightening his arms around her. "That's all I needed to hear, love."

His husky words were smothered on her lips as his mouth covered hers in a hungry kiss. Marguerite's instant response was shameless. She slid her tongue over his lips, enjoying the warm velvetiness of them, and he groaned as she opened her mouth, allowing him to deepen the kiss. Lost in his embrace, all she thought of was how warm and sweet his lips tasted, how blissfully wonderful his hard, muscular chest felt against her breasts.

Marguerite knew she shouldn't be doing this in broad daylight in the open gardens. Anyone could come upon them. She didn't care. Instead, she returned his kiss with reckless abandon, her trembling limbs clinging to him as his thrusting, hot tongue explored the depths of her mouth. His slow, drugging kisses were driving her wild, and she never wanted to let him go.

"Do you have to leave me? Please, don't go, Ashton," she managed to whisper against his mouth.

Tearing his mouth from hers, Ashton stared at her, his jaw tight and hard before planting a tantalizing kiss at the hollow of her neck. "We must stop, Meggie. My ship is waiting. I want to talk with you first." Breathing heavily, he looked at her intently. "I'll be back in two weeks' time. Promise me you won't go to any balls unless chaperoned by your uncle and aunt. When I return, I'll explain everything."

"I seriously doubt I'll be invited to a single one. I'm shunned— remember?" Marguerite smiled up at him, thinking herself the luckiest woman on earth. "Anyway, I've had enough balls to last me a lifetime. I don't understand. What are you going to explain?"

"Never mind, just promise me that when I'm gone, you'll not go near that bastard Bradstone."

"Ashton, how many times must I promise the same thing?"

"As many times as it takes, Marguerite."

A delightful tingle ran through her when he stared into her eyes and molded her to him, pressing her intimately against his sinewy length. "I'm going to miss you, you little minx. Being away from you is going to drive me to drink."

Ashton's words sent shivers of desire coursing through her. Her knees weakening, she put her arms around his neck. "You can drink all you want as long as you kiss me again," she replied. "It is all I think about lately."

Ashton chuckled huskily before his lips covered hers in another delicious kiss.

* * * *

Hours later, while changing for afternoon tea, Marguerite sat at the edge of her bed, recalling the intimacy of the kisses she had shared with Ashton earlier. Smiling to herself, she stood and walked over to the wardrobe. Still smiling, she donned her white long-sleeved blouse and dark blue skirt.

She had begun to loathe the afternoon teas in the drawing room, during which time her siblings and cousin took the opportunity to discuss their forthcoming weddings with their respective fiancés. Lately a visitor or two would drop by with a piece of juicy gossip—usually news of some lucky young lady who had just gotten herself engaged. Afterwards, Marguerite had to endure the embarrassed looks directed her way when they'd realize they were being rude in her presence. She would much rather have stayed in her room and skipped these teas altogether, but it wouldn't be fitting. Afternoon tea at the Hardwood townhome was considered a social must, one she had no choice but to suffer through. If only Ashton could be here with her.

Dear God, she was going to miss him! Two whole weeks abroad. This past week had been horrid. She couldn't imagine having to spend one more day without him much less two entire weeks. Abroad where? In his haste to leave, he had forgotten to tell her.

She was being childish. Marguerite reprimanded herself as she inspected her image in the mirror. He was no longer avoiding her; he was on a business trip handling her uncle's affairs. Surely she could survive two weeks. She would catch up on her reading. It would keep her mind off him until he returned.

Marguerite heard knocking at the door. "Come in."

"Aunt Elizabeth wants Penny and me to get fitted for wedding dresses as soon as possible. Could you please accompany us to Madame's tomorrow?" Winnie asked, entering the room with Penny trailing behind her.

Marguerite smiled. "I wouldn't miss it."

Penny raised an eyebrow. "You seem awfully cheerful. I thought you were miserable. Last night, you almost threw us out of the room."

"She did not throw us out," Winnie said. "We left because she was tired."

Penny insisted, "Nonetheless, she looks happy. She has no reason to be."

Marguerite chuckled mischievously. "I am happy. I'm delirious...absolutely delirious!"

Winnie gasped. "Did you see him?"

"Yes!" Marguerite confessed, clapping her hands.

"See whom—whom did she see?" Penny frowned, her curious green eyes darting from Winnie to Marguerite and back again.

"Never mind, Penny. I need a word alone with Marguerite."

Penny persisted. "I'm not going anywhere, Winnie Wiggins, unless you tell me what is going on."

"Nothing is going on, Penny. Now please go. Mr. Pennington must be waiting downstairs."

"Oh, all right, but I'm still going to find out what you're keeping from me."

When Penny left the room, Winnie turned to Marguerite. "What did Mr. James say when you apologized?"

"We did not talk much."

"You're blushing. Don't tell me you let him kiss you again?"

Marguerite giggled. "I did, and it was wonderful."

Winifred's brow furrowed. "Marguerite, you are allowing yourself to be kissed without a marriage proposal. Do you think this is wise?"

Marguerite was about to answer when Samantha poked her head in. "Winnie, Mr. Cummings is waiting in the drawing room."

"Are you coming, Marguerite?" Winnie asked, after joining Samantha at the door.

"You both go. I need to find my book."

"I'll help you find it," Winnie insisted from the doorway.

"No, don't keep Mr. Cummings waiting. I'll be right down."

"All right," Winnie said, closing the door behind her.

Minutes later, with book in hand, Marguerite left her room. She went downstairs, and on her way to the drawing room, she walked past Uncle John's study. The door was slightly ajar. Wanting to know exactly where Uncle John had sent Ashton, she was about to knock and make her presence known when she heard Aunt Elizabeth mention her name.

"John, do you really think Marguerite loves him?"

"Yes, dear. You should have seen the way she stormed out after him."

"I never thought she'd settle for anyone but that duke of hers. It would be so wonderful. Oh, John! Imagine my niece and...Oh, this is too good to be true. I had hoped when we forced him to chaperone—"

Uncle John interrupted, "Elizabeth, don't be getting too excited. He wants no part of her. He couldn't leave here fast enough. Anyway, I'm not certain he's right for Marguerite. For one thing, he is thirteen years her senior. His travels take him away for months at a time. When he's in England, he shuns society."

"This is true," Aunt Elizabeth agreed. "They seem to get on famously. I've noticed the way they look at one another. Nevertheless, you are right, dear. I shouldn't get my hopes up. Right now, the man is too distracted with Julianna to think of anyone else."

"How can he, Elizabeth? Let's not forget how much he cares for her. I'm beginning to think no other woman will ever hold such a special place in his heart. Poor little thing must be lonely in Spain without him. I bet she misses Windword Hall."

"Oh, John, he's gone after her. I wonder if Julianna will give him the answer he seeks. If she says yes, he'll bring her back with him."

Marguerite could not listen to any more. A fury such as she had never known possessed her. Had her ears deceived her? She needed to make sure. Wanting to burst into tears, she threw open the study door and burst into the study instead.

"Uncle John, is it true? Has Ashton gone to Spain to see Julianna?" she cried.

Uncle John's eyes widened, and Aunt Elizabeth opened her mouth to speak, but Uncle John gave her a stern look.

Marguerite felt their pained silence close in on her. She felt numb as she stood in the doorway. It was true. Ashton loved Julianna Kent and had gone to Spain to ask her to marry him. She still couldn't believe it.

"Aunt Elizabeth, do you wish me to become Ashton's consolation prize should Julianna refuse him? Are you so desperate to marry me off?"

Aunt Elizabeth walked over to Marguerite, putting her arms around her. "Sit down, dear. You look faint."

Crestfallen, Marguerite walked further into the room and sat down on the sofa. Could she have felt more humiliated? Winnie was right. Short of enjoying her kisses, Ashton had never made his intentions clear. She had been so affected by him she had not thought to ask. With no regard for propriety, she had thrown herself at Ashton and had let herself be used.

Marguerite fumed, thinking of how she had begged his forgiveness for bringing up the duke while kissing him. *The hypocrite!* At that same moment, he had been in love with Julianna Kent. Unlike Marguerite, who mentioned the duke, Ashton had not thought to mention Julianna at all. What was it he had said to her before leaving? *When I return, I'll explain everything.* The cad! When exactly was he planning to explain his true feelings to her? When he brought Julianna back with a ring on her finger?

"Aunt Elizabeth, I must have mentioned Julianna to him many times, and not once did he ever say that he knew her...let alone love her. , Samantha, why didn't she tell me about Ashton and Julianna?"

"He swore us all to secrecy."

"Why? I don't understand? Why all the secrecy? I find it

ludicrous."

"Mortimer, what is it? This is not a good time," Uncle John said suddenly, looking toward the door.

Marguerite turned to find the butler standing in the doorway holding a silver tray.

"Miss Marguerite has a gentleman caller in the foyer. Shall I show him to the drawing room, my lord?" the butler asked.

Mortimer walked over to Marguerite and held the tray in front of her, but she did not bother to read the card. "I'm in no mood for company, Mortimer. Whoever it is, tell him to leave," she said with annoyance.

The butler did not budge. "I don't think it would be wise, miss."

His lips thinned with irritation, Uncle John admonished the butler. "Do as you're told, Mortimer. You heard my niece. She is in no mood for a visitor."

"But my lord..." Mortimer insisted.

"Get rid of him at once!" Uncle John blustered.

"Who is it?" asked Aunt Elizabeth.

"Lord Phillip Lancaster, the Duke of Wallingford."

Chapter Sixteen

"Mortimer, please show the Duke of Wallingford to the drawing room," Aunt Elizabeth ordered the butler before turning to Marguerite. "My dear niece, you look as white as a sheet. Take a few minutes to collect yourself. I know you are upset about Mr. James, but the duke mustn't see you like this. The others will keep him company while he waits," she insisted excitedly, her fingers reaching out to pinch Marguerite's cheeks.

Thinking of Ashton and his love for Julianna Kent, Marguerite fought hard against the tears she refused to let fall. "Mortimer, tell His Grace I'll be in shortly."

"Yes, miss," Mortimer replied before quickly retiring from the study.

Once the butler was gone, a smiling Aunt Elizabeth turned to Uncle John. "My darling, isn't this wonderful? Wallingford has finally come to pay our niece a visit. I wonder what has caused him to change his mind."

Uncle John frowned. "Now, Elizabeth, don't get her spirits up. We do not know the reason for Lord Phillip Lancaster's visit. It may not be what you think."

"What else could it be? A gentleman does not call on a lady if he plans to insult her, my dear. The man has finally decided to forgive her." Aunt Elizabeth clapped her hands enthusiastically. "Oh, Marguerite, you are no longer shunned! I knew the duke couldn't resist you for long. I've seen the way his eyes followed you at certain events. Last night, he stared at you during the entire ball. The stubborn man has finally given in."

Marguerite could not respond. She knew she should be jumping for joy—the man of her dreams waited for her in the drawing room—but, at the moment, joy eluded her. A formal visit from Lord Phillip was what she had wanted since arriving in London, but she had never felt more miserable. She could only think of Ashton and the way he kissed her earlier in the garden—only for her to find out a few hours later he had planned to marry Julianna Kent all along. She wondered how many kisses he shared with Julianna and felt sick to her stomach. The idea of Ashton kissing anyone else incensed her beyond reason.

Apparently their love affair was a well-kept secret that not even her cousin, Samantha, could divulge. Samantha lied to her when revealing Julianna's heart belonged to a widowed Spaniard. She had to hand it to her, what an imagination! A fictional widowed Spaniard named Diego de Cordoba, the father of a loveable little girl Julianna felt hard-pressed to resist. *The Three Musketeers, indeed. All for one and one for all—not so!* Marguerite thought furiously. It seemed she was the only Musketeer who had been kept in the dark. Why would Samantha keep this from her?

"Why do you look so wretched? Isn't this what you've always wanted? Your dreams are finally coming true," exclaimed Aunt Elizabeth. "Forget about Mr. James. Hurry, now, and enjoy the duke's visit."

Marguerite hardly heard her aunt's words. Her misery weighed down upon her like a block of steel. Feeling completely betrayed by both her family and Ashton, a furious Marguerite tried to force her confused emotions into order. Suddenly, it all made sense. The family had kept the courtship secret because of Julianna's brother, the strict and domineering Earl of Windword.

Edmund Kent would have Julianna's hide if he as much as suspected his dear sister was involved with an employee of Uncle John's. That had to be it. The Hardwoods loved Julianna so much, they had all agreed to keep her secret. The proud earl would keel over if he knew Uncle John's assistant had snuck into Windword Hall and stolen Julianna's heart and God knows what else. That scoundrel! This was the man Uncle John trusted as a chaperone, the man whom she turned to for protection. Her sisters and she would have been much safer with Lord Roland.

"Marguerite." Aunt Elizabeth grabbed her by the arm, jolting her out of her reverie. She pulled Marguerite along behind her to the door. "You must not make him wait, dear."

"I suppose not." Marguerite nodded in agreement. Shortly after, she left the study and made her way down the long, dark corridor to the drawing room.

The moment she entered the room, Marguerite could see the surprised looks coming from her sisters, cousin, and their respective fiancés when Lord Phillip excused himself and walked over to her.

"Miss Wiggins," he said, bowing down to kiss her outstretched hand as she curtsied before him.

"Your Grace," Marguerite acknowledged politely, withdrawing

her hand from his warm lips.

Lord Phillip said matter-of-factly, "Lady Lorena Bonner explained everything to me last night. I now know it has all been a terrible misunderstanding. You did not realize it was me you were addressing that dreadful day in the park."

"This is precisely so, Your Grace. I'm sorry you felt slighted. If you had stayed long enough to let me explain, you would not have caused me such distress," Marguerite replied, trying her best to smile, but her heart was not in it.

Lord Phillip looked taken aback by her response, as though he was not used to being spoken to in such a manner. "I'm sorry, my dear, but as has been established, it was an unfortunate misunderstanding."

Staring at Lord Phillip, she now wondered why she had been so enticed by him. Granted, with his dark black hair and beautiful gray eyes, the duke had a captivating presence, but Ashton was taller, more rugged, and so much more appealing. She seriously doubted she would ever find another man more attractive than Ashton James.

Determined to forget all about Ashton, Marguerite forced a cordial smile and pointed toward the couch. "Would you like to sit down, Your Grace? May we offer you some tea?"

"No, my dear. I only came to tell you a great injustice has befallen upon you, and I would like to make it up to you by escorting you to the Henley Regatta. Expect my coach sharply at ten." Without another word, and without waiting for Marguerite to reply, the Duke of Wallingford spun on his heel and took his exit, leaving the others in the room awestruck.

A giggling Penny raced over to the drawing room door and called out into the hallway, "She will love to go with you, Your Highness!"

"Hush, you idiot, he'll hear you! He's not a royal duke." Sighing, Winnie rolled her eyes before turning to Marguerite. "Did this really happen? I can't believe you are actually going to the Henley Regatta tomorrow with the Duke of Wallingford."

"I suppose I am," was all that Marguerite could muster to say before walking to the couch, taking her usual seat, and opening her book. They were all so excited with the duke's visit, they hardly noticed Marguerite's lack of enthusiasm.

Penny jumped up and down, clapping her hands. "Marguerite, you'll be the talk of the town—but in a good way! Oh, Mr. Pennington, my sister's reputation is no longer soiled. I do not have to endure the embarrassment of being related to her. Really, Marguerite, you do not know what you put us through. The duke should have apologized to the entire family. A great injustice befell us all. Isn't that right, Mr. Pennington?"

Mr. Pennington looked embarrassed. "This is wonderful, my dear. I'm happy for your sister."

"Mr. Pennington, I'm happy for me. It's not easy having a sister who is shunned by all of London. Papa would be ecstatic if he knew Marguerite was being escorted to the Henley by none other than Lord Phillip Lancaster, the Duke of Wallingford. It serves Papa right he is not here to see it...disappearing in such a way."

Winnie objected, "Be quiet, Penny. Enough about Papa. I'm tired of hearing it. Marguerite's misfortune did not affect you in the least. You did not suffer at all. Isn't that so, Mr. Cummings? It was poor Marguerite who missed out on most of the Season."

Mr. Cummings agreed. "Indeed."

"Hah!" Penny huffed. "Except for a few balls, Marguerite hardly missed a thing. Mr. James escorted her all over town."

Winifred ignored Penny and turned her attention to Mr. Cummings. "Damian, when that duke walked in the door, I almost fainted. He was the last person I expected to see."

"Indeed, my dear, you did look a bit surprised. I'm glad he has made peace with your sister," Mr. Cummings replied. "Now you can finally stop worrying about her."

Seconds later, Aunt Elizabeth and Uncle John entered the drawing room.

"Did he leave already?" Aunt Elizabeth asked, looking about the room. "What did he want? He isn't going to make more trouble, is he?"

Looking as though she were about to burst, Samantha rushed over to Aunt Elizabeth. "Yes, Mother, the duke left, but no, he is not going to make more trouble. You are not going to believe it. Lord Phillip is taking Marguerite to the Henley Regatta tomorrow," she exclaimed. "Isn't that right, Steven?"

Steven Bradstone smiled broadly. "He did ask her."

"Well, he didn't exactly ask," Penny objected. "It was more like an order."

Samantha paid no heed. "Oh, Marguerite, this is all you've ever wanted."

"I know," Marguerite managed to reply before looking down to leaf through the pages of her book.

"The Henley Regatta! Marguerite, you are going to be the most envied woman in London. I told you, John," Aunt Elizabeth addressed her husband. "I knew the Duke of Wallingford had come to his senses. I'm seldom wrong about these things."

"Yes, my dear." Uncle John chuckled. "What a happy day this is for all of us!"

Feigning interest in her book, Marguerite ignored his comment. It was a miserable day...a truly miserable day. She should feel excited to have finally gotten the duke's attention, but she was far from happy. Instead, all she wanted was to retire to her room so she could have a good cry. Ashton was on his way to Spain to be with Julianna, and there was nothing Marguerite could do about it.

* * * *

"Damn it, Diego. What is taking them so long?" Edmund cursed as he stood in the hallway outside Julianna's room, waiting for the doctors to come out. "They've been with her for a good fifteen minutes. I'm going in."

A haggard-looking Diego de Cordoba jerked up from his chair.

"*Por Dios,* Edmund, allow the doctors to examine her properly. Dr. Arango and Dr. Goytisolo are the best in their field. They have come from Madrid, highly recommended. Take a chair and wait like the rest of us."

His stomach churning with anxiety and frustration, Edmund refused to sit. Instead, he leaned against the wall and struggled to keep calm, trying not to go insane thinking about Julianna and what was taking place behind the closed bedroom door. It was useless; the more he tried, the more worried he felt.

"I've waited a month, and my sister has not gotten any better. Nothing has changed since my arrival in Spain. All your doctors are at a loss. I'm taking her to England, where I'll find specialists who will know what to do."

"You forget she is my wife, Edmund. I've summoned a specialist from Germany. He'll be here by the end of the week."

Edmund was about to respond that Julianna was Diego's wife in name only, and would not be in this situation if she had remained in England, but he quickly changed his mind. His friend blamed himself for Julianna's accident and felt guilty enough.

"Julianna has to come out of this, Diego. I don't know what Sofia will do if she doesn't. Your little girl will be crushed...simply crushed," lamented Maria Cristina de Cordoba, Diego's youngest sister, who was keeping vigil outside Julianna's room along with her five older sisters, the Malicious Marias, as Edmund mentally referred to them.

"She will come out of this, Kina," Diego replied firmly. "No more negative thoughts."

"What do I tell Sofia? My niece doesn't understand why Julianna is always sleeping. *La pobrecita!* She insists Julianna is *La Bella Durmiente*—that all she needs is a kiss from a prince to wake her. She keeps begging me to find a handsome prince. *Dios mio*—my heart breaks for her. I cannot tell her her stepmother is not Sleeping Beauty."

Diego's expression was one of pained tolerance. "Tell my daughter we are not looking for just any prince. It has to be a special prince, and that takes time. Just tell her that."

Clad in a dainty pink dress, Kina looked pretty and out of place amongst the sisters, all of whom wore black and resembled four ugly crows while they knitted and bickered in Spanish between themselves.

Huffing with exasperation, Maria Esperanza, the eldest of the de Cordoba sisters, put her knitting down on her lap and shook her head from side to side. "*Esa niña malcriada!* Your wife has spoiled Sofia these past months. Lately, the girl has been unmanageable."

Maria Antonia, the second oldest, quickly agreed. "*Sí, es verdad!* Diego, we have tried to warn you, but you would not listen. Julianna, with her wild English ways, has not been a good influence on your daughter. Look at where it has gotten Julianna! Because of her foolishness, she has been in a semicomatose state for more than a month. Our poor little brother, Gonzalo, had to be the one to find her. He hasn't been the same since the accident."

"Do not mention Gonzalo to me," Kina objected angrily. "My brother is behaving more irresponsible than ever. He should be here by Diego's side and not in Madrid doing God knows what."

"Kina, don't talk that way. What will Lord Kent think? Gonzalo *es un amor*. He is the light of our lives. If only he were here to cheer us up." Maria Antonia's eyes widened with false innocence as she continued, "About Julianna—we don't mean to be rude, Lord Kent. Your sister is a bit reckless. No?"

Edmund wanted to wring the woman's neck, but he kept silent. Why bother? The less he spoke to these people, the better. He had little use for the de Cordoba clan. Except for Kina, whom he found kind and agreeable, Edmund thought the rest of Diego's family to be completely insufferable. He was grateful the younger brother,

Gonzalo, left after the accident and had not returned. Gonzalo de Cordoba was the worst of the bunch.

The Malicious Marias were completely enamored of their little brother, but, much to Diego's chagrin, his brother had grown up to become a spoiled, arrogant young man, one who did nothing but squander his time whoring in Madrid. The last thing Edmund needed was the pompous cretin spouting out insults as well. For the past month, he had often wondered how his sister had been able to live in such a hostile environment. Guilt tore at his gut. He should never have left her here. If she had returned with him to England, this horrible accident would not have taken place.

Edmund looked at his pocket watch. "What the devil could they be doing to her? Why is it taking so bloody long?" he cursed, finding the wait impossible.

Looking up from her knitting, Maria Pascuala, the least attractive and the thorn in Edmund's side, smiled up at him. "Do not lose your patience, *mi querido* Earl of Windword. *Qué pena* that you came all the way from England to find your sister in this condition. Why, she doesn't even recognize you. *Por supuesto que* Julianna should have been more careful," she said with more than a hint of censure in her tone. "My heart aches for you and for her. I wish there was something I could do to ease your pain. I would be *encantada* to do whatever it takes. I did not know Julianna had such a handsome brother and that he was an earl."

Edmund did not respond and did not return the smile for fear of encouraging the woman. A few days after his arrival in Spain, Diego had warned Edmund that his heavy-set, stern-faced sister with the buck teeth had developed a terrible attraction for him, and it was best to ignore her lest she mistake any attention he paid her for a proposal of marriage. When Edmund had frowned in confusion, Diego had simply told him to trust him and stay clear of her. Unfortunately, Maria Pascuala had never married. It wasn't the first time the spinster had misinterpreted a kind and polite gesture to mean an impending nuptial.

Maria Lucia, the mousy, quiet one, or so Edmund had thought until recently, also looked up from her knitting. "*Ay*, Diego, *po-brecita* Sofia. Kina is right. What happens if Julianna does not get better? The girl loves your wife. I knew it was a bad day when you brought that Englishwoman into our lives. If you had married Inés as you were supposed to, none of this would be taking place. *La pobre* Ofelia must be turning in her grave. Your poor departed wife would have wanted you to marry her sister. *Como es debido!*"

An angry tic pulsated at Diego's jaw. "I'm grateful that you came to Aranjuez to accompany me during Julianna's illness, but it is time you return to your husbands in Madrid. *Sí,* all of you must leave. It is unfair for me to keep you here when you are so desperately needed in your homes to tend to your own affairs."

Edmund watched Maria Pascuala's eyes widen in dismay. "I have no husband. I stay," she said in her broken English, trying to control a nervous facial twitch that made the large mole on her cheek appear more animated than usual, as though it had a life of its own. "The earl needs me. It is not his fault his sister is foolish and disobedient."

"Maria Pascuala—*que tonterías dices,*" Maria Esperanza hissed. "You will not stay behind. Where I go, you and Kina go, too. I promised Papa *y* Mama on their deathbeds I would look after you." She turned to Diego. "*Tienes razón, hermano.* I'm more than ready to return to Madrid. There is nothing more we can do here. We will leave this afternoon as soon as the doctors are gone. Julianna should have known better than to go behind your back and ride Diablo. She was warned the horse could not be tamed."

Maria Eugenia, the meanest and most volatile of the five, shrugged her shoulders. "Julianna disobeyed, and now *La Bella Durmiente* will remain as is, sleeping half the time and the other half not recognizing a soul, not even her own husband or brother. *Estos casos no se mejoran.* She is never going to get better. I certainly do not plan to continue taking turns feeding and bathing her for the rest of my days."

"*Silencio!*" Diego's eyes flashed with outrage.

"It is true, Diego," Maria Eugenia persisted, stubbornly. "I would never go against my husband's will in such a reckless manner. Because of her accident, you had to shoot your favorite horse. *Te volvistes loco!* You should not have taken your fury out on *el pobre* Diablo."

His face red and blotchy with anger, Diego moved from the door to stand before his sisters. "*Basta*—all of you—*fuera!*" he shouted, demanding they leave at once. "Get the hell out of my house, out of Aranjuez."

As the shocked de Cordoba sisters put away their knitting and stood to go, Diego grabbed Maria Cristina by the arm. "Not you, Kina. Please stay."

"I can't," Kina replied. "Your sister-in-law insisted on looking after Sofia while we waited to hear from the doctors, but Sofia is not fond of her Aunt Inés. My poor little niece is probably wondering where I am. Please find me if there is any change." She placed a kiss on Diego's cheek before disappearing down the dark hallway with her sisters.

His patience finally giving out, Edmund refused to wait any longer. Not caring whether or not Diego approved, he walked to the door and opened it to find Dr. Arango and Dr. Goytizolo kneeling beside Julianna's bedside, holding rosary beads.

"Bloody hell, what the devil is going on here?" he demanded, startling the doctors who were deeply into their prayers.

"Qué es esto?" Diego asked with furrowed brow, following Edmund into the room.

Taking a moment to make the sign of the cross and put away their rosaries, the doctors rose to their feet and approached Edmund and Diego with dismal expressions on their faces.

"When can I take her to England?" Edmund asked, impatiently.

"Lord Kent, your sister is not fit to travel to England with you," Dr. Arango replied. *"Perdonen, pero no hay mas nada que hacer.* We did not want to give you the sad news, but the prognosis is not good. She has been in this condition for more than a month, and she is hardly responding to any stimulation. She sleeps constantly. When awake, she does not talk or recognize her surroundings. With our deepest regret, we must inform you we have no hope. There is nothing left to do but to pray for her. *Que Dios la bendiga."*

Diego's face drained of color. *"Que dice?"* he demanded angrily. "I refuse to believe there is no hope."

"Dr. Arango and I have arrived to the same conclusion," Dr. Goytizolo interceded. "The marquesa has suffered a severe injury to the head. The residual effects of such an injury are almost always permanent. We are afraid that, in her case, the damage to her brain is irreversible. I wish we could give you better news. This is not what you wanted to hear, but sometimes God takes over where science fails. We will go now and leave you to your prayers."

Nodding curtly and dismissing the doctors, Edmund walked over to sit at his sister's bedside. Grief and despair tore at him while he contemplated Julianna's pale, lovely face as she slept. He would not allow Dr. Arango and Dr. Goytizolo to shake his resolve. *To hell with them!* His sister would get better—once home and in her own surroundings, away from these dreadful people and their chaotic lives.

Seconds later, he looked up to find Diego standing by the side of the bed. The agony they had both suffered during the last few weeks had finally taken its toll and was certainly evident on the Spaniard's face.

"I was supposed to protect her," Diego said, closing his eyes and running his hand through his hair. "I should have gotten rid of Diablo when the horse first showed signs of irritability, but she refused to let me do it. My God, Edmund, the damned animal bit one of my stable boys. How could I have been so reckless? I could never say no to Julianna—not even when she foolishly begged me to take her as my wife."

Edmund gave a choked, desperate laugh, taking Julianna's hand in his before glancing back at Diego. "I wager she promised you she would never ride that horse. I had to watch her closely when she was growing up. The little hellion never did as she was told. Stop blaming yourself. I found it hard to say no to her myself."

"I do blame myself, but I am not giving up. I don't care how long it takes—she is coming back to me. I need her, Edmund."

"Diego, I appreciate all you've done, but your responsibility to her ends now. As soon as Julianna and I return to England, I'm going to have the marriage annulled, but not before I pay a visit to Scotland Yard. I'm more determined than ever to make that filthy rapist pay for the pain and misery he has caused my sister. If the authorities don't want to incarcerate him, I'll kill Bradstone myself!"

"No, Edmund, don't—you mustn't." Her voice was but a soft whisper. At first, Edmund thought he had imagined it, but to his complete and utter joy, he turned to find Julianna watching him, her big brown eyes round and pleading as she begged him again, "You mustn't, Edmund."

* * * *

Archibald Wiggins opened his eyes and, for a moment, forgot where he was. He was soon reminded by the loud snoring coming from the woman who lay next to him on the bed. The chandelier hanging from the painted ceiling had seemed vaguely familiar, but how could he have forgotten the night of "passion" shared with the corpulent female who took up most of the elaborately carved mahogany bed? The two bottles of French champagne lying empty on the floor, and the colossal headache he was suffering, should have given him a hint.

Turning his face to look at his bride, Archibald almost gasped, startled by the sight he encountered. Spittle from her opened mouth drooled down her fat cheek and collected at her pillow. Her hair, usually neat and tidy, was now a cobweb of gray and yellow ringlets resembling straw.

Struck speechless by the way her enormous belly contracted and expanded each time she took a breath, Archie reminded himself for the umpteenth time since their nuptials last night that he was, indeed, a very lucky man. Things could be worse...much worse.

Four months ago, he was a penniless gambler living with his spinster sisters with nothing to his name but three useless daughters destined to become governesses, and no chance of ever being supported by them.

However, always the crafty fellow, old Archie had one last card up his sleeve.

An old gambling buddy of his, Lord Richard Dunhill, had left for Italy years before and had written to him several times offering his hospitality should Archibald ever find himself in Florence. Thinking he would go insane if he spent another day in Crawley with Lavinia and Hyacinth, Archibald had decided it was time to come calling.

Without the spinsters' knowledge, Archibald rummaged through their belongings and pawned a few pieces of jewelry, porcelain, and other pricy-looking keepsakes the sisters probably did not care for and would never miss. His efforts got him on the first ship to Italy, where he had been prepared to finagle his old friend into letting him stay for an extended visit. As luck would have it, upon arriving at his friend's estate, Archibald was informed Dunhill was dead and buried and on an "extended stay" of his own.

To Archibald's further surprise, his good friend, Dunhill, had been auspicious enough to marry an Italian baronessa, and not just any baronessa. He married Alfonsina Porcilini, one of the wealthiest women in Italy. *Also one of the horniest!* thought Archie, recalling the strenuous efforts he put forth in pleasing her last night not once but thrice.

Yawning, he tried to shift position on the bed, but was held captive by the two lardaceous thighs holding him hostage with a viselike grip around his legs. *Bloody hell.* Even in her sleep she was demanding.

Now, Archie, he chided himself. *Your dreams have come true. You are, at last, a wealthy man. Think of the gaming houses you shall visit.*

"Where do you think you are going, *mio amore*?" Alfonsina asked, suddenly waking and ruining his reverie. Marrying his good friend's widow was, indeed, the luck of the draw. He didn't feel so lucky right now. Wanting to get the hell out of there, he again reprimanded himself. *Don't blow it, Archie. She is your queen of hearts. Put on your poker face, and let the chips fall where they may.*

Archibald closed his eyes and tried not to look at her. "*Tu sei una stella—la mia stella—*my star, my lovely wife, my enticing *baronessa*." He responded with as much phony passion as he could muster this early in the morning. "*Ti amo. Non posso vivere senza voi.*"

"Oh, Archibald, I love you, too! *Il mio cuore è per voi.* My heart is for you." Alfonsina pressed her mouth against his. Ragged whimpers of need escaped her lips as her tongue moved into his mouth, demanding a hearty kiss.

Trying his best to think of other things, Archibald returned the kiss, moving his tongue over hers with rough thrusts, trying to prolong the kiss for as long as possible, knowing that, as soon as it was over, she would be expecting other, more taxing, exercise on the rococo bed. Wanting to perform and satisfy the insatiable woman, he tried to bring to mind his favorite memory, that of a lusty prostitute he'd had the pleasure of bedding many years before. The thought of that whore and the things she did to him always managed to stimulate his circulation.

A naughty Alfonsina leaned against the headboard, pushing away the pink satin sheets to expose their naked bodies. "*Mio amore*, make love to me!"

Bloody hell! Archibald stared at the obese, naked woman before him with her mammoth breasts hanging down to her large, flabby belly and realized his flaccid member was not going to harden anytime soon, no matter how many stirring memories he tried to conjure up.

He pressed a kiss on her palm before replying, "My heart is for you, too, my dear, Alfonsina. My passion is willing, but my body cannot follow."

"This is not a problem. We wait. Just hold me, *mio amore*."

Luckily, they heard a knock and covered themselves with the sheets right before two maids opened the door to their suite. *A reprieve!* thought Archie as the maids entered the room, holding breakfast trays.

"Nicolasa," Alfonsina said, smiling. "Did you remember to bring the paper?"

"*Sì*, Baronessa." Without another word, the maids placed the trays on a small table by the window, and, after drawing the curtains, walked out, shutting the door behind them. Alfonsina turned to Archibald as soon as they were gone. "I have a surprise for you this morning, *mio amore*."

Archie did not want any more surprises. He'd had his share of unpleasant surprises the moment he undressed his wife last night. "What is it, my love?"

"*The London Gazette*. I felt you may be a little homesick for news of London."

"Thank you, my dear. This was awfully thoughtful of you. It has been a while since I've had news from home." Archibald slapped her fondly on the buttocks before standing naked from the bed. Quickly donning his robe, he walked over to the breakfast table and sat down for his buttered toast, eggs and ham.

"Is there anything interesting in the paper?" she called out from the bed.

"Haven't had a chance to read it yet, *cara*," he replied as he took a bite of his toast. "Aren't you coming?"

"*Sì, mio amore*. I wouldn't miss our first breakfast together as man and wife, but I need a moment to linger in the memory of the wonderful things you did to me last night, and in anticipation of what we'll do tonight."

It was then that Archie opened *The London Gazette* and almost choked on the toast when he read the society page. He jerked from his chair and dropped the newspaper to the floor in his excitement. Rushing to the bed, he stood before his amazed wife, unable to speak, waving his hands in the air, not knowing whether to laugh or to cry at the irony.

If he had just waited a little longer—just one bloody day!

"What is it, *mio amore?*" Alfonsina asked, concerned. "What has happened? Is it bad news?" She started to get up from the bed.

"On the contrary, Baronessa. Pack our bags, my dear. One of my ducklings is going to marry the Duke of Wallingford!"

Chapter Seventeen

Skirting around the busy maids scurrying up and down the hallway with linens and cleaning paraphernalia, Marguerite and Samantha guided Lady Lorena toward the drawing room.

"I must apologize, Lorena. As you can see, the town house is in utter chaos with Mother in the midst of shutting it down and everyone getting ready to leave for Hardwood Manor this afternoon," Samantha informed their visitor. Smiling, she opened the door to the drawing room and peeked inside. "Good! We can visit in here. It is the only room left where the furniture has not been covered with sheets."

"I'm the one who should apologize," Lorena said as she followed Marguerite and Samantha to the sofa. Once they were seated, she confessed, "I know this is no time for a visit, but I had to come. I hope this isn't too much of an imposition. I wanted to say good-bye before you left for the country estate."

Samantha exchanged a smile with Marguerite and then shook her head. "Don't be silly, Lorena. You are never an imposition. Frankly, I'm delighted you came. Boredom was gnawing away at our nerves before you arrived."

Marguerite agreed. "Indeed, our luggage is ready, and there is nothing left for us to do but to twiddle our thumbs. I, too, am grateful for the visit, but we can't even offer you tea."

"Who wants tea? My curiosity is driving me mad," Lorena declared. "I have to know all about your engagement dinner last night. Marguerite, tell me everything, and do not leave anything out."

Marguerite shrugged indifferently. "It went well, I suppose."

Lorena looked amazed. "Only well—*you suppose?* I bumped into Lord and Lady Alpert on my way here. They told me it could not have been more perfect. The entire *ton* was there."

The entire ton except for Lorena, thought Marguerite. She was furious with Lord Phillip for not inviting Lady Bonner to their engagement dinner. If anyone deserved an invitation, it was Lorena. She would be eternally grateful to Lorena for having gone against the *ton* and taken Marguerite under her wing when everyone else had considered her a social pariah. Phillip had not allowed her to return the kindness Lorena had shown her all summer, maintaining it would be awkward to have a woman whom he courted for five years attend his engagement party. Yet it had not deterred him from insisting his ex-lover, Lady Louise Shasner-Blake, the Countess of Salesbury, and her elderly husband not only be invited, but be seated at the head table as his dearest friends.

"Indeed, Lord and Lady Alpert are correct. The party was a complete success," Samantha chimed in. "We missed you, Lorena. Why didn't you attend?"

Mortified, Marguerite shot Samantha a stern glance, silencing her cousin. Her kind friend showed no sign of feeling slighted, and Marguerite did not want to show Lorena just how angry she was with Phillip, nor would she admit to the dreadful argument she had with him after the party. She was grateful no one had been privy to it. Lorena would feel terrible if she knew she had been the cause of such an ugly spat. Truth be told, she still burned with indignation at the overbearing way he'd patronized her.

Turning to Lorena, Marguerite tried her best to smile. "You, more than anyone, should have been at the dinner, but Lord Phillip felt his mother would have been uncomfortable with you in attendance." She wasn't far from the truth. The old woman had not minced words when it came to Lady Bonner. More than once during the evening, the crusty dowager had referred to Lorena in an offensive manner, and Marguerite had bitten back a few nasty retorts of her own.

Samantha's eyes widened with disbelief. "Did I hear correctly, Marguerite? Are you saying Lorena was not invited to your engagement?"

Ignoring Samantha's outburst, Marguerite went on, "Phillip told me you never got along with the dowager duchess."

"I'm afraid it is true," Lorena admitted. "I find the dowager duchess a bit imposing. Who am I kidding? *Scary* is more like it! If I'd worn boots during our courtship, I would have been shaking in them the entire time. You are in for a battle with that woman, Marguerite. The old bat wants her son all to herself."

Marguerite smiled politely. "Phillip loves her dearly. He insists that, once we are married, his mother will live with us. I suppose Bentley House is large enough for the three of us," she replied, not wanting to elaborate further.

Despite the woman's constant meddling, and irritable disposition, the dowager duchess seemed completely overjoyed at the prospect of having Marguerite as a daughter-in-law. It would not be fitting to badmouth her intended or his ill-tempered, interfering mother to her friend.

Lorena took Marguerite's hands in hers. "Lord Phillip is much older than you, dear. He is set in his ways and quite domineering, but so are most men. Let's not speak about your future mother-in-law. I can see the topic is bothersome to you. Let's talk about more pleasant things. Isn't Bentley House the most beautiful mansion you've ever seen?"

"It certainly is that," Marguerite replied, recalling the magnificent pink sandstone manor. Last night, when the coach had stopped on Hyde Park Corner in Piccadilly, and she had looked up at Bentley House, Marguerite had hardly believed that, before year's end, she would be mistress of such a place. Upon entering, she had been even more impressed. The mansion, with all its paintings by famous artists, and exquisite furniture, took her breath away. It almost made her forget the old dowager and the stuffy, conniving duke who dwelled within its walls.

Samantha smiled in agreement. "It is majestic, but not as grand as Windword Hall. Marguerite and I believe there's no other place quite as lovely."

"Isn't the Kent mansion near your family's estate?" Lorena inquired. "I've never been there. I only briefly met Lady Kent this summer before she went traveling with her brother, the earl. Samantha, you've known him for years. Tell me about the mysterious and elusive Earl of Windword. I hear the earl is a bit of a recluse. They say he blames London for the accident that took his parents."

"My cousin considers him somewhat of an ogre," Marguerite commented before Samantha could reply.

Samantha giggled. "I've never actually said that—not in those words. I think I hear my mother. I better go see what she needs. Lorena, I'm happy you stopped by. I'll see you at my wedding," she said, before hugging Lorena good-bye.

Marguerite did not want to continue discussing the Earl of Windword or his sister, Julianna. It sickened her to think of Julianna Kent. It only served to remind Marguerite of her cheating chaperone, who, to her knowledge, had never returned from Spain, and was probably in Julianna's arms at this very moment. Her heart ached just thinking about Ashton's deception. Again, she tried to suppress the niggling fear that he'd been playing with her emotions all along. The ardor of his kisses had matched hers and had made her yearn for more. How could he have abandoned her so readily?

Forcing her thoughts away from Ashton, Marguerite quickly changed the subject. "I always envied Samantha. I never wanted to leave Hardwood Manor when summer was over. Now I get to stay until I return to London for my wedding in December. Lord Phillip is adamant that the ceremony be held at Bentley House. There has never been a Duke of Wallingford married elsewhere."

Lorena smiled. "Phillip hardly leaves the city. Will he be joining you in the country?"

"He hasn't mentioned any visits."

"You will be separated for three months, Marguerite. Aren't you going to miss him terribly?"

Lorena's question took Marguerite by surprise. She had privately relished the thought of having a bit of space from the controlling duke, especially after last night's row, and was looking forward to her stay in the country, away from all the hustle and bustle that was London. Truthfully, she was exhausted. From the day she had agreed to attend the Henley Regatta with Lord Phillip, she hardly found the time to stop for air—much less think. Her courtship with the duke had taken a life of its own, luring her into a whirlwind of extravagant parties and grandiose happenings. Before she knew it, she agreed to marry him.

Unfortunately for Marguerite, every day since she had done nothing but remind herself that marrying the Duke of Wallingford had been the sole reason she'd come to London in the first place—the focus of her existence since she first set eyes on the man. If this were true, why was she so sad and dreading their future together?

"Marguerite, isn't he attending Samantha's wedding next month?"

"I suppose." Trying to ignore Lorena's questioning brow, Marguerite added nonchalantly, "Did I tell you my sisters are getting married on the same day? Winnie was not keen on sharing Samantha's special day for fear of ruining it, but Aunt Elizabeth insists a triple wedding would be simpler for everyone. My aunt is a saint and a miracle worker, but not even she can plan three separate weddings in such a short time."

"How does your other sister, Penelope, feel about a triple wedding?"

Marguerite smiled. "She's not too keen on it either, but not for the same reasons. Penelope does not want the other two brides sharing *her* special day."

Lorena laughed. "I do hope you'll return to London for my wedding in November. The timing couldn't be better. You'll be able to see to the last-minute fittings and details pertaining to your own wedding."

"Wild horses couldn't stop me from attending, Lorena. As far as the preparations for my wedding, the dowager duchess is planning everything to the last detail, including my dress. There is nothing left for me to do. "

Lorena's eyes widened in horror. "Your wedding dress?" she asked, aghast.

"It's quite lovely, really. Phillip wants me to humor her. His mother wore it on her wedding day. She maintains we not go against tradition," Marguerite said, struggling not to show her frustration and disappointment with Phillip for insisting his mother dictate every aspect of their forthcoming wedding, including choosing the most important dress Marguerite would ever wear.

"That very well may be, but don't you think it a bit intrusive of the old bat?"

A breathless Aunt Elizabeth came into the room. "Lorena! How nice to see you, dear. Marguerite, the Duke of Wallingford is waiting for you in the courtyard. He insists it is most urgent that you meet him there at once."

"What is *he* doing here? I wasn't supposed to see him today," Marguerite mumbled, and then tried to collect herself, horrified that she had let those words spill out of her mouth in front of both Lorena and Aunt Elizabeth.

Lorena stood to go. "You mustn't make him wait. He abhors it."

Aunt Elizabeth used her silk handkerchief to blot the slight sheen of moisture from her brow. "Yes, dear," she agreed. "I've noticed he is quite impatient. You must never make him wait."

After gathering her belongings, Lorena hugged Marguerite good-bye and left with Aunt Elizabeth.

* * * *

Taking her time, Marguerite made her way toward the courtyard. She spotted the duke sitting on a stone bench, impatiently waving at her from afar. He stood as she approached him and attempted to reach out for her, but she would have none of it. The man had deceived her, tricked her. Disgusted with him, she crossed her arms and pointedly looked away.

"I can see you are still angry with me, my dove. Come sit, and we shall discuss it further. You are being unreasonable." His greeting contained a strong suggestion of reproach. "After all, she had no business being at our party."

"I prefer to stand," Marguerite said crossly.

"Sit," he persisted as he traced his forefinger along the curve of her cheek. "We have not settled things between us, little one."

Cringing at his touch, Marguerite walked toward the stone bench, having no choice but to sit and arrange her skirts over its hard surface.

Lord Phillip regarded her with amusement. "Why are you being so difficult, my dear? Indeed, I've never come across such a feisty woman in all my days. Your fire ignites my soul. It is the reason I long to make you my duchess. You will suit your title well, my dove."

Marguerite was not amused or flattered by his compliment. "Your Grace, I cannot forgive the way you underhandedly—"

"Hush!" the duke rudely interrupted her. He sat beside her and grasped her hand. "It wasn't exactly a lie, my sweet."

Marguerite ached to slap the nauseating smirk off his face. She quickly withdrew her hand from his. "What would you call it, Your Grace?"

"An omission."

"You only admitted you failed to deliver Lorena's invitation when I noticed her not in attendance."

"Miss Wiggins, we discussed this last night. I didn't want that tramp ruining my engagement party or my poor mother's health." He ripped out the words impatiently, giving her a black-layered look.

Marguerite bristled at his tone. She could hardly look at him. "My friend is no tramp," she said, full of resentment.

"I forbid you to see her again. You are never to see Lady Bonner again. Is that understood?"

"No, it is not understood!" A furious Marguerite jumped to her feet. She hurled the words at him like stones and turned without waiting for a reply.

The duke's icy hand grabbed her arm before she could walk away. "Don't you dare leave," he ordered in a commanding tone, his fingers biting deep into her arm.

"Let go of me," Marguerite demanded with indignation. "Let go at once."

An angry Lord Phillip promptly released his grasp.

"Of course, my dove," he said, curtly. "Lower your voice immediately, or your blasted chaperone will feel a need to come and defend you. Speaking of whom, I haven't seen him since we started our courtship. Did your uncle finally see the gentleman for a poor choice of chaperone?"

Marguerite fumed. Ashton James is no gentleman. He had returned her passion with kisses that should never have been shared by a chaperone and his ward—especially when the chaperone's heart belonged to another. Poor choice of chaperone, indeed.

"Did you hear me, my dove? What happened to Mr. James?"

"Why do you care?" Marguerite snapped. The duke's mentioning of Ashton made her even more livid with the duke. The last thing she needed was to be reminded of how much she missed her chaperone and how, despite her loathing of Ashton, she caught herself wishing he had never left.

"I don't care really." The duke's eyes anchored hers in a stern gaze. "You will learn to control your tone with me, Miss Wiggins."

"Mr. James is not in London," Marguerite blurted out angrily. "He left for Spain last month in pursuit of Lady Julianna Kent and has not returned."

"For Spain? That's interesting."

Marguerite did not find it the least bit interesting. "It seems she is the love of his life. Are you satisfied?"

"Ah, yes, quite satisfied, my dear. I love that temper of yours. It never fails to amuse me."

Before she could say anything else, the duke rose from the bench. Suddenly his boldly handsome face smiled warmly down upon her. His features were so perfect; he was almost too beautiful for a man. As usual, his change in demeanor baffled Marguerite. He had been furious a second before, and now he was smiling at her as though all was well and they were not in the middle of an argument. The change in his behavior threw her off balance, but it should not have surprised her. During their short courtship, Marguerite had discovered the duke had many faces. He had a way of changing moods with the wave of a hand.

With a pompous flourish, he extracted a small black velvet box from his coat pocket.

"As I was saying, my dove—don't walk off before giving me the opportunity to give you this," he said, opening the box and taking out the most dazzling diamond-and-sapphire ring Marguerite had ever seen. Speechless, she let him slip it on her finger.

When Marguerite was able to take her eyes off the stunning

ring long enough to look at him, she noticed he appeared quite pleased with himself.

"I thought you'd approve of your engagement ring, my dove," the duke said smugly. "Unfortunately, I could not give it to you last night. My mother had it sized, and it was not ready until this morning."

Marguerite took the ring off her finger and handed it back to him. "It is lovely, but I can't accept it. I have changed my mind."

His face froze with indignant shock. "What are you saying?"

Marguerite's stomach knotted, and she stiffened under his withering glare. "I think we may have rushed things a bit, Your Grace. Please take back the ring," she said firmly.

He shook his head. "Miss Wiggins, if you think you can back away from our engagement, you are quite mistaken. You agreed to marry me. This is not a silly matter where you can simply change your fickle mind. I am the Duke of Wallingford. You will not insult me or shame my name. There will be heavy consequences to pay if you try."

"I know who you are, Your Grace," Marguerite said, not able to hold back the cynicism in her tone. "I suffered your wrath this summer. Or don't you remember?"

To her surprise, instead of storming out with a furious huff, the Duke of Wallingford stared at her and then burst out laughing. "What spirit, Miss Wiggins!"

He grabbed the ring and roughly put it back on her finger. "You will make a perfect duchess. You will behave," he said darkly. "We shall tell no one of your little temper tantrum. I will forgive you, and we shall never speak of it."

Lifting her chin with his forefinger, Lord Phillip pursed his lips to kiss her, but Marguerite looked away. "Let us go inside," he said hastily. "I know you are eager to show the ring to your family."

Marguerite's brain was in tumult as mixed feelings surged through her. The duke was so arrogant she no longer thought him appealing. The man was insufferable—completely unbearable. Contrary to what she told Lorena earlier, Marguerite knew she would not miss Phillip during their time apart. Indeed, she would not miss him the least bit. Three months without him seemed like a blessing to her at the moment. What was she to do with the rest of her life?

He was, indeed, handsome, and his title and possessions were most envied in England. The woman he chose to share those with would be considered quite fortunate. However, she was not happy with him, and no amount of convincing herself otherwise was going to change anything. If she felt this way now, how would she be able to live under his dominion? Would she be more content as a lonely governess? Duchess or drudgery? The question had haunted her days and tormented her sleepless nights.

While they walked back to the townhome, Marguerite realized what had just occurred between them had been exactly what had transpired the day he proposed to her two weeks ago. Phillip had not bothered to ask her for her hand in marriage. Instead, he had sat her down in this very place and proudly proclaimed that he decided to marry her and make her his duchess.

Marguerite had been so taken aback she had not been able to utter a word. The man had never proposed to anyone, let alone someone whom he had just recently began to court. Without waiting for an answer, Lord Phillip grabbed her elbow, pulled her along behind him, entered the town house, and announced their engagement to the entire household.

Marguerite did not want to recall the excitement her engagement had generated within the family, much less the exhilaration that had sprung throughout London once the news got out. The duke was right. She couldn't back out now, not before creating a terrible scandal—a scandal that would ruin her and her family forever.

With mounting despair, Marguerite put her hand to her forehead and closed her eyes. Had he proposed only two weeks ago? It seemed like a lifetime. The celebrations and events which followed kept her so busy she'd hardly had a chance to get her bearings. Indeed, she was now the most coveted woman in London. Marguerite Wiggins, the young woman who managed to secure a proposal from the Duke of Wallingford. The future Duchess of Wallingford. Alas, the most wretched woman on the planet.

* * * *

"Your grace, how wonderful to see you!" Aunt Elizabeth smiled the moment Marguerite and the duke entered the drawing room. She stood next to the sofa, where Penny, Winnie and Samantha sat, waiting patiently in their traveling clothes. "I'm so happy you've joined us. It won't be long now. We shall be departing shortly. Isn't it a splendid morning?"

Lord Phillip agreed. "Indeed, it is, Lady Hardwood. It is a most splendid morning, especially for your niece. Miss Wiggins has something to show all of you."

"Oh?" Penny asked curiously. "What is it?"

Putting on a good face, Marguerite walked over to the sofa and extended her hand.

"Marguerite!" Penny gasped. "It's the most beautiful ring I've ever seen. It is much nicer than the one Mr. Pennington gave me or the one Mr. Cummings gave Winnie."

Winifred was about to speak, but Aunt Elizabeth spoke first. "Penelope," she admonished, smiling at the duke, "your engagement ring is a fine ring. You shouldn't compare Marguerite's ring to yours."

Penelope paid no heed. "It is even nicer than the one Lord Steven gave my cousin. Pardon me, Samantha, but look at it."

Samantha laughed. "I love my ring, but I have to agree with you, Penny. Oh, Marguerite, it is, indeed, beautiful."

"Let me have a look," Winnie insisted, taking Marguerite's hand. "I've never seen anything more striking. Your Grace, you've made my sister quite happy."

"Indeed, Marguerite," Aunt Elizabeth agreed. "What a magnificent stone—the same color of your eyes."

With a self-satisfied grin, Lord Phillip acknowledged smugly, "I'm glad you are all pleased with my choice. I was right to follow Mother's suggestion. The old darling insisted a sapphire would suit my future duchess more than a simple diamond."

Marguerite stared at the duke, wanting to wipe the haughty expression from his face. Didn't the pompous, arrogant man realize that, except for Marguerite, every other woman in the room had been given a diamond ring by the men in their lives?"

"There is nothing *simple* about diamonds, Your Grace," Marguerite professed, biting back a few choice words.

"What have we here?" asked Uncle John as he entered the room with Mr. Cummings, Mr. Pennington and Lord Steven following close behind him. "It's a crime to have so much beauty gathered in one place!"

Aunt Elizabeth laughed. "Why, Lord Hardwood, to what do we owe your sudden good humor? Could it be the coaches are ready to go, my dear?"

"Indeed. We can leave as soon as you say, my dear. Except for Mortimer, who will be traveling with us, the rest of the help has just departed for the country."

"How wonderful! I'm eager to return home, but all in due time. I'm guessing these gentlemen want a few minutes to say good-bye to their fiancées."

Mr. Cummings smiled, taking Winnie's hand. "I don't know how I can say farewell. I can't imagine being separated from you, even for a few weeks."

Mr. Pennington followed suit, smiling down at Penelope. "My dear Penny, how will I survive until our wedding?"

"We could pay a visit to Hardwood Manor before a month's time. My fiancée insists Hardwood Manor during hunting season is quite splendid. I don't see why we can't enjoy a little hunting before the wedding," Lord Steven declared, winking at Samantha.

"I agree," Samantha replied. "I'm going to be miserable without you."

"As am I without you, Mr. Cummings," Winnie said, looking up at Mr. Cummings with dreamy eyes.

Assessing the couples before her, Penny rolled her eyes. "Oh please—stop this nonsense. Are you all daft? Surely it will not kill us to be separated until our weddings. I, for one, am going to be quite occupied with all the arrangements. I shall hardly have time to miss you, Mr. Pennington."

Mr. Pennington looked as though he'd been slapped in the face. "I wish I could say the same, my dear, but I'm going to miss you terribly," he responded with a heavy sigh.

"Gentlemen, please sit down," Marguerite said, trying to divert everyone's attention from Penny's comment and poor Mr. Pennington's reaction to it.

"Indeed," Aunt Elizabeth agreed, pointing toward the sofa and chairs. "You mustn't leave. It is still early. Your Grace, please sit down."

Lord Phillip looked at his pocket watch. "I mustn't. My mother is waiting for me at Bentley House. We lunch together every day. The poor darling must be wondering where I'm at."

"Please don't let us detain you further," Marguerite said, her voice sounding a bit too eager. "Go to her at once. Be sure to give her my best wishes."

After frowning at Marguerite, Aunt Elizabeth forced a demure smile when she spoke to Lord Phillip. "We look forward to seeing both you and the dowager duchess at Hardwood Manor for the girls' wedding next month."

The duke shook his head. "My mother will not be attending. The poor darling is not well enough to travel."

"Really?" Penny burst out. "She seemed the picture of health last evening. My wedding will be most memorable. Isn't that right,

Mr. Pennington? The poor darling would enjoy it."

"I'm sure she would," the duke replied, looking a bit distracted as he turned to Marguerite. "Miss Wiggins, I shall see you in a month's time. I hope you will be well until then." They exchanged a polite, simultaneous smile before he turned to the others. "Good day, ladies, gentlemen."

Without another word, the duke turned on his heel and left the room.

"Stuffy, isn't he?" Penny asked Marguerite before bursting into giggles.

"Penny," Aunt Elizabeth objected, but Marguerite could hardly disagree. Her fiancé was, indeed, the stuffiest, most conceited individual she ever had the misfortune to meet. How could she marry him, when being in the same room with the man made her want to run out for air?

"I'm sorry, Aunt Elizabeth, but it is the truth. Mr. Pennington feels the same way."

Mr. Pennington looked mortified.

"Isn't that right, Mr. Pennington?" Penny asked, smiling sweetly up at him.

"Penny!" Winifred snapped. "When are you going to learn to keep your thoughts to yourself? Mr. Pennington will admit no such thing."

"My sister, Winifred Wiggins, the hypocrite!" Penny looked at Winnie with amused wonder. "You know it is true. You told me so yourself just last night. Mr. Cummings can verify that. He was right there with you, shaking his head in affirmation. Samantha, don't you look at me that way. I heard you, Aunt Elizabeth, and Uncle John, two nights ago in the study. All three of you think exactly as I do. The Duke of Wallingford is a stuffy, old duke, and we all know it."

"Well, he is not old," Winifred retorted. "He is two and forty, only twenty-four years older than Marguerite. A perfectly respectable age."

If Marguerite weren't so miserable, she would have burst out laughing. "Shouldn't we be leaving now?" she asked Aunt Elizabeth.

"Indeed, we should," Aunt Elizabeth replied, turning to look at the butler, who had just entered the drawing room. "Mortimer, I'm glad you're here. Summon the footmen. We shall be leaving shortly."

"As you wish, my lady, but I have come to tell you that you have guests."

"Guests? Everyone knows we are leaving for Hardwood Manor. We cannot accept visitors at this time. Go back to the foyer and tell them we are indisposed."

"I cannot, my lady. They are not in the foyer."

"Whatever do you mean?" Aunt Elizabeth snapped at the butler. "Where are they?"

"The man refused to remain in the foyer. I insisted they wait in the hallway. She is the Baronessa Alfonsina Porcilini. They have come all the way from Italy."

"I don't know such a woman. Who is the impertinent man with her who refused to wait in the foyer?" Aunt Elizabeth demanded angrily.

"That will be me, none other than Archibald Wiggins, the baronessa's loving husband. Gooselings, meet Mother Goose!"

Marguerite recognized the familiar voice and turned to see her smiling father standing at the threshold beside a hefty, flamboyantly dressed middle-aged woman with ash-blonde hair clustered in short curls all over her head.

"Papa!" Penny exclaimed, rushing over to his side and throwing her arms around him. "Papa, did you say...*your wife*?"

Archie kissed Penny's forehead, before turning to the baronessa. "*Cara mia*, meet your new daughters. This one is Penelope, my youngest, my copper penny."

"Papa, what do you mean she is your wife?" Penny insisted. "Where have you been all this time? We have been anxiously looking for you."

Ignoring the flabbergasted Penny, Archie walked further into the room. "This one here is Winifred, my eldest, my dear, sweet Winnie."

"Papa!" Penny tugged at his coat, but Archie did not acknowledge her question. Instead, holding the woman's fleshy arm, he made his way toward Marguerite.

"Most importantly, my dear Baronessa Porcilini, this one is Marguerite," he said pointing toward her, "the one who is about to lay the golden egg."

Chapter Eighteen

Lady Louise Shasner-Blake sighed blissfully as she snuggled closer to her lover. "Lancaster, now that we've had our time together, and we are both fully sated, maybe you can answer my question, my love."

"What question?" Lord Phillip asked, staring at the ceiling and enjoying the way her soft, delicate fingers twirled the hair on his chest.

"Did Miss Wiggins like the ring?"

"She did," the duke answered. *A whole lot more than she cares for the likes of me,* he thought, recalling how Marguerite had behaved toward him earlier. *She'll take all the trimmings. It is me she doesn't want.* Anger stirred within him, but the duke kept silent. His pride would never allow him to admit this out loud. "The frigid little chit could not even bring herself to kiss me in appreciation of such a grandiose gift. I suppose she suffers from shyness."

"Not even a kiss? How very proper of her," the countess remarked, her tone dripping with sarcasm. "Regrettably for you, my love, timidity is no virtue when it comes to pleasing a man."

"I better go, Louise, before your husband wakes and finds me in his bed."

"Ah, Lancaster, must you really go?"

"Yes. We had better not tempt the Fates any further," he replied. Not giving her the chance to change his mind, Lord Phillip rose from the huge four poster bed and collected his clothes from the floor, picking up each garment from where it had fallen in the heat of their passion an hour before.

The countess laughed, holding the sheets over her naked body. "I seriously doubt Oliver will wake from his nap this soon. I poured a sedative in his tea. The old fart is probably drooling all over his favorite armchair in the study."

"I know your trusted chambermaid is on the lookout, my dove, but we can never be too cautious. The man is being cuckolded under his very roof."

"What makes today different from any other day? I've never been caught yet," Louise admitted, laughing proudly. "Adultery hints at danger and always has exciting implications. Don't you agree, my love?"

Phillip shrugged. "I wouldn't know. I'm not the married one here."

Giggling, Louise threw a pillow at him. Ducking and warding it off, he proceeded to grab his shirt and trousers from the floor.

"Oh, Phillip, if only Oliver were out for the night. I should be used to it after all this time, but it still turns my stomach when he puts those wrinkly hands on me, not to mention his other disgusting parts. How can I be blamed for wanting to satisfy my pleasure elsewhere?"

"At his ripe old age, one would think Salesbury would have lost interest by now," Lord Phillip said absently as he put on his shirt. "You made your bed, my dove. Now you have to lie in it."

Louise gave a silly laugh. "And *lie*, I do! I'm tired of having to pretend to enjoy his sloppy attempts at lovemaking when being near him only serves to make me ill. If only I had married you, Lancaster," she said, wistfully. "I'm beginning to resent Miss Wiggins more and more."

"Ah, yes, Miss Wiggins. Honestly, I couldn't wait to be rid of her, the sisters, the cousin, the aunt, the lot of them. You should have seen them earlier, my dove. The sister, Penelope, bickering and comparing rings."

"How uncouth, darling. You must have been mortified."

Pulling up his trousers and tucking in his shirt, Phillip heartily agreed. "Indeed. Quite crude, the bunch. Before coming here, I tried to explain to Mother that Miss Wiggins changed her mind about the engagement, but I didn't have the heart to go through with it," he let slip before he could stop himself.

Astounded, the countess rose from her pillow, allowing the sheet to fall and expose her large, generous breasts. "Never mind your mother, Phillip. Are you saying Miss Wiggins actually tried to back out of the engagement earlier?"

"Well, yes, my dear. I was tempted to allow her to do so, but Mother would be crushed—absolutely crushed."

Aghast, Louise shook her head. "I don't have to tell you, my darling, that you are the biggest catch in England. What could Miss Wiggins be thinking? Has she gone insane?"

"The haughty chit was probably trying to act self-important. Far from me to care what is in that little head of hers."

"You should care, darling. She will make you miserable."

"No more miserable than you've made me, my dove," Phillip

replied with biting wit. "The thought of you and your aging count is more than I can bear. Yet, you never cease to rub it in my face."

The countess laughed. "I don't make *you* miserable, I make *Ollie* miserable! Tell me, my love, what did your fiancée think of Bentley House? I noticed the little money-grabbing ingénue seemed quite pleased with her surroundings last night." She continued, "What did the prudish Miss Wiggins think of the well-endowed, naked statue of *Napoleon* at the foot of the stairs? Did you tell her you posed for it?"

The duke threw back his head in a peal of laughter. "Why spoil the surprise? She'll find out soon enough."

"I'm jealous. Why does your mother persist on it being her?" the countess asked, reclining back against her pillow and covering her breasts once more with the sheets.

"I'm beginning to ask myself the same question. I rue the moment Mother set her eyes on Miss Wiggins the night of Lorena's ball." Lord Phillip sat at the edge of the bed and, one foot at a time, slipped on his socks and shoes. "The chit has a temper, and I don't find her insolence the least bit challenging. You should have heard her last night, throwing accusations at me."

"Oh? What accusations could she possibly throw?" Lady Louise asked, her eyes wide with interest as she bit her bottom lip, looking highly amused.

The duke shook his head. "Never mind, Louise," he said, buttoning his vest. "I don't want to relive the argument. This morning was no better. Truth be told, I find Miss Wiggins quite wearisome, but on the other hand, why shouldn't I marry her? I can't very well have you, can I, my dove?"

Lady Louise smiled wickedly. "You just had me, Your Grace. You can have me again, if you so wish," she said, patting the mattress, indicating he join her in bed. "All you have to do is take off your clothes."

Phillip chuckled. "Don't play coy with me, sweetness. You know exactly what I meant. It makes no difference whom I marry if I can't make you my duchess."

Sobering suddenly, Louise bit out, "You have your mother to blame for that, too, Lancaster. Our lives would have been so different, my darling. Why couldn't she have taken a liking to me? What makes Marguerite Wiggins so special?"

"The girl is young, beautiful and carries herself well. My mother fell in love with her on sight. The poor darling is old and demanding heirs. I suppose it is time to give her what she wants.

Nothing has to change between us, my dove."

"How do you intend to beget heirs when Miss Wiggins refuses to kiss you? What if she does not tolerate your bed?"

Lord Phillip donned his frock coat. "Don't you worry yourself about that, sweetness. Miss Wiggins will comply with her wifely duties. She is prudish and temperamental, but she is not daft. After she produces an heir for my mother, the high-strung little hellion can rot alone in her bed for all I care," he said donning his jacket.

Louise smiled. "You promise?"

Completely dressed now, the duke walked over to the side of the bed. He bent down to give the countess a quick peck on the lips. "You have my word, sweetness. After I'm married, I'll continue to come to you when I need pleasuring. As I said before, nothing will change between us, my dove. Nothing ever will," Phillip replied in a much better mood.

Maybe his mother's choice would be a blessing in disguise. Miss Wiggins's apathy toward him could work toward his advantage. She would ask no questions.

"My marriage to Oliver certainly did not tame my desire for you, darling. As you will recall, I broke my silly marriage vows the morning after my wedding, when you sneaked into the study." Louise giggled devilishly. "Indeed, we've managed to fool that dim-witted husband of mine ever since."

The duke stood at the door, staring at the seductive countess on the bed. "We will fool Miss Wiggins as well, my dove," he replied, blowing her a kiss.

How difficult could it be to deceive a frigid and indifferent wife? With that thought, he walked out of the bedroom and proceeded to sneak out of the Salesbury townhome as he had done many, many times before.

* * * *

The moment he arrived in London, Edmund wasted no time in going to the authorities with the name of Julianna's would-be rapist. He went straight to No. 4 Whitehall Place, the official headquarters of Scotland Yard, where he was directed to the chief inspector's office. For the span of an hour, Edmund had no choice but to curb his frustration as he sat before the incredulous Chief Inspector Gerald Littlejohn and his equally skeptical subordinate, Inspector Josephus Appleton.

Chief Inspector Littlejohn took a puff from his cigar and slowly exhaled. "Lord Kent, are you absolutely certain? I find it hard to believe a man of his standing, a gentleman so highly regarded, could stoop to commit such a crime."

"Of course I'm certain. I wouldn't be here otherwise."

"I don't understand. The incident in question took place in the spring. Why would you wait this long to inform us of it?"

"We've been over this," Edmund replied, his patience running thin.

"Humor me, Lord Kent. Let's go over it once again. Why the long wait?"

Clenching his jaw, Edmund intently leaned forward on the leather chair across from the chief inspector's desk, making a concerted effort to rein in his temper. "My sister refused to reveal the bastard's name."

Inspector Appleton, who was sitting next to Edmund, cleared his throat. "Lord Kent, you expect us to believe your sister would keep the name of her attacker from her own brother?" he asked, his chin thrusting forward. "She must have confided in you."

"Damn it! The man threatened her with her life, before she went into hiding," Edmund snapped. "Julianna was distraught and not herself. I refused to pressure her in her condition. I knew that, without the name of the perpetrator, I wouldn't have a leg to stand on."

Chief Inspector Littlejohn shook his head. "Be that as it may, but—"

Edmund interrupted, "I tried to investigate the incident on my own and had my suspicions, but only recently did my sister confirm his name."

"May I see it?" Littlejohn asked, referring to the cuff link in Edmund's hand.

Edmund handed the cuff link over to the chief inspector. "I have it on very good authority the sapphire is from the Royal Collection. There must be some sort of registry for these gifts. A record of who receives what. The bastard's name must be on the list. If not his name, then the name of one of his ancestors."

"That is all very well and true, Lord Kent, but this proves nothing. He can always say he lost it somewhere. It is your word against his. You are both very influential men. You may have stolen it from him."

"Bloody hell!" Edmund slammed his fist on the chief inspector's desk. "Are you calling me a thief and a liar?"

Inspector Appleton quickly intervened. "Of course not, my lord. We will investigate this further. This man is very powerful. We need evidence, and, unfortunately, this cuff link is not enough."

"I have given you a name and the testimony you need to arrest this animal. If you don't arrest him, I'll kill the bastard myself," Edmund declared, meaning every word. "He was not able to hurt my sister in the physical sense, but I'm certain he has raped before and since. A predator does not keep still for long."

Littlejohn nodded his head. "Unfortunately, you are most correct in your assessment. If your accusation is true, there may be many others. Regrettably for us, most victims never report the crime. The women are much too embarrassed and, in this case, fearful of what he may do to them if they did. You said so yourself, Lord Kent. He threatened your sister with death. If what you say is true, this man must be a monster."

"We agree on that much."

"Lord Kent, rest certain that, if this man is guilty of the crime, we will apprehend him," Littlejohn assured him. "Apart from you and your sister, who else knows?"

"Lord and Lady Hardwood and their daughter, Lady Samantha."

"Keep it that way. This is a matter of utmost secrecy. The less people who know, the better. The sapphire cuff link is a good start. We will trace it back to him, but we must catch him in the act. This is the only way we will be able to prove it."

"What do you need from me?"

"Nothing—absolutely nothing except your silence. Let us do our job. Be confident, Lord Kent. This man will rape no more. Without him knowing it, he will be followed—at all times. No other woman will fall prey to his depravity. We will catch him in the act, and he will be prosecuted."

"How the devil do you plan to do that without compromising another innocent victim?" Edmund demanded.

Inspector Appleton smiled. "We have our ways."

Before Edmund could question them further, he heard a knock. A large, hefty man opened the door. "You wanted to see me, Chief Inspector?" he asked, standing at the threshold.

"Don't just stand there, Detective Jones," Chief Inspector Littlejohn instructed the officer. "We have work to do. The Earl of Windword has just shared some very disturbing news. It seems we have a filthy rapist within our midst."

* * * *

Edmund walked out of the chief inspector's office and noticed Lady Lorena and Lord Jackman waiting in the hallway outside another office.

"Mr. James, I see you are back from your business trip," Lady Lorena said, smiling. "Lord Jackman and I came to accompany my dear father, who is in the process of reporting a robbery. Unfortunately, his gold watch was stolen from him when he went walking in the park this morning. It belonged to his great-grand-father. Thank God, they did not hurt him in the process."

Edmund said, "I'm sorry to hear it. Is there anything I can do?"

Lorena shook her head. "Thank you, Mr. James, but there is nothing anyone can do. My brother, Joseph, is with him, but we chose to wait outside."

"What brings you here, Mr. James?" Lord Jackman asked amicably. "Are you also reporting a robbery? I don't envy you—such a disagreeable circumstance."

"Indeed," Lorena agreed. "Speaking of more pleasant matters, I visited the Hardwood town house this morning. I shouldn't have gone today, but my curiosity took the better of me. I just had to see Marguerite. Have you seen her, Mr. James?"

The mention of Marguerite's name excited something deep within Edmund; the thrill of anticipation touched his spine. She had been in his thoughts night and day since the moment he'd left for Spain. He couldn't wait to take the little minx in his arms and show her just her how much he had missed her.

"No, I haven't seen Marguerite. I'm headed there now. I needed to take care of this business first."

Lorena frowned. "I'm afraid that you'll find the town house empty. The Hardwoods left for their country estate this after-noon. It is too bad you didn't get the chance to congratulate her."

"Congratulate her?" Edmund asked. "For what?"

"Oh, Mr. James, you haven't heard! I have wonderful news. Marguerite is engaged to the Duke of Wallingford. Soon all of London will be calling her Duchess!"

Chapter Nineteen

Fury gripped Edmund the moment he opened the morning paper. Staring back at him was the image of the illustrious Lord Phillip Lancaster, His Grace, the Duke of Wallingford, and of Miss Marguerite Wiggins, daughter of Archibald and the late Lydia Wiggins, announcing their engagement for the world to see. Standing between the happy couple, bejeweled and smiling like a Cheshire cat, was the duke's mother, Her Grace, the Dowager Duchess of Wallingford.

Blast them all to hell.

Edmund crumpled the paper and threw it across the dining room. "Damn you, Marguerite," he said, slapping his palm on the mahogany table.

She certainly worked fast, he thought bitterly. The fickle little chit duped him into falling in love with her, and the instant he'd left for Spain, she snatched Lancaster instead. Truth be told, he was angrier with himself than with her. It was foolish of him to think Marguerite began to care for him. He knew she set her sights on the duke. He'd known as much since the first day on that blasted train ride many months ago. Her momentary distraction for Edmund had been just that—a momentary distraction.

To think he had been ready to offer her a proposal of marriage. *Bloody hell!* He always thought of the institution as a nuisance, something he would be subjected to in the future in order to produce heirs. The liberty to come and go as he pleased, to travel the continents for months on end, to sleep with whomever he wanted without having to deal with a whining wife at home, waiting for his return, had meant more to him than any one female, but he had been prepared to give it all up for Marguerite. Losing his freedom would have been a hefty price to pay, but if it meant having her as his wife, he would have gladly paid it. That was before yesterday afternoon at Scotland Yard, when Lady Lorena delivered the dreadful news.

Edmund shook his head with disgust.

"Lord Edmund, you arrived at the wee hours last night. I'm sorry I wasn't there to welcome you. I wish they'd woken me upon your arrival," Ruth said as she walked into the breakfast room. "You shouldn't have come down for breakfast. Godfrey would have brought up a tray."

Edmund stood and put his arms around his old governess's thin frame, greeting her with a hearty hug. "I never take breakfast in bed, Ruth. You know that about me. Have you eaten?"

"Yes, I have, but you sit, my lord. Your breakfast will get cold," Ruth said, settling into the chair Edmund held out for her. "Godfrey told me you are returning to London this afternoon. Tell me it isn't so...You've just arrived."

"I'm afraid Godfrey's right." Edmund shrugged matter-of-factly. "I need to address a matter of utmost importance with Lord Hardwood this morning. Once I've spoken to him, I'll return to the city. There is a situation there that needs handling."

"I'm glad you're finally back home at Windword Hall, if only for this short span. I wish I could say the same for Lady Julianna. Why did she have to run off and marry that Spaniard? Is there any chance she may come visit her old governess anytime soon?"

Without elaborating any further, Edmund nodded as he took his seat. Ruth did not know the true reason for his sister's marriage. He had kept her in the dark, letting her think Julianna had recklessly fallen in love and had run off to Spain with his friend, Diego de Cordoba. The governess would have suffered from constant guilt if she so much as suspected that his sister had been abducted and almost raped last spring—especially since the incident had occurred under her care. Why torture the poor woman with the truth when Julianna would be back at Windword Hall before too long?

Hopefully, his stay in London would be a short one this time. The scoundrel was still loose, but time had run out for the filthy swine who had tried to ruin his sister. Edmund had made certain the bastard would not destroy any more lives. Although the inspectors may have been skeptical upon hearing the man's identity, Edmund knew they would follow through and investigate his claim and would keep Julianna's tormentor under constant surveillance. The moment the bastard tried to rape again, he would be arrested and taken away in shackles.

"I'm interviewing a nice young couple from Manchester, Oliver Clemmons and his wife, Bertie," Ruth said, cutting into his musings. "They aspire to become part of our staff. You are scarcely home, and, now that Lady Julianna is gone, the house is empty except for the servants. It is time to fill it with a wife and children of your own. Let us earn our keep."

The mention of a wife and children made Edmund think of Marguerite, and the anger that swelled inside him made him lose his appetite. "Julianna will be home soon," he said dryly, putting his fork down and grabbing the napkin from his lap to wipe his mouth.

Ruth's face lit up. "What wonderful news! When, my lord? When is she—"

"Ruth, no one knows my sister eloped to Spain. You have kept it that way, haven't you?" he interrupted.

"Of course, Lord Edmund. The neighbors do not know a thing. I've told everyone she is traveling abroad with you—just as you instructed." Closing her eyes, the governess pressed her lips together and shook her head before continuing, "Elopements are viewed upon with such distaste, my lord. You shall announce your sister's marriage when the time is right. No one needs to know she eloped with the Marques of Altamares. We can always say Lady Julianna had a fine wedding with a wonderful ceremony and reception in Spain."

Edmund didn't give a damn what the gossips thought about elopements. His only concern was in keeping Julianna safe. He nodded in agreement for Ruth's sake, knowing full well the news of his sister's bogus marriage would never be revealed. Things were finally falling into place. Once the bastard was caught, Edmund would bring Julianna home. Soon afterwards, her marriage to Diego would be annulled, and no one would be the wiser. Returning Julianna to Windword Hall, where she belonged, had been his one and only objective, the purpose that had kept him centered these past months in London. Now he could almost taste victory.

Pushing aside his breakfast plate, Edmund rose from the table. "Be a dear and ask Godfrey to alert the stable boy so he can ready my horse. I'm riding to Hardwood Manor."

"Of course, my lord," she said, rising fluidly from her chair in search of the butler.

Seconds later, Edmund walked out of the breakfast room, and, after entering the study, he sat at his desk to tackle a mountain load of papers stacked high upon his desk. Unable to concentrate, he gave up trying to organize them. He was not looking forward to the unpleasant task of filling in the Hardwoods on his visit to Scotland Yard.

Edmund knew his news would cause great distress. Lord and

Lady Hardwood would be devastated once he revealed the name of Julianna's attacker, realizing that they had opened their home to the deviant, and had allowed him to get close to the women in the family. For weeks the man had been right under their noses, preying on Marguerite.

Samantha, who had been furious with having to keep Julianna's secret from Lord Steven and Marguerite to begin with, would now find it unbearable to withhold this new information, especially since the abductor was practically family now and would be sure to attend her wedding next month. Unfortunately for Samantha, it was going to be even more agonizing for her to have the secret disclosed. It was sure to destroy someone she loved dearly.

Hopefully, thought Edmund, the animal would be arrested before the blessed event. The man had been a constant thorn at Marguerite's side all summer long. His move toward her in the park had led to her being shunned. Edmund did not know what he would do if that bastard tried to get near her again. He was determined to protect Marguerite no matter what, but—*damn it*—he had wanted so much more than to protect her.

* * * *

After the first restful night in weeks, Marguerite opened her eyes and smiled.

The cozy pink-and-white bedroom welcomed her with warmth and familiarity as she turned on her side. She tried closing her eyes again, but being back at Hardwood Manor made her much too excited to return to sleep. Happier than she felt in weeks, she exhaled a long sigh of contentment and sat up against her pillow to bask in the quiet comfort of her pleasant surroundings.

White, lacy, ruffled drapes with decorative pink bows and tassels shielded the room from complete sunshine, but let in enough light for her to admire the six-light chandelier that hung from the ceiling with six rose silk shades embellished with white and yellow flowers and draped with tiny jewel-like glass droplets. She smiled to herself, thinking of the many other times she had looked up to the ceiling to find the same dazzling chandelier staring down at her.

Every facet of the room brought back happy memories of summers long past. As her gaze wandered about the chambers, she noticed the dark-stained walnut dresser where she had stored her clothes for the past six years. As usual, her room smelled divine, the fragrant scent emanating from fresh tea roses that filled a white porcelain vase that stood upon the dresser.

A puce-colored quilt and the many fluffy pillows used to adorn the cast-iron bed lay on the tapestry chaise where Marguerite had placed them before collapsing into bed last night. She remembered countless pillow fights, and other happy times, when Samantha and Julianna had joined her on that quilt to giggle over some silly happening that had taken place earlier during the day.

Indeed, nothing had changed at Hardwood Manor. It was the one place where she had felt truly happy and completely pampered. From making certain that the vase in her room held her favorite flowers to satisfying Marguerite's penchant for horses by allowing her to have her pick at the stables, Aunt Elizabeth had always spoiled her rotten.

Unfortunately, as she lounged in bed while happily contemplating her surroundings, thoughts of Ashton and Lord Phillip came back to haunt her, and all of the pampering and reminiscing in the world could not make her forget the heartache inside her. Returning to the manor had lifted Marguerite's spirits somewhat, but not enough for her to put out of her mind everything that had taken place during the past month. Not even the prospect of becoming a duchess had lessened the pain of losing Ashton.

Refusing to think of him, she rose and walked over to the window. She needed to go for an early-morning ride. Maybe the beautiful landscape in these proverbial parts could bring her out of her gloomy state.

Opening the lacy curtains, Marguerite noticed a cloudless blue sky with the sun shining brightly over lush green trees. No, she wouldn't think of Ashton. Not this morning—this glorious morning. It would only feed her despair.

She would not think of Lord Phillip either. Remembering him always made her want to gasp for air. Her future with the stuffy duke would arrive soon enough. Today she felt free from him and his doting mother and all their stifling engagements. Yes, she was home at last. *At least for the time being,* she thought with a pang as thoughts of her forthcoming wedding to the Duke of Wallingford resurfaced once again, threatening to ruin her day.

Slipping out of her nightgown, Marguerite went to the wardrobe, anxious to get outside and ride her favorite horse.

A short while later, dressed in her riding habit, and resolute to keep Lord Phillip and Ashton from her mind, Marguerite walked to the stables.

* * * *

"Miss Marguerite, how wonderful to see you. Why, you grow more beautiful with each passing year. When Godfrey announced you were here, I could hardly believe it," the tall, thin, middle-aged governess exclaimed breathlessly as she directed Marguerite to the morning room. "Congratulations on your engagement to the Duke of Wallingford—it is all people are talking about. Julianna is going to be thrilled when she learns of it. May I offer you some tea?"

"No thank you, Ruth. I just came by to see how you were," Marguerite replied absently while admiring the tapestries that lined the halls of the magnificent mansion. "It is wonderful to see you. I've always loved it here. I hope this isn't an imposition."

Ruth smiled and opened the door to the elegant yellow-and-blue morning room.

"Since when have you been an imposition, dear? I always missed you when you had to return to your father at the end of summer. Indeed, I remember the happy Musketeers and how grateful I was that our Julianna had friends like you and Lady Samantha to share her youth. Julianna is having the time of her life abroad. Come, let us sit. I'm so grateful for the visit."

Marguerite and Ruth took their seats on the light blue Queen Anne sofa.

"This room is lovely. It was always my favorite room in the house," Marguerite said, looking about her surroundings. The room was light and delicate, unlike the rest of the mansion with its rich, dark tones and large quantities of highly decorated furnishings and ornaments. Indeed, the room was lovely, but Marguerite had more pressing matters on her mind. The portrait of Julianna that hung above the fireplace only served to strengthen her resolve. Was the lovely girl who smiled from above the mantel Ashton's fiancée, or worse, had she already married him? Marguerite needed to know—no matter how heart-wrenching, she needed to know.

She looked down to the loom-woven carpet beneath her and asked as casually as she could muster, "So is Julianna still in Spain with Mr. James?"

"What did you say about Spain, dear?"

Marguerite looked up to find Ruth frowning. "How daft of me, Ruth—what a silly question. Of course Julianna has not returned.

She would have called at Hardwood Manor if she had."

Ruth's eyes were wide with surprise. "You know about Spain?"

"Well, yes, Ruth. Julianna is traveling in Spain with her brother. Is she not?" Marguerite could feel Ruth's sharp eyes boring into her as she sat in the sofa, her thin fingers tensed in her lap.

"Yes, Lady Julianna was traveling abroad with her brother, the earl. My lord returned last night," Ruth said quickly.

Marguerite gasped. "Without Julianna? Lord Kent returned without Julianna? Is it because of her marriage to Mr. James?" she demanded over her choking, beating heart.

The governess looked distressed, but did not answer.

Marguerite pressed her, "Did they marry? Tell me, Ruth. I must know."

"No—Julianna has not married," an uneasy Ruth finally spoke. "Why would you think such a thing? The earl had to come home to attend to business. Julianna was having such a wonderful time abroad, the earl did not have the heart to bring her back with him. He allowed her to stay with friends."

"What about Mr. James? Is he one of those friends?" Marguerite blurted out before she could stop herself. "Why did the earl leave Julianna and Mr. James alone together in Spain? He is not as strict as Julianna would have us all believe."

Ruth's brow furrowed. She looked taken aback. "I assure you, Miss Marguerite. Lord Kent has left his sister in good hands. Who is this Mr. James you keep asking about?" she asked, perplexed. "I don't know such a person, dear."

"I'm sorry, Ruth. I'm a bit confused. I was under the impression Mr. James went to Spain to propose to Julianna."

"I don't know of a Mr. James. The earl never mentioned such a person. You must be mistaken."

Marguerite did not want to argue with the distraught woman. She could see poor Ruth was telling the truth. The governess had no clue as to the identity of Mr. James.

"Very well, Ruth. I must be mistaken. I'll be leaving now. I didn't know Lord Kent was back. I don't want to impose on his hospitality."

"Nonsense, dear. I know how you love our gardens. Please feel free to wander and stay as long as you like. Julianna would like you to enjoy Windword in her absence."

"Thank you, but as I said, I would not want to impose on the earl."

"Lord Kent would not mind at all, my dear. I remember how

Lady Julianna and Lady Samantha climbed trees and ran inside the mazes while you sat quietly on the stone bench by the lily pond and read your book." Ruth laughed. "Such a serious girl, and what concentration, I thought. Come, you must go to the lily pond and sit a while."

Marguerite followed Ruth outside to the beautiful gardens and shook her head in marvel as they approached the lily pond. No matter how many times she had visited Windword Hall, this spot always managed to take her breath away.

Ruth smiled. "I must go. I'm interviewing the Clemmonses, a nice newlywed couple from Manchester. Bertie is here for the position of cook, and her husband, Oliver, would like to work as our head gardener. But you sit, my dear. You know your way to the stables. Your horse will be waiting for you when you are ready to leave. Come visit me again. You don't know how happy you've made me, dear."

"Thank you, Ruth. Windword holds so many memories for me. I do love the lily pond. I used to sit at this very spot. If Mr. Clemmons is hired as your gardener, ask him to plant tea roses, blue ones. They would look beautiful in these gardens."

"I'll tell him," Ruth said, before she disappeared behind the rock gardens.

A guilt-ridden Marguerite watched her go. Although she held the governess in high esteem, her coming today had nothing to do with wanting to see the dear lady. Indeed, after leaving Hardwood Manor this morning, Marguerite had tried her best to enjoy herself, but as she rode her horse through field after field of wildflowers and rural landscape, thoughts of Ashton and Julianna had overwhelmed her. Perhaps the rat had chickened out or the Earl of Windword had refused him Julianna's hand. Perhaps they had eloped and were on their honeymoon. It had taken three hours of riding like a madwoman to gather up the courage to satisfy her curiosity.

Determined to know one way or the other, she decided to pay a little visit to Windword Hall. Shortly after, she had found herself standing outside Windword's gigantic entrance doors, smiling up at Godfrey, the hall's stiff and proper butler.

At first, she had felt no shame, but recalling how Julianna's governess had been so delighted to see her, Marguerite now felt dreadful. She looked down at the sapphire-and-diamond engagement ring on her finger. How could she admit to Ruth that, while engaged to the Duke of Wallingford, her every waking thought belonged to the man who might very well be Julianna's fiancé?

Trying her best to keep this dreadful possibility from her mind, Marguerite took comfort from the beautiful, tranquil surroundings. Sitting on the stone bench, she stared, mesmerized, at the waterfalls cascading into the lily pond. The gushing sound of water splashing against rock was quite soothing to her senses. She closed her eyes and inhaled the fragrant scent of wildflowers. "I could live here forever," she said, sighing.

"What's the matter, Duchess? Isn't Bentley House good enough for you?"

Marguerite heard the familiar, masculine voice and froze.

Chapter Twenty

Marguerite's heart pounded rapidly as she turned to find Ashton leaning leisurely against a tree, watching her with such intent it almost took her breath away. Staring at his tall form, so magnificent in his riding attire, she wondered if her eyes were deceiving her. The rich outline of his chest and shoulders strained against the fabric of his white, half-opened shirt, revealing a tanned, brawny chest covered with crisp black hair. Tight fawn riding breeches displayed to perfection every inch of his hard, muscled thighs while shiny black riding boots accented his sturdy legs. His dark brown hair looked unkempt, ruffled by the wind.

Always having seen him well groomed and elegantly dressed while attending social functions in London, Marguerite had never witnessed him looking more rugged or more sensual. Even when horseback riding in Hyde Park, Ashton always managed to look quite dapper and neat. At the time, she found him terribly appealing, but she rather liked this rough, earthy side of him. Swallowing hard, it was all she could do to keep from waving aside her injured pride and throwing herself at him. She wanted to tell him just how much she missed him. She wanted to feel his strong arms about her, feel his warm, delicious lips against hers again.

"Ashton!" she blurted, scarcely aware of her own voice, fighting the impulse to run to him. He had been in her thoughts day and night since they had last been together. Now he was here at Windword Hall, leaning casually against the old oak she climbed countless times with Julianna and Samantha in her youth.

"What are you doing here?" Marguerite asked over her choking, beating heart. "Were you looking for me?" she asked, a little too eager. Her voice held a rasp of excitement.

He nodded curtly, his dark eyes mocking her with a coolness that brought her back to reality. "No, I wasn't looking for you, Marguerite. If you must know, I've been riding all morning and had been contemplating a brisk swim in the pond before you and Ruth arrived. I had no inkling you were here."

That explained the open shirt and disheveled look—but, seriously, a swim in the pond? Was he insane? What if the earl had caught him? *My God, never mind the earl!* What if she and Ruth had interrupted him while he was undressing?

The thought made her cheeks warm. Rising from the stone bench, Marguerite squared her shoulders and cleared her throat, trying to hide her disappointment that he had not gone to Windword Hall in search of her. "I don't think the Earl of Windword would approve of you swimming in his pond without the proper bathing attire."

Still leaning against the tree, Ashton shrugged his shoulders. "Thanks for the warning, but I don't think the earl gives a damn," he remarked matter-of-factly.

"Where is Julianna?" Marguerite asked, as nonchalant as possible. "I know everything, Mr. James. *Everything,*" she emphasized.

"What about Julianna?" Ashton's powerful body moved with easy grace as he walked toward her. "What exactly do you think you know?" he asked, coming to stand before her, their bodies almost touching.

Marguerite haughtily tossed her head, trying hard to ignore the erratic sensations that traveled through her at having him so close. "Don't play games with me, Ashton. Are you going to answer me or not? Is Julianna with you?"

A muscle clenched along Ashton's jaw. "No, she's not with me," he answered tersely.

"Oh, I see. You've come to convince the earl for her hand in marriage. He must have refused you in Spain—is that it?"

"Bloody hell, Marguerite!" He looked down at her, his lips twisting incredulously. "You can't possibly think that—"

"I certainly do think it." Furious, Marguerite did not allow him to finish. "Don't act the innocent. I know you plan to marry Julianna Kent."

"Marry my...? Where the devil did you get that idea?"

"You look as though the notion affronts you. Stop pretending to be surprised. I overheard my aunt and uncle say how much you love Julianna, and how you traveled to Spain to bring her home with you. Are you going to deny this?"

"No."

Marguerite stiffened as though Ashton had just slapped her. He had not put a finger on her, but he might as well have. She had wanted him to deny his love for Julianna. She needed him to tell her that Aunt Elizabeth and Uncle John had been wrong, that Julianna Kent meant nothing to him. Instead, he stood before her completely acknowledging all of her worst fears and assumptions about him.

Tears threatened to spill down her cheeks. She turned from him, refusing to let him see the pain his admission had just caused her. "If you think the Earl of Windword is going to allow you to marry his sister, you are sadly mistaken," she retorted as arrogantly as she could muster while trying to reign in her emotions.

"Turn around and look at me, Marguerite."

Marguerite refused, crossing her arms over her chest and stubbornly keeping her back to him. "No. I never want to see you again."

His large hands grabbed her shoulders and turned her toward him, forcing her to face him. She stared up into his cold, dark eyes as though they were probing into her soul. Her intellect knew Ashton James to be a philandering cad; she should hate him and keep her distance, but her heart and body longed for something quite different. She wanted him to touch her, to hold her, to kiss her, to have him dispel the throbbing sadness creeping over her. Damn him! Why couldn't he love her instead of Julianna?

"You seem to know the Earl of Windword quite well, Duchess. Why would the earl object to me? He and I are such good friends."

His words took her by surprise. "In all the time I've known you, Mr. James, you never mentioned you were acquainted with the Earl of Windword, much less mention he is a friend of yours."

"There are many things I never mentioned."

"Indeed!" Marguerite snapped. She shook her head with indignation, not able to hold back her temper any longer. "Exactly when were you going to tell me about Julianna and your feelings for her?"

"I had planned to tell you the moment that I returned from Spain, but circumstances made it impossible for me to do so. You have it all figured out, don't you?"

Marguerite didn't fail to catch the tone of sarcasm in his voice. "What circumstances? There is nothing to figure out. You just admitted everything to me."

"I admitted what? That you owe me an explanation?"

Rage burst within Marguerite. Every nerve of her body itched to slap his arrogant face, but she refrained from doing so. He rigidly towered before her, his eyes meeting hers disparagingly, his lips thinned with irritation when it was she who had been hurt. She was the one who deserved an explanation. No, she deserved a whole lot more than a mere explanation.

Wanting to hurt him, she lifted her chin. "The earl does not think anyone is good enough for Julianna. In this case, I would tend to agree, Mr. James. You are but a liar and a cheat and will make poor Julianna a dreadful husband. Friends or not, the earl will not allow a mere nobody to fancy himself worthy of his precious sister. Why do you want her? Is it her status, her wealth? The earl is no fool. He'll see right through you and peg you for an opportunist. A person like you could benefit greatly from such a match."

Ashton frowned with cold fury. "You certainly would know about that, Duchess. Congratulations. I read about your engagement in today's paper."

"Yes, and I'm delighted," Marguerite spat out, purposely lifting her hand and flashing her engagement ring before his eyes.

The disgust on Ashton's face when his eyes fixed on her engagement ring stunned Marguerite. Why should he be furious when it was he who had left her for another and at this very minute was at Windword Hall trying to sway Julianna's brother into giving his blessing?

Ashton caught her hand, and the tingling sensation of his warm skin on hers caused havoc within her. "You're making a mistake, Marguerite," he said gruffly.

Marguerite snatched her hand away from his clutch. "My mistake was to allow you to play with my emotions. I'm glad you want Julianna. I don't care if you marry her."

Before Marguerite could object, Ashton grabbed her by the waist and pulled her to him; her breasts flattened against his massive chest; her thighs pressed intimately against his hard body. Shocked by the impact of his grip, Marguerite gasped, but she did not move. Instead, she moaned softly as his hands moved gently down the length of her back to explore the soft lines of her waist, hips and buttocks over her riding skirt.

"You care, damn it," he whispered. Highly aroused, it was almost her undoing when she felt his member harden against her. "You most certainly do care." Between each word, he planted delicious kisses on her neck.

"I don't care," she objected stubbornly, before his lips found hers and he kissed her full on the mouth.

Marguerite thought she would melt. Closing her eyes, she parted her lips so he could deepen the kiss when suddenly he stopped. Opening her eyes again, she noticed him staring down at her.

"For someone who doesn't care, you seemed awfully angry just now, Marguerite. Julianna is not the one I want. I'm leaving for London. Come with me." He propositioned her as he bent down to nibble her ear. "Run away with me, Meggie," he whispered huskily in her ear.

"What about Julianna?" Marguerite asked breathlessly, her heart racing, her flesh prickling at his touch.

"I love her very much. Marguerite, she is my—"

Mortified, Marguerite yanked herself from his arms, putting a safe distance between them. "Oh, yes, Mr. James," she interrupted him. "I'll run away with you. We can elope to Scotland. Are you insane? I'm engaged to the Duke of Wallingford. I couldn't walk away even if I wanted to. I don't want to, Mr. James," she lied.

Icy contempt flashed in his eyes. "I thought so," he said bitterly, giving her a frigid smile. Shaking his head, he let out a long, audible breath before turning from her. Without another word, he walked away.

"Go to her, and never come back," Marguerite spat out furiously at Ashton's back, knowing full well the sound of the waterfall would muffle her words, and he would probably not hear her clearly.

Angry tears fell down her cheeks as she yelled after him anyway. Whether he heard them or not, those would be the last words Marguerite would ever say to him. She had no intention of ever speaking to him again.

* * * *

Four weeks after arriving at Hardwood Manor, Marguerite had settled into a routine. Rising at dawn, riding nearly all morning, accompanying Aunt Elizabeth in the afternoons to visit her aunt's many friends at the neighboring estates, sharing evenings with the family and reading in her room had helped steer her thoughts away from Ashton. Even though Ashton had left for London and she had not seen him since, every time Marguerite remembered their encounter at the lily pond, her blood would boil.

Ashton was far from what Marguerite considered a good prospect, but she would have run away with him. At that precise, breathless moment when she had been in his arms and he had held her close, she had not given a thought to Lord Phillip and the scandal the breaking of their engagement would have brought about. Nor had she considered the heartache and embarrassment she would have caused her family. Her only thought had been of

Ashton.

Wrapped in his arms in that irrational moment, Marguerite had been willing to overlook the fact that Ashton held no title and was not a wealthy man. She had not cared about her future struggles or that she might be repeating her mother's folly by agreeing to run off with a cad who did not love her.

Unfortunately, unlike the feelings he held for her, her feelings were strong and all consuming—not those of a simple flirtation. Indeed, she had allowed herself to fall hopelessly in love with a rogue who had been, after a few stolen kisses, looking to make a proper match for himself. Marguerite could hardly admit this out loud, much less acknowledge it to anyone else. Like the rest of England, her family considered the Duke of Wallingford to be the catch of a lifetime. All presumed Marguerite's little summer infatuation for her chaperone had been just that—a little summer infatuation. She certainly was not going to enlighten them otherwise.

Run away with me, Meggie. His words still rang in her ear. The audacity! During the Season, he managed to fool her completely. She thought him to be decent and caring, and put her absolute trust in his character. She knew now Ashton James was as vain and narcissistic a man as any she had ever met. Why hadn't she seen that before? He attempted to seduce her with lovely words and futile promises just to ease his bruised ego. He didn't care about her, nor did he intend to marry her. How could she have been so daft, so ready to forgive the fact he had gone to Spain in search of Julianna? Poor, unsuspecting Julianna—the scoundrel most likely didn't love Julianna either. He was probably using Julianna as Papa had used Mama—only for his betterment and welfare.

The more Marguerite thought of how willing she had been in his arms, the angrier she became. Thank goodness she had come to her senses before agreeing to run away with him, only to have him back out after he'd had his fill of her. With that thought, Marguerite walked into the breakfast room and found Penelope at the table.

"Penny, you are never up this early," she commented, sitting down to join her sister. "Couldn't you sleep?"

A sulking Penny looked up from her plate. "No, I couldn't sleep. I couldn't sleep at all. Why did Papa do this to us?"

Marguerite served herself a cup of tea. "What did Papa do now?" she asked, bracing herself for one of Penny's outbursts.

Closing her eyes, Penny threw her head back and raised the back of her hand to her forehead as though the world were ending. "Everything is wrong," she spat out. "I hate Papa!"

"Penny, you are going to be married within the week. Stop thinking about Papa, and concentrate on your wedding to Mr. Pennington instead. You are going to make a beautiful bride."

Penny shook her head. "I can't stop. It is all I've thought about since he waltzed here, into our lives. Why would Papa marry that woman, Marguerite?"

Marguerite knew precisely why Archie had married Baronessa Porcilini, and so did Penny. Having taken a quick liking to their new stepmother, Marguerite was in no mood to listen to any criticism of Alfonsina. She felt sorry for the kind, amiable woman whose only crime had been to fall in love with their crafty father. Marriage to Archie was certainly not going to be easy. The unfortunate baronessa had no inkling of what was in store for her. Last night, while Marguerite watched the poor enamored fool gushing over Archie, she had been tempted, more than once, to say something but had actually held herself back from giving the lady any piece of advice.

"I, for one, am totally appalled," Penny insisted, closing her eyes and putting her hand to her brow.

Trying to avoid an argument, Marguerite ignored her sister's histrionics and simply changed the subject. "Do you want to come along on my ride? I could use the company. Maybe Winnie would like to come too. I can take you to all the places I told you about in my letters."

Giving Marguerite a look of distaste, Penny shook her head. "I'll pass," she said, turning back to her plate. "My morning is tedious enough. I hate horses, and you know it. Anyway, I'm much too busy with wedding preparations."

"Suit yourself. Are you really going to finish that?" Marguerite asked, noticing the large amount of ham, eggs, sliced fruits, cheese, and other delectable morsels Penny had piled high on her plate.

"I couldn't sleep, Marguerite. The horrid Porcilini woman has deprived me of it, but it doesn't mean I can't eat. The meddler is trying to take the place of our mother. How cruel of Papa to impose her on me, and how thoughtless of him to take advantage of Aunt Elizabeth's hospitality."

"Put down your fork, Penny. I feel you are going to poke out my eye."

Ignoring Marguerite, Penny continued to rant between bites, waving her fork in the air. "Our dear aunt was not counting on having them stay at Hardwood Manor as well. Isn't it enough he lost our cottage and washed his hands of us this entire summer? Why, he got off that train to Crawley so fast, he did not even bother to drop us at the Hardwood's doorstep."

"Aunt Elizabeth and Uncle John do not seem to mind. I think they find the baronessa quite colorful. Her stories during dinner are most entertaining."

"I am not at all entertained. I don't appreciate all the prying questions she asks of us," Penny declared, scoffing.

Watching Penny, Marguerite could not help but smile at the irony of it all. Penny, of all people, shocked at their father's behavior. Why, her little sister had worshipped the ground Archie walked on and had attempted to emulate him from the moment she was born.

"Papa's wife is only trying to get to know you better," Marguerite said while continuing to sip her tea. She took a hot, delicious biscuit and began to butter it.

"You have your own interfering busybody to deal with, Marguerite," Penny said, grabbing a scone and spreading strawberry jam on it before taking a bite. After a few seconds, her eyes sparkled mischievously, and her face split into a knowing, twisted grin.

"Papa told us something last night after you went to bed that may cause you to pause."

"Everything Papa does causes me to pause. What is it, Penny?"

"Are you sure that you want to know? Well, I might as well tell you. The dowager is trying to rekindle an affair of the heart by having his daughter marry her son."

"I don't understand," Marguerite said before taking a bite of her biscuit.

Penny continued to smile devilishly. "Papa knew the dowager duchess before she married the third Duke of Wallingford. She and Papa were young and in love, but the dowager did the wise thing and chose the duke instead. Papa met Mother a few years later. Remember how Winnie was to be called Brunhilda? Papa had insisted, but Mother refused?"

"Brunhilda?" Marguerite asked. "That is the dowager's first name."

"Precisely," Penny exclaimed, putting down her fork and pushing the plate aside. "Wake up, dear sister." She snapped her fingers at Marguerite. "Didn't you ever wonder why the old dowager took such a shining to you? Lorena said the dowager wanted her precious son all to herself until you came along."

"Phillip's mother never mentioned she knew our father," Marguerite said, dubiously. "Papa is toying with you, Penny. He enjoys playing games that way. Even Papa couldn't have been so audacious as to demand our mama name their first daughter after a past love."

"He seemed perfectly serious to me, Marguerite. Obviously, Lord Phillip's mother saw something in you that reminded her of Papa. That old biddy has no notion that Papa has married again. God only knows how she will react when she finds out. She will not be so fond of you then. Will she?"

"I suppose not," Marguerite replied, a bit distracted.

She had, indeed, wondered why the dowager had been so partial toward her. According to Lady Lorena, *"The old hag never approved of anyone, and had made life a living hell for any girl whom Phillip saw fit to court, much less marry."*

It made perfect sense now. Penny was right; the dowager wanted to rekindle her romance with Papa, and it did not matter to her if the bride Phillip chose was right for her son or not. All this time, Marguerite had felt that her future mother-in-law was an interfering, but loving, mother. Now it seemed the dowager and Archie were halves of the same orange—both putting themselves first before their children's happiness. Marguerite did not know which of the two was the more underhanded.

Trying to guide the conversation away from Lord Phillip's mother and her impending marriage to him, Marguerite returned the subject to Alfonsina. "What exactly has our stepmother done now?"

"Oh, *her*," Penny said, distastefully. "She came into our room late last night and insisted on seeing our wedding dresses. Winnie jumped from the bed, ran to the wardrobe, and showed Miss Nosy Parker her dress, but I refused. That Porcilini woman will see the dress at my wedding like all the other guests. That is what she is, Marguerite! She is not my mother."

"Of course she is not, but Alfonsina is only trying to show her enthusiasm."

Penny looked insulted. "You like her, don't you?"

"I do. Papa could have done worse. I hope that poor woman holds on to her purse strings."

"Oh, please, Marguerite! The baronessa's money will run out.

When it does, he better not come running to Mr. Pennington and me. I want nothing more to do with our papa," Penny huffed. "He can take himself and that prying wife of his back to Italy for all I care. It would serve her right if he wiped out her finances. Because of Papa and that woman, Winnie and I have had to share one of the small bedrooms in the manor. They took the last large one."

Marguerite laughed. "Look at your surroundings, Penny. Have you forgotten that not too long ago the three of us slept together in a cottage the size of this breakfast room?"

"That was a lifetime ago." Penny shrugged dismissively. "Anyway, it is easy for you to say. Your bedroom is more spacious and nicer than ours, and you don't have to share with Samantha anymore."

Closing her eyes, Marguerite took a deep breath. "You'll change your mind about Alfonsina soon enough. I heard her say she has no offspring. Since you are the beautiful redhead in the family, she is going to give you her ruby earrings and necklace as a wedding gift."

Penny's face lit up. "Really—did she say that?"

"Indeed. You may not care for her, but she seems fond of you."

"I saw the rubies, Marguerite. The baronessa was wearing them last night. At the time, I thought she looked a little overdone. After all, it was only a simple family meal. She came down those stairs with those rubies and that emerald velvet dress of hers, looking like an ornamented Christmas tree, all sparkling and glittery. Oh, never mind about that. The rubies are magnificent—even more breathtaking than Aunt Elizabeth's. Are you certain you heard right?"

"Yes, I also heard her ask about your honeymoon plans. She wanted to know if you and Mr. Pennington are planning to return to London. She wants you and Mr. Pennington to have the reins of her Italian villa while on your honeymoon."

"The villa—in Italy?" With a nervous giggle, Penny jumped up from the breakfast table. "I better see if the baronessa is up. Indeed, she may need something. Wipe that grin from your face, Marguerite. The poor woman is in a strange land. We must see to her every need and make her feel at home. You wouldn't want her thinking less of the English, now, would you?"

Penny did not bother to wait for an answer as she raced out of the room.

* * * *

Later that afternoon, Marguerite and Aunt Elizabeth came back from their afternoon visits to find Mortimer at the foyer with unexpected news.

"My lady, the Duke of Wallingford and his mother, the dowager duchess, have arrived and are planning to stay until the wedding."

Aunt Elizabeth gasped. "He's here? Now?" she asked, looking horrified.

"Yes, my lady, in the drawing room with the rest of the family. The dowager has taken ill and is resting in one of the guest rooms."

"Taken ill?"

Mortimer sniffed. "The vapors."

Closing her eyes, Aunt Elizabeth brought her hand to her forehead. "Take my things, Mortimer. I'll see to her right away."

"Yes, my lady. The yellow room at the end of the hall." Mortimer took Aunt Elizabeth's cloak and purse and then pointed toward the stairs before turning to Marguerite. "Miss, the duke awaits your arrival and is waiting to speak with you."

Feeling as though the air had been taken out of the foyer, Marguerite wanted to scream. Why had Phillip and his mother arrived a week before the wedding? How rude and inconsiderate of them. *Poor Aunt Elizabeth!* It wasn't enough that her aunt had planned a triple wedding; now she had to execute it while housing and entertaining the Duke of Wallingford and his mother as well. She, Marguerite, would be expected to accompany them at all hours. Wasn't it enough that she would be required to do so for the rest of her life?

The rest of her life—dear God, why had she ever agreed to marry him?

"Thank you, Mortimer," was all Marguerite could say before dragging herself to the drawing room. Seconds later, upon entering the room, she noticed a sober Lord Phillip sitting on the couch.

Her fiancé looked miserable, squashed between Archie and Alfonsina. Her stepmother resembled a rainbow-colored ostrich, dressed in a tangerine gown adorned with an array of multicolored plumes. The poor woman, wearing her coveted rubies, conversed endlessly in broken English in Phillip's ear. Uncle John and Samantha stood behind the couch and exchanged looks when Marguerite entered and Lord Phillip and Archie stood to greet her.

"Miss Wiggins, I've been waiting. We had planned to stay, but

I suppose I must leave as soon as Mother is feeling better. She cannot possibly stay under these conditions. Something in this house has made her dreadfully ill. She was perfectly fine during the coach ride to—"

"Nonsense," Archie interrupted him. "Please stay, Your Grace," he insisted. "I'm certain my in-laws will be adamant that you remain. You and your mother will be quite comfortable here. I welcome the chance to get to know you better. After all, having been blessed with my lovely gooselings, I've always wanted a son. I'm delighted you will be joining our flock."

"*Sì, sì*...join our flock," Alfonsina repeated as she pushed herself from the couch. "Archibald and I very happy here. Right, *mio amore, tesoro mio*?"

"Right, my love. Elisabetta and Giovanni would love them to stay," Archie agreed, continuing to offer Aunt Elizabeth's and Uncle John's hospitality as though it were his own to offer. "There is plenty of room."

Lord Phillip shuddered distastefully. True to his arrogant self, he persisted on speaking to Marguerite, completely ignoring Archie and Alfonsina. "Miss Wiggins, I would appreciate it if you looked in on Mother. She doesn't want to see me. Poor darling threw me out of the bedchambers. She is that upset."

"Phillip, that won't be necessary. We are leaving now!"

Everyone turned to see the tall, bony dowager duchess at the threshold dressed in a high-collared, plum-colored gown accented by a diamond-and-amethyst brooch at the base of her neck, clutching her purse and cane.

Marguerite noticed how Aunt Elizabeth, who had been standing beside the dowager at the threshold, walked into the room and raised her eyebrows at her husband and daughter when she came to stand beside them behind the sofa.

"Brunhilda, my dear. Must you go?" Archie asked, his fat torso eagerly making its way toward the haughty dowager, followed by the equally hefty Alfonsina, who wobbled behind him with a smile from cheek to cheek, her multicolored plumes and short yellow ringlets bouncing with her every step. "Here I thought we would have a moment to get reacquainted. Isn't that right, Alfonsina? Didn't we want to get to know Lady Lancaster a bit better?"

Her jonquil curly cap continued to bounce as Alfonsina nodded enthusiastically. "*Sì...sì*...get to know better. *Duchessa*...Lady Lancaster...*ti prego...per favore*...stay."

Like her son earlier, the dowager completely ignored Alfonsina, giving Archie a black-layered look. "I'd rather not, Mr. Wiggins. You are not as I remembered."

Archibald chuckled, his eyes raking boldly over the dowager's emaciated body. "Time has taken its toll on all of us, my dear."

Highly insulted, the dowager gasped. "Phillip...now!" She ripped out the words impatiently, whacking the cane against the floor. "I refuse to remain here another second."

Lord Phillip quickly raced to the door. Assisting his mother, he called out to Marguerite. "Miss Wiggins, aren't you going to see us out?"

"Of course, Your Grace," Marguerite said walking toward them. Raising their chins in disgust, the dowager and the duke walked into the hallway with Marguerite trailing behind them. Watching them, she thanked God the arrogant pair would be returning to London and not be staying to ruin the last days she would be sharing with her sisters and Samantha before the wedding.

In silence, they reached the foyer. Marguerite smiled politely when Mortimer opened the front door to let them out. "What a shame, Your Grace. You will be returning for the wedding, won't you?" she asked, almost choking on her words.

"That depends on my mother's health," Phillip replied curtly over his shoulder as he assisted the indignant dowager down the front steps.

Standing at the door, Marguerite waved as the duke helped his mother into their crested carriage. Watching the carriage drive away, a sense of joy and relief overtook her.

"Ah, Brunhilda! After all these years."

Marguerite heard her father's voice and turned to find Archie, Winifred and Penelope standing behind her in the foyer.

"When I found out we had both been widowed, I tried several times to renew the relationship. You can't imagine the many times I tried to contact that woman only to be turned down. Brunhilda would have no part of me—wouldn't even agree to see me. She must have changed her mind." Archie chuckled. "A little too late for that, gooselings. Wouldn't you agree? Now give your old papa a hug," he said, extending his arms to all of them.

Ignoring him, Penny laughed. "You missed it, Marguerite. That woman took one look at Mama and fainted. Acted as though she'd seen a ghost."

"Mama's ghost? I don't understand," Marguerite asked, confused.

Winifred rolled her eyes. "The dowager did not see our mother's ghost. Penny has taken to calling our stepmother *Mama,* as of this morning. Mama this, Mama that—I can hardly stand it."

To their surprise, Archibald let out a great peal of laughter. "Indeed, I'm beginning to appreciate my Alfonsina more and more with each passing day. The dowager did not have to see a ghost to want to rush out of Hardwood Manor. Without her even knowing it, your new mama has driven away the evil spirits—that is until your wedding, Marguerite," he added, sobering somewhat. "Never you mind, gooseling! A lifetime of Brunhilda will be a small price to pay for being called Duchess."

Chapter Twenty-One

A week later, as Marguerite was about to leave her room, she heard knocking at the door and opened it to find Flora standing at the threshold. Waving Marguerite aside, the old nanny entered the bedroom and flopped onto the upholstered spoon-back chair on the side of the bed.

"Lady Samantha and your sisters would like a word with you," she said breathlessly. "They are waiting in Lady Samantha's room with Lady Hardwood and the baronessa. Bear with me. I'm a bit out of breath. This is a much larger home than the town house in London, you know."

"Nanny, are you all right?" Marguerite asked, walking over to the chair where Flora was sitting. "It is no easy task rushing from Samantha's room to the other end of the hallway where my room is situated. You mustn't hurry so."

Flora shook her head. "I'm fine. I'm going to miss my Samantha—that is all."

"Don't worry, Nanny. Now that Lord Steven has bought Bellevue Manor just a few miles away, Samantha is going to live close by. I wouldn't be surprised if you saw her every day."

Marguerite's words seemed to revitalize Flora. The old woman looked up with an eager, jovial expression. "I do hope so, Miss Marguerite. It's such a blessing. The timing couldn't have been more perfect with Lady Chamberlain's passing in Paris, and her French relatives wanting no part of the Bellevue estate. My prayers were answered. Not that I was praying for that old cow to take her last breath, you understand, but having my Samantha near means the world to me. If only she could take me to live with her at Bellevue. I'm old, but I'm still capable. I've begged her, but the stubborn girl doesn't budge."

"Of course you are most capable, Nanny," Marguerite agreed, smiling. She couldn't help but feel sorry for her. Never having had children, Samantha had become the old woman's entire world.

"I hope she doesn't forget her old Nanny Flora."

"How can you even think that, Nanny? You are her second mother. Sam has often said so."

"You aren't just saying that, are you, Miss Marguerite?"

Smiling, Marguerite shook her head. "Of course not."

Satisfaction pursed Flora's mouth as she rose from the chair. "Well then, maybe there is hope that she'll change her mind. I'll pack my bags and follow her to Bellevue yet. Now go to her. I've detained you long enough."

"Indeed, I mustn't go to sleep without wishing the three brides good luck," Marguerite said, smiling. "Not that they are going to need it. As usual, Aunt Elizabeth has done the impossible. The arrangements look lovely. She insists everything is in hand for the ceremonies tomorrow."

"Three weddings at the same time. I don't know how Lady Hardwood managed it, but, indeed, she did. Here's hoping everything goes accordingly tomorrow," Flora said. "Hurry on, Miss Marguerite. Don't keep Lady Samantha up too late. She needs her rest if she is going to be the lovely bride I've always envisioned."

A few seconds later, Marguerite, dressed in her nightgown and robe, stood in the hallway before Samantha's door when she heard giggling coming from inside the bedroom. After knocking softly, she entered the room to find Penny, Winnie and Samantha sitting on top of her cousin's big four poster bed, all in nightgowns, and all in the process of braiding their hair.

"Come in." Samantha patted the mattress. "Join us, Marguerite," she said, smiling. "I sent Flora in search of you. Poor dear, she is distraught with my leaving her. I spoke with Mother earlier, and it is decided. Nanny is coming to live with me and Steven at Bellevue. I want to surprise her with the news tomorrow on my wedding day. It will be my wedding present to her. Honestly, I need Nanny as much as she needs me."

Marguerite laughed as she approached the bed. "Nanny is packing her bags as we speak."

"She knows me too well," Samantha replied, giggling. "You just missed Mother and Aunt Alfonsina. They retired to their rooms. I know it is early, but the three of us are much too excited to sleep."

"Excited? I'm a bundle of nerves. I won't sleep a wink tonight," Winifred said, hugging her knees and tucking her bare feet underneath her nightgown after making room for Marguerite on the bed. "We are celebrating our last night as single women. Marguerite, your wedding is only a few months away. Maybe by then I'll be carrying Mr. Cummings's child. Oh, I want a little one so badly. I hope it doesn't hurt too much...childbirth, that is."

Penny's brow furrowed. "Childbirth? I'm dreading tomorrow

night. Two years ago, when we visited Aunt Hyacinth and Aunt Lavinia in Crawley, I overheard the two of them discussing the wedding night. They were saying how the first time hurts and how men are brutes and that our bodies are—"

"Penny, please, they are spinsters. How would they know anything about wedding nights?" Winnie objected.

Penny raised her eyebrows. "I don't know! I'm just saying what I heard. The moment we are married, I'm going to have a talk with Mr. Pennington. My new husband better not force me against me will. I hope he can be patient because it is going to take time for me to let him have his way—maybe days or weeks. Mama Alfonsina told me that I shouldn't worry. Her first time—"

Red-faced, Winifred coughed.

"As I was saying," Penny continued, "Mama Alfonsina told me that—"

"It's a pity Mr. James won't attend our weddings tomorrow," Winifred interrupted. "It just won't be the same without our dear chaperone."

Samantha agreed. "It is a shame he won't be here."

"Indeed, he took such good care of us this summer, watching over us like a hawk." Penny laughed. "It's a wonder we were able to get engaged at all. If only he were in my bed tomorrow night to stop Mr. Pennington from—what? Don't look at me that way. You know exactly what I meant by that. I don't want Mr. James in my bed. I just want him to—never mind. I have every right to be nervous! Mr. Pennington is not a large man like Mr. James, but nonetheless, he is of muscular, stocky build. I'm petite and flowerlike. How am I ever going to be able to breathe with him on top of me?"

Coloring fiercely, Samantha, Winifred and Marguerite exchanged subtle looks of amusement.

"I asked Uncle John, but he said Mr. James is in London on business," Winnie said, ignoring Penny's remarks. "Mr. Cummings and I will be most disappointed if he misses the ceremony. Samantha, it is only an afternoon. Why don't you ask Uncle John to give poor Mr. James the day? What could it hurt? I can't imagine getting married without him. Penny's right; he took wonderful care of us this summer."

"I'm sure Father would if he could," Samantha pointed out. "He is quite fond of Mr. James. It is important business, Winnie. I'm not certain Mr. James can get away."

"What about Lord Phillip?" Penny asked suddenly. "That duke left here so fast last week, I don't know if he will be coming back anytime soon. Thank goodness he cannot back out of the engagement now, not since it became official and news of it was all over the society pages last month. I'm afraid Lord Phillip is stuck with us." She rested back against the headboard in a fit of giggles. "That should make Papa happy."

Winnie and Samantha exchanged exasperated looks.

"Really, Penny," Winifred reprimanded. "Are you certain you haven't gone into the wine cellar and indulged in a bottle or two? Don't pay attention to her, Marguerite," she said, standing and making her way toward the door. "We should all get some sleep."

Penny pouted and was about to retort when Samantha quickly added, "Winnie is right, Penny. You are anxious about tomorrow, and your nerves are making you say silly things. Isn't that so, Marguerite?"

Marguerite kept silent, suffering from the usual suffocating sensation that tightened her throat every time she thought of Lord Phillip Lancaster. Contrary to what they believed, Penny's words were not offensive in the least. The notion of Lord Phillip backing out of the engagement was like music to her ears. In a little more than two months, life as she knew it would come to an end. The nineteenth of December—how she dreaded the date when she would become the Duchess of Wallingford. With every passing day, the calendar marked closer the wretched event. It was the first time in her life when she could actually agree with Penny. Having to be intimate with Lord Phillip made her more than a bit nervous. In fact, the thought turned her stomach. She would have to share a bed with a man whom she could not even bring herself to kiss.

How silly of her—all these years to have been in love with a fantasy. She had concocted a castle in the sky, living a lavish life as a wealthy duchess married to the handsomest of dukes. Yes, Phillip was, indeed, handsome, but he was greatly flawed, and his flaws affected her greatly. What he possessed in looks, he lacked in character. It was a known fact that Lord Phillip loved another, but Lady Louise Shasner-Blake was the least of Marguerite's concerns. She had been prepared to deal with the duke's lover, but his conceit and superiority, his condescending attitude when it came to others, his complete disregard for her opinion, and his obsession with his mother were things Marguerite found impossible to overlook. As his wife, she would always trail behind his mother, his lover, and his self-adulation.

Well, it served her right for agreeing to marry the haughty duke in the first place, thought Marguerite, feeling disheartened, broken and defeated. The mention of Phillip Lancaster had made her cringe, but hearing Ashton's name filled her with sadness. Instead of her castle in the sky, she'd be living in a prison, trapped for the rest of time with a man she did not love or respect while Ashton basked in the comforts of Windword Hall in Julianna's arms.

"Aren't you coming, Penny?" Winnie insisted, standing at the doorjamb. "Marguerite?"

"Yes, I suppose so. Good night, Samantha," said Penny as she and Marguerite stood to join Winifred at the door.

"Good night, cousins. Sleep tight. Tomorrow awaits us," Samantha replied, smiling. "Marguerite, please don't go." She patted the mattress, motioning for Marguerite to stay behind. "I'd like a word before you leave."

After her sisters exited the room, Marguerite perched herself at the edge of the bed and turned to Samantha. "What is it?" she asked, unsettled by the sudden troubled frown on her cousin's face. "What's bothering you, Sam? Don't tell me you are also frightened of the wedding night."

Samantha giggled. "Of course not! I'm worried about you, Marguerite. I can't get married tomorrow and go away on a honeymoon without speaking with you first. I know you don't love Lord Phillip. You love Mr. James. I can see it every time his name is mentioned. Just now you looked as though your heart was about to break."

Samantha's words took Marguerite by surprise. She was about to speak when her cousin continued, "Marguerite, don't deny it. I know you too well."

Closing her eyes, Marguerite shrugged. "I have been holding my feelings in for so long it actually feels good to hear the truth spoken so bluntly. I thought I was doing a good job of hiding my feelings, but you were always able to see right through me. You are right, Sam. I don't love Lord Phillip. I finally have what I thought I wanted, only to find that I want nothing to do with him. Marriage to the duke is no longer my dream—it has become my nightmare."

"Marguerite, don't look so miserable. Mr. James loves you and—"

Marguerite snapped, "Mr. James does not love me. He wants Julianna Kent. How foolish of me to think becoming the Duchess of Wallingford could make up for losing Ashton to Julianna. Dear God, as though I ever really had him. Samantha, don't mention Mr. James to me again."

Pursing her lips, Samantha shook her head. "Do you trust me, Marguerite?"

"Of course I do, but Sam, you knew I was falling in love with Ashton this summer, yet you kept silent about his feelings for Julianna. You saw how infatuated I was becoming with him, and you didn't bother to warn me. You had to have known he wanted to marry Julianna all along. Why did you encourage me to fall in love with him?"

Samantha took Marguerite's hands in hers. "I'm so sorry, Marguerite. There are matters here that do not involve you, matters of a most serious nature which I swore to keep secret for Julianna's sake."

Marguerite withdrew her hands. "Matters of a serious nature? Aunt Elizabeth and Uncle John maintain Ashton's feelings for Julianna had to be kept secret, but I find it ludicrous. Really, Samantha, I don't understand it at all."

"Unfortunately, you will understand soon enough. Mr. James loves Julianna, but he went to Spain to protect her, not to marry her. You must believe that."

"Is Julianna in danger? What are you not telling me?" Marguerite demanded, confused and frustrated.

"Oh dear, I've said too much. Mr. James has known Julianna all of her life. She needed his protection. I can't reveal more without betraying a confidence or putting you in harm's way."

"You are not making any sense, Samantha. The only harm I suffered was getting my heart broken by someone who toyed with my affections."

"Marguerite, in all the time I have been acquainted with Mr. James, I've never known him to be serious about a woman. I don't know what took place between the two of you, but, please, Marguerite, believe me. Mr. James did not toy with you."

"Really? What would you call it then?" Marguerite asked sarcastically. "He had the nerve to suggest I run away with him. Imagine that! I should have slapped him while I had the chance."

Samantha gasped. "He asked you to run away with him?" she exclaimed, looking absolutely shocked. "When—where?"

"A month ago, when I ran into him while I was visiting Windword Hall. Appalling, isn't it? He meant none of it. There is no excuse for his behavior. I've been debating whether or not to tell Uncle John. That corruptive cad deserves to be let go. Imagine trying to seduce me into scandal while acting as my chaperone. If I had said yes, he probably would have had his way with me and then dumped me by the side of the road like the common whore he'd turned me into."

"Marguerite, he would have done no such thing. I never took him for one to elope. How romantic of him to even think it. Oh, Marguerite, he must be mad about you."

"Romantic? Oh, please!" Refusing to listen any more, Marguerite rose from the edge of the bed. "Mr. James has proven to be worse than my father—an opportunist. Julianna is sure to provide that sweet-talking rogue everything I can't."

"You've never been more wrong, Marguerite," Samantha insisted. "I have a confession to make to you. I was romantically drawn to Mr. James for years. Don't look at me that way. Let me finish. Before Steven, I never thought I would be able to forget my feelings for Mr. James. Imagine me, pining for a man who never gave me a second look. Marguerite, I've seen the way he looks at you. He loves you as much as you love him. If he asked you to run away with him, he meant it. He wants to marry you."

Standing with her hands at her waist, Marguerite stared down at Samantha. "You never mentioned an interest in Mr. James. In fact, you never mentioned Mr. James at all before this summer."

"I kept my feelings for him to myself and would be mortified if he ever found out. I was not the only female infatuated with Mr. James. Every female who came in contact with him in these parts wanted him for herself. He never took an interest in any one of us. You saw for yourself how he took London by storm. I have to admit, I was a little jealous of how you were able to wrap him around your little finger. His duties of chaperone went far beyond the call where you were concerned, Marguerite. He couldn't stay away from you. I noticed it. Mother and Father noticed it, too."

"Even if that were so, why are we discussing this now? You know I have accepted Phillip's proposal and I have to marry him. When I saw Ashton at Windword Hall, he said he was a friend of the earl's. Are you are telling me he wasn't there to ask for Julianna's hand, but was coming to report on her welfare?"

"Yes, that is exactly what I'm saying, Marguerite."

Unable to control her emotions, Marguerite turned and walked toward the door.

Samantha called after her, "Marguerite, don't be a fool. He loves you. Don't let him go. I should have spoken sooner."

Marguerite turned the doorknob and quickly left the room so Samantha wouldn't see the hot tears of despair that fell freely down her cheeks.

Chapter Twenty-Two

"Must you cower in the corner? Get up from that floor, you smutty whore. I've had enough of your whining. Get up and undress for me now. I'm doing you a favor—you're wet to the bone."

Lying spread-eagled on his large bed, he opened his robe and took his member in his hand. He laughed when he noticed the girl staring at him, her eyes wide with terror. "Don't pretend you've never seen one of these."

"My lord, please let me go," she begged him. "I promise to keep my mouth shut."

"My dear," he said, chuckling. "I don't want your mouth shut. On the contrary, I want your mouth opened wide...very wide. If you get my drift," he added, his eyes shifting from his shaft to her and back again as he toyed with himself.

She shrieked. "Please, let me go!"

"Get over here," he ordered. "You want it, too. You came willingly into my coach."

Miserably, she shook her head no, hugging her knees and recoiling deeper into the corner.

"You have the nerve to refuse me?" He smiled, thinking of the pain he would bestow upon her before the hour was over.

"You are a gentleman of high regard. I believed you were offering me a ride to my home, a few blocks from the shop." Her hands twisted the dark fabric of her soaked skirt as she tried desperately to explain. "It was storming outside, my lord. My husband is ill. I cannot afford to get sick, too. I recognized you from the society pages. I buy The Gazette to see some of my creations worn by the lovely ladies that come to my shop."

"Naughty little tramp—I don't give a damn about your shop. I know you are trying to distract me, and it isn't working. Get up!" he roared.

Startled and realizing she had no other choice, the sniffling chit rose from the floor. Looking down, she walked over to stand before the bed.

"That's better. Now get naked."

Trembling, she began to unbutton her blouse.

"Hurry, I don't have all night. I'm expected at a family wedding tomorrow. I leave for the country the moment I'm through with you."

Still unbuttoning her blouse, she looked at him with pleading eyes. *"My lord, why me? I'm no prostitute. There are prostitutes who would gladly satisfy your needs for a fee. I'm not one of—"*

"Silence! If I get up from this bed, I guarantee it won't go well for you. I'll start by tearing your clothes off. I wonder how you'll explain that to your sick husband."

"Why me?" she insisted.

"Why not you?" He laughed. *"All the great pickings have left for the country estates. It doesn't hurt to lower my standards a bit until next Season. I almost didn't notice you in the store window, so diligently sewing away. I waited hours for you, my little seamstress. Waited until it was time to close the shop. The rain made it easy for me to abduct you."*

Her blouse fell to the ground as she begged, *"I implore you, my lord. My husband must be frantic, wondering where I'm at. Please don't hurt me! I've never been with anyone else."*

"Silly girl, I'm not going to hurt you. I'm going to ravish you." He waved an impatient hand at her. *"All of it! The skirt comes off too. Let me see what you offer your husband so freely."*

Tears falling down her lovely cheeks, the girl stepped out of her skirt and stood before him, clad in only her undergarments.

"Take them off," he ordered.

Looking horrified, she did as instructed. After a few more seconds of watching her clumsy fingers fidget with strings and buttons, her undergarments fell to the floor and she stood naked in front of the bed. Modestly, she tried to shield her privates from his view with her hands.

"Drop the hands, and let me have a look."

Taking a deep breath, she closed her eyes and dropped her hands to her side.

"You are a beauty, indeed. To think I almost passed on you, so pressed for time as I am tonight, but I couldn't resist. You see, my demon has summoned me. The urge was too great."

"I don't understand, my lord."

"You don't need to understand. You just need to wiggle around, squirm like the worm you are!"

"No, my lord," she objected. *"Please don't make me do this."*
Realizing he was not going to take no for an answer, she began to sway provocatively from side to side. *"My husband, my poor*

husband! This is sinful. I'll never be able to face him again," she cried, tears flowing down her cheeks.

"Your husband is a very lucky man, whore! What he doesn't know won't hurt him. You can stop now." Wearing nothing underneath his silk robe, he crawled to the end of the bed and kneeled before her on the mattress. He looked at her for a few seconds, savoring her anguish and shame. He was happy he had sent Edgar Mason away tonight. This one was too special to share. She was as pretty as they came, with beautiful dark gray eyes and large breasts budded with pale peach nipples. His mouth watered as his hands roamed intimately, cupping her breasts. Enjoying her torment, he played with her nipples, rubbing them gently between his fingers.

She gasped, but it was not a gasp of pleasure. Sheer panic reflected in her eyes, and this caused him to reach full arousal. "Come around and lie on the bed."

Reluctantly, she walked over to sit at the side of the bed.

"Lie down and spread your legs for me."

"Why are you doing this to me?" she asked, whimpering.

"Because I can." He laughed as she helplessly adhered to his orders. "Spread them." His hand moved down over her taut stomach and lower still.

"Stop, I beg you to stop!"

"Now, why should I do that?" Chuckling, he held her down while his finger entered and explored the inner walls of her feminine cavity. He was surprised to find she was moist...very moist. Usually, at the time of entry, his victims were dry as chalk. If he didn't know any better, he'd think that this one was actually ready for him. "You are much too pretty for your own good," he said, taking off his robe and positioning himself over her.

Closing her eyes, she shook her head from side to side and began to scream. As he was about to jam his shaft into her, the door burst open and the room filled with officers from Scotland Yard, who grabbed and handcuffed him before he knew what was happening. Ashton James—what the devil was Miss Wiggins's chaperone doing here?

"I'm going to make you regret the day you were born, you filthy bastard! You'll never terrorize another woman again," Mr. James threatened furiously before being restrained by the officers.

"Are you all right, Miss Tillie?" one of the officers asked, covering the girl with the bedsheets. "Thank you for assisting us, but why did you take so long to scream? We would have stormed the room sooner."

"What? And ruin the best performance of my life? First time I've been ordered to squirm like a worm!" she replied, tittering. "The girls at the theatre will never believe I helped Scotland Yard catch a rapist!" She pointed to the large portrait over the bed. "He said the old lady in the portrait was his mother. He likes her to watch as he rapes his victims. Imagine that!"

The officer in charge spoke in a loud, articulate voice. "Phillip Lancaster, we are taking you in for the attempted rape of Miss Tillie Abernathy." Seconds later, as they dragged him out in his robe and slippers, the duke looked over his shoulder at his mother's portrait.

Mother would not approve...not at all.

Chapter Twenty-Three

Standing on the pebbled driveway outside Hardwood Manor, surrounded by wedding guests, Marguerite threw rice at the newly wedded couples who lowered their heads and covered their eyes while making a dash toward their carriages. Once inside the carriages, each couple waved good-bye as magnificent white stallions began to pull the carriages away.

She noticed how Samantha and Winnie smiled happily, while Penny sat wide-eyed and stone still, waving back at the guests with as much enthusiasm as a dead rabbit about to be thrown into boiling water for stew. Feeling terribly sorry for her younger sister, but even sorrier for poor Mr. Pennington, a silent and defeated Marguerite walked alongside the other guests waving and trailing behind the carriages until they reached the end of the drive.

"Your sister will make my brother, Damian, a good wife," Desdemona Cummings commented to Marguerite once the carriages departed the Hardwood estate and disappeared from sight.

"Indeed, and Mr. Cummings will make her a good husband," Marguerite agreed, swallowing the despair in her throat. "I'm happy my sister was able to find such a decent man," she said absently, looking around for any sign of Ashton, as she had been doing since the start of the day's activities.

What is the use? Marguerite asked herself, disappointment overwhelming her. She had held out, hoping she would see Ashton today, but all of her hopes and prayers had not brought him to her. She felt guilty and selfish. Instead of enjoying the special day, she had wallowed in her own pain and had only gone through the motions, pretending to take pleasure in the day when all she could think of was whether or not Ashton would be in attendance.

The wedding reception was almost over. Marguerite knew she had to accept the fact that Ashton was not going to show up. Still, she continued to look closely among the guests, hoping against hope for Ashton to magically appear, so desperate was she to see him.

Her talk with Samantha last night had left her with many questions. If Ashton's interest in Julianna was solely in helping the

Earl of Windword to protect his sister, why hadn't Uncle John and Aunt Elizabeth told her the truth? Why had they kept silent and allowed her to think Ashton had gone to Spain to marry Julianna? Why did Julianna need protection? Protection from whom?

"Indeed, Winifred and Damian are fortunate to have found each other," Desdemona commented. "Your sister assured me Mother and I are welcome to visit anytime we deem fit. Of course, Mother was more than willing to take her up on it, but I declined for both of us. We mustn't take advantage of Damian and Winifred. They need time to themselves. Poor darling Mother! I would rather not return to Surrey with her, but it is my duty as her only daughter to take care of her in her old age."

Marguerite tried to smile. "Your mother is lucky to have such a caring daughter," she managed to say, scarcely aware of her own voice.

"Miss Wiggins, I know you and I were not the best of friends this past summer, but you are family now. I feel it is my duty to caution you." Letting out a deep breath, Desdemona looked over her shoulder and took Marguerite aside. Anxiously, she moistened her dry lips. "I must have a word with you regarding your fiancé. I feel I must warn you. The duke is not to be—"

"Warn me?" Marguerite asked, wondering why Desdemona looked so worried and serious all of a sudden, quite different from the many other guests who could not stop gushing over her upcoming nuptials to the Duke of Wallingford. "What is it? The duke is not to be what?"

An inexplicable look of withdrawal came over her face as Desdemona shook her head. "How silly of me! Did I say *warn* you?" she inquired with a nervous smile. "I meant *wish* you the best. I wanted to congratulate you, that is all. Let us hurry. We seem to have fallen behind."

Thinking Desdemona's behavior odd, Marguerite hardly recognized the woman as they made their way back to the north lawn and into the formal garden in silence. Desdemona looked different. It had only been a few months, but she had aged considerably since Marguerite had last seen her. Dressed in a simple beige cotton dress, wearing hardly any jewelry with her hair pulled back in a tight bun, Desdemona seemed not to want to attract the least bit of attention to herself. What a difference from the haughty, eye-catching, elegant woman Marguerite had tried her best to tolerate last summer. The one-time flirtatious young lady, who had thrown herself at Lord Roland during their afternoon visits, had spent most of the wedding reception sitting beside her mother, chatting with Aunt Lavinia and Aunt Hyacinth.

By the time Marguerite and Desdemona reached the reception area, most of the guests had said their good-byes and had now taken their leave, but a few remained to mingle amongst themselves.

"I think Winifred made the lovelier bride of the three," Desdemona suddenly spoke. "Her ivory lace wedding dress was elegant yet simple. I much prefer lace to satin and ivory to pure white. She had the longer train of the three, and her headdress was made of real orange blossoms. Winifred's veil reached down to the floor. I noticed that the others didn't. The weather held perfectly. Don't you think?"

"Yes, it held very well," Marguerite acknowledged, only too glad that Desdemona had changed the subject away from the brides to the weather. She did not wish to point out that, although different, each bride had looked equally beautiful in her eyes and that all three had used "real orange blossoms" for their headdresses. Aunt Elizabeth would not have had it any other way. She had made certain her supplier imported them from Florida no matter the cost.

"Indeed, it almost seems like a summer day...perfect for an outdoor wedding. Your aunt was lucky the weather held."

"Aunt Elizabeth was prepared to host the reception inside in case of rain, but she awoke this morning to so much sunshine she changed her mind and moved everything to the formal garden instead," Marguerite said, counting the minutes until the last guests would leave and she could hide in her room.

"It seems the entire *ton* was here today with the exception of the Duke of Wallingford and his mother. I was surprised to find Lord Phillip did not attend the weddings," Desdemona noted, again looking uneasy.

"His mother is ill." Marguerite uttered the words she had been repeating all day to the many guests who inquired about Lord Phillip's much-noticed absence.

Desdemona was about to speak when Lord Christopher Jackman, accompanied by Mrs. Adele Cummings, Desdemona's mother, walked over to them.

"Miss Cummings, are you ready to leave?" Lord Jackman asked Desdemona. "Lorena is waiting by my coach. I think your mother is a bit tired and needs her rest."

"Why, yes...of course," Desdemona replied, turning to Marguerite. "Emily Middleton has invited Mother and me to spend a few days with her family. Lord Jackman has kindly offered to take us, as he needs to return Lady Lorena to Bonner Hall. The Middleton house is on the way."

"Tired? Me?" Adele Cummings frowned. "I seldom get out, Desdemona. Why is this man insisting that we leave so soon?"

Desdemona closed her eyes in frustration. "Mother, most of the guests have gone. It is time."

"Poppycock! Miss Wiggins, where is that handsome duke of yours? I was looking forward to meeting the Duke of Wallingford today."

Frowning at the old woman, Desdemona spoke before Marguerite could reply. "Lord Phillip could not attend. The duke's mother has taken ill. Let us go, Mother. Lord Jackman is waiting."

"Pity! What a shame Lord Eustinius could not make it to the weddings either. Lady Lorena did not want to say at first, but finally she confessed that he is suffering from gout. The man should pay more attention to what he eats," Mrs. Cummings declared loudly before Desdemona grabbed her by the arm and pulled her along behind her. Lord Jackman simply rolled his eyes and nodded good-bye as they walked away.

"Miss Wiggins," Lady Rosalind Blythe called out, waving to Marguerite from across the lawn. "Be a dear, and come join us!"

Dear Lord! Not Lady Blythe and her husband. Poor Lord Frederick was hard of hearing, and when he wasn't shouting a loud "Huh? What is that, my dear?" he was napping and snoring in his chair. Worst of all, Lord Roland and Bernice were also sitting at the table. Marguerite had tried to ignore Lord Roland's presence all day, but she couldn't very well ignore Lady Blythe's insistence that she join them.

Could her day get any worse?

"Miss Wiggins, Miss Wiggins!" Lady Blythe waved and called out even louder.

Marguerite had no choice but to smile and make her way toward Rosalind Blythe's table. She would have to grin and bear it. It was late afternoon, and most of the guests were gone. *The reception will soon be over,* she reassured herself when Lord Roland rose from the table and pulled out a chair for her to sit.

"You must forgive Uncle Freddy. He can't very well get up and act the chivalrous gentleman when he is gracing us with a nap, now, can he, Miss Wiggins?"

"Indeed," Marguerite replied stiffly, taking pity upon the old man, who was drooling all over his morning coat. Once Marguerite was seated, Lord Roland went back to sit beside Bernice.

"Have you heard the news, Miss Wiggins? Miss Blythe has just this morning agreed to become my wife. Now Uncle Freddy will be my stepfather-in-law as well. Isn't that jolly? My parents are delighted. We have kept it all in the family. Haven't we, little one?" he asked, taking Bernice's hand and winking at her.

"Congratulations," Marguerite said graciously, feeling sorry for the reticent Bernice, who smiled shyly at her from across the table. She tried not to think of what the poor girl would have to endure in the future, being married to such a disgusting, lascivious man. It made no difference to Marguerite that he was now officially part of her family or that he was engaged to be married. Lord Roland Bradstone still made her feel uncomfortable.

"Bernice, my love. Let us take a walk. Excuse us," Lord Roland said, standing to draw Bernice's chair and assisting her from the table.

Let us take a walk. Marguerite cringed inside, remembering how much she had dreaded those awful words during the summer. The man had been relentless in his pursuit of her. She would never forget that afternoon in the park when he had tried to lure her away from the others. If Ashton hadn't come when he did...

"I'm so pleased. I never dreamed my Bernice would make such a match," Lady Rosalind Blythe suddenly exclaimed as they watched Lord Roland walk away with the timid Bernice. "She is going to make an exquisite bride, indeed. You, Miss Wiggins, dressed in that beautiful white bridesmaid's gown, with your headpiece of flowers and ribbons. You look much the bride yourself. If it weren't for the light blue trim, I would have thought there were four brides instead of three in the church this morning. You do look lovely. Tell me, where is that handsome fiancé of yours? He is nowhere to be found, and I so wanted to see him again."

"His mother has taken ill," Marguerite said for the umpteenth time.

"Oh, dear, what a disappointment," Rosalind said, shaking her head.

"Huh? What did you say, my dear?" Lord Frederick suddenly stirred. "What appointment?"

"Go back to sleep, Freddy. I refuse to repeat everything I say solely for your deaf ears!"

"What?" Lord Frederick wiped his sleepy eyes.

"Go to sleep, Freddy!" Rosalind insisted.

"Yes, dear," Lord Frederick replied and, to Marguerite's amazement, fell right back to sleep, snoring within seconds.

Marguerite turned to Rosalind. "How did he do that—fall asleep so quickly?"

Lady Blythe glanced at her husband and shrugged. "Never mind Freddy." A devilish look came into her eyes. Smiling slyly, she continued, "I had such a delicious encounter with the Duke of Wallingford the last time I was in London. Talking about delicious, where is that scrumptious Mr. James? Why isn't he here?"

"Mr. James could not make it to the weddings. He had pressing business in London," Marguerite answered quickly, stiffening at the mention of Ashton's name.

"Such a handsome fellow that Mr. James. I was eager to see him as well. Let us get back to Lord Phillip. I wished to thank your fiancé for the wonderful carriage ride he gave me." Rosalind licked her lips suggestively. "You remember the night of Lady Samantha's engagement party, after Bernice left with Lord Roland. I don't think I've ever enjoyed a ride more in my life. It was everything he said it would be, surpassing all my expectations. Be sure to tell him that when you see him and ask him to give my regards to his coachman, Edgar. Won't you, Miss Wiggins?"

"What? Yes, I'll tell him," Marguerite said, not paying much attention. Rosalind's mentioning of Ashton's name had, once again, stirred up feelings she had been trying hard to suppress.

"Rosalind, is Miss Wiggins feeling well?"

Marguerite hardly heard Lord Frederick as terrible regrets assailed her. Why had she acted so rashly? Why hadn't she waited for Ashton to return from Spain to confront him about Julianna Kent? Instead, because of her injured pride, she had become engaged to a man who did not love her and now made her skin crawl. *Dear God, that awful Duke of Wallingford!*

"Miss Wiggins," Lord Frederick persisted. "Rosalind, she looks sad, as though she is about to burst into tears. Miss Wiggins, is there anything I can do for you?"

"Leave her alone, Freddy!" Rosalind snapped. "Don't look so troubled, Miss Wiggins. The carriage ride meant nothing—absolutely nothing. I ran into Lord Phillip earlier that afternoon. When I said I would be attending your cousin's engagement party, he offered to show me London after the party. Really, Miss Wiggins, there is no need for petty jealously. You were not even engaged to Lancaster at the time."

Jealously? Did the woman just say jealousy? Lady Blythe could have the Duke of Wallingford on a platter for all Marguerite cared.

"Carriage ride?" Lord Frederick demanded, the lines on his wrinkled brow furrowing even deeper. "What carriage ride?"

Rosalind took a napkin and wiped the spittle from Lord Frederick's chin. "Be quiet, Freddy. Can't you see I've offended the woman?"

Lord Frederick lifted a bushy eyebrow. "Why would you want to offend such a lovely creature, Rosalind? Miss Wiggins, I apologize for whatever my wife has said to you to make you look so forlorn. Miss Wiggins..."

Marguerite snapped out of her thoughts only to realize Lord Frederick was speaking to her. "Apologize...forlorn? I don't understand, Lord Frederick. You'll have to excuse me. I'm the one who must apologize. I didn't get much sleep last night. I'm embarrassed to admit I was not listening carefully."

"That has been known to happen, my girl. Lady Rosalind never pays attention to anything I say." Displaying decayed yellow teeth, Lord Frederick grinned at his wife as though she were a small child. "It was all in your mind, Rosalind. The girl is not offended. She simply is in need of a good night's sleep."

"Indeed." Rosalind nodded, looking relieved. "How many times does a young woman get to be a bridesmaid in a triple wedding? Never in a lifetime! I probably would have lost sleep as well."

Marguerite returned the smile as best she could. Sleep had eluded her last night, but it had nothing to do with the weddings and everything to do with Ashton. She had spent the night tossing and turning, mulling over the words Samantha had said to her before she had rushed out of her bedroom.

He loves you, Marguerite. Don't let him go. I should have spoken sooner.

Could it be true? *Oh, Ashton!* If only she could see him one more time. Had she ruined her one chance at happiness by mocking him when he had asked her to run away with him? The moment he admitted to loving Julianna, she had been too furious to hear any more. Why hadn't she allowed him to explain when they were alone at Windword Hall? Why had she rashly refused him and thrown the duke in his face?

If Ashton loved her, she would gladly run away with him to the far corners of the earth—and to hell with the Duke of Wallingford and the scandal it would bring.

"Miss Marguerite." Flora approached the table and whispered in her ear, "Lord and Lady Hardwood need to see you in the study. It is of the utmost urgency. We have to find your father."

Chapter Twenty-Four

Returning his gold pocket watch to his vest pocket, Edmund sat down at one side of the walnut partners desk in the Hardwood study while an anxious Lord and Lady Hardwood stood at the windowsill, watching the dwindling wedding reception below.

Bloody hell—what the devil had he been thinking, upsetting the Hardwoods on such a special day? In his haste to speak with them, he had forgotten there was a wedding reception taking place. Unfortunately, he was reminded the instant he arrived at Hardwood Manor and spotted the guests, many of whom were in the process of climbing into coaches and making their exits.

Thinking that the sooner his neighbors heard the news of Wallingford's arrest, the sooner they could start to put it behind them, Edmund had slipped into the mansion without being noticed. Once inside, he had asked Mortimer to direct him to the study and had ordered the butler to fetch Lord and Lady Hardwood while he waited. Minutes later, when the Hardwoods entered the study, Edmund had wasted no time in telling them of Wallingford's capture—but that had been twenty minutes ago, and Lady Hardwood had become more and more distressed by the second.

"Lord Kent just checked his watch, John. It is six in the evening. How much longer is a morning wedding supposed to last? Why can't they all go home?" she complained to her husband.

Hardwood put his arm around his wife. "Everyone seems to be leaving, dear. The guests will be wondering why we are not downstairs to say good-bye. Why is it taking so long for Flora to fetch Marguerite?"

Elizabeth Hardwood shook her head. "John, I'm too rattled to care about the guests. If only Marguerite could stay down in the gardens for the rest of her days and not have to hear the terrible news we are about to tell her."

Leaving her husband's side, Lady Hardwood began to pace the room. "The scandal of it all," she spat out, her brow crinkled with worry as she wrung her hands. "I'm delighted he is going to be put away for the rest of his days, but poor Marguerite! How is she ever going to forgive us?"

"Now, now, Elizabeth." Lord Hardwood walked away from the window and took his wife in his arms, trying to calm her. "Maybe it won't be so bad." He rolled his eyes at Edmund over her head as though he didn't believe a word coming out of his own mouth.

"Isn't this so, Kent?" Hardwood went on. "You said so yourself. Wallingford is insane. He will probably be sent to an asylum. The Wallingfords are practically royals. Word will never get out. No one has to know Marguerite was engaged to marry a rapist."

Elizabeth disentangled herself from her husband's embrace. "There will still be scandal, John. It matters little if Lord Wallingford will be known as a rapist or a raving lunatic—no matter what, gossip will follow my poor niece until her dying day. At best, people will think that the duke did not want to marry our Marguerite. They will wonder why. Oh, my poor, darling! All kind of speculation will surround her. She is destined to live the life of a lonely spinster. No one will ever want her again."

"Such melodrama, my dear. It is not as bad as all that. Engagements have been known to be broken. I'm certain someone will want her. Maybe we can send her to live abroad until people forget."

"Live abroad?" Lady Hardwood snapped. "Who do we know abroad? How long is Marguerite to be gone? It is going to take a lifetime for this scandal to go away. Engagements have been broken before, but not an engagement to the Duke of Wallingford. Don't accuse me of being melodramatic, John Hardwood, when we have a crisis on our hands. People will never forget."

"Kent will help us," Lord Hardwood announced in desperation. "We will send her to the de Cordoba fellow in Spain, the kind Spaniard who is taking care of Julianna. Please, Kent. Didn't he assist your sister in her time of need? Would you write your friend a missive and have him take Marguerite as well?"

Edmund was about to respond when Lady Hardwood flung her hands in the air. "John, do not bother Lord Kent with that silly notion. Even if the Spaniard were to agree, I seriously doubt a few months in Spain can remedy the situation. People will wonder about Lord Phillip's whereabouts. They won't rest until they know why the engagement was called off. Marguerite will forever be known as the jilted bride who almost married the Duke of Wallingford. Oh, dear, such a sweet girl. Ruined! What are we going to do?"

"I don't know, dear." Sighing heavily, his shoulders slumped in defeat, Lord Hardwood returned to the window. "I've been asking myself that question since Kent came back from Spain with the dreadful news. The last person in the world whom we would have thought—the illustrious Duke of Wallingford, a filthy rapist! I've been trying to come to terms with that for weeks. Marguerite will never forgive us for not telling her the truth. I've questioned the wisdom of having kept it from her in the first place. The poor girl thinks she's to be wed in December."

Elizabeth Hardwood shook her head. "As soon as we found out the identity of Julianna's attacker, we should have let Marguerite know, and the devil with Scotland Yard. I've dreaded this moment and haven't slept since the day you told us, Lord Kent. Now the animal has been arrested, I must face Marguerite. I cannot tell you what this is doing to me."

"I'll be leaving for Spain to bring Julianna home as soon as I can make the necessary arrangements. At which time, I will be happy to speak with de Cordoba about sheltering Marguerite until the furor regarding the engagement settles down. Diego will not refuse me. I trust him implicitly. His home will be opened to her for as long as she needs. There is nothing more I can do here, but to leave you to your privacy," Edmund said, rising from his chair. "I apologize for ruining your daughter's wedding day."

"Don't go, Kent. We need you. You were right to come to us today. My niece needs to know. She won't understand why we didn't tell her before. You have to help us explain to Marguerite," Lord Hardwood begged Edmund, who had walked to the door and was beginning to turn the doorknob to make his exit.

"I see her!" Lord Hardwood called out suddenly. "She is with Flora and Archibald. They are walking across the lawn, making their way to the study as we speak."

"Oh dear!" Elizabeth Hardwood stopped pacing long enough to close her eyes and put her hand to her forehead. "Please stay, Lord Kent. The poor girl is going to be crushed," she said, dismally. "My husband is right. Marguerite is fond of you. We need your help with the explanation."

Edmund stood at the door, wishing he could just walk away. Lord and Lady Hardwood needed him, but he certainly didn't need this. The last place he wanted to be was in the Hardwood study, waiting for Marguerite, but he couldn't walk out on them now. Not with the way the Hardwoods were staring at him, their eyes desperately pleading with him to stay. He was grateful to them for having kept Julianna's secret. Now their cooperation in keeping the secret could very well ruin a cherished relationship with their favorite niece. He owed them, damn it. The least he could do was to help them relay the news of Wallingford's arrest to Marguerite.

"I'll stay as long as needed," Edmund consented, but cursed inwardly as he walked back into the room and stood by the bookshelves. Their niece was far from *fond* of him. She made that very clear the last time they were together. The news would be humiliating enough for her. He had no business being present while her world came plummeting down upon her. Bloody hell! Why the devil was he obligated to stay and watch the woman he wanted go to pieces over losing another man? Wasn't it enough that he had saved Marguerite from marrying a savage—a lunatic who raped women in his mother's name? Hadn't he witnessed enough last night? A sobbing Wallingford repeatedly shouted the name of his lover, Lady Louise Shasner-Blake. He hollered at his mother when the dowager appeared at the police station and blamed her for his disdain of women as he was being dragged away by male nurses in white coats. The dowager turned to Edmund for consolation. Those images were still vivid in his mind, and it took him most of the night to deliver the grief-stricken old dowager to Bentley House and leave her in the care of her servants.

"Damn that horrid duke! Why did he have to set his sights on Marguerite?" Lady Hardwood said.

"Elizabeth, do not swear, my dear. It isn't like you—Flora!"

At that precise moment, Flora burst into the room, followed by the corpulent man whom Edmund recognized as Archibald Wiggins, Marguerite's father, the louse on the train who had provided his three daughters with a list of men to pursue during the Season before disappearing and leaving them to face the future on their own.

"Flora, where is Marguerite?" Lord Hardwood asked the maid.

"A guest stopped her along the way, my lord, to ask why the duke is not with her today. She'll be in shortly," Flora replied breathlessly.

"Thank you, Flora. That will be all."

"Hardwood, what is so urgent that I was not allowed to finish the piece of wedding cake I was so enjoying? Who is this gentleman?" Archibald Wiggins stared at Edmund with a glimmer of recognition. "I feel as though I know you. Have we met before?"

Edmund had been about to introduce himself, but all thoughts of Archibald Wiggins disappeared from his mind the instant he noticed Marguerite standing at the threshold. Staring at her in her lace bridesmaid's dress, Edmund was certain no bride had been able to outshine her today. Hell, truth be told, no other woman had ever come close to surpassing her in his eyes.

Her shiny black hair, worn in a loose chignon at her nape and adorned with a crown of blue and yellow flowers, Marguerite was a captivating vision in white. The blue trim in her dress accented the cobalt blue of her eyes, and the frilly white gown did nothing to hide her tantalizing womanly curves beneath. As always, it was hard for him to keep his head when she was around. No matter how many times he saw Marguerite, her beauty stunned him.

It shouldn't be like this, damn it. What was Marguerite Wiggins but a mere slip of a girl filled with haughty aspirations and puffed-up dreams of becoming a duchess? What made her so damned special, so different from the others? What magic did she possess to have made him fall so deeply and desperately in love? He had fought his desire for Marguerite all summer long, but she had made it impossible for him to resist her charms. The moment he had held her in his arms and had tasted her luscious lips, he had wanted her in his bed, not simply as a lover but as his wife. He ached for her—there was no doubt about that. Instead of contemplating her with disdain for her fickle ways and the manner in which she had treated him, all he could think of was how absolutely magnificent she looked and how, in a few seconds, he was going to break her heart by ruining her dreams of becoming the Duchess of Wallingford.

Lady Hardwood pointed to the two leather chairs at each side of the partners desk. "Marguerite, dear, please sit down. You too, Archibald. Help me, John," she said, turning to Hardwood with pleading, worried eyes as Flora left the room.

"Certainly, dear." Lord Hardwood cleared his throat with an awkward little cough. "My dear niece, come in. Shut the door. We have an urgent matter of the utmost importance to discuss."

Marguerite shut the door and came closer into the room. "What is it, Uncle? Flora said that you wanted to—Ashton!" she gasped when she spotted Edmund standing by the bookshelves.

Had he imagined it, or had her voice held a rasp of excitement when she said his name just now? *Bloody hell!* What the devil was he doing? Why was he putting himself through this? As usual, one look at Marguerite and he had lost all rational thought. He quickly reminded himself that, while playing him for a fool, this tempting, gorgeous angel, with her beautiful sapphire eyes and her seductive young body, had maneuvered herself into his heart—toying with him, causing his loins to burn for her while she yearned for another man. Nonetheless, he didn't want to break Marguerite's heart. He did not want to witness the proud beauty before him reduced to tears, completely broken and desperate.

"Marguerite, I have something to tell you. As soon as I've done so, I'll leave," Edmund informed her, his voice cold and exacting.

* * * *

"No! You mustn't leave," Marguerite burst out, her heart pounding madly against her chest. *Ashton!* She could not take her eyes off him, standing before her, so big and strong and wonderfully handsome. As always, he took her breath away. All she wanted was for him to take her in his arms. This was her chance, the opportunity that she had ruined a few weeks ago at the lily pond.

"Uncle John, I need to speak with Ashton. Nothing is more important to me at the moment."

"Dear, this is urgent. It is about the duke," Uncle John insisted. "I'm afraid you are not going to like what we are about to tell you."

At the mention of the duke, Archibald's brows furrowed. "What about the duke?" he queried. "Gooseling, this is pertaining to Wallingford. I think you should listen to your uncle. What is it, Hardwood? For God's sake, man, do not keep us in the dark."

"Never mind the duke," Marguerite objected, walking to stand before Ashton. Not caring what the others thought, she blurted out the words that had been going through her mind all of last night and most of the day. "Ashton, did you mean it when you asked me to run away with you?"

"Run away? *Gooseling!*" Archie objected, rushing over and positioning himself between Marguerite and Ashton, his eyes bulging with indignation. "Who is this man who wants to run away with my daughter?" he demanded, pointing his finger in Ashton's face. "What nonsense is this?"

Ashton's mouth twisted into a threat, and Archibald quickly retreated.

"It is no nonsense, Papa. I must know if Ashton has come to take me away."

"Archibald, calm down. He is her chaperone." Uncle John attempted to pacify her father, but he would not be pacified. Scowling darkly, he stood glaring at Ashton with his stocky arms akimbo while he angrily tapped his foot on the wooden floor.

"Chaperone—what sort of chaperone asks a young lady to run away with him? I demand his name," Archie burst out. "I should have known better than to allow Elizabeth to watch over my precious daughter. She has always been too lenient."

"Wiggins!" Uncle John raised his voice. "I won't stand here and have you throw blame at my wife. Elizabeth has done her best."

"Indeed, I have, Archibald Wiggins." Aunt Elizabeth defended herself. "You may have insulted by poor sister, Lydia, anytime you pleased when she was alive, but you will not insult me, not under my roof."

Ignoring the ramblings surrounding her, Marguerite looked into Ashton's eyes for a sign that he might actually care for her, but his eyes told her nothing. His expression was a mask of stone, his eyes flat, hard, passionless. Marguerite could not read his thoughts, but she needed to reveal her true feelings to him. Desperately wanting to explain, to make him see how much she loved him, she reached out and clutched at his strong, manly hand.

"His name is Mr. James, Papa." Marguerite tore her eyes away from Ashton to address her father. "You met him on the train to London last summer. He is all I think about. He is all I want. I'll toil for the rest of my days as long as he gives me another chance. I love him with all of my heart, and if he should ask me again, I'll run to the end of the earth with him. There, I said it! Now stop insulting my dear aunt when I owe her everything."

"I knew it, John! She loves him," Aunt Elizabeth hooted triumphantly. "She's been miserable ever since he left for Spain. I told you it was her injured pride which led to the engagement to that beast Wallingford. Oh, this is what I wanted all along!"

Uncle John cautioned, "My darling. You mustn't get ahead of yourself. We do not know if Mr. James returns her feelings."

"*Mister* James? Hardwood, did you say *mister*? A mere commoner! Never mind if he returns her feelings. Daughter, you are engaged to the Duke of Wallingford. What about the scandal this will bring? You will be ruined for life," Archibald exclaimed, his voice hoarse with frustration. "Don't you want to be called Duchess? You are going to give up everything for this...this nobody?"

"Happily, Papa. I don't want the Duke of Wallingford, and I don't want to be his duchess." Marguerite gave Ashton a little smile and said, "I'd rather be called Meggie."

"Meggie?" Archie spat out the name as though it were venomous. "Unlike your sisters, you've always insisted people use your proper name," he cried out before walking over to flop himself unto Uncle John's leather chair, hiding his face with his hands. "Elizabeth, talk some sense into her. She's gone daft. This man shall not whisk her away."

"Archibald Wiggins, stop your ranting. Your daughter has a mind of her own. You certainly must know that by now, but Mr. James is not here to whisk her away," Aunt Elizabeth corrected. "He is here to tell her that the Duke of Wallingford has been arrested."

Archie's head jerked up. His white, bushy eyebrows shot up in surprise. "Arrested? The Duke of Wallingford? Bosh! What kind of gibberish is this?" Balking, he rose from the chair and walked over to Marguerite. "My poor gooseling! Is this some sort of cruel joke, Mr. James? Who has sent you with this absurd piece of gossip?"

"Archibald, Mr. James will tell you everything if you let him speak. Now let him speak," Aunt Elizabeth pleaded.

"Let him speak? Who is stopping him? The scoundrel says nothing. Daughter, I fear you have made a terrible mistake. He keeps quiet while you pour your heart. This man does not love you."

Marguerite felt her face color. Her body stiffened in dismay. Papa was right. She had allowed her feelings for Ashton and everything Samantha had said last night to influence her into making a complete fool of herself. She had hoped, once Ashton heard the truth, he would fall to his knees and propose marriage. When he neither spoke nor moved, Marguerite felt more than crushed. Looking down, she noticed that she was still holding Ashton's hand.

"The Duke of Wallingford being arrested is too fantastical to be believed. Has Lancaster changed his mind about marrying my duckling? Is this why you are all telling such tall tales?" Archibald asked worriedly as Marguerite quickly let go of Ashton's hand.

Trying to keep her composure, Marguerite straightened herself with dignity. She had walked into this room with her heart wide open. She would leave with it in tatters, but at least she was through with all the lies and pretenses.

"Indeed, Papa. It seems I have made an error in judgment. If it were not so laughable, I would cry," she managed to say, tears brimming as she turned to leave the room in utter humiliation. Before she could do so, Ashton reached out for her and pulled her to him.

"Don't," he said, speaking only to her, ignoring the others.

She tried to wrench herself away, furious for allowing Ashton to see her crying over him. She needed to get away, but his hand tightened on her arm.

"Don't you dare go, Marguerite. Not now—not after everything you have just said to me. Leave us," he ordered the others. "We need a moment alone."

"Do as you are told, Wiggins," Uncle John insisted in no uncertain terms, physically forcing Archie out of the room.

"What about the duke? What are we to tell Wallingford?" Her father's voice resounded in the hallway right before Aunt Elizabeth shut the study door.

Alone with Ashton, Marguerite looked to the floor. She could not face him, so desperate she must have seemed for him earlier, but Ashton was insistent as he raised Marguerite's chin to meet his gaze.

"Look at me, darling. I must know," he demanded, his deep voice raw with emotion. A brief shiver rippled through her as Ashton caressed her cheek with his knuckles, the touch of his hand almost unbearable in its warmth. "Did you mean it, Marguerite, when you said that you loved me?"

Had he just called her darling?

His dark eyes were tender and warm, no longer cold and hard as they had been before. Looking into them, her defenses began to subside. Mesmerized by the attractive, tiny crinkles at the corners of his eyes and the fullness of his warm, tempting lips, Marguerite could barely breathe, thinking only about how much she loved him and how shamelessly she yearned for him.

"Yes, I meant every word," she spoke in a weak, tremulous whisper. "I humbled myself in front of you. I told my father I was willing to toil for the rest of my days for another chance with you. Ashton, what more could I have said to convince you?"

"You'll not have to toil a single day," Ashton said with a low chuckle. "You'll want for nothing. All you have to say is yes." His face darkened with passion, his eyes holding her captive, he took her hand and pressed a kiss on her palm.

"I love you, Marguerite. God help me, I do. Marry me, and you'll make me the happiest man on earth," he whispered hoarsely.

"Ashton—yes—of course, I'll marry you." Her heart felt as though it would burst with joy when Ashton locked his hands around her waist and drew her close. Melting against him, she put her arms around his neck. "I want nothing more."

"How would you feel about being called Countess?"

"Countess?" Marguerite giggled at the absurdity of his question. "Countess of what?" she moaned softly as he pressed her to him.

"Countess of Windword, my beautiful, willful, magnificent Meggie. Rumor has it that the Earl of Windword is a terrible chaperone and has fallen hopelessly in love with you," he drawled. He stifled her little gasp of shock by pressing his lips to hers, kissing her madly, making her forget everything but how wonderful it felt to be in his arms.

Epilogue

Three weeks later, after securing a special license, Edmund Ashton James Kent, the Earl of Windword, and Miss Marguerite Wiggins were wed in a small, intimate ceremony at the lily pond at Windword Hall. After the service and the customary refreshments, Edmund carried Marguerite up the grand staircase into his bedroom.

While Edmund made passionate love to his countess for the first time, exploring, arousing, and pleasuring her naked body with his own, the sound of horse hooves against cobblestone could be heard from their bedroom window. Edmund paid little attention to the sound as Marguerite melted against him and his world was filled with only her.

* * * *

"Where to, Your Grace?" the coachman, Edgar Mason, asked the Dowager Duchess of Wallingford while their coach drove away from Windword Hall.

"Just drive, Mason. I don't care where to," the dowager replied stiffly, holding in one hand the sapphire-and-diamond ring that had just been returned to her by the earl's butler. In her other hand she held the matching cuff link that had been bestowed upon the first Duke of Wallingford by the king of England many years ago—the same cuff link her son had lost when he had tried to abduct Julianna Kent, the cuff link whose perfect match he had given as an engagement ring and that Scotland Yard had kept as evidence but later returned in view of the fact that there would be no trial.

Opening the divide partition, the dowager instructed the coachman, "Mason, return to London at once. Take me to the Countess of Salesbury."

It was only fitting that Lady Louise Shasner-Blake have the ring now. The dowager would keep the matching cuff link as a reminder that they were the only two who would mourn the loss of her son. Phillip would be locked up in an insane asylum in

Australia for the rest of his days, lost to them forever.

* * * *

Several evenings later, an English marquesa in Spain read a missive from her brother informing her that he and his new bride arrived in Madrid that evening and would travel to Aranjuez the next day to return her to England.

After crumbling the missive and throwing it across the room, the marquesa walked to the mirrored armoire and began to take off the black attire she had worn to attend Mass at the *Iglesia de San Antonio* earlier. After removing her tortoiseshell *peineta* comb, along with her lace mantilla and gown, she took off her underclothing and donned a robe. Gazing at her image in the mirror, her hand over her pregnant belly, the English marquesa felt blissfully happy that her husband had proven to be as poor a chaperone as her brother Edmund.

"My darling little one," the marquesa spoke to her unborn child as she got ready for bed. "When your uncle hears of you... sparks are going to fly!"

* * * *

Confident Julianna received their missive and would be packed and ready to return with them to London when they came for her in the morning, the newlyweds, after enjoying a wonderful meal of roast suckling pig at the famous *Casa Botín* restaurant in Madrid, checked into a nearby inn off the Plaza Mayor for the night.

Hours later, the guttural sound of gypsies singing and playing guitar, stomping their feet and clapping to the rhythm of a flamenco tune resonated from the street below. Edmund and Marguerite stirred in each other's arms.

"Edmund? Are you asleep? I was trying not to move so as not to wake you."

"Bloody hell," Edmund spat out, annoyed. "It is three in the morning. Don't these people ever sleep?"

Marguerite giggled as she turned in his arms, giving him her back, and curling into the curve of his body. "After a night filled with boundless indulgences, you wake up grouchy, my love?" she mumbled over her shoulder while adjusting her pillow.

"Who can sleep with all this noise, Marguerite? One would

think it was three in the afternoon and not three in the morning. I've been awake since I kissed you good night."

"It serves you right, Edmund. I haven't slept much since the day we were married. Now close your eyes and try to count sheep."

Edmund gave out a deep chuckle. "Night after night of endless pleasure and you are complaining already, my love? How can this be?" he teased, placing a kiss on her shoulder as he lifted a lock of her hair to play with it gently.

Marguerite's lacy nightgown crept up onto her thighs as she snuggled closer. The contact of her curvy backside nestled against him hardened him, making him want her once more.

"We are only several days into our honeymoon and you want me to count sheep?" Edmund asked hoarsely.

The little minx kept silent, but somehow he knew she was smiling. She moaned softly when his hand raised her gown further to caress the skin of her warm, silky thigh. When his hand traveled upward, her breathing became heavier, letting him know she wanted him as well. Not bothering to wait for an answer, he lifted her gown above her hips and over her shoulders, quickly discarding it to the floor. "To hell with sleep."

"Shame on you, Edmund Kent!" Marguerite giggled devilishly, turning around to face him. "Aunt Elizabeth surprised me with that lovely nightgown as part of my trousseau. She would be sad to know how little use you have for it."

"Marguerite," Edmund groaned. The light from the window rippled on her full, naked breasts and it was all he could do not to devour every inch of her. "We won't tell her."

"Oh, Edmund—call me Meggie. I love it when you call me Meggie." Marguerite traced her fingertip across his lips before he bent to kiss her.

Raising his mouth from hers, Edmund gazed into her eyes. "Meggie," he whispered as she wrapped her arms around him and welcomed him into her warmth.

About the Author:

Born in Havana, Cuba, Maggie Dove is a happily married housewife and mother of two who has lived in the U.S. since she was five. Her family owned one of the oldest newspapers in the Americas and, as the granddaughter of a famous Cuban writer and publisher, writing is in Maggie's blood. She's had twenty-six of her letters to the editor published  in The Miami Herald. *Call Me Duchess* is her second published novel and the second book of the Windword Trilogy.

Visit her website at: www.maggiedove.net

Also by Maggie Dove:

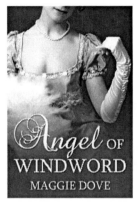

Angel Of Windword
by Maggie Dove

eBook ISBN: 9781926704654
Print ISBN: 9781926704739

Historical Romance
Novel of 83,500 words

Having traded the blissful existence of her beloved Loire Valley, Angelique Beauvisage finds that Windword Hall has more than one villainous skeleton in the closet.

Evil forces are at play surrounding Angelique Beauvisage, but she has no clue. Sensuous and suspense-filled, *Angel Of Windword,* begins with a murder that takes place four years before and turns into a perilous cat and mouse game played by two reluctant lovers, who spin a web of deception that only their love can unravel.

Also from Eternal Press:

The False Light
by Diane Scott Lewis

eBook ISBN: 9781770650596
Print ISBN: 9781770650657

Romance Historical
Novel of 124,316 words

Forced away from France by her devious guardian on the eve of the French Revolution, Countess Lisbette Jonquiere must deliver an important package to further the royalist cause. In England, she discovers the package is full of blank papers, the address is false, and she's penniless. Stranded in a Cornish village, Lisbette toils in a bawdy tavern and falls in love with a man who lives under the shadow of his missing wife.

Immersed in poverty, Lisbette realizes what sparked the revolution in her homeland. Her past catches up to her when desperate men hunt her down: they demand the money her deceased father embezzled from the revolutionaries. Lisbette learns the truth of her father's death, and her lover's involvement in his wife's murder.

Once again, Lisbette faces the threat of losing everything.

CPSIA information can be obtained at www.ICGtesting.com
Printed in the USA
BVOW02s0954251113

337264BV00001B/15/P